Pr

"Coffman enriches the historical...
Her writing is deft, capable...evocative."
—*Publishers Weekly*

"Ms. Coffman pens a heartfelt,
old-fashioned romance that delves
into the shadows of the human soul."
—*Romantic Times* on *The Bride of Black Douglas*

Praise for Deborah Hale

"A wonderfully romantic romp with characters
as easy to engage in as a box of the
finest chocolates... Ms. Hale has penned a
charming, witty romance that's a simply delightful
way to spend an afternoon."
—*Old Book Barn Gazette*

"With this novel, Deborah Hale has outdone
herself! ...*A Gentleman of Substance* has a nearly
flawless plot, well-dimensioned characters, and a
flame that will set your heart ablaze with every
emotion possible! Well done!"
—*Affaire de Coeur*

ELAINE COFFMAN

was born in San Diego, California, reared in Midland, Texas. She received a degree in elementary education from North Texas State University, and worked on her master's degree in language and learning disabilities at Texas Tech. She has researched her family, owned ranches, drilled oil wells, taught elementary school and, during all of this, miraculously managed to raise three well-adjusted children. She lives in Austin, Texas, when she is not tromping around Italy. She considers herself an upbeat, positive person who sees her glass as half-full. "I love people, especially children, so color me friendly."

DEBORAH HALE

turned to historical-romance writing as a way to blend her love of the past with her desire to spin a good love story. Deborah lives in Nova Scotia, Canada, between the historic British garrison town of Halifax and the romantic Annapolis Valley of Longfellow's *Evangeline*. With four children under ten (including twins), Deborah calls writing her "sanity-retention mechanism." On good days she likes to think it's working.

ELAINE COFFMAN

**The Bride of
Blackness Castle**

Deborah
Hale

A Gentleman of Substance

HARLEQUIN®

TORONTO • NEW YORK • LONDON
AMSTERDAM • PARIS • SYDNEY • HAMBURG
STOCKHOLM • ATHENS • TOKYO • MILAN • MADRID
PRAGUE • WARSAW • BUDAPEST • AUCKLAND

ISBN 0-373-83521-3

HARLEQUIN SPECIAL Vol. 1

CONTENTS

CONTENTS

The Bride of Blackness Castle

Elaine Coffman

Prologue

*Scotland, in the years
following the battle of Culloden Moor*

He was not taller than any mortal man, but the curses and dark prophecies that haunted him made him seem that way. He was the last laird and sole survivor of what had once been known as "the mighty clan Macqueen."

Alone and bitter, he walked the walls of Blackness Castle—long ago a stalwart fortress, now neglected and partially roofless. Yet, like the broken man who possessed it, it was noble in its desolation—a heap of crumbling griffins and grotesque carvings that rose majestically from a base of tumbled-down stone.

Night after night he was there, crouching against the salt-laden winds to gaze far out over the ocean toward the Arctic, looking as wild as the island he lived upon, as fierce as his Celt and Viking ancestors, and as cold and unforgiving as Scotland itself.

There had been a time when he had laughed and loved, a time when he was known by his Christian name, Robert Macqueen. But those who had called him that were gone, lying as cold and silent as the Stones of Callanish. Only he was left behind—a man, once so capable of emotion, now dying inside. A man who hated as deeply as he had once loved.

To those who lived in the Shetlands, he had become the Wolf of Blackness Castle. Many thought the name appropriate, for it was rumored that when the moon was full and shining down upon the windswept parapets, his long black hair grew longer and his eyes changed from blue to tawny yellow.

They swore by all that was holy that what they said was true, for there was not a soul on the island who had not heard the eerie notes of his mournful howl as it came rolling across the bogs and peat moors, a sound as chilling, and as lifeless, as the fog.

"He searches for his lost mate," they would say, for everyone in the islands knew the tragic story that haunted the last laird of the clan Macqueen.

He was a man of myth and legend, a man they whispered about behind locked doors, a man they pitied, a man they feared. For he lived in a magical place, where the Atlantic met the North Sea, where roaring and swirling currents turned the giant millstones beneath the water, grinding the salt that flavors the sea.

Perhaps the castle was haunted, just as the village folk believed. Perhaps, too, it was the place where the water horse lived—a malicious Shetland spirit that drowned anyone who tried to ride it....

Anyone, that is, save the Wolf of Blackness Castle.

Chapter One

Be not forgetful...
some have entertained angels unawares.

Lady Anne Crofton sat demurely in the boat. Her manner was deceptive, for there was absolutely nothing demure about Lady Anne.

She kept a sharp eye upon the ruffian who rowed the small craft toward shore. It was obvious his brain was as rum-soaked as the ship's captain. She should have known better than to book passage on a ship named *Misadventure*.

A wave slapped the boat and threw a shower of water over her, drenching her best clothes and her parasol, and soaking her only hat. The toothless brute on the working end of the oars had the audacity to laugh. Her patience was wearing tissue-thin, and she swore inwardly that if he did one more thing to irritate her, she would find another use for her parasol.

They were drawing closer to the shore, and Anne searched the land with mounting excitement for the home her father had written her about, a place called Ravenscrag Castle. But the island looked completely deserted, save for a roofless ruin of a structure that must have dated back to the days after King William.

"Are you certain we're in the right place? I don't see anything that looks like the castle my father described."

"Eh…it's wot the cap'n said, miss. This be the place."

Anne could barely understand a word he said, perhaps because she had never heard anyone completely toothless speak before. It sounded as if he were speaking a foreign language.

The boat struck bottom and scraped across rocks to come to a stop. The seaman leaped out, then took her bags, one by one, and stacked them just beyond the edge of the water, on the shore. Then he climbed back into the boat and looked at her, as if she were holding up his departure.

She closed her parasol and rose majestically to her feet. "I did not relish being carried to shore by a smelly brute, anyway." With that, she yanked her skirts up to a modest length and climbed out of the boat into water that came to her thighs. When she caught him leering at her, she smacked him, hard, beside the head with her parasol. "If you don't want your bloody eyes to be as gone as your teeth, stop your leering and weigh anchor!"

She knew the rowboat did not have an anchor, but he seemed to get the message, for he did as she ordered.

Once he started rowing, she turned her back on him and the ship anchored offshore and concentrated on making the last few feet to dry land. Walking through deep water wasn't easy, especially dressed as she was.

Once ashore, she surveyed the area around her. She fervently hoped the ruined castle was not her new home, but as it was the only choice she had for making inquiry, she decided to leave her baggage where it was and head in that direction.

As she walked along, her shoes squishing with each step, she saw someone riding toward her. The dark chestnut horse drew closer and she could see the rider was a man. His hair was long, and as black as the cape that hung around his shoulders. When he drew even with her, he stopped.

He did not dismount, but sat towering over her, with the most piercing look in his eyes—eyes that were as hard and blue as sapphires. He was a handsome man, but his brooding male vitality held her at bay. There was a dangerous quality to him that set her heart to beating faster. It also made her wary.

This was not a man she would be able to crown with her parasol. Just the thought gave her a sudden vision of him yanking her parasol out of her hands and breaking it over his knee. She decided that she would be wise to be guarded around him, for she knew he would not hesitate to use anything he learned against her.

"What in the hell are you doing here?" he asked suddenly, his voice so hard and brittle that she flinched and took a step back. "You are on private land."

Anne's first instinct was to turn tail and run, but she was too terrified to do more than squeak out an apology. "I do beg your pardon, sir." She cupped her hand to shield her eyes as she stared up at him.

He looked her over with thorough devotion, and she had a feeling he knew one of the buttons on her drawers was missing. There was something in that look that made her aware of him as a man. If he had the same awareness of her, she was doomed. She knew what could happen to a woman alone in a deserted place.

He obviously thought her an intruding inferior. Why not let him add *simpleton* to the list? "It was not my choice to be left here, sir. You see, the ship's captain was too drunk to find his head in broad daylight, much less my destination. I fear they have set me upon this place by mistake." She paused for a shaky breath. "Where am I?"

"Where are you going?"

"I am on my way to see my mother. She is a widow… That means she doesn't have a husband, that is, not at the present time. Widows were married once, you see, but their husbands died, and that is what made them a widow.''

Anne was feeling pretty good about the way things were going, until he pinned her with a cold, angry look. She melted into a quivering lump of fear. ''I am all she has in the world.''

''How unfortunate for her.''

She smiled at him and dipped in a hastily modified version of a curtsy. ''Thank you.''

She saw him squeeze the reins in his hands so tightly that his knuckles turned white. ''You...are...*English*.''

He obviously hated everything English, including the word, for he literally spat it out. She decided to nail down a few Scots ancestors and family members before he put those white knuckles around her throat. ''My speech has lost its Scots flavor, I fear. After my father died, my mother sent me to her aunt in England.''

He seemed restless, anxious to have this conversation over and her on her way. ''So, where does this unfortunate woman live?''

''In a house, of course. It is a modest cottage with a thatched roof. It is quite small...barely big enough for two. The garden is tiny, and she has only one cow, three chickens—''

''Enough!'' His eyes seemed to glow with anger, and she wondered if she had come face to face with the devil himself.

She took a step backward.

He leaned forward, catching the bottom of her chin with the handle of his whip. While she stood there in terrified silence, he lowered the handle, dragging it along the neckline of her dress. ''I would caution you to stop playing games with me, mistress. I am not some callow youth with an Adam's apple bigger than his brain. I tend to get nasty when I am angered, and it isn't a pretty sight. I asked you where your mother lived. I expect to be given a location,

not a description of her house and everything in it. Now, I
will ask you one more time. Where are you going?''

''I...I...'' The words came out in a gravelly croak. Terror
had sucked the moisture from her throat. She couldn't have
spat if he set her on fire. She knew she had better get to
talking fast, or he might be tempted to do just that, so she
took a deep breath, giving her mouth just enough time to
recover, before she tried again. ''I do not have anything
exact, sir. I only know my mother wrote that her cottage is
not far from a castle.''

''And the name of the castle?''

She looked around her, as if frantically searching for
something. ''Oh, no, I think the captain has kept my paper...the one with the name written on it. Oh, dear! What
shall I do?''

''You might try thinking.''

''Oh, I didn't think of that.''

''Obviously.''

She rolled her eyes in her best imitation of deep thought.
''It's no use. I can't remember anything....''

He leaned forward and looped the whip around her head
and pulled her toward him. ''You'd better pray something
shows up fast, otherwise I might he forced to take other
measures.''

''Oth— Other measures?''

He smiled nastily. ''Of a passionate nature.''

''I remember now.''

He withdrew the whip. ''Somehow, I knew you would.''

''I remember only that part of it contained the name of a
bird.... Something like Sparrowcroft... No, that's not it....
Wrenfields... No, that's not right, either.'' She shrugged her
shoulders and smiled at him. ''Wrong again.''

''Ravenscrag,'' he said through gritted teeth. ''Ravenscrag Castle.''

''That's it! I am certain that's it. Are you familiar with
it?''

"I am familiar with it. The question is, are you? The castle there is haunted. It is a place of great tragedy. There is a man who is reported to be a monster. He turns into a wolf at night. Are you certain you want to go there?"

"Is this monster dangerous?"

"No one who has seen him has ever come back, so who's to say?"

"I think I will bypass the castle and go straight to my mother's cottage. Am I very far away?"

"No. Ravenscrag Castle is on the other side of this island. Across the bay. The place you seek should be beyond that."

She wrinkled her nose as she looked at him. "This is an island? But I was going to an island. One called Shetland."

"The Shetlands are a group of islands. The one you seek is across the bay." His voice held a warning. "There are no villages here."

"You mean to tell me I have been dumped, parasol and baggage, upon the wrong island?"

"Catastrophic, isn't it?"

"How will I ever get off of this island, if no one lives here? I can't very well swim.... What would I do with my baggage?"

"It will be a pleasure to help you on your way. I will have someone take you across."

"I don't want to be a bother."

"You are a bother now, mistress, and I am anxious to rid myself of you...one way, or another. I do not take to having strangers snooping around my island."

"I have yet to snoop," she announced.

"You are a woman. You will snoop."

"I am a different sort of woman than most."

"For once you have spoken with something that resembles wisdom."

"If I am such a bother, sir, I will see myself off this island, even if I have to swim across. I shall leave my baggage here, and send someone for it later. Good day."

She opened her parasol with a fluttering snap, and held it over her head as she turned and marched with as much dignity as she could muster, through the rocky sand. She had walked a fair distance when she heard the thundering sound of a horse approaching. A second later, a strong arm whipped out and grabbed her. Suddenly she was airborne, uncertain whether she was more terrified that he might take her with him, or drop her on the spot.

"You aren't going to kill me, are you?"

"The thought crossed my mind. Now, be quiet, or I may start thinking about it again."

She snapped her mouth closed, unable to see anything but the ground beneath them for quite some time. When he finally stopped, he yanked her from his horse and stood her on her feet. When she gained her balance, she saw two men standing in front of the ruined castle, staring at her.

"This baggage has more baggage waiting where she came ashore. Get it, and take her across the bay. She lives not far from Ravenscrag."

The men left to do his bidding and he turned to her. He was unbelievably tall. "I will ask you this once. Do not lie to me, for if you should, I can promise you will not like what I do to you. Do you understand?"

Anne was terrified he knew she had passed herself off as something she was not. "I understand."

"Why are you here?"

She looked at him blankly. "But...I told you. I have come from England..."

"To spy on me?"

She blinked. "I am not a spy, sir. Do I look like a spy?"

"No, but you have the brains for one."

"I am no spy, and that is the truth."

"It had better be. I detest lies, and I do not deal mercifully with those who tell them. For your sake, I hope you have been truthful with me, for if you have not, there is no place safe where you can hide. I am not making light with you, mistress. Believe me when I tell you, I am not a nice man.''

She gulped. ''I believe you…with all my heart.''

''Good.''

Chapter Two

Darkness was where he belonged. It was his comfort, his strength, the place of refuge where he could go and remember. In the deepest part of his heart existed a tomb and a dungeon, and when the darkness came, their doors were thrown open and he was consumed with grief—and filled with an insatiable thirst for revenge.

It was night, and the darkness was all about. The new maid, Marta, had come by to light the candles, but that had been some time ago. They were all burned down now, and they sputtered and flickered, leaving a legacy of tawny shadows to dance upon the wall.

Marta looked at the lord of the castle and moved closer to the housekeeper, Grizel. "Do you think the devils will come for him again tonight?"

"They cannot come for him, lass. They are already here. His devils come from within. It is only at night that he lets them out."

Marta shivered and looked around her. She rubbed her arms. "It grows colder, I think."

"Aye. The wind of remembrance blows coldest when it comes from the graves of those who cannot rest."

"What graves?"

"The ones we spoke of earlier."

"Oh...you mean the graves of his wife and son?"

"Aye, and those of the entire clan...save the laird, of course."

Marta glanced back at the Macqueen. "He must be very sad and very lonely."

"Aye, he lives in the dark part of his soul, where pain and torment wait."

A look of compassion swept over Marta's face. "Have you ever heard him laugh?"

"Not since the tragedy, but before that, yes." She closed her eyes as if remembering. "I can still recall the sound of his laughter shaking the very walls of Ravenscrag Castle."

"Ravenscrag? He did not live here, at Blackness?"

"No. He came here only after Ravenscrag was taken from him by the English."

"The English..." She spat on the floor. "The curse of Cromwell be upon them all!" Marta narrowed her eyes and looked back at the somber figure hunched over his tankard. "I can't imagine him ever laughing."

"No, I don't suppose you can, any more than you can imagine the way he has suffered. Everything and everyone he loved—all those he was closest to—they are all gone."

Tears slipped down Marta's rosy cheeks.

Grizel gave her arm a pat. "Don't cry for the dead, lass. They are at peace."

Marta sniffed. "I'm not." She took the corner of her apron and wiped her eyes. "I was crying for the Macqueen."

"You could not cry enough tears to equal his grief. His pain is too deep." Grizel picked up a candle and held it toward Marta. "Go to your room, lass. Try to get some rest. In time, you will learn, like the rest of us, to live with the constancy of his torment. Go on, now. I will snuff out the candles."

Marta reached for the candle, then paused, her gaze going

back to the Macqueen. "If you don't mind…I think I would rather wait for you."

Grizel's expression softened, and she nodded. "Come along, then," she said, and the two of them put out the candles and slipped quietly from the room, leaving the master of Blackness Castle to grieve alone in the darkness.

The Macqueen sat at the head of the table in his great carved chair, his head bowed with grief, his mind focused not upon what was happening around him, but upon what had already passed.

His eyes were cold and lifeless, and his face was unshaven. His gaze was fixed upon the rich burgundy of the liquid inside the tankard before him. Upon its dark, glossy surface danced the image of Ailis, his wife. Ailis, with her long flaxen braids, their small son, Colin, held fast to her side. Ailis and Colin, radiant and happy, floating on the surface of the wine. Ailis, forever silent, cold as clay, and Colin, sleeping eternally in a grave no bigger than his tiny bed.

With a ragged curse, he reached for the crystal decanter of wine and knocked it from the table. Crying out in agony, he buried his face in his hands.

The sound, more mournful than the howl of a wolf, echoed down the long corridors and empty hallways, then faded away. Nothing moved. Not a sound could be heard. For some time, he sat motionless, and then, after a while, he lifted his head.

The darkness of the night called out to him, and he rose from the table, the heavy legs of his chair scraping across the uneven stone floor. He lifted the tankard to his mouth and swallowed the last drops of forgetfulness and tossed the goblet to the table. It rolled to the edge, teetered, then fell to the floor with a hollow clang.

Standing silently near the door, Manus Finlay stood in the shadows and watched, as he always did. He had been the Macqueen's friend and faithful ally since he had found him lying wounded upon the bloody fields of Culloden Moor, some five years before.

As the Macqueen approached, Manus removed his friend's cape from a peg, and he handed it to him as he passed by. As if in a trance, the younger man took the cape and threw it around his shoulders. A moment later, he had disappeared through the door.

Once he was gone, Manus turned to follow in silence.

Chapter Three

Lady Anne Crofton went to bed with a glass of warm milk. She could not sleep even after drinking the milk, so she lay in the darkness, watching eerie shadows move silently about her room. Something about them reminded her of the stories she had heard of the haunted island across the bay.

She wouldn't have given those stories a second thought, had it not been for two facts. The first was that her father was somehow involved, and the second, that she could not stop thinking about her frightening visit to the island.

It was that tall, dark man with the piercing eyes and the angry set to his jaw who had first told her about the beast. But when she had inquired about the story, she had learned that the beast the man on the island had talked about did not live here, at Ravenscrag, as he had led her to believe, but on the island where the crumbling old castle lay in ruins. She shuddered at the thought. No wonder he had wanted her off the island as soon as possible, or that he had been suspicious of her, accusing her of being a spy. And then there was the matter of the way he had threatened her with what he would do if he ever learned she had told him a lie.

She trembled at the thought. The truth was, she had told him nothing but lies. And she had a suspicion her father had told her a few of them as well.

Try as she might, she could not remember more than a few snatches of the conversation she had had with her father. They had talked of the enmity between him and the half-mad creature who lived on that devil-possessed island, but her father had not revealed much, keeping the discussion vague and, obviously, from his own point of view. Lady Anne was a woman who formed her own opinions. Just because he was her father, that did not mean she trusted him. In truth, she hardly knew him, having seen him for the first time since she was a baby when she came to the Shetlands only a few weeks ago, after the death of her mother in Cornwall.

Because of this, she thought it prudent to be cautious. After all, her mother had disliked him enough to leave him, and she had continued to hate him until the day she breathed her last. And now that he had sailed for England, it would be longer still until she and her father got to know one another.

By the time Anne finished that thought, she was hoping she'd find someone to tell her the truth about what had happened between her father and the creature who lived in the ruins of Blackness Castle before he returned.

Blackness Castle... Why did the very name intrigue her? The sound of it haunted her dreams at night. Even now, she could feel its pull...something magnetic that drew her like the power of suggestion.

Throwing the covers from her body, she combed her fingers through her mane of thick black hair, pushing the long length of it behind her as she climbed from the bed. She went to the window and drew back the drape. Darkness surrounded the island, making its outline vague. Not that it mattered. She could feel its presence.

Above the island, the moon danced among the dark, brooding clouds that rolled restlessly overhead. A cold rush of wind swept over her, as though a door had been left open somewhere in the house. A breath later, she thought she heard someone calling her name.

Anne... Come.... Come into the darkness.... Come and share your warmth with me....

What she heard was only the wind making eerie noises as it blew through the old, drafty turrets and crenels of Ravenscrag Castle. Yet she could not shake the feeling of a presence.

She gave in to a bit of self-admonishment. "You have been listening to too many ghost stories. Keep this up and they will lock you away in an oubliette and leave you there to forget." The reminder sent a shiver up her back, which was followed immediately by an unquenchable thirst to know even more. One step was all she took. Now she was closer to the window. Pressing her nose to the pane, she searched the darkness that lay beyond.

Was he out there? Now? Was that what she felt? His awful presence? Did he lure young women to their deaths among the treacherous rocks?

Logic told her that was ridiculous. Curiosity said the best way to answer her questions was to go to the island again, where she could see for herself.

Yet the thought of going to the island caused an uneasiness to sweep over her. She had been frightened the day she was there, and she was famous for being too curious and too headstrong for her own good. Even now, her mother's word of caution reached out to her: "God fashioned hell for the inquisitive."

Anne stood at the window, staring at the grotesque outline of Blackness Castle. Its broken towers and jagged walls were as black as the name they bore. He was there, she knew, walking the walls as the village folk said, with his hair wild and flying about him. A madman. A howling beast...

The Beast of Blackness Castle.

She heard the door open, and although she knew it would

be her maid, Fanny, she quickly dropped the drapery and turned away.

Fanny stopped and looked at her bed. "Were you in the bed, milady, or did you leave the window open when a storm blew through? What a frightful mess! The covers are going every which a way."

"I couldn't sleep."

"I would never have guessed."

The two of them laughed, and Anne was reminded that laughter was, indeed, good for the soul.

"I'll straighten it up and then you'll sleep better," Fanny said. She turned to the bed and busied herself with setting it to rights, clucking and tsk-tsking as she did.

Anne stayed where she was, waiting for her heart to stop its rapid pounding. She took a deep breath.

"Have you been staring at that devil again, milady?"

Anne glanced back at the window, thankful she had allowed the drape to fall back into place. She did not want to look at the darkness or see that awful place the beast called home. "Fanny, do you believe the stories they tell about him in the village?"

"Of course I do, milady."

"What kind of stories do you hear?"

Fanny punched the pillow into a nice puff. "Horrible stories. It is said that he offers sacrifices of young virgins and he drinks their blood. That is what makes him go mad—virgins' blood."

Anne laughed. "Oh, Fanny, surely *you* don't believe such stories…do you?"

Fanny looked a bit shamefaced. "I…I don't know, milady."

"Have you ever seen him?"

Fanny looked properly horrified. "Oh, no, milady. And I wouldn't want to. They say he has a curse upon him, you know. He has the evil eye."

Anne did not bother to hide her amusement. "I think he

is probably a poor, miserable man who has gone slightly mad—more to be pitied than feared.''

"I don't believe that for a minute. There isn't a soul in the village what isn't afraid of him and his devil's lair. People who go there never return.''

Anne scoffed at that. "I was rowed to the island when I first came here, and I survived, as you can see.''

"You went to Blackness Castle? Alone?''

"I was left on the island by mistake. I was supposed to be taken here, but the captain of the ship was a fool.''

"It was the perfect time for the beast to put his curse upon you.'' Fanny eyed her with an open air of speculation. "Lord protect us! You do seem intrigued with him and his wicked castle, more and more. Oh, milady…''

"Fanny, I am not bewitched. I am simply a curious sort, and certainly not on the receiving end of any curse.'' She tapped her finger against the side of her face. "I would give anything to know what the bitterness is between the beast and my father. Have you ever heard anyone speak of it?''

"Not to any great length. All I know is that his family was murdered. They are all buried here, you know…at Ravenscrag.''

"His family? You mean his wife and children? Or his parents?''

"I don't know, milady, but I think I remember hearing someone say it was his wife and child. Murdered, they were, and by the English, it is said.''

Anne turned her head away. "Oh, how awful! Did it happen here, do you think?''

"Yes, it was here…perhaps in this very room.''

"I asked for information, not white hair. What are you trying to do, frighten me?''

"The more you know about the enemy, the more you can withstand him, I always say. Will there be anything else, milady?''

"No, that will be... Wait a minute. Take that empty milk glass when you go."

Fanny bobbed downward in something that faintly resembled a curtsy, while brilliant red strands of her hair fell down across her eyes. With a quick puff of air, she blew them out of her face. "Yes, milady." She picked up the glass and headed for the door. As she passed through it, she said, "Good night, milady. Don't worry about the beast coming to get you. I hear he never leaves the island. They say he cannot, for his heart is buried there and he cannot leave until he finds it."

"Good night, Fanny. I am *certain* I will sleep now."

When Fanny closed the door, Anne turned toward her bed. "Well, with that bit of cheerfulness, I suppose I will try to get some sleep." She climbed into bed and doused the light. She closed her eyes and waited for sleep.

...he never leaves the island. ...he cannot, for his heart is buried there and he cannot leave until he finds it....

Anne pulled the covers higher over her shoulders and lay in the darkness, staring at the drape that covered her window. She wondered what was going on across the bay—on that tiny island where a man existed who was as steeped in mystery as the great ruins of his castle. And what the connection was between the man she had met that day and the beast.

As always when she thought of the beast, a cold draft of air seemed to move over her. Her body trembled in response. She found herself wondering what he was like, and yet, deep inside her, she knew that she really did not want to know.

She closed her eyes, refusing to think about the crumbling castle and the man who haunted it. Instead, she focused her thoughts on her father and wondered when he would be home.

Chapter Four

The old longing was back, and the thirst for revenge was strong. The Macqueen stood on the castle wall and stared out across the expanse of thrashing black water toward the battered coast of the Shetlands, his gaze locked upon the dim glow of lights from the windows of Ravenscrag Castle, the ancient home of the lairds of the clan Macqueen. His home…until it, and everything else he loved, had been taken from him by the English.

The pain of remembrance caused him to throw back his head and shout. It was a long, mournful cry. The wind ripped the ribbon from his hair, sending the long black mass swirling about his head. Hard drops of freezing rain pelted him and splattered upon his face.

The rain came down harder and faster. The wind rose and whipped his great black cape about him. Overhead, black, boiling clouds blocked the moonlight and cast the world below into complete darkness. Not even the torches that burned along the castle wall could penetrate the inky cover of black. Below him, the angry sea pounded against the rocky summit and sent a fine mist shooting upward, where it leaped the parapets to settle upon his cape, but he did not seem to notice, any more than he noticed the deafening sound of the towering waves that slammed against the rocks.

A storm was settling in. He had known since early this morning that this storm would be worse than all the others, for the throbbing ache in his old wounds had awakened him even before daylight penetrated the gloom of his chamber. Even now, he could feel the pain more intensely than he had this morning, and he prayed it would grow stronger still. For then, and only then, would he be certain that he would never forget.

One by one, the lights of Ravenscrag began to disappear as the storm worsened. A blinding bolt of lightning ripped across the sky. A second later, an exploding crack of thunder sent a stab of pain deep inside his ears. To his right, a dull beam of light penetrated the darkness as a lamp appeared.

Manus stepped through the doorway and shouted, his voice barely audible over the roar of the wind and the waves. "I ken we've a bonny storm brewing! Would you be coming inside now?"

The Macqueen stood with his legs widespread as he faced the wind and stared into the heart of the storm. He did not turn his head to look at Manus. "Go back inside, I'll—"

The words froze in the Macqueen's throat, for just as he was about to speak, he saw the faintest glimmer of light reaching out from the wildly thrashing sea. As quickly as it had come, the light disappeared. For a moment, he thought his eyes had deceived him, for he could see nothing. Then, suddenly it appeared again, the faintest gleam of light.

A ship. Before he could think further upon it, Manus quickly covered the distance between them and reached his side. He held the light aloft and stared into the Macqueen's face. "You look like you have seen a ghost."

"No ghost, but a ship…floundering not too far offshore."

Manus glanced in that direction. "Will she be coming aground, do you think?"

"Aye. She will be upon the rocks before we can get down there. Alert the men."

Manus grumbled something inaudible, then said, "You know what they will be saying…that it was you and your curses that caused the wreck. You will receive no thanks for risking your life." Manus paused to watch the great black cape of the Macqueen disappear through the doorway.

Grumbling, he turned away and did what he had been doing for five years: He followed the Macqueen.

Chapter Five

It appeared that all aboard were dead by the time they reached what was left of the ship. Robert and his men searched among the rocks and wreckage for survivors, fighting the waves to reach each body, only to discover that the life they hoped to save was already gone.

"We're too late!" Manus shouted through his cupped hands.

"Aye!" Gavin McDougal shouted back, holding a lamp aloft.

The Macqueen was about to tell his men to return to the castle when Gavin held his lamp aloft and waded out into the water. "Look! Over there…is that someone clinging to a piece of drift?"

Already the Macqueen was making his way between the rocks to wade deeper into the water, fighting his way, inch by inch, falling and being driven back by the sheer force of powerful waves. When he reached the driftwood, he threw his arm around the man. This time, he fought against the weight of a limp body and the water's power. At last, he pulled the man to shore.

Weak and trembling from exertion, the Macqueen stared down at the body stretched out on the sand before him. "Gavin! Bring the lamp!"

Gavin hurried to his side. "Is he dead?"

"I don't know. Hold the lamp higher."

Gavin raised his arm. The lamp cast a small circle of light upon the face of the man Robert Macqueen hated more than anything in the world: Sir John Crofton.

Manus approached. "Is he dead?"

Robert could not take his gaze from the devil's own face. "Aye, much to my sorrow, I think he is."

Manus looked down at the man and gasped. "Sir John! 'Tis the murdering bastard himself."

"Even in death he has cheated me."

"At least this way you won't have his blood on your hands."

"I can think of nothing I would like better." He nudged the body with his boot. There was no movement, no response.

Manus stared down at the despised face, then looked around at the bodies scattered upon the sand. "'Tis a pity we couldn't save even one of them."

"It is a greater pity that we couldn't save *this* one."

"What do you want to do with him?" Gavin asked. "Shall we leave him here for the scavengers?"

"No. Bring him back to the castle. I'll hang his black heart from the tower."

Gavin wedged his lamp in the sand, then picked up the body of Sir John, his brawny arms flexing as he heaved the Englishman's scrawny body over his back. Suddenly a gush of water rushed from Sir John's mouth. It was followed by a choking cough.

Gavin started and glanced at Manus, who turned to look at the Macqueen. "He lives," Manus said, in a disbelieving voice. "What shall we do with him, now?"

"Take him to the castle. Nothing has changed," Robert said. He said nothing more as he stood with his arms crossed in front of him, but he never took his gaze from Sir John's body as Gavin hauled it toward Blackness.

Manus gave him a questioning look. "What will you do with him? Toss him into the dungeon?"

"Of course not. We will give him the finest care, to ensure his speedy recovery."

"And then what?"

A slow-spreading smile curved across the Macqueen's face. "And then, we will kill the bastard."

Across the bay the next day, Lady Anne Crofton sat before her embroidery frame, her face pale, her eyes glistening with tears, as she listened to the words of Captain Singleton.

"The dead have all been accounted for, but your father's body has not been found. More than likely, it was swept out to sea."

Anne barely looked at the splendid uniform, the gleaming medals, awarded to only the bravest of English soldiers, that the captain sported. Her father's ship was lost, and her father was dead. It was too soon, she thought. Too soon after the death of her mother. Too soon for her to get to know him. "Where did the wreck occur?"

"Not far from here. It seems the *Albatross* was blown off course and broke up on the rocks near Blackness Castle."

"On the island?"

"Yes, just below the castle... At least, that is where the bodies were pulled from the water."

"And my father was not among them?"

Captain Singleton looked down. "No, I regret to say he was not."

"And he is the only passenger not accounted for?"

"Yes."

Anne was silent for a moment. Then she put her embroidery away, and rose to her feet. "Would you be so kind, Captain, as to take me to the place where you found the wreckage?"

"A lady such as yourself should not be going to such a

rough place. It is quite difficult to reach, especially with a small boat.''

"I do not mind. I am not afraid of a small boat. I often went out alone in England."

"It is a difficult journey. The way is treacherous...covered with boulders and many large rocks."

"I would like to see the wreckage, Captain. If you will not accompany me, then I will go alone."

Captain Singleton's face turned red. His expression said he was quite put out at her request, but he clicked his heels together with true military dispatch, and said, "As an English gentleman and an officer, I cannot allow you to make such a journey alone. I will, of course, accompany you. When would you like to go?"

"Now."

This time, all the color drained from Captain Singleton's face. His mustache drooped with obvious disappointment. "Now?" he sputtered. "You wish to go now?"

Anne nodded her head. "If you please."

"As you wish," he replied, but this time he did not click his heels.

Lady Anne walked from the room, pausing momentarily at the door. "I will only be a moment, Captain. I will change clothes and meet you down at the boat."

Chapter Six

The Macqueen paced the floor back and forth in front of the enormous fireplace in the library. He was waiting for Dr. Burris to finish his examination of the murdering English bastard. Only an hour ago, he had come from the chapel, where he had gone down upon his knees in supplication as he prayed to God for the sparing of Sir John Crofton's life. He did not feel one whit of remorse in asking for Sir John's healing so that he could have the satisfaction of killing him. And why should he?

The Macqueen cursed and turned to brace his hands upon the mantel. As he stared into the flames, the face of his dead wife took shape, and he saw Ailis as he had seen her last, standing upon the walls of Ravenscrag Castle, with their three-year-old son, Colin, in her arms, the two of them waving goodbye as he rode off to fight the British, leading "the mighty clan Macqueen" toward a rendezvous with death.

In the hallway, just outside the room, Marta and Grizel passed by, their arms loaded with laundry. Seeing the Macqueen standing before the fire, his broad back turned toward her, Marta stopped and peered at Grizel over a stack of neatly folded laundry.

"He is such a handsome man, and yet so sad. Why is it

that no one here will speak of the tragedy that struck him? Everyone I ask tells me to tend my own flock.''

''It is wise to heed good advice.''

''You can say that, because you know what happened. Why can't you tell me?''

''No one loyal to the Macqueen enjoys talking about his sorrow.''

''Yet everyone here knows the story, except me. Someone must have told them.''

Grizel stared down at the stack of laundry in her arms for several seconds before she turned to look at Marta. With a resigned sigh, she said, ''I can see by the fire in your eye that you will not rest until you have heard it all. Very well. Go and find Manus Finlay. He knows the story best. Let the burden of telling you be upon him.''

Marta's face brightened, and she thrust her stack of laundry on top of the stack Grizel carried. While Grizel muttered something about not being able to see, Marta went to find Manus.

She found him cleaning guns in the armory. When she told him why Grizel had sent her to find him, he was reluctant to speak of the Macqueen's misery, but, as she had been with Grizel, Marta was persistent.

''I will have Grizel's head for sending you here,'' he grumbled, ''but I ken you will not let this rest until you have heard the whole story.''

''No, I will not. I think I have a right to know. I have already proven my loyalty by coming to work here...even when I know there isn't another lass in the village who would do so.''

Manus turned his faded eyes upon Marta, his resigned sigh telling her that she would learn, at last, of the death of the Macqueen's wife and son, the slaughter of the members of the clan Macqueen, and the curse upon the Macqueen's head.

She took a seat beside Manus and listened quietly as he told the tragic story of the clan Macqueen.

"You mean they were all murdered? Every last one of them?"

Manus nodded. "Down to a man, they were butchered...all of them, save the laird himself, and now he is cursed with the memory of seeing his men cut down right before his eyes, their blood mingling with that of a hundred clans, to stain the fields of Culloden scarlet."

"And the Macqueen was the only member of the clan to survive?"

"Aye, he was the sole survivor, although he was gravely wounded. When I found him, I feared he had lost too much blood to live."

"But he didn't die." Marta's tone possessed a hint of optimism.

"No, but it wasn't because he did not pray for death. He cursed the English with every painful breath he drew, and he cursed his own inability to end his own life. It would have been much easier, and far more noble to die there, just like the other Macqueens. But it was his fate not to join the clan he led to their deaths."

"So you saved him and brought him home?"

"I could not bring him home straightaway. He was at death's door. I took him to an abandoned crofter's hut and nursed him back to health. When he was well enough to return home, some three months later, I went with him. It was on our journey to Ravenscrag that the Macqueen made a vow to raise the sons and daughters of the slain Macqueens, and to make the clan as great and mighty as it had once been.

"But you said they were all dead."

"Aye, it was a vow he could not keep. From the moment we first set foot upon the Shetlands, the Macqueen had a premonition that something dreadful had taken place. He fully expected to see Ravenscrag torn apart, stone by stone.''

"And it wasn't."

"To his surprise, Ravenscrag was as strong and splendid as it had been the day he left. It was only when we rode closer that he saw just how the British deal with those they call enemy."

Marta shivered. When she spoke again, her words came slowly, and her tone was low. "They were all dead."

"Aye. Down to the lowliest servant. As we passed by the graves, he dropped to his knees beside his horse and cursed God for making the innocent pay. He struck his chest and cried out in anguish, but it was when he discovered the graves of his wife and son that I feared he had lost his mind.''

"What did he do?"

"He was overcome with grief, ye ken. That is what made him wish for death. He remounted and rode his horse at a dead run, right up to the gates of Ravenscrag, praying all the while that someone would slay him. From high upon the walls above us came the sound of mocking laughter, and he looked up to see the flaming scarlet coats of the English soldiers. He stood up in his stirrups and held his arms out, making himself a bold target, but not one of his tormentors fired a shot.''

"Why?"

"Because they were told to hold their fire. Sir John preferred to let the Macqueen live, rather than to end his suffering by allowing him to join those he loved in death.''

"A fate worse than death," she whispered.

"Aye," he said, "a fate worse than death. So, now you know." Manus looked tired and worn. He sighed wearily, and it reminded her that he was an old man. "Go back to your work, now, and speak no more of this to anyone.''

Marta turned away, then paused to look at Manus over her shoulder. "But what about the curse?"

"That *is* the curse…to remember when you want to forget. To seek death over and over again, and each time be denied."

"No wonder the Macqueen hates the Englishman. It was Sir John who brought the curse upon him."

"Night after night he has walked the castle walls, praying for a way to seek his revenge. And now, after five long years, his prayers have been answered…."

Chapter Seven

Manus came into the kitchen, where Robert sat, hunched over a bowl of soup. "The English captain is snooping around the wreckage. He has a lady with him."

Robert tossed the spoon to the table and stood. A moment later, he yanked his cape from a hook. "Who is the lady? Did you get a good look at her?"

"I was quite a distance away and could not see her face. Perhaps it was Sir John's daughter."

"His daughter? I didn't know he had a daughter. How did you learn of her?"

"I only heard about her. Apparently the mother died, so the girl came to live with her father."

That had a strangely familiar ring to it, and Robert could not help thinking of the girl who had walked out of the water like a silkie and onto his island that day. It wasn't the same girl, he assured himself. He could never be attracted to a daughter of that English pig. "How old is she? What does she look like?"

"Old enough to be wed, and from what I hear, she is comely enough to turn a man's head. Other than that, I do not know. I have yet to see her, ye ken."

"Old enough to be wed… She is English, and the spawn

of a murdering Englishman. No right-minded Scot would come within a mile of her.''

Manus said nothing.

''If it is his daughter with the captain, what would she be doing here?''

''It could be that she is curious about her father's disappearance...or it could be that the woman I saw wasn't the Crofton wench.''

''It doesn't matter. Let them snoop. They will find nothing.''

''What if they find out he's not dead?''

''Finding out he is alive is one thing. Taking him from us is another.''

''You cannot fight the English and win. You, of all people, should know that.''

''I don't intend to fight the English. I have what I want.''

''If they learn he is here, they will come after him.''

''Let them come.''

''Are you not afraid...even after what you've seen them do?''

''What can they do to me, that they have not already done?''

''They could take your life.''

At that, Robert gave a shout of mocking laughter. ''You cannot kill someone who is already dead.'' He turned away and made his way to the castle wall. He wanted to see for himself.

He stood on the wall, the wind whipping his hair and cloak as he looked down at the English captain and the woman. Even from where he stood, he could see that she was quite small, and when the wind blew her cape from her head, he saw that her hair was as black as her father's heart.

As he watched them, he kept thinking of the girl who had come here that day. He did not want to think of her, but his mind had a habit of getting its own way. He narrowed his eyes and watched the two snooping around below. Soon, the girl he tried to forget was out of his mind.

But he knew that was not where she would stay.

Lady Anne pulled her wool cape more closely about her, to ward off the penetrating wind. She stepped over shattered boards and bits of rope left from the wreckage, and paused a moment to look at the broken remains of the ship that lay scattered over the rocks. From what she could see, it was easy to understand how all lives aboard the *Albatross* had been lost. It was not easy to understand why her father's body had been the only one not recovered. Not unless one figured that the beast had had something to do with it.

"Where were the bodies found?" she asked the captain who followed closely behind her.

"We don't know for certain, since Macqueen's men discovered the wreckage. They could have been moved, but they were all lying among the rocks that line the shore, or in shallow water."

"All but my father."

"Yes."

She stood amid the wreckage and stared out over the water. "It would be a horrible death, I think, to drown."

"Horrible, but it's a quick death, I am told."

"Then I can be thankful for that, at least."

Captain Singleton glanced at the sky overhead. "It grows dark, and you are cold. We should be returning."

"Yes, I suppose there is nothing further for me to do here." She paused, looking around her. "I don't know what I expected to find here."

"Sometimes it helps the grieving to see the place where a loved one was seen last."

She called her father's wolfhound, Pharaoh to her side, and waited for him to appear from beneath the rocks. Suddenly, she felt someone watching them, and she turned to stare up at the walls of Blackness Castle.

She drew in her breath. He was there, just as the rumors said, a figure of a man, black against the purpling close of day, the wind whipping his hair and clothes, making him look every inch the beast he was reported to be.

"Don't be alarmed. They say his mind is not right. He is a sort of legend in these parts."

"I have heard of him. They say he is a beast, Captain…the Beast of Blackness Castle."

"The Scots are a superstitious lot. Don't believe all their supernatural drivel."

"Of course I don't," she said, and turned away, stepping lightly over the stones that lay wet and glistening beneath her feet. Captain Singleton held out his hand to help her into the boat. Just as she took his hand, she caught a glimpse of something shining in the water.

"Just a moment, Captain." She bent down and put her hand into the icy water. She could see now that it was a golden chain, catching the last of the sun's rays as it lay among the black rocks in the sand. She caught the chain between her fingers and lifted it, but as she raised the chain, she realized it was connected to something. A second later, she pulled a gold watch out of the sand.

Paralyzed, she stood there, looking at the watch in her hand.

"What is it?"

"A watch." She opened the case and saw the inscription: *To my beloved John, on the occasion of our marriage. Elizabeth.*

Elizabeth. It was her mother's name, and although Anne had only seen her father's watch a few times, and from a distance, she knew this watch was his.

"Whomever the watch belonged to, it is of no value to them now. Come, my lady, let us be off."

She took the captain's hand and climbed into the boat. She called Pharaoh, and he came running out of the rocks, his nose to the ground. Suddenly, he veered off to the left, sniffing in earnest now, and she knew he had picked up a scent.

A scent of what?

The thought had no more than formed when Pharaoh stopped. He began to whine and bark. A moment later, he began to dig, unearthing a bit of white cloth.

"Pharaoh! Come!" she called, and waited patiently for Pharaoh to return to her, a white scrap of linen still in his mouth.

Captain Singleton laughed. "Seems he found a bit of treasure. It's a pity you cannot train him to sniff for gold. There might be more where that watch came from."

"Yes," she said absently as she took the cloth from Pharaoh's mouth.

She looked down at the linen square, which she realized was a man's handkerchief. There, in one corner, embroidered in white, were the initials *J.C.C.* Her father's name was John Charles Crofton, and this was his handkerchief. She knew it was his, because he had given her one just like it to use one evening when she was telling him about her mother's death and she started to cry.

Her father had been here. She was certain of it. The question was, if he were dead when he came ashore, why would someone go to the trouble to bury his handkerchief? It did not make sense. What made sense was that her father must have been alive, and whoever rescued him had buried the handkerchief in order to fake his death. And who had a better reason to do that than the man who owned this island?

Pharaoh began to whine.

"You have taken his plaything, my lady."

Anne smiled sweetly, "Why, so I have." Then, with a laugh that was a bit higher-pitched than she would have liked, she gave the handkerchief back to Pharaoh.

A moment later, she was staring solemnly into the water, her hand in her pocket and stroking the cold gold casing of her father's watch. As they rowed past the point, she took one last look back at Blackness Castle.

The beast was gone.

Chapter Eight

As his prisoner grew steadily stronger, Robert felt himself coming alive.

He had lived for this moment for five years—waiting and watching, learning a patience he had not known he possessed. And now it had come to pass. At last, he had Sir John Crofton where he wanted him: in the dungeons of Blackness Castle.

Gavin McDougal put the key in the lock. The iron door creaked open. He stepped back and handed the Macqueen the lamp.

"Shall I accompany you?"

"No. Wait here. I won't be long."

Robert ducked his head as he stepped into the small, damp cell. On a straw pallet in the corner lay Sir John. Unaccustomed to the light, Sir John put his hands up and turned his head away. "Have you come to let me go?"

The Macqueen laughed. "I will make a bargain with you."

"One you do not intend to keep, I'll wager. Well, let's hear it. What do you want in exchange for me?"

"I will let you go, when you return my wife and son to me."

"I told you before that I had nothing to do with their

deaths...or the deaths of anyone at Ravenscrag. They were all in their graves when I arrived.''

"They were murdered to make room for you. Not that it matters, for I don't believe you, anyway. Your hands are as red as your scarlet coats, and nothing will wash it out. Certainly not lying.''

"I am not lying. How can I convince you?''

"You cannot, so don't waste what little energy you have left in trying to do so.''

"Then I beg you, as one human being to another, let me go. I will petition the king and request that all your possessions be returned to you, including Ravenscrag.''

"All my possessions? Save the ones I desire the most. What will you do about my wife and son?''

"You can marry again, and have many children. You are still young.''

"It isn't as easy as that. You took something priceless from me. I intend to do the same to you.''

"Please. Let me go.''

The Macqueen laughed. "You will never leave here.''

"What do you intend to do with me?''

"I will keep you here. Forever. And each day you will die a little more than you did the day before, and each night you will pray for death, but it will not come. I will be as merciful as you were. I will not kill you. I will let you live. I will let you live so that you will regret until your dying day that you reaped the profits of another's suffering.''

"I have told you—I did not have anything to do with the death of your wife and child. There was no one here when I arrived.''

"I do not believe you.''

"What would make you believe me?''

"This conversation is finished.'' The Macqueen turned and started toward the door.

Sir John ran after him and grabbed his hand, going down on his knees before him. "Please. Tell me what I can do. I will do anything…give you anything it is in my power to do.''

''I want my wife back.''

Sir John's eyes were wild, rolling from side to side, as if he were searching for something he could say, something that would change his fate.

The Macqueen shoved his hand away and stepped through the door. He handed Gavin the lamp. ''Lock him up.''

''Aye.''

''No!'' Sir John screamed. ''Wait! I have a daughter.…'' Sir John seemed to catch himself. ''I am a family man, and although my wife is dead, I understand how a man feels about his family. I would not do anything to deprive a man of his family.''

''As I said before, I do not believe you, just as I will never believe anything you say. You are English. It is in your blood to lie.''

''You bloody bastard! You are the devil incarnate!''

The Macqueen walked off. The iron gate creaked heavily behind him.

Sir John's shrill voice cut through the dungeon's damp air. ''Do you hear me? You are a devil!''

A muscle in Robert Macqueen's jaw flexed. ''Then you would do well to remember one thing—you cannot bargain with the devil.''

Chapter Nine

Lady Anne knew this was the day she would go to the island again. There were too many questions that remained unanswered, and the island was the only place to answer them.

She was exhausted by the time she had rowed around the point that blocked Ravenscrag from view. Although she had often gone out alone at home, she was not as familiar with these waters as she was with those of Cornwall. As a precaution, she hugged the shore, knowing she must keep it in sight. It would make the trip longer, but that could not be helped.

The waves here were higher, the currents stronger, than she was accustomed to, and the weather was bitterly cold. Already, her gloves were stiff and crusted with ice. Inside, her fingers were numb. Beneath her soaked clothes her body felt warm, and yet her teeth chattered from the cold. Her throat was dry and scratchy. Her eyes teared and made it difficult for her to see.

She had to go on. She had gone too far to turn back, and there was no place along this rugged, lonely coast for her to seek shelter. She realized her foolishness and her over-confidence. She was too headstrong, and she possessed too much pride, and now that pride was asking her to pay a dear, dear price.

How she wished she could go back to Ravenscrag, turn back the clock and be standing in her bedroom, faced with the same decision she had been faced with this morning. Only this time, she would choose to stay home.

From out of the stormy grayness ahead of her, she could make out the dim outline of the island, but she knew her strength would be gone long before she reached its shore. Her head felt light, and she had difficulty focusing. She stared down at her aching arms and realized that the oars were gone, and yet she had no recollection of having let them go. She was doomed now. Without the oars, she was completely at the mercy of the sea, and well she knew that the sea had no mercy.

She was tired...so tired that even the knowledge of her own approaching death did little to shake her. Her only thought now was to lie down, to rest, to close her eyes and to feel warm again.

Dying wasn't so bad. You lay down and you went to sleep. She felt herself slipping downward. Her head struck the seat behind her, and a stabbing, blinding pain shot through her skull.

Robert had been watching the boat for some time now, unable to fathom what kind of fool would set out in a small rowboat at the onset of such a violent storm. One moment he was watching the occupant of the boat battle his way forward. The next, the boat was unmanned and drifting wildly. Whoever the fool was, he had either gone overboard, or had succumbed to the cold and lay frozen in the bottom of the boat. It served the half-wit right if he was carried out to sea.

It was only when the boat drifted toward his island that the Macqueen turned and went inside, calling to Manus and Gavin as he went.

It was almost dark by the time they reached the point where the battered boat was being shoved closer to shore by each pounding wave. The Macqueen held the lamp aloft as he stood on the rocks and watched Gavin wade out into water up to his knees.

Gavin grabbed at the rope tied to the bow, and missed. He caught it on the second try, then turned and put the rope over his shoulder, tugging the boat forward until it rested upon solid ground.

Robert saw the dark cloak covering the man who lay unmoving in the bottom of the boat. He called out to Gavin. "Is he dead?"

"I don't know, but if he isn't, he should be! His cloak is frozen stiff!"

Manus moved forward. "Let me help!"

Together they lifted the body from the boat. "Light as a feather!" Manus shouted. "'Tis but a lad."

"Is he alive?" the Macqueen called back.

Manus shook his head. "I can't tell!"

"Bring him up to the house, then, and be quick about it!"

They carried the lad up the stairs to the Macqueen's chamber, for there was a warm fire going there, and his bed was covered, appropriately, with wolf furs. When Gavin and Manus had placed the lad on the bed, the Macqueen sent them to find Grizel and Marta. "And bring a bottle of warm brandy and a jar of honey."

As soon as they left the room, Robert turned and placed his hand on the pale skin of the lad lying so silently before him. He had seen this lad before. He was certain of it, but he could not recollect where.

The lad's face was icy-cold—too cold for Robert to tell if he was dead or alive. With a sudden movement, he grabbed the two sides of the lad's shirt to rip it apart, so that he could place his ear to his chest to listen for a heart-beat.

The fabric had barely been ripped apart when Robert sucked in his breath. Transfixed, he could only stare. The sound of the door opening behind him shook him out of his stupor. He cursed.

Marta let out a shriek. "''Tis a girl! Oh, my Lord... 'Tis a girl, and the Macqueen has bared her to the waist!''

"Stop yapping and get out of the way," Grizel said, giving Marta a bump with her hip. She stopped next to Robert and looked down at the girl. "Is she still alive?"

"I...I don't know. I was going to listen for a heartbeat. That is why I... Oh, hell. I'm no good at this. You see what you think."

Grizel nodded. Placing the bottle of brandy and the honey on the chest by the bed, she leaned forward and put her ear to the girl's chest. She remained that way for so long that Robert thought the girl must be dead. Grizel finally pulled her head back and covered the girl. "Her heart beats, but faintly. We must get her out of these clothes. Marta, help me."

Marta scampered around to the other side of the bed and looked at Grizel.

Grizel turned to the Macqueen. "If you would lift her, Marta and I will pull the cloak from under her. The rest we can manage."

Robert lifted the girl off the bed. Even soaking wet, she did not weigh as much as one of his hounds. But when they pulled the cape from her, a long, curly mass of black hair fell to the bed like glossy ropes of wet seaweed. Somehow appropriate, for a creature plucked from the sea.

This was the woman who haunted his dreams at night. Had she come back here on purpose? Or was her appearance an accident, a result of the storm?

Grizel placed a dry, folded blanket beneath the girl, and Robert lowered her onto the bed again. He turned away and saw Manus and Gavin standing nearby. ''Send someone to build up the fire,'' he said to Gavin. ''Tell them to keep it going all night.''

Gavin nodded and left. Silently Robert and Manus followed him from the room leaving the women behind to minister to the girl.

Anne moaned and stirred in her sleep. she was dreaming again—strange dreams, in which the familiar and the unknown seemed to melt together into a whole. She could hear the crashing force of waves against her boat, and felt the rocking motion as surely as she tasted the tang of the sea on her lips, heavy with salt. She knew she was dying, and yet, when she looked on the other side of the boat, the sea was as calm and as smooth as glass.

Then, from out of the darkness, he came, a creature not quite man and yet not completely beast. Grotesque though he was, she felt no fear of him as he lifted her and carried her over the water toward the darkness that lay beyond, a darkness she feared she could never leave.

She couldn't let him take her there, for once she was within the walls of his lair, there would be no escape. Not ever.

She moaned again, thrashing the bed wildly, repeating the same word. ''No... No... No...''

From out of the darkness, a voice came to her—a strange voice filled with reassurance. ''There, there. You are safe now. Sleep, and do not fret.''

But she wasn't safe. She must leave. Now. Before it was too late. If only she weren't so weak. If only her body would obey. Her throat was dry and swollen, her chest burned as if filled with hot coals. One moment she felt as though she was being boiled alive. The next, she was shivering from the cold.

Someone was trying to kill her. She had to escape. She had to...

The soft voice spoke to her again, but the words seemed too far away for her to comprehend. Someone lifted her head. She felt a sweet, burning liquid slide down her throat, and felt the sharp stab of pain when she swallowed. She turned her head from side to side. She did not want any more. It hurt too much. "Noooo…"

"Just a little more, child. It will help you rest, and keep the bad dreams away."

Three more times she swallowed, each time fighting against the pain. Then she felt her body relax as she drifted off to sleep.

They had lied to her. The dreams came again, only this time they were worse than before. She was lying in a great bed in an unfamiliar room. She was not bound, but she could not move. It was as if she were held to the bed by some invisible binding. She heard a key turn in the lock. Her heart beat wildly in her chest. Then the door opened, and she saw him standing in a pool of pale white light.

His eyes were yellow, his nose was long, and his teeth were pointed and sharp. It was the face of a predator, a wolf. The sight of him terrified her. And yet she felt a craving, a thirst, for him that she could not have explained. She wanted to feel the heat of his skin and the strength of his arms around her, wanted to know the things he could teach her, things for which she had no name.

She felt her arms lift, stretching out to him in a beseeching manner. The thought that she had done it frightened her, and yet she could not stop herself.

He was beside her now, and she felt the weight of him on the bed beside her, felt, too, the warm caress of words spoken softly against her throat. "I am yours, my beautiful one, my lovely creature from the sea."

She wanted to rebuke him, to scream and keep on screaming until he went away, but the words, the resistance, fell away from her, as shed skin falls from a snake.

"Come to me, my beloved…."

Tears spilled down her cheeks. Her body shook with heaving sobs. And yet not a sound came from her lips. *This is a dream. Soon I will awake, and I will be home. This is only a dream. Nothing is real....*

Her fingers spread outward. The bed was solid beneath her. Her eyes fluttered open for a mere second, just long enough for her to see the candle that burned next to her bed. It was real. She took a deep breath, and the scent of the wax filled her nostrils, and she knew then that this, too, was real.

"No," she whispered. "You aren't real. This isn't happening to me."

"I am real, and your body knows it. It is only your mind that won't accept the truth."

She lay still, unmoving, attempting to focus all her energy into her mind. She was trying to understand how something unreal could appear so real, how the imagined could interplay with reality. Her mind swirled in a mist of confusion.

She felt his mouth on hers. Such a beautiful feeling it was—one that sent a ripple of sensation cascading through her. Was this real, or was she dreaming it as well? His hands caressed her body, touching her intimately. It couldn't be a dream. Not this mouth. Not these hands.

She was surrounded by his warmth, his nearness, and bewildered by her unrestrained desire for him. She fought against him, against herself. She could not give in. She had to resist. But whatever it was that consumed her, it was stronger than she. At last, she lay passive, her body drenched in sweat.

Need. Wanting. Desire. They coiled around her like a sweet perfume, seducing her with promises of the exotic, the unknown. And still his hands were upon her, coaxing, leading, persuading, seducing....

She gave in to the aching need, the incredible pleasure. Paralyzed with wanting, she felt herself relax and open to him. She moaned and stirred restlessly.

"You belong to me. You will always be mine."

His voice seemed to come to her from far away.

"You are tired. Rest. Rest and regain your strength. Then I will return, to give you the pleasure you want. Wait for me, little beauty. Wait, until it is time for me to come."

His words flowed out of him like a song. The words were familiar to her, but the melody was one she had never heard. He kissed her again, and her heart fluttered inside her like a trapped bird.

"Rest, my love, my adorable one, my gift from the sea. I will be back...."

His words sounded faint and distant. She willed her eyes to open, and she saw him, standing far away, nothing more than a specter, cursed and wicked, a vague shadow against the night. With his midnight hair and great black cape, he was almost impossible to see.

I will be back....

A gloomy hopelessness swept over her. She knew what she must do. She had to get away from him, from this place. She could not stay here to be consumed by this beast, this creature of darkness and despair.

She was so sick. She could not lift her head. How could she even think she could get away? She tried to reason with herself, to plump up her spirits with a shot of courage, but it was no use. Her mind was empty, all her thoughts sucked away by her gripping fear. No wonder he was so understanding, so kind in telling her to rest, so magnanimous in giving her time to heal.

He knew she was trapped here, trapped by her own pride and foolishness. She understood now why animals sometimes froze when they stared into the face of death.

She closed her eyes and wept.

When she awoke, the room was filled with a soft, diffuse light, and Anne knew it was early morning. She had no idea how long she had slept—whether a few hours or a few days.

Yet the need to flee, to get away from this dark, demented place, was still strong within her.

"You cannot stay here," she whispered, forcing herself to a sitting position. "You must leave. Immediately. It may be your only chance."

She raised her head. Dizziness gripped her. The warmth of the bed beckoned. "Get up, Anne. You must get up."

She could not give in. Her life was at stake. "Be strong, Anne. Do not weaken."

She felt the smooth coldness of the stone floor beneath her feet. She looked down and saw she was in a flannel nightgown, one much too large, and miles too long.

She had no idea where her clothes were, or her shoes, for that matter. But she could not waste precious time searching for them. Not if she was to take them by surprise. "They do not expect you to try anything so foolish when you are so ill. If you are to escape this place you must go now. Go, and don't look back."

The halls were deserted, yet she had no idea how to get out of the half-destroyed shell of the castle. Her instincts told her that as long as she was going downward, she was getting closer to the sea.

Her body ached and trembled from exhaustion and she had almost given up hope of ever finding her way when a cold waft of air washed over her. A moment later, she heard the shrieking of seabirds.

She came to an iron gate made of closely set bars. She gripped the bars and pushed. The gate did not give. Her head was swimming and she was so nauseated and dizzy that she felt she might faint. "Please, God, show me the way. Grant me strength...."

She began to search the gate for a lock. Running her hands over each of the bars, she found nothing. There had to be one someplace.

She braced herself against another wave of dizziness by placing her hand on the wall beside her. Her hand closed around something sticking out of the wall. She knew without looking that it was a key.

One turn, and she was outside.

Though the storm had passed, the weather was cloudy and still quite cold. The threat of rain, or perhaps snow, was in the clouds. Already the wind was up, bitter and bringing a burning sting to her cheeks. The flannel nightgown she wore was drafty. "Don't think about the cold," she told herself out loud, needing the comfort of a voice, even if it was her own. "Think about how wonderful it feels to be free, to be away from that moldy and crumbling old castle, away from the creature who dwells there. Think about how warm you will be when you reach home."

Chapter Ten

Robert spotted her as he walked along the wall. As he watched her stumble and fall over the rocks below, he knew she was heading for her rowboat, foolish enough to think she could make it to Ravenscrag. At death's door. Weak as a kitten. Barefoot, and— "God's teeth! She is wearing nothing but a flimsy nightgown."

He whirled around and disappeared through the turret door. A dozen flights of stairs later, he found Manus.

Manus listened to the Macqueen. His weathered face registered disbelief. "Escaped? She was out of her head with fever for five days. Where did she get the energy to climb out of bed, much less make it down to the rocks?"

"How the hell do I know? All I know is, she is down there, barefoot and wearing a nightgown big enough for you and I together. Of all the idiotic—" he caught himself. "We had better go after her. If she gets in that damn leaky boat, she will be nothing but bait for the fish."

"I can bring her back by myself. There is no need for you to go. She doesn't weigh any more than a clump of wet seaweed."

"I'll come with you."

"I think perhaps the lass is afraid of you."

His words turned Robert's face hard, and he knew the

expression in his eyes was bitter. He did not understand why it pained him so deeply to think the lass was so afraid that she would risk her life to escape his very presence. Perhaps the gossip was right. Perhaps he had turned into a beast—a raging wolf who walked the Shetlands at night, seeking those whom he might devour. It was obvious that she believed that to be the truth of it.

He saw Manus was looking at him strangely. "You cannot mean to leave her out there, to let her try to reach Ravenscrag alone. It would be sentencing her to death."

"I am aware of that."

"Give me the word, and I'll have her back here before she grows any colder."

"It has been my intention all along to go after her. My indecision comes from my inability to decide what would be best for her once we've caught up with her."

"We should bring her back here. She will need looking after."

"True, but she will also try to escape again. And again, if necessary. She will try until she succeeds, or kills herself."

"Then what should we do? Take her home?"

"Yes," Robert called back to him, for Manus was already headed down the narrow passageway that led to the caves below. He went after him.

With a grim set to his jaw, Robert hurried through the ancient caves that he knew like an old friend. There was little doubt in his mind that he and Manus would reach her before she found her boat. What concerned him was whether or not he could let her go.

She was not alone. Anne could feel someone, or something, behind her, moving across the rocks that led down to the water's edge. She knew she was being followed, even before she stumbled and fell.

The frigid wind had taken the last of her strength. She

was too weak to get up, too weak even to move. She could do little more than lie there, watching them silently, as she waited to see what they would do to her.

There were two of them, but neither of them was a creature, some half-human form of life that lived in the darkness. They were two men she had seen before, but that did nothing but frighten her more.

The older of the two was short and bent, and he walked with a painful gait. He had rowed her to the big island that day when she first came here. The other she remembered vividly, for how could she forget the way he moved, as gracefully as water over rocks? His torso was lean and long, and his stride covered a great distance. Like that of the beast who walked the castle walls at night, his hair was unbelievably long and black, but, unlike the wild hair of the beast, his was tied back. To her relief, this time he wore no great, swirling cape.

Thankfully, the creature himself had not followed her. She had been wise to flee in the daylight, while he lurked behind the castle walls, afraid of the light.

The powerful one reached her first, and stopped a few feet away to look down at her, irritation and anger gripping his face. How she remembered that look.

She was shivering uncontrollably now. She was tired. Too tired to fight. Too tired to care what they did to her. Not even the thought of being served as the creature's next meal frightened her. It wouldn't be so bad…as long as she was a *warm* meal.

In spite of her weakness, and the intense burning in her lungs, she began to laugh at the direction of her thoughts. Was she demented, or had her fever reached her brain? Once she started laughing, she could not stop. She laughed until her heart felt as if it would explode, and the fire burning in her lungs seemed to suck away each breath she drew.

She was barely mindful as the man swore, then leaned

over and scooped her up as easily as if he were skimming a leaf from the surface of a limpid pool.

His voice was deep and rich. "Her skin is like ice. Give me your cape."

"Is she laughing or crying?" the old one asked.

"Both. She is delirious, and in spite of her icy skin, her breath is hot and feverish. Perhaps our lass wasn't so foolish after all. Coming out here just might have saved her life."

"By freezing her to death?"

"We could not have brought her fever down like this, and certainly not this quickly."

"You aren't going to leave her out here, are you?"

"No, I thought I'd do something more cruel, like rowing her out further and tossing her into the water."

She might be delirious, but there was nothing wrong with her hearing. She could not seem to make the words in her head come out her lips. All she could do was to struggle weakly against the strong band of arms that held her and mutter incoherently.

"I think you've frightened her," the old man said.

"Something I should have done sooner."

"Shall we take her back with us?"

"Only long enough to cover her warmly. Then you and Gavin can take her home."

Manus eyed him speculatively. "Are you certain you want to send her back?"

The Macqueen's body stiffened. "Why wouldn't I? I have no need for a woman underfoot." Without another word, he turned and carried her back to the castle.

Anne opened her eyes only once, but it was enough to burn the imprint of his features into her memory. His face was like a mountain sculpted by the harshness of the elements, yet possessing a raw and breathtaking presence. Like the mountain, he was both beautiful and mysterious, and yet there was something seductive there, despite the threat of danger.

He looked down at her, and for a moment their gazes met and held. His eyes were not the glowing yellow eyes of the creature that had come to her during the night, but a cold, frigid blue that looked as fathomless as the sea that battered the coast.

He might not be the beast, but still he frightened her. "Don't throw me in the water."

He cursed. His body jerked to a stop. When he spoke, his voice was as cold and biting as the wind. He turned toward the old man. "Here. Take her."

She felt herself thrust into another pair of arms. She blinked and looked up into a pair of gray eyes that were gentle and warm. His ancient face wore the weathering of time, and his look was full of wisdom. Somehow she knew he would understand. She lifted her hand and tried to touch his face. She desperately wanted to say something, but her effort came out nothing more than a dry hiss. Her eyes closed. Her hand fell away.

When she awoke again, she was home.

Since her recovery, Anne had returned to the window each night, to stare out at the grotesque outline of Blackness Castle, at those broken towers and jagged walls that were as black as the name they bore.

He was there, she knew, walking the walls, as the village folk said, with his hair wild and flying about him. A madman. A beast. The creature who had come to her. She would never forget his glowing amber eyes. Who was he? Did he really exist? Or was he something that had stepped out of her illness, a phantom of her delirium?

Behind her, the door opened and Fanny came rushing in. As was her custom, she dropped the drapery and let it fall back into place, then turned to see that Fanny was fixing her bed.

"Are ye still starin' at that devil, milady?"

"There is little else to occupy my time during such bitter

cold and deep snows.'' She shivered and drew her shawl higher as she moved to stand before the fire. She held out her hands to warm them.

''Someone ought to go to that island and find the beast. A creature what devours human flesh is not to be pitied. He should be chained in a dungeon...or shot.''

Fanny smoothed the top blanket and removed the last of the wrinkles. ''There,'' she announced, pausing to look at her mistress. ''It is wonderfully pleasurable to see the bloom in your cheeks again, Lady Anne. I don't mind admitting I doubted your ability to recover when they brought you home. You looked quite dead, milady. Pale as a gutted fish, and talkin' out of your head.''

The corners of Anne's mouth turned up at Fanny's vivid description.

Fanny went on with her work for a few seconds, then paused and looked up to direct her stare in Anne's direction. ''Milady, were you afraid you were going to die?''

Anne shook her head. ''No. I felt too awful to die.''

Fanny's eyes gleamed with amusement. ''Sometimes living is worse than dying.''

''Yes...'' Anne did not know why her thoughts took off suddenly in the direction of the tall, black-haired man, but her reply was interrupted by her recollection of the cold emptiness in his eyes.

Sometimes living is worse than dying....

She remembered the way he had stood there, looking down at her, wrapped in the silent manliness of grief.

''Will there be anything else, milady?''

The sound of Fanny's voice startled her and broke her concentration. ''What?''

''Will there be anything else?''

''No...thank you, Fanny.'' Anne put her fingers to her temples.

''Are you all right, milady? Do you have a headache?''

''No headache, just troubling thoughts.''

"I suppose that comes because you haven't quite given up on finding your father alive. It will go much easier for you, once you have learned to accept his death."

"I don't think my father is dead at all."

Fanny gaped at her. "You don't think he is dead? But how could you think that, milady?"

"I have my reasons, Fanny. But I think he is being held prisoner on that island...by that madman."

Fanny made a clucking sound. "If he is in the clutches of that devil, then he is worse than dead."

"I know. That's why I have to find a way to go back, a way to discover if my father is alive."

"I would not risk my life again, if I were you. Besides, if the beast has him, he would never turn him over to you. There is too much hatred in his heart."

Anne sighed and sat down in the rocking chair next to the fire. "I know. That is what worries me. But I can't leave my father there. Although I hardly know him, he is the only living relative I have. His health is poor. The doctor did not think he had a long time to live, even in the best of conditions. He had tried to persuade him to seek a warmer climate."

"You cannot sacrifice your life, milady, for that of your father. He has lived his life. You are just starting yours. You will marry one day, and raise a peck of little ones. Your husband and your children will be your family. You will not be alone."

Although Anne heard Fanny talking, she was not taking in what she said. Her thoughts were trapped a few sentences back, as she heard Fanny's words repeated in her head, over and over.

You cannot sacrifice your life for that of your father....

How ironic it was, that what Fanny said she could not do was the very thing she knew she *must* do. When the idea came to her, it seemed so perfect, she was amazed she had not thought of it before.

"Are you feeling unwell, milady?"

Anne leaped from her chair and hurried toward Fanny, who took a step backward. Anne laughed and took Fanny's hands in hers. "Dear, dear Fanny, I did not mean to alarm you."

"You gave me a fright, milady, coming out of that chair like the devil himself were nippin' at your heels."

"I know...I could hear your knees knocking."

Fanny blushed and looked down. "I am sorry, milady."

"Don't be. You have no idea how much you have helped me."

"Me, milady? How?"

"You have just given me the answer to this dilemma."

Fanny looked at her with a puzzled look in her eyes. "I have?"

"Yes, you have."

"What was it, exactly, that I gave you, milady?"

"The perfect plan to bring my father home."

A bit of Anne's excitement was stolen by the look of pity on Fanny's face. "Oh, milady, don't you understand? If your father is there, the beast will never, ever, allow your father to leave Blackness Castle, much less that evil island."

"I understand the beast would never set my father free, of course, but he might be persuaded to exchange him for another prisoner."

Fanny's brows arched with surprise. "Another prisoner? Who might that be, milady?"

"Me."

Chapter Eleven

Manus heard the roar of the Macqueen, and stopped just outside the door. He gave Gavin a questioning look. "Do you think we were a wee bit hasty in telling the Macqueen who the girl was?"

"Aye. He has been in the devil's own black mood since we told him she wanted to go home to Ravenscrag. Though I think his mood would have been worse if we hadn't told him and then he'd learned she was Sir John's daughter."

"I can't imagine how it could be worse. One minute he is raving, and the next he is sullen and quiet. He lashes out in a fury at anyone who disturbs him, and then he goes through the castle bellowing because he is alone. There doesn't seem to be an end in sight."

"Dare we go in?" Gavin whispered.

"Aye. We all need companionship during our sufferings."

"What if he doesn't want companionship?"

"He doesn't know what he wants. The pain is too sharp. He cannot think. He is like a lion with a thorn in his paw. He doesn't know how to get it out, yet to walk on it causes more pain." Manus took a step, then paused, looking back at Gavin, whose feet seemed embedded in the stone floor. "Are you coming in, or not?"

"Aye...if you are."

Manus opened the door, and the two of them stepped into the great hall, just as they heard a splintering crash, followed by the clang of metal. They looked toward the table and saw eating utensils rolling across the floor.

"He's been drinking again," Gavin said, stopping behind Manus, as if the old man offered some sort of protection.

"Aye, drinking and brooding. He is always this way when the devils go to tormenting him. When the pain becomes unbearable, he strikes out at the first thing he sees. Tonight, it was the dishes on the table."

"Yesterday, it was Marta's mop bucket, which he kicked down the stairs."

"And two days before that, he put his hand through a glass. That particular display cost him nine stitches in his arm."

"And now he's at it again," Gavin whispered, "acting as ornery as a penned stallion."

The Macqueen's voice seemed to explode within the room. "If the two of you have anything to say, you can say it to my face. You don't have to whisper behind my back."

Manus winked at Gavin, who grinned at him through his rusty red beard. "I was just wondering if you had changed your mind about letting the lass go," Manus said, "because if you have, it would be easy enough to go after her and haul her back."

"Why would I want her back? I've more important things on my mind than nursing some kelpie that beached herself on my island."

"Better things? Like torturing her father?"

Robert threw down his tankard and crossed the room in a few long strides. He stopped a hairsbreadth away from Manus.

Gavin swallowed loudly and stepped farther back, his tall form seeming to shrink, but the old man stood his ground, never flinching or looking away. His gaze was steady as he looked the Macqueen in the eye.

"What I do with her father is my own business, and you of all people should know the bastard deserves much more pain and suffering than I could ever hope to give him. He should be down on his knees and praying that locking him up is all I do. I have not tortured him...yet."

"Keeping him chained in that hole is torture enough. Why don't you kill the poor bastard and go on with your life?"

"I am warning you, Manus. Stay out of this. I make my own decisions. When I want your opinion, I will ask for it."

"I hear your warning, but I cannot remain silent any longer. You have suffered much, but you have allowed your loss to turn you into a bitter man. Look at what you've become. You are so tormented by the past that you come dangerously close to being the beast you are rumored to be. Your only pleasure is indulging your grief."

"My grief is just that—*my* grief." The words came out like a snarl.

"You cannot stop the birds of sorrow from flying over your head, but you can prevent them from nesting in your hair. What is gone, and what is past help, should be past grief. Time passes, and so does our grieving. You need to let it go. It has been over five years. Even the sea has its ebbings."

"Are you finished?"

"Almost."

"And what is left? The thrust of the final blow? A knife between my ribs...or is it to be my back?"

"If I were younger, I would never let you remain standing for saying that."

"If you were younger, we wouldn't have gotten that far. I would have flattened you at the beginning of this conversation."

Manus did not say anything, and the room grew tomb quiet.

Robert looked at the old man who had saved his life, the man who had been like a father to him. He did not want to have words with Manus...or Gavin...or Grizel...or even Marta. He did not want to have words with anyone. He wanted to be alone—to be away from them all. He wanted to leave—now—and take his sorrow and his bottle of whisky with him. His grief was too heavy to share.

His insides were on fire from drinking too much. His head ached abominably. Ever since that English witch had beached herself on his island, his life had been in torment. It was bad enough that she was as lovely as a sunlit loch. Did she have to remind him of everything he had lost? The soft feel of a woman lying next to him. The beckoning look of desire. The feeling that what he did, what he thought and where he went mattered, mattered to someone who cared about him, not because of who he was, or what he could provide, but because he was her sun and moon and stars.

Ailis... His heart wrenched. When she was taken from him, the world had turned suddenly dark and cold. Grief had changed him and made him hard. There was no gentleness in his life now, no softness, no woman's loving caress. There was only torment and nagging guilt, and always the vivid red stain of innocent blood on his hands.

Blood that he could never wash out.

As if Manus were privy to his thoughts, his next words hit him with a broadside. "As your friend, as someone who has watched you suffer, I have only one word of advice, one warning. Take a careful look at yourself. Vengeance follows close on the heels of guilt. Are you certain that is not what you are feeling, what has caused you to harden your heart?"

Plain and unvarnished came the words of truth, striking him sharply. "And if it is?"

"There are times when a hard heart is worse than a bloody hand."

"Advice that comes too late. It has been too long. I don't know how to undo my hate. I have nursed this cub, and now it will eat me."

"Perhaps that is why *she* came. She seems to be a quiet, gentle sort...the kind to teach you the power of forgiveness."

Robert scoffed at that. "The power of forgiveness would turn to hate in a heartbeat. The moment she learned I held her father..."

"We often hate what we fear."

"If she is afraid of every blade of grass, then she should not sleep in a meadow. She came here of her own accord. I did not invite her."

"I was wrong to try to make you see reason. The fires of hate burn too strong within you. You have lost all feeling."

"Perhaps that is because you are knocking at the door of a deserted house. I am empty inside, Manus. It is only my body that perseveres. There is, I fear, nothing more stubborn than a dead man." He turned abruptly, and walked back to the table. "Go to bed. I want to be alone."

Gavin, who needed no further encouragement, hurried from the room.

Robert saw the look of both hurt and pity in his friend's eyes, saw the way his old body seemed to go stiff. He owed Manus more than a liberal dose of his own bitterness.

Manus gave a curt nod, then turned and walked from the room, taking his hurt, his pity with him. Once he was gone, there was nothing left behind but the haunting sound of his last words. "I pray that you are not lashed by your own stubborn tail."

Robert filled his tankard, then took his chair before the huge fireplace. He was soon lost in reflection...upon the words Manus had spoken.

How could he change? How could he give up the thing

he had lived with for so long? How could he forgive, rather than hate? He could sooner change squares to circles.

He had waited so long. For years he had thought of nothing but the time when he would have Sir John Crofton at his mercy. And yet, when that moment came, he had not felt the elation, the sense of triumph, he had imagined. He hated his inability to feel anymore. Hated the weakening of his thirst for revenge, the need to strike out and hurt because he hurt. Even as he thought these things, he knew, deep down in the most secret part of him, that the thing he hated most was what he had become.

It had taken a tiny slip of a girl, delirious and out of her head, to show him just how far down he had gone. He could not remember a woman ever being frightened of him, and certainly not to the point that she would prefer death to his presence. And yet her act of desperation had proven one thing: Her driving need to escape him had been greater than her fear of death.

He did not known how long he sat there, but it was long enough for him to down the last bit of whisky.

Grizel's voice announced her presence. "It grows late, and you do not need anything more to drink."

He picked up the empty tankard and tipped it toward her. "There is nothing inside." He laughed. "It bears a striking resemblance to me and my life, does it not?"

"It is only your eyes that cannot see. If you were truly dead inside, you would not feel so much pain. Your heart is heavy. Take it out on sleep. Things will not seem so grim on the morrow."

"Too many devils chase me tonight, Grizel. I cannot sleep. There are many decisions to be made."

"It is always better to sleep on things than to lie awake thinking."

"When I am bedeviled, I cannot sleep. Sleep then becomes my enemy."

"Aye, I know. I have heard your cries in the night, when

you are tormented by dreams. Perhaps tonight will be different. Perhaps the whisky has dulled the memory. Sleep is what you need.''

"Sleep," he said, staggering to his feet. "A beautiful fruit…such a bitter taste."

Grizel walked with him to his room and removed his boots when he fell across the bed. She drew the furs over him, then doused the candle and crept quietly from the room, leaving him to seek the counsel of his pillow.

He dreamed of Ailis again.

Beautiful Ailis, with the musical voice and the fair, fair skin. Only, when he reached for her as he always did, hungry to take her in his arms, her long golden hair turned an inky black, and the face that leaned into his kiss was not the face of his dead wife, but the face of the spawn of the devil who took her life.

He talked in his sleep. He tossed and turned in the bed, then awoke with a start. He sat upright, his body drenched in sweat. The black-haired witch had robbed him of his dreams again. As she had done nightly since she had first come to his island. She who managed to cover his wife's pale golden image with her devilish black one.

Even in his sleep, she mocked him, tormented him. He wanted to put his hand to each side of his head and press until he crushed the image of her lying pale and cold in front of him. Even now, he could not rid himself of the memory of her that burned within him like a red-hot brand.

He wanted her—had wanted her since the first moment he had looked down at her. He climbed out of bed and threw his cloak about him. He needed the cold shock of the wind upon him tonight to clear his jumbled thoughts.

He walked the wall, willing his thoughts to remain on his dead wife. He stopped and braced his hands against the wall and stared out over the sea that stretched endlessly before him. Her soul, her sweet, sweet spirit, was out there…

somewhere just beyond his reach. "Ailis, my love, my life. How can I bear it?"

He dropped his head down between his shoulders. "I will never be at peace. I will know only torment for the rest of my days." He threw his head back then, and cried out in agony. The mournful sound of his wail drifted over water that lay as dark and cold as death.

A sharp, stabbing pain cut into his chest. Hot tears scalded his face. Consumed by grief and abject loneliness, he cried out again, his tears mingling with the sound of anguish, as he repeated, "Why? Why? Why?"

His heart stilled. A cold, cold chill passed over him. He felt the warm touch of Ailis's hand upon his cheek. She did not speak. She did not have to. He knew why she had come.

She wanted to be free of the chains that bound her to him, even in death. She wanted him to release her, to let her go, so that she could rest in peace. The thought terrified him. She was the only link to sanity he had, just as his hatred of the man who had killed her was the only thing that kept him alive. Without either of them, he would go as mad as the wolf they reported him to be.

"No! Do not ask this of me. Do not ask for what I cannot give!" He could not let her go. What would become of him, of his hatred, if she left? "Don't go, Ailis. You promised to be with me always."

The warm hand upon his face turned suddenly cold. The shimmering image of her moved over the wall, then began to slowly drift away from him and out over the water, growing fainter.

"Hate me!" he cried. "I left you alone and unprotected. I caused your death. I murdered you! Haunt me! Haunt me, and don't let me forget!"

She hovered in one place for a moment, as if she were undecided, as if his words had reached her, but then she held out her hand.

He leaned over the wall and stretched out his hand toward

her, begging her to return to him, to bring her memory back. But the specter of Ailis, the love of his life, moved away. Gradually the image grew dimmer and dimmer, until she was gone completely from his sight.

He dropped down to his knees, overwhelmed by anguish, and grieving over his loss so completely that he did not feel any pain when he began to beat his head against the stones of the wall.

It was only when Grizel and Manus came for him and drew him to his feet that he realized he was bleeding.

Chapter Twelve

This time, Anne rowed herself toward the island with ease. Even before she reached there, she knew the beast was watching her. She could feel his presence, the debilitating power of his gaze. The strangest feeling crept over her, and she knew the castle, the island itself, was drawing her, as if it had dominion over her will.

Come. Come to me, it seemed to say. This is where you were meant to be. This is where you belong. I am waiting…waiting…waiting…

The day was clear and not too cold. The sun seemed to favor the island—especially the castle itself—with its light and warmth. It must have been something in its day, for there was a magnificence to it even now, when more than half of it lay in crumbling and tumbled ruin.

She reached the edge of the island just below the point where the battlement towers of the castle seemed to rise out of thick stone, like a fist reaching toward heaven. It was at least an hour later when she stood beneath a Norman archway and knocked on the studded oak door.

A young woman with belligerent red hair tied in a kerchief answered the door. "Come in, Lady Crofton. We were expecting you."

"You saw me coming."

"Aye, 'twas the master himself who saw you."

"The master—?"

"The Macqueen, milady, the last laird. If you will follow me, I will take you to him. This way, please."

Anne followed her. "I did not come here to see the Macqueen. It is the bea— It is the man they call the Beast of Blackness Castle that I wish to speak with."

The girl said nothing. She continued down a long, dim passageway, lit intermittently by burning torches. They passed many doors, all closed. The warm, accepting feeling Anne had in the boat earlier was gone. She felt an uneasiness creep over her, as if this immense castle were empty and she were here alone, without another living soul on the entire island—none, that is, save this girl, and the creature.

They went up a narrow, winding staircase and stepped into a sparsely furnished medieval gallery. Sunlight squeezed through the cracks in the drapes to provide the only light. Suddenly, the girl stopped before a door that was much larger than the doors they had passed.

"*He* awaits you in there." She paused, then stepped to one side.

The castle was abnormally quiet. Not even the usual sound of wind blowing around the merlons and through the embrasures could be heard. The girl turned the handle. Anne felt a shiver creep over her, and she almost cried out for the girl to stop.

The door creaked, then swung open. With a fast-beating heart, Anne looked down, her gaze fastened upon the folds of her cape, where a slice of the dark green gown beneath was exposed.

"You may go in, Lady Crofton."

With a deep, steadying breath, Anne lifted her head. A moment later, she stepped through the doorway, understanding at last what was required of those unfortunate queens who faced the headsman's ax. She knew now how they felt, knowing they took the last steps they would ever take upon this earth.

The moment she was inside, the door closed behind her. Instinctively Anne flinched and looked behind her.

"It is not locked."

Her head whipped around.

He stood unmoving, a somber black figure in a dark, poorly lit room, supernaturally tall, imperially slim. One solitary candle burned low on the massive carved table that stood next to him. The light caught, and illuminated his face—just enough for her to make out his features.

He was staring intently at her.

She felt herself trembling, and realized that she was gripping the soft wool of her cape almost savagely. Her stomach cramped violently. He narrowed his eyes, as if to see her better in the dim light, and she recalled the golden-yellow eyes of the beast she had seen during her illness here. There was something strange about her attraction to him, an attraction laced with fear. He reminded her of a cat waiting at a mousehole. Foolish, foolish, she called herself, and that was what she had been, to allow this evil place to seduce her with a feeling of welcome and well-being. She wondered now just how dear a price she would pay for her foolishness.

"What are you doing here?"

His voice was smooth and seductive, with an undertone of authority. All the life, all the vitality, seemed to have drained from her body, for she trembled when she heard his voice. "I will state my purpose to the… That is, I wish to speak to the…the other man."

His sensual mouth curved slowly into a smile. "There are many men here."

He was the cat, and he was toying with her. She took a deep breath. She would end the game now, with an act that went beyond the brazen, to border on stupidity. "I wish to see the one they call the Wolf of Blackness Castle." There.

She had said it. At least the floor had not opened up to throw her into a bottomless pit.

"You are very bold to use such rashness. He despises that name."

She was really trembling now, and she prayed her voice did not quiver. She knew she must speak with conviction. "It was the only way I had to identify him. I could not afford to lose the opportunity. It is imperative that I speak with him…a matter of life and death. I meant no disrespect."

"Whatever the reason, rashness is not always fortunate. Why did you take such a grave risk? Was it impudence? Stupidity? Or simply to hide your fear?"

"It is said that boldness wins the favor of the gods."

"And what is the favor you seek?" His gaze swept over her. "I admit you have a great deal to bargain with, but it remains to be seen whether he will be interested in what you offer."

She gasped. "I am afraid you have mistaken my intentions."

"Have I?"

"Yes."

"Then why are you trembling?"

She realized she could not get anywhere with a man whose very presence drained all the strength from her. Hoping to quell her trembling, she took a step back and came flat against the door. Held by his relentless gaze, she felt trapped, like a flower pressed between two transparent pieces of paper.

"Perhaps it is time for you to tell me why, exactly, you are here. And no lies this time. I *know* who you are."

"What I have to say must be said to *him.*"

"Him? You mean the beast?"

Wringing her hands, she looked around her, hoping *he* had not heard. "I thought you said he abhorred being called that."

"He does, but only when it is used by others."

"Others? You mean strangers?"

"I mean others…beings other than himself."

"But you just called him the b— Oh, God!"

He took a step toward her.

"You! All along, it was you!" Blind with fear, she stretched her hand out and felt her way along the wall until she came to a table. She stepped behind it and realized her mistake. In her effort to put something solid between them, she had placed herself away from the door and farther into the room.

He must have read her mind, for she thought she saw a flash of amusement cross his face. He continued coming toward her.

Instinctively she reached behind her and, finding her way by groping with her hands, she retreated, like an animal being stalked.

He closed the distance between them.

Unable to take her eyes off of him, she bumped up against a window. She had no choice now but to stay here, for to turn would give him cause to grab her. She was terrified of what he could do…what he might do. After all, she had, as he had said, lied to him. That thought caused her to press backward. She did not care if she broke the glass and fell through. It was a way to escape.

She pressed harder. The glass did not give.

"You tried this once before, if I remember. I cannot help but find you interesting. If you are so frightened as to risk death in order to escape, why did you choose to come here in the first place?"

Never had she been this frightened. She knew he sensed her fear, knew, too, that it amused him. His lips curled and his eyes seemed to glow with a light from within. She felt a tingling sensation of both horror and amazement that traveled the length of her spine. How long, she wondered, before he turned into the beast she knew him to be?

This was her own foolish fault. It was her boldness that both challenged and attracted him. She had played right into his hands. What was left but to admit it? "I—I am not sure. I have a history of making bad choices."

"Yes, I seem to remember. And this you consider a bad choice?"

"Yes. A very bad choice. I realize that now. I should not have come here. I should not have allowed my idiotic curiosity to bring me here again. My actions were rash and foolish. I have interrupted you and your household. My only choice is to admit it, to beg your pardon, and leave."

"There are other choices."

He was so close now, she could hear him breathing. "I don't want to hear them."

"Then tell me why you are here."

"I would rather not."

"I will ask you one more time. Why are you here?"

Was this how one died? By suffocating with fear? What would he do if she did not tell him? The possibilities were too awful for her to imagine. "I have a proposition to make."

"Go on."

"I am Sir John Crofton's daughter."

"I have known that for quite some time. Now, go on."

This was it. She drew in a deep, deep breath—perhaps her last. "I know my father was not lost at sea. I know he reached your island with the others, and that he was alive. If you did not murder him, then he is here, now, being held as your prisoner."

"And what makes you certain he was here? How can you think that I would let the bastard set foot upon this island?"

"The day after I received word of his death, I came over here, to your island."

"Why?"

"I found it strange that my father's body was the only

one lost. I had heard stories about the quarrel between you. I wanted to see for myself.''

''And did you?''

''Yes. My father's dog accompanied me. It was Pharaoh who found my father's handkerchief, buried in the sand.''

''It could have washed up and been covered in the storm.''

''But my father's watch could not. Gold is quite heavy. The moment it slipped out of his pocket, it would have gone straight down, instead of washing up on the beach.''

''You found a watch....''

She reached into her pocket and withdrew her father's watch. ''I found this lying in the shallows, near the shore. I know he was here.''

''And if he was?''

''I want to know where he is...what happened to him....

''You think I killed him?''

''I know you hate him enough to take his life.''

''What if I didn't?''

''Then he is here.''

''And what will you do if he is?''

''If he is here and alive, then I have a proposition to make.''

''Now we get back to the *proposition*. I take it I am supposed to release your father in exchange for a few favors. What's it to be? A sampling of your body?''

Anne clenched her jaw, afraid that if she said anything, she would say too much.

''Don't tell me you are offering me your sacred and treasured virginity?''

She turned her head away and closed her eyes. He was a master at humiliation. She would not let this coldhearted monster have the satisfaction of reducing her to tears.

When his fingers touched her face, her body jerked in response. She had no fight left in her, and that made it easy for him to turn her toward him. She could not help looking up into his eyes.

"Tell me the truth. I hate lies even more than I hate being called the beast. If you discovered your father was alive, what were you going to propose?"

She was shamed to the depths of her soul when a tear slipped down her cheek. "To exchange my life for my father's."

The Macqueen swore. "The bastard is not worth saving. He is a murderer. He deserves whatever happens to him."

"I would take his punishment."

With an oath, his hands came around her and, grabbing the drapes in each hand, he gave a mighty jerk. Sunlight flooded into the room.

He stared down into her face.

She could see him clearly. The face of the beast was a mystery no more. She stared at him in confusion. He did not resemble in the least the beast she had seen during her illness. His eyes were not yellow, or anything close to it. They were blue. Such a deep blue that they were almost black—and so cold that she shivered. He looked more like Lucifer than the beast...Lucifer, the fallen angel, with his beguiling, tempting ways.

"You must love him a great deal, if you are willing to give your life in exchange for his."

"I do not know him well enough to love him in the way you mean. I was raised by my mother in Cornwall. She died a few months ago. I have no other relatives. That is why I came here. We had been together only a short time when my father disappeared."

"I seem to have heard this story before...only a different version. Are there more?"

"No, only this one, for it is the truth."

"Why would you make such an offer?"

"He is my father. I owe him my respect."

"You don't owe the bastard your life!"

"My father has lung fever. He is dying. I can do nothing to help. I would not want that on my conscience."

"I am tempted to take your offer, if for no reason other than to call your bluff. I know what you are thinking. You believe in the basic goodness of mankind, therefore you think I would not stoop to do a woman harm. You do not know how wrong you are."

"It does not matter. That is not why I came here."

"Then come, little captive, for I am giving you the opportunity to prove it."

"You will spare my father's life?"

"Only if you remain here, as my prisoner."

"I will remain. You have my word."

"Then God help you, for you have no idea what you have done."

Chapter Thirteen

The next morning, Robert paced back and forth across the solar. He was in a foul mood, angry at himself. He had allowed a woman—a woman who was the daughter of his sworn enemy—to distract him. It was something he had never done before, and because of it, he had made a foolish bargain.

He realized now that keeping her and releasing her father was not enough. The crux of the matter was that Sir John would go free and unscathed. Yet how could he punish Crofton without bringing dishonor to himself? Like it or not, he had made a bargain. There had to be some way to drive a nail into that murderer's heart, and still keep his word.

He stopped abruptly, giving thought to an idea. It might work. It just might work. He grunted his satisfaction at the idea, then left the solar.

A short while later, Robert walked into the dungeon and ordered the guard to unlock Sir John's door. The moment it creaked open, he picked up the lamp and stepped inside.

Sir John was sitting on a stool, shielding the light from his eyes. "Have you come to gloat, or have you decided it is time to kill me?"

"Neither. I have come to tell you that your daughter is here."

Sir John sprang to his feet and wobbled a bit, then reached out to steady himself by bracing his hand against the damp stone wall. "Why did you involve my daughter in this? There was no reason to bring her here. I'm the one you want. What do you want with her? What do you intend to do with her? She is not part of this thing between us. She is innocent."

"Your daughter came of her own accord. She has come to bargain for your life…something that is a surprise, if what she said is true."

Sir John's face was like stone, and his eyes blazed, but he did not speak.

"Tell me, is it true that she has just come to Ravenscrag, that the two of you hardly know each other?"

The hardness in his face softened somewhat. "It's true. My wife left me when Anne was three weeks old. She took her to her family in Cornwall, and raised her there. It was only after Bess died that she came to me."

"Interesting. I wonder where she has learned to have such love and devotion for a father she had never seen."

"What do you mean?"

The muscles in Robert's face tightened, but his hard expression did not change. "She has come like an angel of mercy, and offered herself as my prisoner…in exchange for your miserable life."

Sir John paled. "You cannot accept such an offer. I will not allow her to settle my debts."

This was going better than he had expected. His appetite was whetted by his first taste of blood. He went for the throat. It was only a matter of time before he closed in for the kill. "My, my, such fatherly love and devotion for a child you never saw until she was a grown woman. I had no idea the protective paternal instinct ran so deep. Of course, I have no experience in such matters, seeing as how you murdered my only child."

As the Macqueen had known he would, Sir John ignored

his last comment. "She is young. She has much to look forward to. I am an old man…"

"And you are dying."

Sir John's expression was a startled one. "She told you…"

"Something interesting you chose not to reveal."

"You are not a man of compassion. I knew it would do no good."

"Oh, but I am a man of compassion. I am compassionate enough to accept her sacrifice. I will spare your life."

"God's blood, I hope you suffer for this," Sir John said, and his eyes blazed with a rage of utter frustration and bitterness. Without warning, he sprang to his feet. His hands went for the Macqueen's throat.

Robert easily subdued him and shoved him back against the wall. "I would suggest that you refrain from becoming physical. You might tempt me to keep your daughter and end your miserable life, as well."

Obviously weakened, Sir John's legs gave way, and he slid down the wall to sit on the floor, his breathing heavy and rasping. He coughed violently. When the coughing subsided, he rested his head back against the wall. "What do you want of me?"

A slow smile curved the corners of the Macqueen's mouth. He had his man. And he had his answer. Now he knew the way to drive the stake through Sir John's evil heart.

"It is a little late for fatherly intervention, I'm afraid. Your life is spared. The girl is mine. However, it would suit my purpose to have your blessing."

"You fool. Do you honestly think I would ever accept you as a suitable mate for my daughter?"

The Macqueen regarded him impassively. "Did I mention marriage? There are ways to enjoy the fruit without buying the tree."

"I will not agree to it. I will never agree to it. Take my

life. Take it now, and be done with this thing. I grow weary.''

"What is done cannot be undone. I have given my word. Your daughter will remain here.''

"You cannot do this.''

"I did not come here to ask your permission. The deed is already done. You are free to go. You will be returned to Ravenscrag on the morrow.''

"You miserable fiend. I will return, and I will have my daughter back, if I have to start a bloody war. And when it's over, I'll see my daughter properly wed.''

"I'm afraid there is one major flaw in your plans. Lady Anne has agreed to become my wife. Even the king doesn't have the authority to take a woman from her lawful husband. The matter is out of your hands.''

Sir John closed his eyes and threw back his head, a tormented scream ripped from his throat. *"Noooo…"*

But the Macqueen was already gone.

Manus looked up when the Macqueen entered the gallery, but he said nothing.

"Bring Lady Anne to me in the chapel.''

Manus gave him a strange look, but chose not to reveal what he was thinking. With a nod, he departed.

The Macqueen was waiting in the chapel, near the altar, when the door opened and Lady Anne stepped inside.

Manus closed the door behind her.

The Macqueen did not miss the way Anne's gaze darted toward the door, or her look of panic when she saw that Manus had gone.

"Why have you brought me here, to the chapel?''

"You do not like chapels?''

"I do not think the chapel an appropriate place for the plotting of wickedness.''

"And here I thought we understood each other. You are expecting wickedness, when in truth, I have a proposition to present to you. One that will make you very happy, I am certain.''

''What is your proposition?''

''I am prepared to offer you your father's freedom…the chance to walk out of these gates a free man, with this thing between us settled forever.''

Her expression was confused. ''Are you jesting with me, or is it your turn to play the simpleton? We agreed to that last evening.''

He feigned a surprised look. ''Beg pardon, Lady Anne, but we did not.''

She gasped. ''We did!'' she said, her tone loud and angry. ''You granted me my father's freedom in exchange for my remaining here. You gave me your word.''

He feigned indifference. ''Obviously you have read something into the bargain that was not there. What I granted you was your father's *life*. Not his freedom.''

''By all that's holy! You tricked me!''

His jaw clenched. He spaced his words evenly, and kept his tone low. ''On the contrary. I gave you precisely what you asked for. Your exact words were 'I came to offer my life in exchange for my father's.' ''

Anne paled, as if she realized the blunder in her choice of words. ''But, in the end, I asked you if you would set my father free, and you agreed. I remember what you said— 'Only if you remain here, as my prisoner.' ''

''You err again, little captive. What you asked was, 'You will spare my father's life?' ''

''They were right to call you the devil. You are the prince of deception.''

''The error was yours, mistress, not mine. Direct your anger, and your poetic names, where they belong.''

''You knew I was asking for his freedom. There could have been no misunderstanding, no matter what words I used.''

''You would do well to learn a man can only agree to

what is stated. He cannot be held accountable for another's thinking or logic. If you intended to trade yourself for your father's release, then you should have asked for it.''

"But I—''

"A bargain is a bargain. You gave your word, as did I. Your father's life will be spared, and you will remain here.''

She winced at his words. One pale, slim hand came up to her forehead.

Silent as a sunrise, he waited…for her to make her next move.

It did not take long. Her hand dropped away from her face. When she turned her face up to his, the expression he saw was wary. She was ready to do battle. She would be cautious now. She would not make the same mistake twice. She learned fast, clever girl. How could he ever have thought her a simpleton?

"What happens now?''

He raised his brows. "Why, nothing. We will go on with our lives. You will take up residence here. You will be free to come and go…as long as you remain on the island. If you should try to escape, you will be placed under guard.''

"And my father?''

"Will remain alive.''

"Where?''

"In the dungeon, where he is now.'' Her lower lip quivered, and he wondered if she was going to cry. She did not. It pleased him to learn that she possessed such strength of control.

"And if I want my father to be free…free to leave the dungeon, free to leave this castle and this island, free to return to Ravenscrag to live in peace for the rest of his *natural* life?''

"Then you will have to come to me with another proposition, or accept the one I offered you.''

"I am your prisoner already. I have nothing further to give you…nothing I can exchange for his freedom.''

Her sadness touched him. He would have done anything in his power to end the sadness he saw in her face and in her eyes. He would have, save for the fact that he wanted her, so much that he was willing to risk it all for the chance to have her. He picked up her hand. It trembled in his. "I beg to disagree with you, lass, but you are not as impoverished as you think." He brought her hand to his lips and pressed a kiss there.

His move plainly surprised her, and her expression was startled. Her eyes were large and round with surprise, but she said nothing.

He did not release her hand, but went on to say, "You have overlooked something...something rare and priceless that you can only give once."

She jerked her hand back. "I will not be your whore!"

"I have not asked you to be."

She spun around and walked angrily across the room. She stopped in front of the altar and stared down at it, hugging her middle with her arms. She trembled—whether from frustration or anger, he was not certain. He only knew she was trying to get control of herself.

He heard her release a long sigh. She stopped trembling, but she did not turn around. "What were you suggesting? If you were not thinking of my becoming your...your harlot, then what is this rare and priceless thing you were thinking I could offer?"

"You could become my wife."

She whirled around. "Your wife?"

He narrowed his eyes. "The only way you will gain your father's freedom is to give me your hand in marriage."

"I cannot."

He came to stand next to her. She turned to face him as he spoke. "The decision is yours. In either case, you will remain here."

Her eyes filled with tears, but she did not cry. "Why would you want to marry the daughter of a man you despise, a woman you do not love?'' she asked, with a lost look that stabbed into the heart of him.

"It is the only way to give you what you ask for. The only way to settle an old debt.''

"An eye for an eye," she whispered. "My father was responsible for your wife's death, so you force me to become your wife.''

"I will not force you. The decision is yours.''

She seemed to grow smaller before his eyes. When she looked at him, her entire being seemed consumed with sadness. "You have my word.''

"I am not an easy man to dupe. The words are short, but the possibilities are endless. I am a man of precise definition. I have your word...on what?''

"You have my word that I will become your wife, but only when you have released my father and agreed to let him live in peace for as long as he lives...without being murdered.''

"You will have to learn to trust your husband.''

"When he becomes king of England.''

He was amused, but he did not show it. It would not do for him to reveal that now. She wanted her father released before they wed. He could not trust her any more than she trusted him. "You will become my wife, then I will release your father.''

He saw by the expression on her face that she realized she had no leverage to use to gain her way. It amused him to see her fury at being forced to yield. She would make a fine wife...someday.

"You will never be satisfied with this arrangement. Never!''

His eyes bored into hers. This time he allowed the desire he felt to warm in his look. "On the contrary, little captive, I plan to be quite satisfied on our wedding night.''

Chapter Fourteen

The Macqueen did not keep his word.

It wasn't that he did not marry Anne Crofton, for he did, some three months later, and he changed her name, as he said, "from that vile, evil name, Crofton, to one more suitable—and honorable, as well."

And it wasn't that he did not release her father as he had promised, for he had kept his word on that, as well.

The sad truth was that when it came to fulfilling his claim to be satisfied on his wedding night, Robert Macqueen had told a lie. He had not come to her since they married, not even to consummate the union.

There had been a few times, Anne would have to admit, when she thought they came dangerously close. One time in particular stood out in her mind. It had happened when he wanted her to tell him about herself, about her life. Apprehensive and nervous around him still, she had been quite reluctant to tell him the things he wished to know.

"Why the continued shyness? I want you to tell me."

"No."

"We will start with your mother. What was her name?"

"Bess... Elizabeth."

"Tell me about her."

"She was born a little girl. I didn't know her then. She

grew up to be a lady. She was betrothed to my father, whom she had never met. They were married. They had a daughter. They named her Anne. A few weeks later…''

He started laughing. ''We seem to be back where we started, with you playing the simpleton.''

''And you the ogre.''

He shrugged. ''It is a role that comes naturally to me, I suppose, but that doesn't mean I can't change.''

''It doesn't mean you will.''

''No, it doesn't, but we can talk about it—perhaps even reach a compromise.''

''I have made bargains with you before, milord. You will have to forgive me if I am reluctant to stick my hand into that same fire. I am still recovering from the last time.''

He looked as if he had decided to let things ride a bit. As she expected, he turned the conversation back to her. ''All right. Tell me more about your mother. How did she look?''

''She looked average.''

He lost his temper at that point, and actually had the audacity to *command* her to tell him everything.

She would have died first, but she knew better than to give him any ideas. So she remained willfully mute.

He stared at her, as if trying to smother the flames of anger that burned hotly within him.

''What are you going to do to me? Lock me in the dungeon, or have me whipped for disobedience?''

She had never seen anger disappear so quickly in anyone. There must have been something in her defiance, her manner or her words that penetrated his harsh exterior, something that was able to go through all the layers of pain and hurt to the core of the man inside, for he did something she had never heard him do before.

''I have offended you and caused you pain by my callous disregard. For that, I apologize. My manner, I know, is abrupt, and my way exacting. I cannot promise it will change. You are ten-and-seven, while I will see my thirtieth summer soon. My age has given me more of life's experiences—most of them unpleasant—which have made me demanding, critical, and difficult to live with. I can only ask you to try and understand…to be patient.''

Since he had given a mile, Anne felt charitable. She gave an inch. "I will work on not being offended."

He did not smile—he rarely did—but amusement lit up his eyes. "I find myself sitting here looking at you, and trying to remember what it was like to be your age."

"You make me sound like a child, while you portray yourself to be positively creeping with age."

"I am a man of many years and great regrets. I became laird of my clan at a very young age…too young to shoulder such a responsibility. Times were hard. Life was harder. My life seemed to be building up to some sort of climax, and when it came, it was more than I could handle. I was surrounded by suffering and consumed by darkness. My pain was so great that there were times I thought God had handed me over to Satan.

"I was convinced my life was over, until I saw the darkness penetrated by the thinnest beam of light, and I saw something there, something I envied, something I wanted. I knew longing, but saw no way to have what I longed for. I had been out of touch with myself for too long, and life had gone on around me. They say God works in mysterious ways, and I have proof of that. I saw hope coming toward me with her arms outstretched, an angel of mercy and light."

He paused to study her face, as if he were looking for something. He smiled softly, then leaned his face toward hers and kissed her firmly on the lips. The power of it almost knocked her off her perch. When he spoke, she could barely hear what he said over the loud hammering of her heart in her ears.

''The Arabs have a saying—'When the angels appear, the devils vanish.' I never understood that until now.''

She did not understand, exactly, what he was trying to say, but that did not matter. What did matter was that after that night, she knew she would never be afraid of him again.

It was a sad state of affairs to have to admit it, but she was still a virgin after three months of marriage. Anne remembered what Grizel had said to her a few weeks back. ''I have a feeling, lass, that you have decided being married to a beast isn't so bad after all.''

That was at least partly true. Aside from her continued state of maidenhood, it wasn't so bad. In fact, her only displeasure was her husband's lack of interest in making her his wife in the truest sense. She would have never believed that she would come to feel this way. But how could she not?

Since the day of their marriage, she had not seen the beastly side of him at all—if, indeed, there was one. She saw only pain. And, through his suffering, she had begun to understand the man he was.

She did not, however, understand his unbelievable self-restraint. For she knew he desired her.

That should have pleased her. It did not. What it did was make her furious.

How dare he humiliate her by leaving her a virgin....

Suddenly it occurred to her: What if he had intended from the beginning not to consummate the marriage? It would be the perfect revenge, for what better way to torment her father than to marry her, letting her wither on the vine like an old maid, with no love and no children?

She took back everything—no, just the things that were kind and in his defense—that she had thought. He was a beast. He had tricked her into this marriage, and now he was going to trick her out of it. How easy she had made it, playing into his hands like a simpleton.

Anne could not remember ever being so angry. Well, she wasn't ready to give up yet. What she wanted and intended to have was desire gratified, and that meant everything that went with it. She had some thinking to do, and a walk was the best way to do it.

In order to make her way outside from her room, she went through the keep, which lay mostly in ruins. Only the forge, weaving room and laundry were still in use, the laundry having the best access to the bailey.

The fragrant, steamy smell of soap and water greeted her when she stepped into the laundry. Although it was Wednesday, the day Grizel and Marta did the laundry, it appeared to be empty. She ducked under the drying clothes, and was about to walk between the wooden tubs when she heard Marta talking.

"I swear on my grandmother's grave that the sheets have not shown any proof of it. If you ask me, I'd say she was still a virgin. Now, I ask you, why would that be? It was his idea to marry her in the first place, wasn't it? So, why did he marry her, if he did not intend for them to live together as man and wife?"

Anne paused and crossed her arms in front of her and nodded in agreement. Perhaps she would get the answers she sought here, in the laundry, and the walk outside would not be necessary.

"You must be mistaken about the sheets, lass. Whatever the reasons the Macqueen had for taking the lass to wife, I would wager my best cotton drawers that remaining celibate was not one of them."

"I am not wrong about the sheets, Grizel. There has been no consummation. In fact, I don't think they have slept together at all. Not once. At least, their beds don't show the proof of it."

"Perhaps they went someplace else."

"And where would that be? The stables? The pigsty? Strapped to the porticullis? Floating in the dye vats? Even if the Macqueen were so disposed, I cannot imagine Lady Anne accepting such conditions.''

Anne nodded her head vigorously at that. She peeped through a pair of drawers and saw Grizel twist the sheet in her hands.

"No, I cannot imagine it, either,'' Grizel said. "If what you say is true, then there must be a reason.''

"But what? Lady Anne is more than comely.''

Lady Anne puffed up, then smiled as she thought, *I never suspected Grizel had such wisdom.*

Grizel went on. "We both know what a devil he was to live with when he let her go…after she tried to run away. He was in love with her then, if you ask me.''

Anne's head snapped up in surprise. *In love with her?* She narrowed her eyes. *Piffle! A man does not avoid a woman he is in love with.*

"Aye, she has tormented him since the first time she came here,'' Grizel said. "I think he wanted her, even then.''

"You don't suppose he is angry now, because he let his heart rule his head, do you? He waited a long, long time to have Sir John in his lair, and then when he had him, he allowed his desire for Lady Anne to change all that.''

"He did not have to let him go,'' Grizel said. "He could have taken what he wanted.''

"He had to let him go if he wanted her as his wife. He could not marry her and hold her father prisoner.''

"He could have, but he is not the sort of man to do such a thing. He may be a beast at times, but he is an honorable one.'' She paused. "Perhaps he is sorry he let her father go. I have never seen anyone so tormented. If he makes a go of it with Lady Anne, he will have to turn his back on his past. If he continued his pursuit of Sir John, then he will lose his wife.''

"That must be it—'' Marta paused.

Anne started to turn away.

Marta went on. "Unless something happened to change the way he felt about her."

Anne jerked to a stop.

"What do you mean, something happened?" Grizel asked.

"You remember the way Lady Anne was in the beginning? A regular shrew she was, independent and headstrong. Outspoken, too, and using her wit to bait him, playing the dimwit when it pleased her. She rowed herself to this island more than once, and when things did not suit her, she was ready to row herself away. She would have made good her escape, too, if she had not been so ill."

"So what has changed?"

"*She* has changed. She is meek and docile now."

Grizel chuckled. "That is because she is in love with him. Love will turn the biggest shrew into a sheep."

Anne gasped. *A sheep? How dare they call her a sheep!* She had heard enough....

She left, going back into the keep, where she wandered around aimlessly for most of the afternoon. She had no idea where Robert was, nor had she seen Gavin or Manus. Not that it mattered. She did not feel like talking to anyone right now. She wanted to be alone.

Somehow, she found herself in the solar that led to her husband's chambers. She opened the door and went inside. She had never been here before, and she was shocked at the spareness of it. Except for the bed and a large chest, the room was entirely bare.

Something about the meager furnishings touched her. It also reminded her that the rest of the castle did not look much better. There were not the usual trappings—tapestries, fine carpets, beautifully carved furniture, or anything that would even hint at luxury or wealth. She had not fully realized the extent of his losses until now.

"He has nothing," she said, her gaze resting on the large chest at the foot of his bed. Curiosity got the best of her.

She went to the chest and opened it. His clothing was as scarce as the furnishings. As she touched the fabrics, she realized they were of very fine quality, but they were old and worn and sadly in need of replacement. .

She sat down on the floor and looked through the chest, learning more about him than she had before. There was little here, and certainly nothing of great value, save for an ornate silver dirk and a leather bag that contained a few silver coins. Mostly, it was a collection of relics from the past—a family Bible, a child's spinning top, a blue silk ribband, and a journal of some sort.

Anne removed the journal and opened the lock, not knowing that inside lay a horror of great darkness.

The journal's first entry was filled with suffering and anguish, for it told of the Battle of Culloden, the loss of his entire clan. The next entry was as harrowing, as pain-racked, as the first. Page after page, she read the outpourings of his agony, his aching pain, the grief he had felt when he returned to Ravenscrag and discovered his wife and son were dead, along with all the women and children of the clan.

On and on she read, page after page of his suffering—his spirit somber, his words moving and powerful, touching her and bringing tears to her eyes. And then she read about the dreams, the horrible dreams that had such a profound influence upon him.

She shivered when reading of the grinding influence of nocturnal scenes chillingly, fearfully and vividly described—scenes that were relentless and cruel, scenes of ghosts and visitations, of lost souls and fallen beings. It was little wonder that this poor, desperate man was forced to banish sleep by night, why he was destined to suffer disturbed and distorted mental peace by day.

And yet, underlying it all was a message from a man of true benevolence; a man who had once believed in fidelity and home life; a man of constancy, tenderness and loving kindness; a man who had once held with the concepts of

forgiveness and mercy; a man who had changed because of
the acts of man's inhumanity, from a man of passion and
feeling, into an ever-suffering soul of violence, a beast of
ceaseless and unquenchable rages, a man of great emotion,
as well as cruelty; a creature unredeemed, who carried his
hell with him, and never once strayed from his arrow-
straight course toward his own destruction.

And then she read about herself, learning of his true feelings for her, his delight in her beauty, her kindness that was
sometimes at war with her defiant manner.

She has come into my life bringing goodness, flooding
the darkness with light, and giving me hope. She is my
salvation, my restoration, the healer of the past, the
promise of tomorrow, my angel of mercy, my guiding
light.

She paused. Those words had a strange ring of familiarity,
and she tried to recall where she had heard them before.
And then she remembered the time he had told her about
himself, the time she had not understood what he was trying
to say.

*I saw hope coming toward me with her arms outstretched,
an angel of mercy and light.*

She closed the journal and replaced it in the trunk. Just
before she closed the lid, she removed a soft, worn linen
shirt. She went to his bed and lay across it, tucking his shirt
against her chest, feeling his nearness, his presence, assured
of it by his scent.

She looked around his room, with its meager furnishings,
its bare floors. The windows were covered with old, faded
drapes that were more holes and tears than fabric. She
thought about his pitiful collection of clothes, the few me-
mentos and possessions he had in his trunk to show for a
life that had mainly been losses. And then she thought about
his home, his castle, and how much it reminded her of him.

Like Blackness Castle, he was a tall and solid mass of crags, once mighty and strong, a place of refuge, shelter and protection that was now nothing more than a burned-out hull, lonely and abandoned, battered by the elements and lying in ruins.

It was all there, in his journal. Past and present, dream and reality, hopes and disappointments, all blended into one credible whole. There, too, lay the explanation of how a man of strength and compassion, a beloved laird with a fine mind, could turn into a brooding, sullen man capable of vindictiveness and given to black moods.

Nothing and no one had ever touched her this deeply. Never could she remember feeling such anguish for another human being. She had judged him, when he needed understanding. When he sought kindness, she had given him hate. She grieved that she had been cold and indifferent. He was a man grievously wronged and greatly misunderstood, and she was as guilty of it as anyone.

His pain, his suffering, and the unfairness of it all, were more than she could contain. She buried her face in his shirt, feeling as if he were here, with her, and began to cry. Once she started, she could not seem to quit. She cried in a tortured way, her sobbing wretched and passionate, her heart full of regret.

She did not cry for a man who had set out to destroy himself, a man who wanted desperately to forget.

She cried for a man who could find no reason on earth to go on—or enough joy in life to make him want to live.

Her last thoughts were a reminder that she would stay here, waiting for him in his bed. That way, she could tell him she understood now what he had tried to say to her, the pain he wanted to forget. Knowing she truly loved him, she waited, crying herself to sleep, thinking about all the things she wanted to say.

She did not get the chance to tell him.

For before her husband could return, her father's men stormed the castle and took Lady Anne Macqueen away.

Chapter Fifteen

The Macqueen exploded with rage when he returned and discovered his wife was gone. Not even Manus and Grizel together could soothe the ranting, the madness, the passion of his anger. "Get out of here! All of you! I don't want your sympathy, or your pity, damn you!"

They all agreed the Macqueen was like a wild man, completely out of touch. He destroyed everything in his path, roared at anyone who got in his way.

Grizel and Manus watched helplessly until he went for his gun, returning with the intent to go to Ravenscrag. Alone. He was determined to bring her back. That was when Manus picked up a piece of firewood and knocked him unconscious.

For two days, they kept him drugged and tied to his bed.

On the third day, he was calm, and acting like himself again, rational, yet determined as ever to get back what was his, the part of him that had been stolen. But even then, they would not untie him, until he promised to wait one more day.

After she was brought home, Anne sequestered herself in her room for two days, refusing any food that was brought to her and every entreaty that was made. Her father would not talk to her. And she vowed to starve herself until he relented, or the undertaker carried her away.

On the third day, Sir John sent for her. He was ready to talk.

"I want to go back. You had no right to take me from my husband."

"I had every right. You are my daughter, and the bastard forced you to marry him."

"He did not force me to marry. It was my idea."

"Regardless, I am having the marriage annulled."

"You cannot have a consummated marriage annulled."

"I can, because you will swear that the marriage was not consummated, or you will never see daylight again. I would rather see you dead than sacrificing your life to a monster to save mine."

"Father, you cannot have this marriage annulled."

"It is already being done."

"Then you will have to stop it." She was surprised at her own calmness, in spite of her father's wrath. "I will not tell them the marriage was not consummated. They would soon know it for a lie."

"What are you talking about? What lie?"

"I am with child. That is something I cannot lie about, or hide. Before long, it will be obvious, and then they will realize the truth."

Her father suddenly looked older, his body more bent, his forcefulness turning to wistful regret. With a weary sigh, he said, "Anne, I do not have long to live. I have never done anything for you. I saw this as a way to make amends for all the years I was not there."

She went to her father and put her arms around him. "Don't you understand? You don't have to make amends for anything. And certainly not by destroying a marriage I want very much."

"You are in love with him?"

"Painfully so." She did not expect him to understand, so she was not surprised when he didn't.

"Of all the men, why this one?"

"Perhaps it was God's way of righting a wrong that was done a long time ago."

Her father did not say anything, but after a while, he patted her hand and told her to go. "I am tired now. I would like to rest."

She came to her feet and, after kissing him on the head, started toward the door. Just before she walked out, she turned and said, "When may I return? I am most anxious to see my husband."

Her father's voice was soft. It sounded weary. "Send Joseph to me. I will send him to Blackness Castle with an invitation for your husband to come after you."

"No tricks. I will have your word."

"No tricks," he said, putting a spark of life into his voice. "You have my word."

When Robert Macqueen arrived at his former home, he paused at the front door, uncertain he would be able to go inside. He could not help wondering if all the agony he had once felt here would be waiting for him. He could not step back into the memories, the pain.

When he thought about the reason he was here, what he stood to lose if he did not, it was enough. He knocked. Loud.

He was shown into the library, where he found Sir John waiting for him. He was offered a seat.

"No, thank you, I prefer to stand."

"How about a glass of port...or brandy?"

"This is not a social call. I came for my wife."

"Anne will be down shortly. In the meantime, I have something I have been needing to say to you for a long, long time."

"I have no interest in hearing anything you have to say.

Whatever it is, it has no bearing on anything now. You waited too long. Do not think you can ease your evil conscience just before you die.''

"I met with my solicitor this morning. I have deeded Ravenscrag back to you. The signed documents are on their way to London. I have included a letter to the king, which confesses my wrongdoings, and explains my desire to set things right. You may have noticed my carriage is packed and waiting. As soon as you are reunited with my daughter, I will be leaving for Italy. The weather is dry there, and better for my health.''

Robert's expression remained hard and unmoved. He did not trust this man. And for good reason. The last decent thing he had done was to bring Anne into the world.

Sir John rose unsteadily to his feet. "I know it is difficult for you to trust me, or to believe anything I say. Only time will prove the truth. Unfortunately, time is the one thing I do not have. Before I go, I have one more thing I wish to say. It is not something I find easy, but it is necessary. Although I did not kill those you loved, I am guilty, because I was the one who stood to benefit the most from it. For that, I am eternally sorry. I do not expect you to accept my apology, any more than I can change what happened. My only hope is that perhaps I can, in some way, atone for it.''

With a slow, obviously painful gait, he walked to a door on the opposite side of the room. When he opened it, Anne stood behind it.

Sir John motioned for her to come forward.

Anne walked silently into the room, and paused beside her father.

Sir John took her arm and walked her to where Robert stood. He took her hand and held it out.

Robert was so emotionally charged at the sight of her, looking lovelier than he had ever seen her, that it took him a minute to comprehend just what was happening.

When he reached out and took Anne's hand in his, and

drew her to him to rest against his side, Sir John said, "What I took, I give back. A wife for a wife."

Anne turned to her father and kissed him, thanking him for giving her back her happiness.

Then she put her arm through Robert's, and together they stepped out into a sun-filled world. Her thoughts were of the future, with her husband at her side. When her father's carriage drove off, she waved until it was out of sight, until Robert took her in his arms and kissed her soundly.

Breathless and a bit giddy, she looked into his face, knowing the question he was going to ask.

"What did you do to make him change?"

"I talked to him."

"You *talked?* Or did you plant some little seed, and leave it to sprout? Was it something you told him that made him see things differently enough to apologize?"

"How did you know?"

"I know how you are."

She began to laugh. "All this talk about seeds and sprouting is uncanny...and so near the truth. I must confess, I told a small lie."

Up went his brows. "You?"

"Only a wee little one."

"What was this insignificant lie?"

She poked him in the chest. "I did not say it was insignificant, only tiny. In truth, it was very significant, I think."

"Are you going to tell me, or leave me hanging in suspense?"

"When I first arrived, my father was completely unreasonable. He already had his solicitor working on an annulment."

"The bastard."

"Please, I am speaking of the way he was, in the past."

"All right—the erstwhile bastard. Now, tell me what you said to change his mind."

"I told him I was going to have your child."

Robert grinned at her and kissed her again, even more soundly this time. While she was still reeling from that, he swung her up into his arms and carried her up the stairs.

"Where are you taking me?"

"To your room. Which one is it?"

"The last one...on the right." She began kissing his face, his throat, his ear.

"If you don't stop that, we may not make it to your bed."

"My bed? Why, Robert Macqueen, whatever are you thinking?"

"I am thinking it is time to make an honest woman out of you."

"An honest woman? But we are married."

"True, but my wife has a bad habit. She does not always tell the truth. The only way I can help is by turning fiction into fact, and I better start working on it now."

"Oh, Robert, I thought this moment would never come."

He kissed her. "I must admit I was beginning to wonder a bit, myself. You are a hard woman to convince. I was running out of devices."

"Do you mean you were contriving?"

"A man does what he has to do." She was laughing when he carried her into the room and kicked the door shut.

A moment later, he lowered her to the bed, and then he followed her, covering her body with his own. She had never experienced such delicious weight. She had wanted this for so long. She was eager to have him know how much she wanted this, and she was eager to explore every part of him.

"Kiss me," he whispered, his lips brushing hers.

She needed no further invitation. His mouth against hers was warm, inviting. She wondered how anything could ever be any better than this. How had she done without it? If only she had known. She realized, then, that the time was not right, that if she had known earlier, she might not have waited, that she would have missed the one true and great love of her life. It wasn't just a matter of enjoying the things he did to her when he kissed her, or the things he was doing to her body now. It was not the ritual. It was the man.

She knew that she would love this man until the day she died, and then, if it was possible, she would love him longer, stronger, for all eternity.

He removed the last of her clothing. She did not realize he had done so until she felt the cool brush of air against her skin. He warmed her, bringing his body against her, aligning himself perfectly with her. She felt a sudden and urgent craving for him, and her arms went around his back to press him closer. He groaned, and then she felt his hand as it smoothed over the skin of her legs, across the flat surface of her belly, then lower, to where she ached.

He smothered her face with kisses, then took her mouth as swiftly as he had captured her heart. This kiss was different from the others, more intense, more demanding, and it made her want something that she could not have named.

Her hands came down, learning the texture, the shape, of his back, then dropping lower. He lifted his body slightly, then brought his knees between her legs. Willingly, she let them part. She could feel him against her now, touching her in a way that made her arch her back. With a gasp, she realized her movement brought him inside her.

It was all the invitation he needed. She heard her own intake of breath, then felt him come into her with a driving swiftness. A sharp pain caused her to cry out softly, and he paused, even though she knew what it cost him to do so.

She decided the pain was worth the wait. Something inside her was building with such intensity that she was star struck. She wanted more of him, all of him, everything he could show her, all he could teach her about her own body, and his, as well. "Love me, Macqueen," she whispered. "Love me as much as I love you."

"God help me, but I already do," he said, and he began to move, taking her with him. It was a ride, a journey that she would remember even when she was old, for she realized then that there was something magical between them, something that opened like a secret cave, and when they stepped inside they found a room filled with treasure.

She was rich. Rich with loving and being loved. Rich in the joy of knowing she had found not a husband, but her lifelong mate. "Hold me," she whispered, her arms going around him. "Hold me until I ache. I love you, Robert Macqueen. So much it frightens me."

A breeze stirred, and blew through the window. She felt the cool chill of it, the ripple of goose bumps left behind. She rubbed his arms and felt the chills there. "An angel just went through the room," she said.

Robert chuckled and rolled over, his body partly covering hers, and then he kissed her. "Don't think this is going to cool the heat of the moment. Inside, I still burn for you. I have since the moment I first saw you. I love you, little captive."

She smiled at his choice of words, finding them somehow appropriate. "I am your captive," she said, biting his ear. "Forever."

"Forever isn't long enough."

She kissed him and thought how beautiful it was... whenever they agreed.

*   *   *   *   *

A Gentleman of Substance
Deborah Hale

Chapter One

The Lake District, 1812

A clod of rain-soaked earth fell on the coffin, landing with a heavy, wet slap. From her place behind the lichened stone wall of Saint Mawe's churchyard, Lucy Rushton felt that sound like a physical blow. A tiny whimper escaped her clenched lips, but the damp autumn wind snatched it up and carried it away. They were burying the earthly remains of Captain Jeremy Strickland, mortally wounded in a minor skirmish of Wellington's peninsular campaign. That "minor skirmish," Lucy reflected with bitter irony, had cast her into every woman's worst nightmare.

Unwed and pregnant by a dead lover.

In vain, Lucy bit down on her lip, praying the pain would wake her from this horrible dream. She'd worshipped the handsome, dashing Jeremy Strickland from a distance for most of her twenty years. Suddenly taking notice of her, the captain had returned Lucy's regard, wooing her with an urgency peculiar to young men off to war. Overlooking the waterfall at Amber Force, he begged the happiness of her hand in marriage. In a secluded glade on the banks of tranquil Mayeswater, he persuaded her to consummate the union of their hearts. He'd promised to return at the earliest opportunity, to wed her in a splendid ceremony.

Even knowing her condition would eventually expose her to censure and ostracism, Lucy could not bring herself to regret what she'd done. Far worse to stand here and watch them bury her dearest love, having denied him the joy of their communion. Without the memory of his ardent kiss and tender embrace to sustain her.

The meagre clutch of mourners at the graveside bowed their heads as Lucy's father, the vicar of Saint Mawes, led them in a final prayer. One man towered above the others, a tall severe-looking person whose somber funeral habit was little different from his normal attire. Lucy fixed the formidable Drake Strickland, Viscount Silverthorne, with a baleful glare.

The viscount had selfishly decreed his half brother's funeral a private affair, closed to all but family. Otherwise, Saint Mawe's would have overflowed with tenants and villagers, sincerely mourning the gallant, agreeable young officer. Rather than skulking behind the wall, Lucy might have taken her place among the throng, free to vent her grief in public.

As if drawn by the animosity of her gaze, Lord Silverthorne suddenly turned his dark, inscrutable eyes upon Lucy. She met his stare without flinching, channeling all her resentment into an answering glare.

How dare you bar me from him on this of all days? her look challenged Drake Strickland. *It is your fault Jeremy enlisted in the army in the first place. Always trying to live up to your impossibly high standards and never succeeding. Always trying to make his own mark. Always trying to emerge from beneath your shadow. If not for you, he would be alive today.*

At that moment, Vicar Rushton intoned the benediction. "Earth to earth. Ashes to ashes. Dust to dust."

Rising tears quenched the passionate rage in Lucy's eyes.

Looking away from the hateful Lord Silverthorne, she pressed her arms protectively over her flat belly, where Jeremy's child had just begun to grow within her. This was what her love and her dreams had finally come to—ashes and dust.

The Dowager Marchioness of Cranbrook peered down the length of Silverthorne's formal dining table. Her wrinkled mouth puckered in distaste. Though she regretted the death of her favorite grandson, her ladyship was not unduly distressed. In seventy-five years she had buried three husbands, five sons and four grandsons. Losing loved ones was an inevitable part of life—no sense railing against events one could not change. Plenty of other circumstances were amenable to her influence. It was upon those the marchioness chose to focus her attention.

"Drake, what is this dish?" Suspiciously, she sifted her spoon through an unfamiliar variety of stew, heavy in cabbage. "It's barely palatable. And black bread? My servants dine better than this. You must come to London with me, if only to secure the services of a proper cook."

From the moment of her arrival, the marchioness had lost no opportunity of urging her grandson to come to London in search of a wife. At the head of the table, Viscount Silverthorne rolled his eyes, heaving an impatient sigh that was audible above the tattoo of rain drumming on the windows.

Impudent cub! Her ladyship bridled. Did he think her eyesight and hearing too feeble to mark his insulting behaviour?

"I regret our cuisine is not to your taste, Grandmother," Drake replied with tight-jawed civility. "We are not accustomed to such exalted company." He inclined his head to her and to his other guests—his cousin, the Honorable Neville Strickland, and Lady Phyllipa Strickland, widow of yet another cousin.

Acknowledging Drake's nod with a dyspeptic smile, Phyllipa picked daintily at her meal. A bland, sallow creature, her cloying solicitude set the marchioness's teeth on edge. Neglecting the food altogether, Neville concentrated on his wine.

"Personally," Drake continued, "I find Mrs. Maberley's cooking both toothsome and nourishing. I wouldn't trade her Lancashire hot pot for all the glazed pheasant and oyster puddings in London. I'm a plain man. I prefer plain clothes, plain food...."

"But not plain women, I'll wager," Neville quipped, twirling his quizzing glass by its string.

The marchioness held her breath, waiting to hear Drake's reply. Neville was either very drunk or very stupid to be baiting his cousin in such a way. More than once Drake had discharged the young dandy's mounting debts with no more than an ominous grumble about the sin of profligacy.

"Speaking of women..." Phyllipa broke her meek silence. "Who was that young lady watching us at Jeremy's funeral this afternoon? She looked positively distraught."

Drake appeared confounded by the question. "Young lady? Oh, that was just Lucy...Miss Rushton. The vicar's daughter."

"Indeed." Neville grinned broadly. "Does she hang about looking picturesquely mournful for all the burials?"

"If Miss Rushton looked mournful, she has every right. She's known Jeremy since childhood...." For a moment Drake fell into a pensive silence. Recovering himself, he continued brusquely, "Besides, you know girls that age. They have an exaggerated sense of tragedy—particularly about young men dying gallantly for their country. Too many people nowadays have romantic notions of war."

"You don't consider Jeremy's death a tragedy?" challenged Neville.

"I consider it a waste." A sharp crack of thunder from the storm punctuated Drake's pronouncement. "Jeremy had no business gadding off to Spain, as though the army were an amusing diversion. He had responsibilities. To me. To our people.''

"Your people?" Neville chuckled. "My dear fellow, you talk as though your tenants were your subjects.''

Her ladyship had followed the volley of conversation between her grandsons like a match of battledore and shuttlecock, looking from one to the other. Now she stared expectantly at Drake, waiting for a crushing return.

She felt distinctly disappointed when he took a deep breath and replied forbearingly. "It is a question of duty, Neville. If such a concept is not altogether foreign to you. My tenants and employees depend on me. The mines, the mills, the tannery—when they turn a profit, families can feed their children and send them to school. They patronize the local shops and keep money from draining away to Liverpool or Manchester.''

"Fah, Cuz. You sound like a merchant, not a viscount. Gentlemen aren't meant to grub for guineas in dreary factories and counting houses. That's what tradesmen are for.''

"You think it vulgar to possess a comfortable fortune, rather than living off the gaming tables or the charity of relatives?" His restrained, quiet tone told the marchioness Drake was growing more vexed by the minute. Neville was twice a fool to mistake his cousin's cold, contained wrath for weakness.

Neville ignored the warning signs. "Old fellow, you are too modest. A comfortable fortune?" He gestured about the dining room, recently restored to its former glory. "Why, you have one of the vastest fortunes in England. You're prudent to stay clear of London, though. Prinny might try to touch you for a loan.''

The marchioness glowered in Neville's direction, but he took no notice. "Of course, it isn't vulgar to possess a fortune—only to have earned it." He laughed immoderately at his own jest. No one else joined him. "I can't think why you went to all the trouble, when you might have married an ugly little heiress with an uncouth tradesman for a father.''

''By all means, feel free to pursue that course yourself, Neville.'' Drake's tone sharpened. ''I prefer to build something beneficial and lasting, by my own initiative.''

''I fear I am not temperamentally suited to such earnest labor. I am one of society's lilies of the field. I sew not. Neither do I spin. Yet King Solomon in all his glory had not so richly embroidered a waistcoat as mine.'' Neville sprawled back on his chair, displaying an expanse of that waistcoat.

The marchioness thought it in rather questionable taste for mourning. Still, she was not altogether displeased with Neville. He'd provided her with excellent leverage to use on his cousin.

''There sits the heir to all your hard-won wealth, Drake.'' She waved scornfully in Neville's direction. ''How long will take him to run through your fortune? Six months? A year?''

''I expect to live a long, healthy life, Grandmother.'' Drake's words sounded clipped and precise, his voice menacingly soft in volume, like the first rumblings of thunder.

''What my cousin means, Grandmama, is that he expects me to be worm food when he is enjoying a vigorous old age. Staggering about the countryside. Minding his mills and mines. Wolfing down heaping bowls of boiled cabbage and tripe. And celibate—is that not also part of your regimen, Cuz?''

''For pity's sake, Neville, stop plaguing the poor man,'' snapped Phyllipa.

The marchioness looked at Clarence's widow with a faint glimmer of interest. She hadn't thought the vapid creature capable of snapping.

''Drake is our host,'' Phyllipa continued primly. ''He has just lost his only brother. Besides, your bickering will upset poor dear Grandmama.''

"Fiddlesticks!" exclaimed the marchioness, when no pithier oath came readily to mind. "There's nothing I like better than a good family row. It's obligatory to quarrel after a funeral. Keeps everyone from dwelling on morbid thoughts of mortality."

Neville raised his glass to her. "What a philosopher you are, Grandmama."

"Save your oily tongue, coxcomb! I've been flattered by men more skilled in proper subtlety than you'll ever be."

His grandmother caught Drake in the ghost of a smile. She had no intention of letting him get complacent. "Your cousin has a point, Drake. No one cheats death forever. What becomes of your fine enterprises when you're gone? You need sons to inherit your title and carry on your work. Come back to London with me and take your pick from this season's marriage market."

"I'd sooner swim in a cesspit." Drake wrinkled his aquiline nose expressively.

"Exasperating cub!" The marchioness was not used to being flouted. "Were you counting on Jeremy to supply you with heirs? Now you'll have to do the deed yourself, my boy."

Drake rose abruptly from his chair. The "boy" cut quite an imposing figure these days, his grandmother grudgingly admitted. Though his long, angular face gave him a gaunt look by times, he had the lean muscularity of his late grandfather. A far cry from the sickly child whose life the family had despaired of.

"Consider this discussion closed, Grandmother. I am not a child you can cane into submission. Now, if you will excuse me, I mean to go for a ride before I retire."

"Oh, Drake, you can't be serious!" Phyllipa gestured toward the room's large windows, each composed of over a hundred small panes. Judging by the force with which the rain thrashed against them, it was being driven by a fierce westerly. "Hear that wind. It's raining fit to sink Noah's Ark."

Already halfway to the door, Drake shrugged his wide shoulders. "Never fear, Phyllipa. I have yet to dissolve in water. Besides, I prefer the impersonal hostility of nature to Grandmother's cherished family quarrels. Good night, everyone. I trust the lack of company won't spoil your enjoyment of my port, Neville."

He closed the door quietly, but firmly, behind him.

Tipping his chair back, Neville hoisted his feet up to rest on the edge of the highly polished mahogany table. "Not in the least, my dear fellow," he chuckled in reply to his absent cousin. "Not in the least."

For twopence, the Dowager Marchioness of Cranbrook would have garrotted her grandson with the string of his own monocle.

Drake was well soaked by the time he reached the stables. The chill rain had not cooled his smoldering temper, though.

"Evening yer lordship." One of the stablemen touched his cap in greeting, surveying his master with obvious puzzlement. "Is there aught I can do for you tonight, milord?"

Compared with Silverthorne's dining room, the stables looked invitingly tranquil. Drake inhaled the soothing aroma of leather, horses and sweet dry hay.

"I fancy a ride before bed. Saddle up the Spaniard."

The big black stallion strained eagerly to get out into the storm. Pointing his mount toward an expanse of open countryside, Drake rode into the darkness. Gusts of wind drove the rain into his face, taking his breath away. Rivulets of water ran down his cheeks like tears. Abandoning a lifetime of painstaking civility, he gave himself up to the savagery of the storm. Fury and anguish warred within him, as he allowed himself the luxury of experiencing raw emotion for the first time since receiving word of his young half brother's death.

For fifteen years he had striven with might and main to resurrect Silverthorne from the ashes of his late father's ruin. To what end? For Neville to mortgage it to the hilt and gamble it all away? For Phyllipa's nasty little Reginald, to do who knew what? Whatever else his grandmother might be, Drake admitted she was no fool. He *had* been relying on Jeremy to provide him with an heir. Now, if he hoped to salvage his life's work for the future, he would have to perform that odious chore for himself.

He'd gone to London once before, in a flush of youthful naiveté, and there been so abominably used as to sour him on the idea of matrimony ever since. Why could Jeremy not have taken a wife before rushing off to fight Napoleon's armies? What had possessed him to take up a commission in the first place? Heedless. Imprudent. Unreliable.

Suddenly, Drake pulled his mount up short and headed back home. He'd let his self-control slip quite enough for one night. He had no intention of handing everything to Neville on a silver platter by catching his death of ague. Before he returned to a warm bed and a scalding cup of Mrs. Maberley's cambric tea, however, Drake had one stop to make.

A faint light flickered in the old stone sanctuary of Saint Mawe's. Drake tethered his horse by the eastern wall, sheltered from the wind. It was foolish of him to come here, he supposed. However, since he'd already indulged in an orgy of foolishness by riding out on so wild a night, he might as well purge it from his system. Something compelled him to kneel by Jeremy's grave and ask, *Brother, why did you desert me?*

Cautiously, Drake picked his way through the old graveyard, following a winding route around the haphazardly arranged tombstones. So loud was the wind and so fiercely was he concentrating to avoid a fall, that he scarcely heard the sound of weeping until he was almost on top of the source. His leg brushed against a small figure huddled beside Jeremy's grave.

What was a child doing loose in a graveyard, on such a night? If Drake had a weakness, it was for the lost and the helpless, anyone in need of his aid. Abandoning his plan to commune with his brother's ghost, he hoisted the little stray into his arms and carefully wended his way back to the church. Finding the vestry door unlocked, he pushed it open with his shoulder. Only when he had settled into a pew and relinquished his burden, did he recognize Lucy Rushton.

"What the...? Miss Rushton, what are you doing here?"

Though admittedly not the most perceptive of men, where women were concerned, Drake could tell the girl was fighting to master turbulent emotions. Distractedly, she pushed the rain-soaked hair out of her eyes. The wetness made it look quite brown. Ordinarily, it curled in delicate tendrils around her face, a warm shade of dark honey.

"Forgive me, your lordship." Her words sounded muffled, as though by a head cold, but the tone was icily formal. "I know you endow my father's living, but I had no idea you counted the graveyard as your personal property. Excuse me for trespassing."

For some reason, her haughty reply made Drake want to smile with admiration. She looked so forlorn—drenched and dripping, eyes and nose ruddy from crying, face pale and pinched. Yet there was a spark in Lucy Rushton that no amount of rain or misfortune could quench.

"You know very well I don't own the graveyard." Fishing in his pocket for a handkerchief, he handed it to her in a conciliatory gesture. After all, he had no more quarrel with her than she could reasonably have with him. "Even if I did, you'd be welcome to come and go as you pleased."

Many a time, on rides about his estate, he'd come upon Lucy Rushton sitting under a tree or perched on a stile. An open book spread over her uptucked knees and a plump apple half-eaten in one hand. Engrossed in her reading or her daydreams, she seldom noticed him. Yet, from those brief encounters, he'd absorbed a measure of her contentment, going on his way in a strangely lightened mood.

Lucy scrubbed at her eyes, which only succeeded in making them redder. "Would I be welcome? I wasn't welcome this afternoon when you buried Captain Strickland."

She made a thorough job of blowing her nose. Loud and wet, it sounded intentionally rude.

"Not welcome?" Drake looked at her in frank astonishment. "What nonsense, I..."

"It was very badly done, barring everyone but family. Who were those people, anyway? That ridiculous creature with the garish waistcoat and quizzing glass. He didn't appear the least bit grieved. I'd swear he was gloating."

"Cousin Neville, the son of my father's brother." Drake didn't try to deny Lucy's opinion of his cousin.

"I recognized your grandmother, but who was the younger lady? I've never seen her at Silverthorne before."

"Lady Phyllipa Strickland, widow of my cousin Clarence." If asked, Drake could not have said why he answered her peremptory interrogation so readily.

"Oh." His account of Phyllipa's identity appeared to confound her for a moment. Her inexplicable indignation rapidly gathered strength again. "Those people may be Captain Strickland's relatives. But I doubt if they knew him or cared for him as well as many of his old friends...."

Her words trailed off as fresh tears sprang into her wideset brown eyes. Drake reached out to take her hand, but she pushed him away. In the split second they were in contact, he could feel her trembling.

"You must be freezing. I'd offer you my coat, but I fear it would do little good, sodden as it is."

"F-f-father..." She was shivering in earnest now, her teeth chattering rhythmically. "F-f-father keeps a s-s-spare surplice in the v-v-vestry."

Rising from the pew, Drake strode down the side aisle to

fetch the vicar's spare surplice. He wrapped it around her as best he could.

"Believe me, Miss Rushton, it was never my intent to slight you. I only wanted to spare my tenants any obligation to attend the funeral. If you'd spoken to me beforehand, I would have welcomed you to join the family. Jeremy was very fond of you."

In the perverse, puzzling manner of women, Lucy greeted his attempt at kindness with a fresh effusion of tears.

"Dash it all, what's the matter now? You always struck me as a sensible person. I must say, I find your reaction to Jeremy's death exaggerated quite out of proportion. Just because you didn't get a front row seat for his funeral is no cause to go courting consumption by keeping a graveside vigil in the pouring rain."

Bluster had no better effect than solicitude. Lucy Rushton bent her head practically into her lap, weeping in loud sobs that racked her delicate frame.

"There, there." Drake patted her shoulder in an awkward gesture of sympathy. He was beginning to wish he'd stayed back at Silverthorne. "Don't take on so. I'm sorry if I said anything to offend you." He tried to recall what he'd said that might have caused this outburst. "You must stop. Otherwise you'll make yourself ill."

Then, as though she considered his warning an invitation, Lucy Rushton vomited all over the flagstone floor, the kneeling bench, and Drake's Hessians. Fortunately for the boots, she had little on her stomach but broth.

Afterward, Drake wondered what had prompted his uncharacteristic flash of insight. Grasping Lucy Rushton by the shoulders, he looked her straight in the eye. "You're carrying my brother's child," he said with complete conviction.

Her chin trembled, but she did not flinch from his look. With only the barest nod, she confirmed Drake's preposterous charge. His hands slipped from her shoulders, limp with shock.

Lucy unwadded his handkerchief and daubed at the mess on the chapel floor. "Go ahead. Say what you're thinking. I'm a harlot—a wanton. I deserve everything that's coming to me."

Suddenly the stock around Drake's throat felt very tight. He had a powerful urge to dig up Jeremy's corpse so he could have the satisfaction of strangling his brother. Damn him! With his golden good looks and ingratiating manner, Jeremy'd always had more women than he knew what to do with. Drake hadn't cared how much of his allowance the young fool spent on trinkets for actresses and barmaids. But to take advantage of an innocent like Lucy Rushton was utterly insupportable!

"Wanton?" His lips twitched involuntarily at using such a word to describe her. "Nonsense. My dear child, you could not behave in a wanton manner if you tried."

He scarcely knew what to make of it when she flared up, "I am *not* a child! I am every day of twenty. I have been to Bath."

Signifying what, exactly? Drake wondered. He opened his mouth to explain he'd meant no offense, quite the contrary.

She cut him off. "How do you know what I'm capable of? You know nothing about me. Just go away and leave me alone."

"Perhaps I would rather stay and commiserate. It appears Jeremy's death has put us both in a spot of bother."

"Bother?" Sharp and shrill, the word echoed off the chapel's stone walls. "Is that what you call it? When my condition becomes known, I will be a social outcast. My child will be farmed out to strangers or to the harsh mercy of a foundlings' hospital. What bother of yours can compare with that?"

"Only that I shall have to marry, against my inclination,

to provide myself with heirs. Otherwise that foppish cousin of mine stands to inherit Silverthorne.''

''Forced to marry? Poor man. You make it sound as appealing as a hanging. Jeremy did not shy from it as you do. He planned to marry me on his next leave.''

Drake wished he could believe that as sincerely as she appeared to.

''A pity he did not marry you before he went away. It would have spared us both considerable distress.''

Her anger collapsed on itself, like a punctured bubble. ''Forgive me, your lordship. I have abused your patience inexcusably this evening. I must get back to the vicarage before father misses me. I trust you'll keep my secret for as long as need be.'' She rose to leave.

''How far along are you?'' Drake called after her.

His abrupt question stopped Lucy. ''I beg your pardon?''

''How long...since you conceived the child?''

She answered without hesitation. ''Six weeks.'' Musing softly, she added, ''We only made love once. The day before he left.''

Drake drew a deep breath. He was about to dive headlong into murky, uncharted waters. Unfortunately, his bothersome conscience would let him do no less. He must speak now, before she hurried away again, or before he lost his nerve.

''In that case...I propose...a mutually beneficial solution to our problems.''

Chapter Two

"**M**arried? Drake you can't mean it." A morsel of egg slid from his grandmother's spoon and fell quivering onto her saucer.

Neville and Phyllipa exchanged a glance, two pairs of eyebrows raised in surprise and consternation. Drake felt a rush of satisfaction at having ambushed his family so neatly. This was their payback for last night's dinner.

"I assure you, Grandmother, I am quite in earnest." Drake cheerfully tucked into his breakfast.

"To the vicar's daughter?" Phyllipa blinked her bulging eyes. "But you are a gentleman of substance, Drake."

"All the more reason I can dispense with the bothersome task of pursuing an heiress," he replied with exaggerated good humor.

"Decided to dive into the cesspit after all, have you Cuz?" Neville weighed in with his contribution. "I marvel at how rapidly your scruples deserted you."

"If you'll recall…" Drake could not keep the muscles of his jaw from tensing. "I was speaking of that matrimonial cattle market they call *The Season*, not of marriage in general. Were you too drunk to mark the difference?"

Breathing on his quizzing glass, Neville made a show of

rubbing it clean with his napkin. "My dear fellow, you un-derestimate my capacity for good port."

"And you underestimate my reluctance to have you in-herit Silverthorne. Taking Grandmother's warning to heart, I followed her advice and secured a wife with the utmost dispatch."

"But it's so unromantic!" Phyllipa wailed.

"Which suits me admirably, for I am the least romantic of men. I find nothing disagreeable about this arrangement. It is honest, practical and expeditious."

They all looked so dumbfounded, he could not help warming to his subject. "Just think if I'd gone about it the usual way. I'd have had to abandon my business concerns for weeks on end to attend a lot of tiresome routs and balls in London. There, I would have stayed up later than is good for me, eaten food that disagreed with me and drank an intemperate quantity of spirits." He cast a pointed glance at Neville.

"I would have strained to hold my gorge while a pack of silly girls preened for my inspection. I would have pranced through a succession of tedious terpsichorean ex-ercises, whose sole purpose is to provide an immoderate living for mincing dancing masters."

After pausing for a sip of coffee, Drake continued. "Hav-ing fixed on my choice—the least objectionable female des-perate enough to consider me for a husband—I would pay the lady my addresses. Which is to say, a compound of meaningless pleasantries and insincere flattery. My proposal accepted, I would commence negotiations with her father, resulting in a marriage contract. The driest batch of legal quibble ever penned by a lawyer's clerk, a monument to cold-blooded self-interest. The whole operation is so ex-ceedingly romantic, it fair takes my breath away!"

Such a long speech, all in one go, did leave him rather winded. Still, Drake felt a tremendous sense of relief to have had his say on a subject that had long vexed him.

"When is the wedding?" Phyllipa finally squeaked.

Drake beamed as though she had wished him warm congratulations. "Day after tomorrow. I have to speak with the vicar and obtain a special license. I trust you'll all stay on for the nuptial festivities. We will need witnesses."

The Dowager Marchioness rose from her place. She had a majestic presence for so small and ancient a person. Grasping her walking stick, she stalked toward the door. "No doubt the funeral meats will coldly furnish forth the wedding table." She quoted from *Hamlet*.

Drake almost grinned. *Touché, Grandmother.*

"I, for one, will not condone this farce with my presence." With that malediction, she marched from the room and quit Silverthorne within the hour.

In a pool of pale autumn sunshine, on the stoop of a modest thatched cottage, Lucy Rushton sat reading aloud from Milton's *Comus*. On the bench beside her sat Widow Sowerby, tenant of the cottage, a pair of knitting needles clattering busily in her tiny nimble hands. Never once did she look down at her work, but gazed unseeing on the pastoral beauty of Mayeswater.

For years it had been Lucy's habit to drop by Mrs. Sowerby's cottage and read or talk while she knitted. Preoccupied with her grief for Jeremy and her fears for the future, she had recently neglected her self-imposed duty. Today, in spite of her new misgivings, or perhaps because of them, she had sought comfort in doing for others.

"Come now, lass, out with it. What's troubling you?" The tempo of Mrs. Sowerby's knitting slowed.

Lucy glanced up from her book. "Troubling me? No…I mean, nothing. Nothing is troubling me. I am quite well. Whatever makes you think that?" Fortunately, Mrs. Sowerby's cataracts prevented her from noticing the blush that smarted in Lucy's cheeks.

The old woman chuckled. "Just because my eyes don't

work no more, doesn't mean I can't see what's plain. I've counted seven times you've sighed since you last turned the page, and four times you've lost your place. Don't try to fool Old Fanny that you haven't got some'ut weighing on your mind."

Lucy sighed for the eighth time. "I might as well tell you, Mrs. Sowerby. Everyone in Nicholthwait will know by tomorrow night. I'm getting married."

"Is that so?" Mrs. Sowerby nodded over this information, and perhaps the marked lack of enthusiasm in Lucy's announcement. "Anyone I know?"

Lucy nodded, then remembered her friend couldn't see her. "Everyone knows him. I am to marry Viscount Silverthorne."

Mrs. Sowerby's knitting needles froze in midstitch. "His lordship? This is unexpected news. Most lasses would be singing it to the rooftops—a match like that."

"It is a great honor." Not to mention a great burden, sharing her life with the man she held responsible for Jeremy's death. If she could have seen any other way to provide decently for her child, she would have taken pleasure in refusing Lord Silverthorne's proposal.

"Oh, aye. A big estate. A title. A large fortune. Most lasses could ask naught more from a marriage." The two women, sat silent for a moment. "Then again, you aren't most lasses, Miss Lucy. I think you want more from a husband than his brass or his family name. You'd fancy a man with a ready smile and a way of saying your name that makes your heart beat faster."

Lucy thought of Jeremy Strickland, his eyes as blue as the summer sky reflected in the glassy surface of Mayeswater, his golden hair ruffled by the upland wind. As her eyes began to water, she felt a pang of exasperation. She had always been of a sunny, optimistic nature. A sensible person, as the viscount so plainly put it. Lately it took nothing to make her weep. She hated having her emotions so out of control.

"Your description does not sound very much like Viscount Silverthorne, does it?" Lucy hoped Mrs. Sowerby would mistake the break in her voice for a chuckle.

"I suppose not. Nothing glib about his lordship, poor lad."

"Nothing poor about his lordship either," Lucy reminded her friend tartly. "They say he has the Midas touch."

Mrs. Sowerby felt at her knitting to find where she'd left off. "As I recall, the golden touch didn't make that Midas fellow any too happy."

"You're hinting at something, so you might as well tell me plainly. Why do you call Lord Silverthorne a 'poor lad'?"

Now it was Fanny Sowerby's turn to sigh. "Perhaps you should ask him, my dear. Let's just say he had a childhood I'd not envy any lad."

Something in Mrs. Sowerby's tone gave Lucy a pang as she thought of her own idyllic girlhood, full of books and dreams and the small beauties of nature. The only passing shadows on those years had been the deaths of an infant brother and sister. Deprived of other children, her parents had lavished all their love on her.

Just then, Lucy noticed the long shadow cast by Mrs. Sowerby's crab apple tree. Though she was curious to hear more about Lord Silverthorne's unenviable childhood, she'd promised to meet him at the vicarage within the hour.

"I'm afraid I must be getting back home, Mrs. Sowerby. I'm sorry I was so distracted, and spoiled the reading for you."

"Never you mind about that. I'm grateful for the company. Not many lasses would bother with a blind old woman."

"That would be their loss." Lucy stooped to bestow a gentle kiss on the woman's weathered cheek.

Mrs. Sowerby dropped her knitting and caught Lucy's hand. "I wish you and his lordship every happiness. He's a fine man, for all he don't say much. Once a month, like clockwork, I'll hear him ride up to my gate. Never says a word, just checks to see how I'm getting on. Once he came by when it was raining, and my roof was leaking like a sieve. The next day a crew shows up from the big house with orders to rethatch it."

Lucy could not think what to reply. Mrs. Sowerby's story contradicted her lifelong perception of the stern autocrat.

"He needs a bit of happiness in his life," Mrs Sowerby added. "Deserves it, too, with all he's done for folks round here. If there's a woman can make him happy, I fancy it's you."

"I'll try, Mrs. Sowerby."

The old woman waved Lucy on her way. Then, perhaps thinking her out of earshot, Mrs. Sowerby mused aloud, "And you might just be surprised at how happy he can make you, my dear."

Lucy turned away, sighing for the ninth time that afternoon. She doubted it was in the power of any woman to make his lordship happy. And she was certain any chance of her own happiness had died on a Spanish battlefield with Jeremy Strickland.

At a wary distance from the vicarage, Drake sat on his horse trying to screw up his nerve for an interview with Vicar Rushton. He had made his initial marriage offer to Lucy in a momentary surge of moral obligation. Jeremy had used her abominably, and Drake felt it his duty to rectify the situation. He relished breaking the news to his family. Their opposition had only strengthened his resolve. During his ride to the vicarage, a host of doubts had risen to assail him.

Could he manage to put up with a wife underfoot all the time? He'd lived a solitary existence, apart from his years in school—years he'd hated. Ragged and bullied by high-born louts with no interests beyond their own pleasure, he'd fought hard for the simple right to be left alone. It went against his grain to surrender his hard-won privacy.

He wasn't thinking only of himself, either. What kind of life would it be for Lucy and the child—mewed up at Silverthorne with a man temperamentally unsuited to marriage and fatherhood? Desperately as he wanted an heir to supplant Neville, he could not consign Jeremy's son to a bleak, joyless childhood like he had suffered.

"It's no good," Drake muttered through clenched teeth.

"Do you not think so?" Lucy suddenly emerged from a wooded path nearby. "Most people would call this a fine day, after that dreadful storm. Or were you referring to the view?"

Drake looked down the lane to Saint Mawes vicarage, a cosy stone house, green with ivy and hemmed in by an inviting miscellany of trees and shrubs. Not merely a house, the vicarage looked like a home. The sight of it stirred a long-buried wistfulness in Drake Strickland's practical, impervious heart.

"No, indeed." He strove to sound impassive. "The view is very well."

Planting herself squarely in front of his horse, Lucy looked up at him, a challenge glittering incongruously in the depths of her wide, soft eyes. "Then I must assume you are having second thoughts about marrying me?"

He fixed his gaze on a point just above the crest of her bonnet. "By no means, Miss Rushton." Drake surprised himself with the ease by which he delivered this bold-faced lie. "I see clearly where my duty rests." At least that part was true.

"How priggish you sound. As your wife, will I be subjected to daily sermons at the breakfast table?"

Drake felt the sting of her rebuke. This was not the Lucy Rushton who had won his distant regard—the generous, unpretentious girl who read to Widow Sowerby and wandered the countryside with a book under her arm. That winter in Bath of which she boasted, had spoiled her completely. Turned her into one of those tart-tongued brittle creatures he despised.

"I can assure you, madam, I will subject you to as little of my objectionable discourse as appearances permit."

"If that's how you feel, perhaps we should call off this ridiculous charade." With those bold words, her face went white and she swayed as though buffeted by a strong wind. Drake vaulted from his saddle, sending his startled horse skittering sideways. He caught Lucy just before she hit the ground.

It took a moment for her to recover, a moment during which Drake found himself torn by conflicting emotions. Part of him protested that it was most indecorous for the scion of Silverthorne to be kneeling in a country lane with a half-conscious woman in his arms. Even if she was his intended bride. Another part felt a passing qualm of guilt that he had subjected Lucy to an unpleasant exchange, in her delicate condition. An overwhelming sense of protectiveness conquered all other feelings.

So small and childlike in his arms, she needed him as much as any of his tenants or employees. But she was not a child—she was a woman. Through the light fabric of her dress, he could feel her delicious feminine curves. This whole arrangement would work better if he did not find her so dangerously attractive. All the same, Lucy and her baby were his responsibility. Though it might prove the most difficult undertaking of his life, he must do right by them.

"Where am I?" Her eyelids fluttered. "What happened?" She struggled to sit up.

"Easy now." Drake gently restrained her. "Do let me know the next time you feel faint. You gave me quite a turn."

She quit trying to get away from him, but her whole body

stiffened, reluctant to yield. "I seem to make a habit of discommoding you, my lord. It's a habit I am eager to break, I assure you."

What a prickly temper! Drake frowned. Making any overture toward Lucy Rushton was like trying to engage a hedgehog. Were all expectant mothers like this? he wondered.

As he slackened his hold, Lucy pulled free of his arms. Jumping to her feet, she slapped the dust from her pale-blue dress. "Forget what I told you last night. I absolve you from any moral obligation to me."

Drake unfolded his tall frame from the crouched posture in which he'd held Lucy. "That is the trouble with moral obligations—one can never quite absolve one's self." He tried to smile, to show he was partly in jest and hopefully to ease some of the tension between them. The muscles of his face didn't seem to understand what he was asking of them. They could only manage a lopsided grimace.

"If you wish to reconsider your decision to marry me, that is your right. In fact, I urge you to weigh your options carefully before choosing the course that will best serve you…and your child," he added almost under his breath, in case anyone should be within earshot of their conversation.

"Options?" She gave a bitter little laugh. "I have no options, Lord Silverthorne, as you are well aware."

"Of course, you do. You must. If you choose not to marry me, I'll still provide for you…both. I'll give you money to go away until the child is born. If you choose not to keep him, I'll secure him a good home."

"That is very generous of you."

"It is my duty."

"Ah yes, that irksome word again."

Drake was tempted to launch into a lecture on the importance of ideals like duty and honor, but he restrained himself. "Bear in mind, if you choose to go your own way,

I will never be able to acknowledge Jeremy's son as my heir.''

"I understand.''

"However, it would leave you free to forget the past and, one day, make a marriage more to your liking.''

"I will never forget Jeremy.'' She declared it as a fundamental truth. "And I will never love any other man. It would be wrong of me to marry a man I could not love.''

"What if the man knew you could not love him?'' Drake asked quietly. "What if he did not want your love?''

"I suppose…'' Lucy looked over at the spire of Saint Mawes, rising from behind the vicarage. "Won't it be a sin to speak marriage vows we have no intention of keeping?''

"I doubt we will be the first couple to do so.'' Drake scuffed the grass with the toe of his Hessians. "Or the last.''

Lucy made no reply. Assuming she must be weighing her options, Drake held himself still and silent. He'd had his say, whether or not she'd listened to him. In the end it all came down to her life and her child's. She must be free to choose, without pressure from him. Yet, as the minutes passed with no sound but the occasional swish of the horse's tail, Drake found himself earnestly hoping Lucy would not change her mind. Perhaps her doubts had tempered his resolve. Or perhaps he wanted a son of Jeremy's to call his own.

Finally she spoke. "Very well, sir. I will marry you.''

Drake suddenly realized he had been holding his breath. "I must speak to your father.'' He gasped out the words. "Then I must hunt up Squire Lewes and have him issue us a special license. Is tomorrow too soon?''

"For the wedding?'' A faint blush mantled Lucy's cheeks. "Considering our reason for marrying—the sooner, the better. First…'' She laid a hand on his coat sleeve. "Can we make a private vow, truthfully, with only God as our witness?''

"What a clever idea.'' Drake found himself smiling

"Like in business—a prior contract. What did you have in mind?"

Her hand slid slowly down his sleeve, and after a moment's hesitation, clasped his hand. "I, Lucy Rushton, promise to raise my child, with you as his father. I vow to treat you with the respect due to a husband. I will never burden you with unwanted affection or be jealous of your interest in other women."

That summed up the whole situation quite well. Drake cleared his throat. He liked the feel of her hand in his—too much so, perhaps. "I, Drake Strickland, promise to raise your child as my own and treat you with the respect due to a wife. I'll never…"

"Burden," Lucy prompted him.

"Oh, yes. Never burden you with unwanted affection or be jealous of your interest in other men." For some reason, he had trouble saying that last sentence with conviction.

Lucy let go of his hand. "You needn't have added that last part. I told you, I will never care for any man but Jeremy."

"And I have no interest in any woman." Though he stressed the words most emphatically, Drake could not forget the way she'd felt in his arms. "I believe that sets us even. Now, shall we go break the news to your father?"

Chapter Three

All things considered, her father had taken the news quite well, Lucy reflected as she sat before her dressing table preparing for bed the following night. Though the best of men and the kindest of fathers, Vicar Rushton had a vague, preoccupied air, that had deepened over the years since the death of his cheerful, practical wife. Lucy often had the feeling he was only half listening when she spoke to him.

When Lord Silverthorne…Drake, had formally asked for her hand, her father only shook his head and chuckled, "Well, well, well. Bless my soul!" Perhaps he thought they'd been courting for ages under his nose, but couldn't bring himself to admit he hadn't noticed. He raised no objection when Drake requested a hasty wedding, without benefit of banns, blithely agreeing to conduct the ceremony himself.

The ceremony. If their union lasted fifty years, Lucy knew she would always cringe at the thought of her wedding—brief, awkward and decidedly unfestive. As she spoke her vows to love and honor her husband, forsaking all others, her thoughts resonated with earlier promises to do nothing of the kind.

"Will you be needing anything else, your ladyship?"

asked the serving girl who had just finished unpacking her trunk.

The silver hairbrush slipped from Lucy's fingers, but made scarcely a sound as it landed on the thick pile of the carpet. Glancing around her bedchamber in alarm, she wondered if Lady Phyllipa had managed to enter without her noticing. Then she realized the girl was addressing her.

"Excuse me…Mary, is it? I'm afraid it will take me some time to become accustomed to my new title. As a matter of fact, plain 'ma'am' is good enough for everyday use."

She retrieved her brush from the floor and checked it over for dents. Such luxuries would take some getting used to.

"Let's see?" She surveyed the spacious, elegantly appointed room. The very style of it emphasized that she was far out of her social depth. "The fire's been lit. You've turned down the bed and given it a pass with the warming pan. You've unpacked my clothes. I doubt I'll require anything further tonight." Back home at the vicarage, she'd have tended to those chores herself. Would she ever get used to ordering a houseful of servants?

The girl curtsied. "Very good ma'am. I hope you rest well your first night at Silverthorne."

Feeling a blush begin to prickle in her cheeks, Lucy turned back to her dressing table. If young Mary was privy to the gossip buzzing around Nicholthwait about Lord Silverthorne's hasty marriage, she probably doubted her mistress would get any sleep at all on her wedding night.

"Thank you. I'm sure I shall." Lucy tried to sound more certain than she felt.

She heard the door of her bedchamber open, and Mary let out a squeal of surprise.

"Excuse me, your lordship," the girl gasped. "I was just on my way out."

Lucy jumped from the stool in front of her dressing table. Her hairbrush tumbled to the floor for the second time. She heard her bridegroom reply heartily, "How convenient,

Mary. I was just on my way in. By the way, tell Talbot I said not to be stingy with the champagne below stairs to-night.''

Drake's long lean frame filled the doorway as he stood there bidding Mary good-night. His dark hair clung to his head in damp curls, leading Lucy to guess he had bathed in the short interval since dinner. A pair of bare feet and firm bare calves showed below the hem of his lordship's olive green dressing gown. Was he wearing *anything* beneath that dressing gown? Lucy wondered, her throat constricting.

They'd politely danced around the subject in their discussions, but she thought she'd made plain her reluctance to share his lordship's bed. Unwanted affection, indeed. She had loved Jeremy in a way she could never love again. It would be like the worst kind of infidelity to give herself to another man with her beloved barely cold in his grave. But what if her new husband insisted? She hadn't the strength to resist him physically. To call for help would mean the end of her marriage and the exposure of her secret.

In the few seconds it took for Lord Silverthorne to close the door behind him, Lucy's pulse sped to double time. She took a step back. ''Why are you here?''

He swept her a casual glance, a glint of amusement in his dark eyes. ''*Not* to claim my marital rights, if that's what you presume.'' As though to prove his innocent intentions, he sauntered over to the velvet-upholstered chaise before the hearth. ''I merely wish to convince our household that I am an attentive husband.'' He lowered himself onto the chaise. ''If our marriage is to serve its purpose, everyone must believe I sired your child. I took a rather circuitous route to get here. By my count, five of the servants saw me, as well as Lady Phyllipa—an unexpected bonus. With any luck, tales of my ardent regard for you will spread far and wide.''

''I see.'' Lucy's heartbeat slowed again. Something made her ask, ''Was it necessary to arrive in quite this state of undress?''

She could see a wedge of his tanned chest, lightly matted with dark curly hair. How different Drake Strickland was from his brother. Jeremy had been of an elegant, compact build. With his fair complexion and blond hair, he'd made Lucy think of gold and ivory. Spare and rangy, with a fiercely masculine presence, Jeremy's brother was a creature of bronze and sable.

Drake leaned back on the chaise with an air of polite indifference that enraged her. "Merely useful costuming in our charade of a marriage. I did not want anyone mistaking my intentions." One dark brow cocked expressively. "Why all this virginal prudery, my dear? Surely it's nothing you haven't seen before."

The cruelty of his words smote Lucy. Had Lord Silverthorne taken her to wive purely for the pleasure of humiliating her? A passionate rage overcame her. She fairly flew the distance between them, striking his cheek with her hand. "Never speak to me that way again, do you hear?"

She gasped with pain as Drake clutched her wrist. "Keep your voice down, woman, or the whole house will hear you. If you're so afraid of seeing something improper, get into bed and draw the hangings." None too gently, he pushed her toward the bed. "I will see myself out after a suitable interval."

Part of Lucy could not believe she'd dared to strike Viscount Silverthorne, a man she had looked on with awe and more than a little fear for most of her life. Would anything cure her of such reckless impulsiveness? Another part was glad she had slapped him, would slap him again if need be. Insufferable creature!

"I will retire to bed when I am ready, sir. Not when you command." She sat down on the stool and began pulling the bristles through her golden brown curls. Her hands trembled.

In the looking glass, she saw Drake shrug his wide shoulders. "I did not command. I merely suggested."

Lucy could see the red mark on his cheek where she had slapped him. Coupled with her other contradictory emotions, she felt a sudden pang of shame. More disturbing still, she felt an inexplicable desire to anoint that tiny welt with a kiss.

"I'm sorry I slapped you." She tossed the words carelessly over her shoulder.

He chuckled faintly. "This?" He pointed to his cheek. "I hardly felt it, I assure you." Then his expression turned gravely earnest. "I apologize for my flippant observation. It was uncalled for."

Lucy could not bring herself to utter false assurances of forgiveness. Deliberately, she laid the hairbrush on her dressing table, and rose from the stool. "I believe I will retire now. I have not slept well of late."

Drake made no reply, but she could feel his eyes upon her. Suddenly, she was conscious of her swollen, tender breasts, pushing against the light fabric of her nightgown, and a warm tingling sensation below her womb. What other unsettling symptoms had pregnancy in store for her? Lucy scowled to mask her embarrassment.

Perhaps he marked her expression and thought it was directed at him. "I'm your ally, not your adversary," he said quietly.

"I know." Snuffing her candle, Lucy climbed into bed and drew the covers up to her chin. "It's just that…" She hesitated, unable to put her feelings into benign, neutral words.

He appeared to understand. "…you can't help thinking how different this night would be if you were Jeremy's bride?" He had his back turned to her, hunched forward on the chaise. "Perhaps you even wish I were lying in the churchyard in his place?"

Lucy shut her eyes and forced her breath to a slow steady rhythm. If Drake looked to see why she hadn't answered, he might believe she had fallen asleep. For several long minutes, she heard nothing but the soft crackle of the fire. Then he spoke again, his voice almost too low for her to hear.

"I wouldn't blame you if you did. But the die is cast now. What we cannot change, we must endure."

He sounded so bereft. It suddenly occurred to her that Drake had lost a beloved brother. At the same time, her pride smarted from his implication that their marriage was an ordeal he must endure. She hated these overwrought, contradictory feelings he constantly provoked in her.

Neville Strickland drained the last drop of port from his glass with a sigh of appreciation. When one had to abide a sojourn in the godforsaken wilds of Cumbria, one must needs take advantage of minor consolations. He fancied a drop more, but the decanter sat on a sideboard clear across the room. He could not work up the ambition to go after it. Perhaps a servant would happen by soon, to extinguish the dying fire. With a discreet belch, Neville slouched further in the thickly upholstered armchair and let his heavy eyelids slide shut.

He heard the door open, and footsteps enter the room. Presuming it must be a servant, he roused himself to order another drink. Then he heard the welcome clink of a heavy stopper being lifted from the mouth of the decanter. Say what you liked about old Drake—the man did have his servants well trained.

Neville coaxed one eye open in time to see Phyllipa emptying the last drop of port into a tall dipper.

"Greedy little pig," he grunted.

With a muted shriek, she rose several inches off the floor, sending the port stopper crashing onto a silver salver. "Good Lord, Neville, you frightened me near to death! I thought you'd gone to bed."

"Tsk, tsk, Phyllipa, do you know nothing of logic? There is port in the decanter—at least there *was*—ergo, I must be on hand to drink it. Besides, my bedroom is only two doors down from the bridal chamber. How would I get any sleep with the floorboards creaking under my cousin's strenuous performance of his conjugal duties?''

Phyllipa shot him a withering look. "How crude you are, Neville. You must be drunk."

"You sound exactly like Grandmama." He pried his other eye open. "You make it sound as though people lie or talk nonsense when they're drunk. In my experience, it is quite the contrary."

"And we all know you have vast experience of being drunk." Phyllipa took a long draft of her port.

"Do I detect a hint of malice? Nurture it, by all means. It might save your character from being thoroughly insipid."

She responded in the most provocative way possible—by ignoring him. Pretending she hadn't heard a word he'd said, Phyllipa seated herself opposite him and took another drink, smacking her lips with enjoyment. Such deliberate aggravation was not to be borne.

"Drowning your sorrows?" he sniped. "How long do you think before that toothsome little vicar's daughter drops a dozen Silverthorne brats to supplant young Reggie?"

Phyllipa's eyes bulged to a gratifying degree. If she'd been any closer, Neville was sure she'd have spit on him. "Damn you, Neville! You can sit back and laugh. You'll never live long enough to see a ha'penny from Silverthorne. But darling Reggie...it is too bad!"

Having goaded her into such an outburst put Neville in a better humor. "There, there, old girl, I share a measure of your disappointment. True, I didn't expect to outlive Drake with his monastic regimen, but I could have lived like a king on my expectations."

The port in Phyllipa's glass gleamed like liquid rubies in the flickering firelight. She tipped it toward him in a mock toast. "Here's to the death of expectations."

"Don't bury the corpse unless you're certain it's past revival," quipped Neville.

The glass to her lips, Phyllipa hesitated. "What drunken foolishness are you talking now?"

He'd managed to stop her from consuming the last of the port. Neville congratulated himself. "What if the bride is barren? She didn't look robustly healthy to me. What if she miscarries? Stillbirth? Maybe she'll bear him a daughter?"

"Even a fool like you wouldn't pin your hopes on that." Phyllipa gave him a sour look. "There hasn't been a female born in the Silverthorne line since the Norman Conquest. Clarence reminded me of the fact every day while I was carrying Reggie."

"Must you be so literal?" Neville smelled that last drop of port luring him from the bottom of her glass. "I'm only saying—a lot can go wrong."

"Yes?" Phyllipa stared at him with intense expectancy.

"I'm sure if we put our heads together, we can shipwreck this 'honest business arrangement' of Drake's before it produces any troublesome progeny."

A hopeful smile spread across her long, pasty face. The port in Neville's stomach sloshed around menacingly. Gad, the woman looked positively gruesome when she smiled.

"What must I do?" she asked eagerly.

Neville marshaled his wits for several moments of intense concentration. He hadn't had an actual plan in mind, but surely he could devise one. After all, mischief was on his list of favorite pastimes, second only to drinking.

"You must stay on at Silverthorne and ingratiate yourself with the bride."

Phyllipa's thin upper lip curled in distaste.

"It won't be so difficult," said Neville. "You've been ingratiating yourself with somebody or other for as long as I've known you. And this is in a worthy cause. Sow seeds of discord between the newlyweds and get them to come down to London."

"London? Whatever for? What is your part in all this?"

"Patience, my dear." Neville beamed in admiration of his own genius. "While you are chipping away at the foundations of Drake's marriage, like a good little sapper, I shall be mounting a marvelous ambush to topple it completely."

"What sort of ambush?" Phyllipa sounded dubious.

Neville fumbled for his monocle, then screwed it up to his eye. He thought it gave his face a look of wisdom and mystery. "Never you mind. Suffice it to say, it will send our disaffected young bride bolting for the Continent like a hare with a greyhound on its tail."

Phyllipa let out a high-pitched giggle that sent shivers down his spine. The port was obviously working on her. "Then if Drake wants to remarry, he'll have to endure the public disgrace of a divorce. After that, no respectable woman will have him. Oh, Neville, you are too clever!"

He gave a wan smile in return. Her flirtatious glance made him distinctly nervous. He desperately needed another drink. "Shall we toast our alliance, then?"

"By all means." Weaving over to Neville's chair, she dribbled a generous splash of her remaining port into his glass.

"Here's to the restoration of my expectations and Reggie's inheritance." Neville savored the rich body of the port on his tongue for a reverent moment before swallowing. Phyllipa settled on the floor beside him and rested her head against his knee. As he recalled a saying about necessity making strange bedfellows, Neville felt the wine in his stomach begin to curdle.

The fire in Lucy's bedchamber had subsided into a handful of glowing embers. By the sound of her deep, even breathing, Drake judged her to be sound asleep at last. He had one final prop to plant in their little charade. With any luck it would fuel all the right sort of rumours, so no one would be suspicious when Lucy's baby arrived "early."

By rights he should have done it before she got into bed, but he hadn't been anxious for her to strike him again. Drake reached up and touched his cheek gingerly. Contrary to his earlier protestations, it stung like the very devil. The little spitfire could muster considerable strength when roused.

Not that he could blame her, after his churlish remark. Drake had no idea what had compelled him to say such a thing, or why he hadn't warned Lucy he would be coming here tonight. This whole marriage business had propelled him into territory he'd never expected or wanted to tread. Deliberately throwing her off balance helped him to regain some of his own equilibrium. Drake refused to consider that he might have provoked Lucy in the hope that he would feel her touch, however untender.

From his dressing gown pocket, he drew a small flask and uncorked it. Stealthily he approached the bed, reaching under the blankets to deposit the flask's contents. Warm from the heat of his body, she would probably not even notice it. Until tomorrow morning, at which time he hoped she would play along with the ruse. Drake felt his hand brush her flesh.

Before he had an instant to savor the sensation, she sat bolt upright, throwing off the bedclothes and letting out a piercing scream. Dropping the flask, he managed to arrest her hand within inches of his face.

"Once a night is my limit for that kind of abuse, madam."

"You deserve it for frightening me near to death. What are you doing? As if I need ask."

Drake released her hand. He trembled with the effort to suppress his raging urges. He smelled her hair and the faint tantalizing musk of a woman's body roused from sleep. For the first time in his life, Drake felt overwhelmed by powerful impulses beyond his control. It scared the hell out of him.

"Get it through your head, woman, that I am not racked with lust for the dubious pleasures of your body," he lied, in what he desperately hoped was a convincing manner.

"Eeeuu! What have you got all over the sheets and my nightgown?"

"Keep your voice down," Drake snapped. "It's a few drops of pig's blood. To convince the servants that *I* have relieved you of your virginity."

"Oh. I hadn't thought of that."

Drake rescued the flask and shoved it back in his pocket. "I have learned to pay attention to details." Retaining a tenuous grip on his self-control, he backed away from the bed. "The way you have splashed it about will likely cause talk of my enthusiastic performance."

"You might have warned me and done the deed before I lapsed into a sound sleep." Lucy pulled the bedclothes up around her.

"Let's just say I was not eager to feel the sting of your wrath again so soon." Drake prayed she would attribute the breathlessness of his voice to anger.

"Have you any other nasty surprises in store for me tonight, your lordship?"

"None." Drake did not trust himself to say more.

"In that case, I'll thank you to leave."

"With pleasure." He stalked from the room.

In the gallery he could hear the muted sounds of celebration rising from the butler's pantry. At least someone was getting a bit of pleasure out of his benighted marriage.

Back in his dressing room, Drake found the bathtub still set up and full of water, long since gone cold. Perhaps eager to take part in the festivities below stairs, his valet had neglected to drain it. Letting his dressing gown fall around his ankles, Drake stepped into the narrow tub. As he sat down in the chilly water, he half expected a hissing cloud of steam to rise from his fevered body.

What in heaven's name had he let himself in for?

Chapter Four

As the footman set breakfast before her, Lucy smiled wanly. In the weeks since her wedding, she had come to dread the morning meal. In the first place, her persistent nausea was always at its worst before noon.

She glanced down at her plate, mounded with food. Eggs, bacon, hotcakes, kippered herring, broiled veal kidneys in quantities fit to sustain a grown man at field labour. Lucy averted her eyes, before the sight made her vomit. What she would have given for a modest saucer of dry toast and a cup of weak tea! Somehow she could not bring herself to dictate special requests to Lord Silverthorne's cook. His cousin kept the kitchen in a constant hop as it was.

"Not indisposed are you, my dear?" asked Lady Phyllipa as Lucy toyed with her breakfast.

"Not at all." Lucy shoved a forkful of eggs beneath the veal kidney. "I fear my appetite is not equal to Mrs. Maberley's generous portions."

"Yes." Phyllipa laughed. A high-pitched tinkling sound, like a spoon tapping wildly on a wineglass, it often sounded in danger of shattering. "Drake's cook does consider it her mission in life to fatten everyone up." She cast her cousin a teasing look. "I doubt she'll ever succeed with him."

Drake responded with a derisive grunt as he bolted

mouthful after mouthful of his breakfast. Simply watching him made Lucy's gorge rise.

Pushing her plate away, she tried to work up a smile. "You must find the food and the society here very dull after what you've been used to in London, Cousin Phyllipa."

From the other end of the breakfast table, she marked the black frown Drake directed her way. No doubt he was angry with her for daring to insinuate that his cousins should leave Silverthorne. Well, too bad about him. If he had told her his marriage proposal included a honeymoon with Lady Phyllipa Strickland, she never would have accepted.

"I find nothing wanting in your society, Lucinda dear," Phyllipa replied in her usual patronizing tone. Evidently, she had not recognized the broad hint. "Though I'll own I have been pining for London of late. There are so many merry doings in the autumn, particularly if one is as well connected as Drake."

Lord Silverthorne's frown deepened into an outright scowl. Obviously, he could not abide the notion of his boon companion, Lady Phyllipa, departing for the south.

More than once in the past weeks, Lucy had broached the subject. Phyllipa's answer was always the same.

"I spoke to Drake about my returning home, but he would not hear of it. Protested that you could not spare me so soon. He is counting on me to help mold you into a proper viscountess, and I cannot let him down…after all the dear man has done for me since my poor Clarence died."

A spark of resentment deep within Lucy began to smolder. She was heartily sick of constant sermons on aristocratic protocol and proper ladylike deportment. As interpreted by Lord Silverthorne and proclaimed by Lady Phyllipa, this consisted of doing a great deal of nothing. At least nothing enjoyable, stimulating or improving. Riding was for hoydens. Reading was for "blue stockings." Tramping the countryside was entirely beyond the pale.

Small wonder Jeremy had joined the army to escape his overbearing brother.

An awkward, expectant silence in the breakfast room recalled Lucy from her musings. Both Drake and Phyllipa were staring at her, waiting. She desperately tried to recall what Phyllipa had been talking about. Evidently she'd been asked a question, but she had no idea what.

"Don't you agree, my dear?" Phyllipa prompted her.

If they expected her agreement, Lucy was sure it was something she would naturally oppose. Still, she must do her best to conform to their ways. For the sake of her child—the reason she had wed Drake in the first place.

"Of course. I do." She made every effort to sound sincere, but sincere about what?

Lady Phyllipa spread her thin lips into a tight smile. "You see, Drake? Lucy is as anxious to get down to London as I am."

Silently Lucy cursed herself. With Drake glowering at her, how could she retract her agreement and explain that she simply hadn't been paying attention?

"What a welcome you would receive, my dear." Phyllipa gushed. "Everyone would be avid to meet the new Lady Silverthorne."

That, thought Lucy, was precisely her fear. She knew just what sort of *welcome* she would receive at the hands of the ton. Like some pitiful curiosity at the fairground—a dwarf donkey or a three-legged chicken. The vicar's daughter masquerading as a viscountess. They would watch her like a flock of vultures, ready to rend her to pieces at the first misstep.

Abruptly, Drake rose from his place, hurling down his napkin. "We have been over this before." He glared at Lucy, his tone icily formal. "I have pressing business matters to attend. I've recently bought a mining operation at High Head. The place has been losing money for years, and lately I've heard tell of dangerous conditions. I need to get to the bottom of the trouble and set things to—''

''I fear Neville is right about you, Drake.'' Phyllipa looked surprised to hear herself agreeing with Neville about anything. ''You are overburdened with a sense of 'noblesse oblige.' Do you mean to say this great hole in the ground is of more importance than your own wife?''

''Enough!'' Though Phyllipa had been speaking, Drake addressed himself to Lucy, with cold loathing in his eyes. ''I have business to attend, if you will excuse me. I may not be back in time for dinner this evening.''

Though she struggled to suppress them, tears welled in Lucy's eyes. She had borne his grim censure for the past four weeks. Together with Phyllipa's constant carping and her own unrelenting biliousness, she could bear it no longer. The sight of her distress did nothing to soften her austere, exacting husband. With a final look of glacial disdain, he strode from the breakfast room.

''My poor Lucinda.'' Phyllipa caught her hand.

For an instant Lucy regretted her resentment of Drake's cousin. Despite her nagging and condescending airs, at least Phyllipa tried to be sympathetic.

''Don't worry your head about it. I'll go talk to Drake.'' She set off after him.

He had not gone far when Phyllipa caught up with him.

''Drake Strickland, how could you? We all know you married Lucy for one reason only, but must you flaunt the fact by paying her so little mind? Could you not see how crushed she was by your refusal to take her to London?''

Trying manfully to control his temper, Drake felt his back teeth grinding. The situation was intolerable. Other men had wives who nagged them. *His* wife enlisted an expert to nag him on her behalf.

''Lucy and I are staying at Silverthorne. If you are so anxious to get home, Phyllipa, by all means, go.'' Drake reminded himself that by *home,* he meant his own town house in London. He had put the place at her disposal after the death of his cousin Clarence.

Phyllipa sighed. ''Much as I would love to get back to London, I know my duty, Drake. Lucy is so very attached to me. She depends on me to steer her through these early days in her new position. I could not think of deserting the poor child.''

''My wife is not a child.'' She was very much a woman, and Drake wished to heaven he could ignore the fact. ''Sooner or later she must learn to manage on her own.''

Phyllipa blinked her eyes in a look of mild reproof. ''Only yesterday I mentioned to her how I should like to get back to London before the snow flies. If you could have seen the tears in her eyes as she pleaded with me to stay another fortnight, you would not be so unsympathetic, Drake.''

Another fortnight in the company of Phyllipa and her odious little Reggie? Drake wondered how he would bear it. Mentally he added another item to his tally of grievances against his wife.

''Of course Lucy couldn't object to my leaving if the two of you came along with us for a visit. That is why I broached the subject. Didn't you hear how eagerly she greeted the idea? She has never been there, you know, but I can tell how she longs for it. She gets such a sweet wistful look when she talks about spending last winter with her aunt in Bath. Why, only the other day she said to me, 'Phyllipa, do you suppose Drake is too ashamed to take me out in society?' ''

To cover his acute discomfort, Drake made a few derisive noises deep in his throat. Ashamed? What nonsense!

''It quite broke my heart to hear her,'' continued Phyllipa. ''I hastened to assure her that nothing could be further from the truth. However, when she learns of your latest answer on the subject, I fear she will take the news very hard.''

Drake suspected his cousin Clarence might have been glad to die and escape this woman's fretting and badgering.

"Nonetheless, I have made my decision."

Shaking her head dolorously as she started back for the breakfast room, Phyllipa cast him a reproachful look. Drake chose to ignore it. Beneath the frigid surface of his composure, resentment seethed. If Lucy had cause to complain of their marriage, why did she not speak to him directly, instead of setting her bosom companion, Phyllipa, to hound him?

He gained the entry hall with a mixture of relief and exasperation. Relieved to be making his escape for another day. Exasperated at how his wife and her crony had made him a fugitive from his own home.

"Begging your pardon, sir."

Drake spun around to find the cook waiting on him, neat as a pin in her starched apron and cap, with every grey hair smoothed into place. A tiny scrap of a woman, somewhat plump from sampling her own good cooking, she'd been the only motherly influence in his life. Drake smiled in spite of himself.

"I am at your service, Mrs. Maberley. What can I do for you this morning?"

"Well, your lordship." She addressed Drake's knees, a purplish flush creeping up above her high collar. "I'd be most obliged if you'd start interviewing for a new cook."

Drake didn't think he'd heard right. "Surely you're not giving notice, Mrs. Maberley." The very idea! "Did I forget to mention how much I enjoyed your seedcake the other night?"

The cook shifted from one foot to another. "Very kind of you to say so, I'm sure, milord. I am giving notice, as soon as you can find a replacement."

"I couldn't possibly replace you, Mrs. Maberley. At best I'd get someone to prepare our meals. You have been the heart of Silverthorne for as long as I can recall. How often

I used to steal down the back stairs, when I was a little fellow, to find a bit of seedcake or gingerbread for bedtime tuck.''

A nostalgic smile momentarily lit Mrs. Maberley's motherly features. ''You were such a spindly little shaver in them days, Master Drake. A body couldn't help wanting to fatten you up. You still want filling out,'' she added tartly.

''So you won't desert me…I mean *us*.'' He had a devil of a time over that collective pronoun, Drake mused. Try as he might, he could not think of himself as part of a couple.

Mrs. Maberley shook her head. ''It's been many a year since you were a lad scavenging for a bite at bedtime, Master Drake. And likely you thought me an old woman back then…''

If only Jeremy was here, Drake thought. His charming half brother had always known exactly what people wanted to hear. What's more, he'd been able to deliver it with an air of candid charm that ensured he always got his way. Though a trenchant observation or a mordant jest slipped easily enough from his own tongue, Drake had never mastered the skill of putting his deepest feelings into words.

''Never,'' he protested. ''Well, perhaps a little…''

Mrs. Maberley nodded knowingly. ''I am getting on in years. Thanks to the handsome wages you pay me, I've been able to save a little nest egg to retire on. You need some fresh blood around Silverthorne, to do everything up proper for your new missus.''

Suddenly Drake understood. ''Has my wife been giving you any trouble, Mrs. Maberley? Is that why you want to leave?''

''Oh, no, your lordship, not at all. Her ladyship's a lovely girl.''

''But…?'' Drake prompted. He could sense it coming. What airs was the vicar's daughter giving herself as mistress of Silverthorne?

The cook looked torn between a desire to avoid trouble and a need to voice long-stifled complaints. "It's just that her ladyship isn't partial to my cooking. Her plate always comes back to the kitchen hardly touched."

Drake opened his mouth to explain Lucy's lack of appetite. Then he shut it again. Was it too early for the symptoms of pregnancy to be appearing, if Lucy had conceived on their wedding night, as they wanted everyone to believe? If it had been a case of equine gestation, he would have known instantly.

"I promise I will speak to her ladyship, Mrs. Maberley. I doubt she meant any intentional insult. Do say you'll stay on. If you feel the workload is becoming too much, I'll engage you a battalion of scullery maids."

"It's not just her ladyship, milord. There's Lady Phyllipa and Master Reginald. Always pestering me for special dishes and trays sent up to her room. Complains the boy won't eat what I give him. Then I catch the young rascal stealing my fresh jam buns out of the pantry. I wouldn't mind it if he et his supper like a good boy. *He* don't need no fattening up, I can tell you."

"They won't be staying much longer, Mrs. Maberley," Drake assured her. One way or the other, he'd have them out by the end of the week. If his wife couldn't manage without her friend, she could go off to London with them and good riddance.

"I'm sure I don't *want* to leave if I don't have to."

"And I...that is, we...don't want you to go. So it's all settled. If anyone gives you trouble, do as you like with them. Tell Lady Phyllipa to go whistle for her tray. Give Reggie a good smack if you catch him in the pantry. I'll stand behind you completely." Drake hoped his cook would mortally offend Phyllipa into leaving Silverthorne posthaste.

The pedestal clock in the entry hall chimed nine. Drake bowed to Mrs. Maberley. "If you will excuse me, I must be off now. Thank you for bringing these matters to my attention.''

Minutes later as he rode away from Silverthorne, Drake added yet another black mark against his wife to the rapidly growing list.

''That man!'' Phyllipa chuckled as she reentered the breakfast room. ''You mustn't mind him, Lucinda. He's been too long a bachelor—that's his trouble. I can tell what you are thinking, my dear, but it simply isn't true. Drake is not the least bit ashamed of you. You mustn't on any account think that is why he refuses to take you to London. What matter your humble origins or your rustic manners? Your beauty and sweetness of temper more than compensate for those deficiencies.''

Ashamed of her? Lucy felt the blood drain from her face, leaving behind a frigid mask. For weeks now, she had tried to follow Lady Phyllipa's advice and mold herself into the kind of wife a man in his position needed. For her baby's sake, she owed Lord Silverthorne that much. Had he offered a word of encouragement? Recognized and applauded her efforts?

Hardly. The more strenuously she tried, the more quietly antagonistic he became. She had grown to detest his frosty politeness and his look of silent censure. Now to discover he was ashamed of her. If her husband had returned to the breakfast room at that moment, Lucy would have throttled him!

If she stayed a moment longer, she feared she might throttle Lady Phyllipa in her cousin's place. ''Please excuse me, Cousin Phyllipa.'' Lucy pushed away from the table. ''I feel the urgent need of fresh air. I believe I will take a walk.''

''Not to visit those common people in the village, I hope,'' Phyllipa cautioned. ''What would the viscount think of his wife consorting with those so far below her new station?''

Of all the strictures imposed by her position, this rankled Lucy the worst. She longed to stop by Mrs. Sowerby's cottage for a talk or drop in for tea at the vicarage. Apart from Sunday matins, she'd scarcely seen her father since her marriage. She'd invited him to Silverthorne of course, but Phyllipa made them both feel so ill at ease. In recent weeks, he'd begun to turn down her invitations on various pretexts. Perhaps it was just as well, thought Lucy. Though she didn't want her father to worry on her account, she was hard-pressed to keep up the pretense that all was well in her new life.

"I don't plan on going into Nicholthwait." Lucy strained to keep her tone civil. "I only mean to stroll in the garden and sit under the great elm."

Phyllipa squinted in the direction of the windows. "The weather does look unusually clement. Perhaps I shall join you in the garden this morning. Get a taste of this fresh air and see if I can fathom why you and Drake are so addicted to it…"

Lucy heard no more, for she was out the door before Lady Phyllipa finished speaking.

Returning to her bedchamber to fetch a shawl, Lucy deliberately took a roundabout route. In the main gallery of the east wing, she paused for a moment beneath a portrait of Jeremy Strickland, aged sixteen. Even then, his features had shown the promise of manly beauty. The artist had managed to capture that engaging light in his eyes. Lucy almost fancied he was looking out at her from the painting, knowing she was carrying his child, understanding how much she still loved him.

How hopeless her love had seemed when he was a poised and handsome young man of sixteen and she, a timid, graceless adolescent adoring him from a worshipful distance. She had lived for his school holidays, gazing raptly at him in church every Sunday morning, prowling the fringes of the estate praying for a glimpse of him. Year after year.

Then one day, long after she had stopped hoping for it, the miracle had happened. She had not even heard he was home. Hurrying back to the vicarage from picking wildflowers, she'd collided with Captain Strickland on a wooded path by the lake. He had called her by name, and for the first time, he had truly looked at her.

"There you are, ma'am." The housemaid's voice shattered Lucy's bittersweet reverie. "Lady Phyllipa's looking for you."

Lucy touched a finger to her lips. "You haven't seen hide nor hair of me, Mary. Is that clear?"

The girl raised her eyebrows knowingly. "Odd. Could've sworn I saw her ladyship. Must've been a shadow." She glanced up at the portrait of Jeremy. "What an awful shame about poor Captain Strickland. We so miss his high spirits around here."

Feeling her eyes begin to sting in an ominous fashion, Lucy turned away without another word. She now understood why Jeremy had chafed under the tyranny of his formidable brother. She must stand up to this unfeeling despot and she must do it now. Otherwise she and her child might never know a moment's unfettered happiness.

Chapter Five

He had not been at High Head colliery for more than half an hour, when Drake scented something foul in the wind. And it was not the miners. Oh, they weren't a promising lot by any means, shifty and evasive in answering his questions. Irritatingly servile, yet obviously mistrustful of his intentions as the new owner.

Only the mine's overseer, an affable fellow named Janus Crook, appeared ready to be the least bit forthcoming.

"This here could be a real going concern, your lordship, if you don't mind my saying so. That's a good vein we've tapped."

Drake cocked an eyebrow. "The previous owners assured me of that as well, Mr. Crook. However, through my inquiries I've discovered High Head has been steadily losing money for some years. How do you account for that?"

The overseer's rather prominent ears turned scarlet. "Not my place to criticize my betters, your lordship, seeing as the previous owners was gentlemen like yourself...."

"Save your breath, man." Drake did not try to hide his exasperation. He knew what the fellow was hinting at, for he'd seen it often enough in his other business ventures. Scions of indebted noble houses trying to raise some capital by dabbling in business ventures they knew nothing about.

Arrogantly refusing to take the advice of smart young chaps like Janus Crook, whom they considered their social inferiors. Drake didn't care a tinker's damn for those pompous fools. What he regretted was the damage done to the local people.

"You'll soon discover I run a much tighter ship, Mr. Crook. I won't tolerate waste or corruption. I demand loyalty and an honest day's work, but I believe in paying for it."

Grinning with indulgent tolerance at his new employer, the overseer shook his head. "A noble goal, your lordship, but if you don't mind my saying so, I think you're wasting your concern on these louts." He jerked his head toward the office window, and the miners milling about outside. "As shiftless and surly a lot as you'd ever want to meet. They stole the last owners blind. If you ask me, I'd say sack the lot and bring in a new crew."

Drake could scarcely believe what he was hearing. "Where can these people go if we dismiss them?"

"Not your lookout, is it governor? Leeds. Sheffield. Who cares, eh? Long as they're not being a drain on your operation."

Drake drew himself up to his full impressive height. "Much as I appreciate your advice, Mr. Crook, that is not how I do business. My policy is to keep Westmoreland folk at home. Pay a man a fair wage, treat him with respect and he will be your ally in the quest for success. Another point on which I won't compromise is safety. I've heard rumors of dangerous conditions at High Head."

The overseer looked genuinely shocked. "Can't think who'd be spreading malicious lies like that, your lordship. High Head colliery is as safe as any in Britain."

No great boast, Drake mused. He'd heard of atrocities in the Welsh mines that made his hair stand on end. "If it's all the same to you, Mr. Crook, I'll judge that for myself."

"As you wish, your lordship. Always at your service."

To his surprise, Drake found little fault with the operation. Some of the equipment was not in top repair, but otherwise he was fairly well pleased at the end of his tour. The morose silence of the miners made him uneasy, though. They went about their work listlessly, almost tentatively, as though used to getting away with doing as little as possible. Perhaps Janus Crook was right about the people of High Head after all.

Late in the afternoon, following a brief inspection of the accounts, Drake took his leave, promising to return for a more thorough scrutiny later in the week. He rode back to Nicholthwait, preoccupied with plans for putting High Head on a more profitable footing. Remembering his intention not to return to Silverthorne for dinner, he stopped to eat at a small inn outside Eastmere.

As he ate, Drake contemplated his mistake in marrying Lucy Rushton. Alienating his servants, clinging to the detestable Phyllipa, angling for an excursion to London—she was no longer the sweet, unspoiled creature he'd once thought her. Perhaps she never had been. With a shudder of distaste, Drake ordered another tankard of ale.

What he resented most was the mysterious, potent power she exerted over him. Though he'd tried to shut her out during the past weeks, Lucy drew his eyes at every opportunity, intruded upon his private thoughts, and boldly invaded his dreams. How dare she hold his body and his emotions in such thrall, when she obviously held his most cherished ideals in contempt!

Darkness had fallen by the time Drake reached Nicholthwait. He rode silently through the village, aware of hearth light shining through chinks in the window shutters, hearing snippets of talk and laughter. Thinking of what awaited him back at Silverthorne manor, his hackles raised in a chill of aversion.

Absently drawing the brush through her unbound hair, Lucy sat by her bedroom window watching the well-lit drive for some sign of her husband's return. After pondering her choices all day, she had finally come to a decision. She would take her trip to London, like a dose of castor oil—unpleasant, but necessary to purge Lady Phyllipa from Silverthorne.

Ever since dinner she had been nerving herself to broach the subject with Drake. The wait for his return from High Head was becoming intolerable. Just as Lucy was beginning to fear the brush had rubbed her scalp raw, she caught a glimpse of a tall erect figure riding up the drive. As Drake passed beneath her window, illuminated by the bright lamps of the main entry, she saw his mouth grimly set. Somehow he looked weary, too. And sad. Perhaps a few weeks' diversion in London would be just the tonic for him. An opportunity to forget about business and indulge in a little enjoyment for a change.

As she waited by her chamber door, held open a crack, listening for the sound of Drake's brisk step, Lucy rehearsed her speech. Her nerves had worked themselves up to a tense pitch by the time she finally heard him approaching.

"Your lordship…" She swung the door wide to block his path, but affected mild surprise at seeing him. "I am pleased to see you home at last. I was hoping to have a word with you."

He said nothing, but swept her with a scornful glance. Lucy wondered if she had neglected something in her evening toilette.

"Will you…that is…won't you come in?"

She stepped back into the room and Drake followed her just past the threshold. He drew the door closed behind him, but not tightly enough to latch.

"Do I take it this is an official invitation into your bedchamber, madam?" he asked coolly. "To what do I owe this unexpected honor?"

His tone stung Lucy like gust of cold wind. Just once she

wanted to put *him* on the defensive. "I thought it wise, your lordship. I fear your servants might grow suspicious of an infant bred from a single act."

"I have your word that my brother got you with child on his first try."

Lucy flinched as though he had struck her.

"Was there anything else you required of me, your lady-ship?"

She grasped for one of her rehearsed speeches, but her mind was suddenly a blank. "London," she blurted out. "It would do us both a power of good to make the journey to London."

A spark of antagonism blazed in the depths of Drake's dark eyes. "London again?" he growled. "I grow tired of hearing about your longing for London. I have urgent busi-ness that keeps me here. Let me hear no more talk of Lon-don."

"So, it is true. You are too ashamed of your wife to introduce her in society."

Drake's lip curled in disdain. "You can quit this pity mongering, woman. I assure you my heart is quite imper-vious."

His words and his manner fanned a month's worth of smoldering resentment in Lucy. It flared into a blistering blaze. "If you have a heart, Drake Strickland, I do not doubt it is impervious to any tender emotion." She trembled in an effort to contain the power of her rage. "I don't care if you are ashamed of me. I am who I am, and I will not change—least of all for you."

"When have I ever asked you to change?" In response to the heat of her anger, Drake became colder and more restrained. His voice sounded menacingly quiet, his words clipped and precise.

There he stood, as hard and uncaring as an effigy of cold black marble. It goaded Lucy beyond bearing that he should provoke her to such a pitch of turbulent rage, while remaining so aloof and impregnable himself. She longed to throw herself at him, pounding on his chest, battering him into some answering flicker of feeling.

"You needn't condescend to ask." Her voice sounded ragged and breathless. "You have others to issue your edicts. Besides, your lordship underestimates what he can convey with a haughty look. I know just what you would mold me into."

"If you are so aware of my displeasure, I wonder that you made no effort to win my approval." All that displeasure and more was etched plainly on his arrogant features.

"No effort!" Lucy fairly shrieked. "You have no idea of the effort I have made, without receiving the least sign of encouragement or appreciation from you."

Drake's black brows knit in a frown of cold vexation. He folded his arms across his chest. "If you think I mean to encourage your recent behavior, madam, you are mistaken."

Years of ingrained propriety fell before Lucy's consuming anger. "Then to hell with you! I don't care twopence what you think of me." She snapped her fingers beneath his nose.

His hand shot up, gripping her wrist in a hold that brought tears of pain and rage to her eyes. "Remember your promise, my dear," he urged her in a grating whisper. "You vowed to treat me with the respect and honor due a husband."

A thrill of victory blossomed momentarily in Lucy's heart. As he crushed her arm in his forceful hold, she could feel the answering waves of wrath pulse through Drake. His nostrils flared as his breath came fast and shallow. He wanted to toss her over his knee and thrash her within an inch of her life, and she had the satisfaction of knowing it. She'd lured him out of the fastness of his granite citadel into open combat.

"For a time, I thought I might have been mistaken about your character, Viscount Silverthorne." She willed her voice not to break. "Now I see I was right in the first place."

Abruptly, he loosed her wrist, casting it from him as if it were some loathsome form of reptile life. "I thought I knew your true character, madam," he replied stonily, retreating once again into his icy fortress. "Now I see I was entirely deceived."

Beneath his scornful words, Lucy heard a note of genuine disillusionment. Why should she care for the opinion of this insufferable tyrant? Though Lucy insisted to herself that she cared not one whit, she knew in her heart that she did want Drake's approval. What sort of life stretched before her if she did not have his regard at least? What sort of family life could she hope to make for her child? She turned away, determined not to give him the satisfaction of seeing her cry.

"You drove Jeremy to his death trying to escape your domination." She hurled the indictment over her shoulder. "I serve you notice here and now that I will not allow you to grind me or my child beneath your heel."

She heard a sharp hiss of indrawn breath. Her missile must have found its mark. After a moment's silence Drake spoke again, his tone betraying no sign that she'd inflicted a wound.

"Much as I would like to stay and continue this charming tête-à-tête," he mocked her with biting sarcasm, "I have had a busy day. And I fully expect to have several more before the week is out. If you will excuse me, madam, I believe I will retire for the night."

Not trusting herself to speak or to face him, Lucy waved her hand in what she hoped he would take for a gesture of indifferent dismissal. She held herself in expectant stillness waiting for the sound of his departure.

"Do give me some warning before you next invite me to your boudoir." Drake casually leveled his parting shot. "I will take the precaution of wearing armor."

Lucy heard her bedroom door close with quiet finality. Only when Drake's footsteps had died away in the distance did she bolt for her bed. There she pummeled her innocent pillow into a tattered heap of cotton and feathers.

Chapter Six

It took Lucy several hours to calm herself sufficiently to get to sleep. Tossing and turning in her bed, she thought of all the scathing remarks she wished she'd hurled at Drake. Worst of all, she knew with galling certainty that he had marched off to his own bed for a peaceful, untroubled night.

She woke late the next morning, having scarcely slept at all. In a particularly rebellious mood, she dressed in a serviceable old gown she'd brought to Silverthorne from the vicarage. Phyllipa or no Phyllipa, she intended to pay some calls on her friends in Nicholthwait today.

Descending the stairs, she looked forward to a quiet breakfast without the company of her husband and his cousin.

She nodded to the butler. "Mr. Talbot? Since I've come late to breakfast, tell Mrs. Maberley not to bother with a full meal for me. Tea and bread will be quite sufficient."

"Are you certain, ma'am? It would be no trouble…"

"Quite certain, Mr. Talbot. In fact you may tell Mrs. Maberley that from now on I will take tea and bread for my breakfast."

As the butler set off for the kitchen, Lucy let out a long, shaky breath. There, that hadn't been so difficult. Her stomach felt less upset already.

Slipping into the quiet breakfast room, she startled at the sight of Drake sitting at the head of the table. He acknowledged her with a cool nod. She replied in kind. For a wild instant, Lucy found herself wishing Phyllipa had been there to ease the tension with her prattle.

As she took her seat, she noticed the rise and fall of Drake's fork picking up tempo. As rapidly as humanly possible, he consumed his breakfast. Evidently, he was as eager to get away from her as she was to see him go. With a flush of vindictive satisfaction, Lucy noted the dark shadows beneath his eyes. Perhaps he hadn't slept as soundly as she'd assumed.

She was beginning to fidget and wonder how soon Talbot would bring her tea, when she heard the muted sounds of a commotion in the entry. Drake must have heard it, too, for he looked toward the door. At first Lucy could make nothing of the words, except their tone of anger and urgency. Then, quite clearly, she heard *mine* and *cave-in*. Dropping his cutlery in midbite, Drake rose from his chair and strode out of the room. Lucy followed.

In the entry hall stood Talbot, Silverthorne's normally phlegmatic butler, engaged in a shouting match with a stranger—by far the dirtiest individual Lucy had ever seen. Spying Drake, he tried to shoulder his way past Talbot.

When Drake approached, the stranger lunged forward, clutching the lapels of his coat. "Cave-in at High Head, sir! A whole shift of men trapped!"

Drake responded immediately. Grabbing the stranger by the arm he propelled him out the door. Lucy presumed they were headed for the stables. As she stood there, momentarily stunned by the turn of events, Talbot brushed off his coat where the stranger had laid hands on it.

"Why did you not show the man in at once, Mr. Talbot?"

"As I informed the caller, ma'am—" he thrust back his shoulders and drew himself into a severely straight posture "—a few minutes either way wasn't going to matter. His lordship slept poorly last night, and I felt he should be able to enjoy his breakfast in peace.''

"His lordship slept poorly?" Lucy savored the taste of those words. Innocently, she asked, "What was the trouble?"

"His lordship did not choose to confide that information."

Hearing the clatter of hooves in the forecourt, she looked outside just in time to see Drake and the messenger riding off at full gallop. With a pang of shame, Lucy remembered the cave-in at High Head, the trapped miners and their families. She had no business gloating over a minor victory in her running battle with Drake when there might be something she could do to help.

Immediately an idea came to her. It would mean issuing orders to the Silverthorne servants—particularly the formidable Mr. Talbot and the cook, who wore a constant frown of disapproval. In the end she would likely receive a stern lecture from Drake as well, for breaking any number of edicts on the proper conduct of a viscountess.

Both considerations gave her pause. Life at Silverthorne had been intolerable enough for the past month. Did she need to make it worse? On the other hand, who else had the means and the authority to bring relief to the people of High Head?

Swallowing a lump in her throat and wiping moist palms on the skirt of her gown, Lucy gave her first true order as Mistress Silverthorne. "Mr. Talbot, kindly inform the hostlers I want a sturdy wagon and a good strong team. Have them harness up the little tilbury as well. In the meantime, I want the household staff to round up supplies for me."

"Supplies, ma'am?" The butler looked bewildered.

"Lord Silverthorne has set off for High Head and I mean to follow. I'll need blankets, cotton for bandages. Food, of course. I'll speak to Mrs. Maberley about that. Well, Talbot, don't just stand there. We have work to do."

"Yes, ma'am." The butler acknowledged her with a twitch of his head. Then he blew a shrill whistle that brought several young footmen scurrying.

For the next hour the elegant halls of Silverthorne echoed with footsteps proceeding far more quickly than their usual sedate pace. From her headquarters in the front entry hall, Lucy marshaled her supplies, diverted only briefly to don her gloves, her bonnet and a thick shawl. The wagon appeared without delay and was soon piled high with commandeered food and other supplies.

"One more thing, Mr. Talbot." Lucy stood on the tips of her toes and whispered in his ear.

The butler's face went white. "B-b-but your l-l-ladyship," he sputtered. "That's the last of his lordship's French stock. God knows when we shall see decent brandy again as long as Boney's got a stranglehold on the Continent."

Lucy put her hands on her hips. "I have every confidence in General Wellington, Mr. Talbot. Now, go and get me that brandy. I will take full responsibility for disposing of it."

Talbot trudged away with the air of a man ordered to present his children for ritual sacrifice. Lucy turned her attention back to the wagon.

"What a fine idea," she commended the two footmen who covered her load with a heavy sheet of canvas.

When she ordered the driver off the tilbury gig, the man gave her a puzzled look. "Who's to drive you, ma'am?"

"I shall drive myself, of course." Lucy tried her best to look confident—and taller. "I'm very good with horses."

"I must protest, madam." Mr. Talbot reappeared with a small wooden crate lovingly cradled in his arms. "That's no journey for a lady to make by herself. I feel certain his lordship would not approve."

Lucy felt equally certain, but she had no intention of letting that stop her. There were people in trouble who needed her help. For the first time in weeks, she felt strong, confident and alive. "As you see, Mr. Talbot, his lordship is not on hand to consult."

The butler began to sputter again. Lucy relieved him of the crate of brandy, tucking it under the driver's seat of the gig. "If it will put your mind at rest, Talbot, I do not intend to go all the way to High Head by myself."

The butler's craggy features betrayed visible relief.

"No indeed." Lucy accepted a hand up into driver's seat. "I'll stay close to the supply wagon at all times. I also mean to stop at the vicarage and enlist my father to accompany me."

"What is all this to-do? Where is Viscount Silverthorne? Will someone kindly tell me what is going on?" Phyllipa emerged from the entry hall. She stared at the supply wagon and Lucy's gig, as though the whole scene were some kind of apparition.

Talbot briefly explained the situation.

"This is ridiculous! Lucinda, come down at once. Rest assured I would never have let you get this far if I had known what was going on. I was in the nursery with Reggie. The poor child has suffered a dreadful bilious attack."

Undoubtedly brought on by eating too many stolen sweet buns, Lucy thought. She wished Phyllipa would be quiet for a minute so she could get a word in.

"I've finally got him settled," Phyllipa continued with no foreseeable break, "only to discover that in my absence Silverthorne has been turned upside down and the lady of the house is preparing to drive off to some dreadful mine. Really, Lucinda, you must remember your new station. It is out of the question for a viscountess to undertake such a madcap escapade. Whatever will his lordship say when he finds out?"

She finally paused for breath.

"He can say what he likes," replied Lucy. "I'm going and that's all there is to it. As you are so fond of reminding me, Phyllipa, I am *Lady* Silverthorne, now. Short of throwing yourself in front of my horse, there isn't much you can do to stop me.''

With that, Lucy twitched the reins against the rump of the bay gelding, who set off smartly. Unfortunately, Lady Phyllipa did not accept the invitation to hurl herself into its path.

It was well into the afternoon by the time Lucy and her father reached High Head. The wind felt chillier at this altitude than down in the valley around Mayeswater. It had blown in a bank of fat, dark-bottomed clouds that were beginning to spit heavy drops of rain.

A crowd had collected some distance from the mouth of the mine—a shaft cut horizontally into the side of a steep hill, now choked with fallen earth and rock. Lucy could see boys running back and forth with barrows and handcarts, tipping what debris the digging crews had unearthed. The rescuers must have made a good start, for they had managed to tunnel their way out of sight.

''Excuse me,'' Lucy called to a man on the fringe of the crowd. It was obvious why he had not joined in the rescue effort, for one of his shirt sleeves hung empty below the elbow. ''I have food and supplies. Is there anywhere I can set up to get these people out of the rain?''

''Aye, miss. There's the overseer's office. Though I don't imagine he'd care for folks crowding in there.''

''Where is he? I shall ask him myself.''

An old man in the crowd cackled, ''We ain't seen aught of Mr. Crook since last night. Skinned out for parts unknown if you ask me. Didn't want the new owner breathing down his neck. Still, you'd best not take over his office without permission, lass.''

''The *lass* is Lady Silverthorne,'' barked the driver of the supply wagon. ''Her husband owns this mine.''

The old man exchanged a glance with the one-armed fellow. He shrugged. ''If you're t'new owner's wife, lass, I reckon you can go wherever you please. Can we show you the way and give you a hand getting set up?''

''By all means. Thank you.'' Lucy uttered a silent prayer that she would not find Drake in possession of the overseer's office. He would surely pack her off back to Silverthorne before she had a chance to climb down from the gig.

In fact, the building was eerily empty. Lucy could see her breath in the still, cold air. The five-room dwelling, which evidently served as both office headquarters and residence for the overseer, had certainly been vacant all day.

''Let's get some fires going.'' Lucy issued her first order. ''This being a colliery, we'll have no shortage of fuel.''

Her two drafted helpers looked at each other for a moment, then turned on Lucy with eager smiles. ''Right, ma'am. Fires. Unload the wagon. See to the horses.''

''A commendable set of priorities, gentlemen. I will be along to help you in few minutes.'' Lucy turned to her father. ''I need you to go out to the crowd and bring back anyone who has relatives trapped in the mine. It will be a while before I can do much for them, but you can be of help immediately. Besides, filling this building with bodies might help to warm it up.''

''What's that you say, my dear? Oh, the people outside.'' Vicar Rushton looked altogether confounded by the flood tide of events that had overtaken him. ''We must get them out of the weather, by all means.'' At the door he hesitated, looking back at Lucy. ''Do you think I'll be able to make myself heard over that wind?''

Lucy dropped a fond kiss on her father's cheek. His fluffy white side-whiskers tickled her nose. ''Use your lectionary delivery.''

''Of course.'' The vicar's ruddy countenance blossomed with a confident smile. ''Reading from the gospel according to Saint John…'' he declared in tones of clerical resonance.

''That's the way.'' Lucy patted his shoulder. ''Now go

round them up. If they're nervous about coming, tell them it's all been approved by the new owner.''

"Has it, indeed?" The Reverend Rushton gave Lucy a shrewd questioning look. Perhaps he understood more of what was going on around him than he cared to let on.

Lucy held her head high. "Once his lordship hears what we are doing, I believe he will endorse the idea." Everything but her own part in it, she silently reminded herself.

The vicar nodded. His long fringe of white hair danced wildly around his red face. "I expect you're right. I've known few men with so genuine a concern for the working people."

Lucy scarcely looked up from her work for the next several hours. When she finally had a moment to do so, she glanced around the room with a flush of pride and satisfaction. Kettles of coffee, tea and soup steamed away on the hob of every hearth. Relatives of the trapped miners sat huddled in small groups, talking amongst themselves in tones of quiet encouragement. A short time ago she had dispatched baskets of cake and sandwiches to the rescue crew, along with three bottles of Drake's French brandy. Lucy hoped the men she had sent with those provisions would return soon with heartening news of the rescue effort.

As she wended her way through the crowded rooms of the building with a fresh tray of sandwiches, Lucy noticed one young woman sitting off by herself. Her thin fingers clenched around a mug, the woman stared listlessly out the window. Even her high-waisted dress did not conceal her bulging belly. Lucy's heart immediately went out to her.

Sinking down onto a stool beside the woman, she held out her tray. "Would you care for a sandwich? They aren't very dainty I'm afraid, but they're good and nourishing. You'll need to keep your strength up."

The woman set her cup down on the wide window ledge beside her. She took a sandwich from the plate and nibbled at one corner of it.

"I'm Mrs. Strickland. The vicar who brought you in here is my father. I hope we won't have to wait much longer for good news of your husband."

The woman gave Lucy a queer look. "My name is Alice Leadbitter, ma'am. And it ain't my husband who's down the mine. In fact, he's helping them dig. Only wish I could. It's so hard to wait and not be able to do anything. My boy's down in that mine, Mrs. Strickland. Poor little mite. He'll be that scared." Her lower lip began to quiver, and Lucy could see Alice Leadbitter's eyes misting with tears.

"Your son? Mrs. Leadbitter, you can't be any older than I am. How could you have a son working in a coal mine?"

"I'm twenty-four. My Geordie is eight years old. He only started working last month."

A boy of eight employed at such dangerous, backbreaking work. Lucy could hardly believe her ears. She'd heard tales of child labor in the big industrial cities to the south, but here in the Penines? Drake would soon put a stop to that practice. But where was Drake? She'd seen him ride out for High Head at a furious speed. All afternoon she'd kept glancing over her shoulder, expecting him to blaze down on her with a stern lecture about her conduct.

"I didn't want him to go." Mrs. Leadbitter wiped her tears with the back of her hand. "I told John the lad was too young to be working. John said he'd started working on his pa's farm when he was a good bit younger than our Geordie. We needed the money, with another mouth to feed soon.

"So there was nothing for it but to put Geordie to work. Then this happened. How long will their air last? What if the gas builds up and explodes? I'll never forgive myself if…if…"

Lucy reached for the woman's hand and gave it a reassuring squeeze.

"Beg your pardon, ma'am."

Lucy glanced up to see Anthony Brown returned from

delivering food to the rescuers. "The fellows up to the mine shaft nearly tore me to pieces getting at that grub. They said could you send more?"

"That we shall, Anthony. But first, what is the news? Mrs. Leadbitter's boy is in the mine, so she's naturally anxious to know how soon he'll be out."

The man flashed Alice Leadbitter an apologetic glance. "'Fraid I wouldn't know that, ma'am. Don't know as the chaps doing the digging have any notion how soon they'll break through. They've shifted a pile of earth and rock, though, I can tell you. There's one fellow there—a stranger. Big tall man, digging for all he's worth."

"My husband," Lucy cried, barely aware of the pride in her voice.

"Oh, that explains it," said Anthony. "I offered him a drink from one of them bottles. Well sir, he takes a swig and then he says, 'Best use this brandy's ever been put to.' Another swig and a sandwich and he was right back to shoveling again."

Lucy nodded. "Go ask the women over at that table to refill your basket, Anthony. I'll be with you directly." She turned to Mrs. Leadbitter. "You heard what Anthony said. My husband is personally leading the dig. He's a very determined man, Mrs. Leadbitter. He'll get your Geordie out safe and sound."

Alice Leadbitter's reply was drowned out by a low, rumbling sound in the distance.

Someone cried, "There's been another rock slide!"

A furor erupted in the overseer's office as anxious women rushed to the windows. Lucy sat rooted to her chair. Drake was out there now, burrowing toward the trapped miners. What if he was now entombed, himself? Or crushed by a falling boulder? With a start Lucy came to herself again. She and Mrs. Leadbitter were holding each other's hands so tightly, their knuckles had gone white.

Chapter Seven

The first of the injured rescue crew arrived at Lucy's make-shift aid station within minutes. She pushed down her paralyzing fear for Drake's safety by concentrating on her duties.

"Bring him this way. Put him on the bed. Shift that settee into this room as well. Has anyone seen my basket of bandages?"

Peering closely at her first patient, Lucy recognized him as the stranger who had appeared at Silverthorne that morning. Had it been this very day? Lucy felt as though she'd been at High Head for a week at least. The man's leg was distended at a painful-looking angle below the knee. Fortunately the fractured bone had not pierced the flesh of his leg.

Lucy glanced around, hoping to spy the doctor she had sent for. She did not feel confident to set a broken bone. The man's other injury, a gash on the forehead, she immediately tended with a clean cloth and hot water.

"Will he be all right, Mrs. Strickland?"

Lucy looked into the anxious face of Mrs. Leadbitter, who now held the man's hand as tightly as she'd recently held Lucy's.

"It could have been much worse, Alice. Once the doctor

gets here, he can set your husband's leg." Lucy handed over her cloth and water basin. "Since you're here, I'll leave you to wash and bandage his forehead while I see to the others."

She hesitated, wanting to ask John Leadbitter a question, but not daring. Part of her cried out that she could not stand the suspense—she must know the worst. Another part of her shrank from finding out how bad the worst might be.

It would serve her right if something awful had happened to Drake. After all, she had wished him dead instead of Jeremy. No use trying to excuse herself by pleading the extremity of her grief or insisting she hadn't truly meant it. She had been a wicked, ungrateful creature and now she might never have the chance to say she was sorry.

"Mrs. Strickland, the doctor's here. Do you want a word with him?" Anthony Brown interrupted Lucy's self-indictment.

"Yes, thank you, Anthony." She picked her way through the chaos, thankful for the distraction and an excuse to postpone her fateful question.

For the next hour, as she conferred with the doctor and administered aid to the injured, Drake was never far from her thoughts. He had not come in for medical attention, which might mean he'd escaped harm. Or was he beyond medical help? Lucy shivered as an icy hand clutched her heart.

"Don't tell me you find it cold, Mrs. Strickland." The doctor chuckled as he sewed up a gash on a patient's shoulder. "With the fires going and all the bodies crammed in here, it feels like an anteroom of hell, if you'll pardon the expression."

"Cold? No, doctor. Only a chill down my back. Perhaps a draft from the door opening."

"Perhaps." The doctor sized Lucy up with a glance. "You may be experiencing the symptoms of shock, ma'am. Hardly surprising after what you have been through today." He patted her hand in a fatherly way. "We have the worst under control now. Why don't you go find a seat and treat yourself to a bowl of that good soup I smell?"

At the mention of food, Lucy's stomach made the most unladylike growling noises. She flashed the doctor an embarrassed grin. "I believe I'd better follow your prescription, sir."

As she sank onto a corner stool, her hands gratefully clutching a warm mug of lamb broth, Lucy could only echo Alice Leadbitter's conviction. She would never forgive herself if anything had happened to Drake. True, he was proud, antagonistic and thoroughly preoccupied with his business concerns. But he was a man of his word. A man who took his responsibilities seriously. Lucy had even begun to suspect he cared about people in that distant, impersonal way of his.

In short, Drake was the complete opposite of his brother, and she had not been able to forgive him for it—until now. She'd been unfair, expecting him to be a replica of Jeremy, just as he'd been unfair expecting her to be a duplicate of Lady Phyllipa. He had done her an invaluable service, rescuing her reputation, providing her child with a name and a future. How had she repaid him? With petulance and childish spite.

If only God would grant her one more chance to make it all right. Lucy heaved a sigh. As a clergyman's daughter, she knew the futility of trying to strike bargains with the Almighty.

Gradually, as she tried to screw up her courage to ask about Drake, Lucy overheard snippets of conversation around her. Several men from the rescue party, those with only slight injuries, were huddled near the fire devouring soup and sandwiches while passing around a bottle of Drake's brandy.

"Damnedest thing I ever saw…"

"…diggin' like a man possessed."

"Who'd he say he was?"

"Ant'ny Brown claims he's the new owner."

"I reckon Ant'ny's been at the barley jar." The speaker tipped a swig of brandy.

"John Leadbitter says he's some high-muckety-muck from down Mayeswater," said the next man, holding out his hand for the bottle. "Lord or earl or some'ut."

The other men responded with sceptical chuckles. "I never seen no lord or earl wield a shovel or hoist a barrow like that. Whoever he is, he knows how to work and that's a fact."

"I feel a might guilty sitting here warm and fed while he's still at it." The others squirmed in their seats, stroking their bandages like treasured badges of privilege.

Lucy wanted to hurl herself onto these gruff, grimy men in delighted relief. She settled for closing her eyes and breathing a silent prayer of thanks. God might not make bargains, but he did dispense grace. Unworthy as she was, she had been granted a second chance.

Drake set his lips in a tight grim line to stifle the exclamation of pain that rose in his throat every time he hefted his shovel. He'd come through the hail of rocks and dirt without any visible injuries, fired more desperately than ever to dig out the trapped miners. They had been so close before the last rock slide. Drake had felt a faint draft of warm air on his face. Now they had to shift this new debris before more fell, with half the crew too badly hurt to continue.

A twinge of pain in his back, about halfway down his left side, had gradually intensified to its present agonizing pitch. On top of that, his head throbbed with a pulsing, dizzying ache. It made him stagger when he heaved his shovel of dirt into the waiting cart. Drake sucked in a breath of raw night air through his clenched teeth. With vicious strength, he thrust the point of his shovel at the wall of earth before him. In the flickering light of the torches, he could imagine the oily, deceitful face of Janus Crook mocking him.

In truth, his pride pained Drake almost as much as his back or his head. For hours now, as he'd gone about his work with ruthless singularity of purpose, he had overheard enough to know that the overseer had duped him. Drake took little comfort from knowing the previous owners and even the miners hadn't suspected Crook until it was too late.

With mealymouthed duplicity he'd told the owners and the workers each what they'd expected to hear. Playing on their natural prejudices, feeding their mutual mistrust, all the while defrauding High Head colliery of a small fortune. Drake wouldn't have put it past the villain to have caused this crisis to cover his escape. If he found a single scrap of evidence to support such a notion, Drake vowed he'd prosecute the blackguard to the fullest extent of the law... provided they could find him.

"I can't keep up with you, mate." One of the other men leaned on his shovel. "I need a minute to catch me breath."

Acknowledging the comment with a terse nod, Drake continued the mechanical rote of digging, wincing slightly each time he hefted the loaded shovel. If he stopped for a rest now, he feared he might never be able to get started again.

"Reckon we'll get to 'em before their air runs out?"

Though he grunted something vaguely affirmative, Drake felt a lethal garrote of fear tighten around his throat in response to the fellow's words. As a boy, one of his governor's favorite punishments had been shutting him in a cupboard. He knew that terrifying sense of the walls slowly closing in, the darkness threatening to suffocate you. Even now the thought of it made his legs go weak. That was what drove him to keep digging, long after his body screamed to stop. Because those men were his responsibility, and because he knew what they must be feeling.

"Mug of soup or coffee, lads?" The little one-armed fellow appeared with his basket.

"Anything for you, Mr. Strickland?"

Drake shook his head doggedly. Several drops of sweat rolled down his brow, but he dared not break his rhythm by stopping to brush them out of his eyes.

"Maybe you ought to come back down the hill with me, sir," said Anthony. "You don't look well. You've been at it for hours. It's time you took a rest."

"Once we get the men out," Drake growled, each word costing him an effort.

"If you say so, sir. Your wife's done a first-rate job taking care of everyone. If it wasn't for her, folks would still be out waiting in the cold. Lord knows what you lads would have done for food, let alone doctoring for the blokes who got hurt."

Drake didn't have any spare strength to answer, but he let his thoughts turn to Lucy. Slowly the tightness in his throat began to ease. What was she doing here? Had his stern lecture made some impression on her after all? Drake doubted it. He remembered the golden sparks of defiance flashing provocatively in her brown eyes. She'd sworn she would never change.

Perhaps she hadn't.

The thought robbed Drake of what little breath he had. He'd had the nagging feeling Janus Crook reminded him of someone, and just then he realized who. Phyllipa. Why had it never occurred to him that she had nothing to gain by befriending Lucy? Was it possible that Phyllipa had pitted him against his wife in the same way Crook had pitted owners against miners? The more he thought about the past weeks at Silverthorne, the more likely it seemed.

Nothing galled Drake as much as being made a fool. Phyllipa would pay for her meddling, he vowed as his shovel struck a particularly savage blow. It met with far less than the usual resistance, burying itself halfway up the handle. When Drake withdrew it, he once again felt the brush of warm stale air against his cheek. Before he could gasp out the marvelous news that they'd broken through at last, he heard a high treble voice from beyond the barricade of stones and dirt.

"I hate this dark!" a child's voice cried. "I want out! It's crushing me! It's choking me!"

Those were the very words he had cried as a boy, even after he'd learned the futility of uttering them. Drake staggered back, dropping heavily onto a wheelbarrow loaded with dirt. The sound of that child's anguish galvanized the other rescuers. They attacked the remainder of the fall with renewed energy, hollering encouragement to the miners within. As Drake sat paralyzed on the dirt-filled barrow, he began to tremble.

Surprised to realize she had fallen asleep, Lucy woke to find herself slumped in her corner seat. She rubbed her eyes and stretched. Every muscle in her body protested how she had overtaxed them in the past twenty-four hours.

The fire had died to a bed of faintly glowing embers, which cast a dim orange light over the room. Two middle-aged women had fallen asleep slumped over the table where they sat. Four others, still awake and watchful, clustered together in a tight circle near the window. The injured rescuers had vacated their place in front of the hearth, in favor of their own beds. Shamed by Drake's tireless example, one or two might have returned to the mine.

At the thought of Drake, alive and unhurt, Lucy drew an easy breath. Then she shook her head over her own folly. How ridiculous to have fretted over the safety of a marble man like Lord Silverthorne. At this very minute he was probably plying his shovel with the relentless power of Mr. Watt's steam engine, immune to cold, or hunger, or despair. Once he finished, he would surge down the hill to give her a thorough dressing-down for conduct unbecoming a viscountess. She had promised herself to treat him with greater forbearance from now on.

It would not be easy.

Just then, one of the women by the window broke into quiet sobbing. Lucy understood. By her reckoning, the time must be coming on three in the morning. It was an hour Lucy loathed. Too soon for even the earliest risers to be up. Too late for any but the most debauched of nightowls. An hour when human spirit and energy were at their lowest ebb. Troubles always looked their worst at 3:00 a.m.

Lucy felt her own eyes tingle with tears of sympathy. In this one day, so crowded with toil and anguish, she had drawn close to the people of High Head. She could name to a man every miner trapped below. She knew all the reasons they had to live—a new bride, a baby on the way, an ailing mother, a growing family. It would take more than Drake's relentless effort to free those men. In the end, there was no guarantee they would find anyone alive. Lucy quailed at that thought.

Whatever this day would bring, she did not mean to meet it crying in the corner. Hauling her weary body up from the stool, she laid a new fire in the grate and set a kettle to heat. A quick glance over her food stores assured her she would soon have to send the wagon back to Silverthorne for additional supplies. Treading quietly so as not to wake the sleeping or intrude upon the private vigils of the others, she made her rounds to check on the injured men. Finding her father dozing in an armchair, she hunted up a spare blanket and covered him.

John Leadbitter moaned restlessly in his sleep. His wife reached over and stroked his cheek with her hand to calm him. The poor soul. This one day had etched deep lines on her brow. Lucy's heart ached with shared worry.

Her gaze strayed to the window, and the distant, flickering torches that lit the rescue efforts. *Please, Drake,* she silently willed her husband. *Get the boy out safely. At least get him.*

Were her tired eyes playing tricks on her? Lucy rubbed them again and stepped closer to the window. The torches bobbed about, moving down the hill. Her stomach con-

stricted. Not another rock slide. That would stall the rescue
efforts dangerously.

Then, on the clammy upland wind, she caught the distant
rumble of excited cries and hoarse cheers.

"Alice," she whispered, her voice tight with emotion.
"They're coming down the hill. I think it's good news!"

Mrs. Leadbitter flew from the room before she had fairly
got the words spoken. Lucy followed, pausing only to grab
her shawl and to alert the other women. She emerged from
the overseer's front door into a courtyard boiling with jubilant tumult. At the center of it all was a sturdy little figure
perched on a man's shoulder. Lucy saw Alice Leadbitter
hurl herself at man and boy, bringing the child down into
her waiting arms. Her thin shoulders heaved with the effort
to exorcize a day's hoarded tears in the space of a few short
minutes.

Lucy skirted the crowd, making her way up the path to
the mine. Her feet and her heart, so heavily weighed down
only moments ago, suddenly felt lighter than air. She practically flew up the path, stopping only to confirm the obvious—all the miners had come out alive.

"That you, Mrs. Strickland?"

Lucy noticed a slight, wiry figure bringing up the tail end
of the joyful procession. "Yes, Anthony." She clasped his
one hand warmly. "Isn't it wonderful?"

"Aye, ma'am, close to a miracle, you might say. Are you
looking for your husband, by any chance?"

Lucy nodded. She hadn't quite realized until that instant
what had compelled her to come here.

"That's good." Anthony Brown shook his head in grim
puzzlement. "He's still in there." He jerked his head toward
the tunnel. The opening looked none too solid. "Just sits.
Don't say a word. If you asked me, he pushed himself too
hard trying to dig them men out."

"But he did get them out, Anthony. Every single one.
Alive." Lucy could barely contain her admiration and won-

der at what Drake had wrought. "You go on. I'll see to my husband."

Lucy gave an involuntary shudder as she passed into the mouth of the tunnel. The air felt surprisingly warm. The muted glow of the disappearing torches scarcely penetrated the debris-choked passageway. Lucy startled at the sound of a rock tumbling down a dirt slope. Then she heard another sound very nearby—a man's rapid, rasping breath.

Groping toward the source of that respiration, she stumbled upon Drake. Compelled by some remnant of elation, she threw her arms around his neck.

"I'm so proud of you. To have helped rescue all those men."

He did not respond at first, receiving her embrace with weary passivity. When she tried to back away, however, he clasped her to him with such desperate force it took her breath away.

"There were children in that pit." His words rasped with emotion plumbed from the stormy depths of his soul. "Little boys trapped in the dark."

Lucy felt his wide shoulders shudder as one harsh sob after another came retching out of him. The pressure of his cheek against the swollen flesh of her breast was almost as painful as hearing a strong man weep. Instead of pushing him away, Lucy cradled his head in her arms and held him closer still.

So Drake Strickland was not made of cold marble after all, but vulnerable flesh and blood. With a pang, Lucy experienced the birth of a strange new feeling for him. She bent her head forward, until her cheek brushed his hair. He smelled of sweat and coal dust and courage.

Chapter Eight

"Hush, now. Everything's all right."

In response to Lucy's comforting words, Drake fought to bring his rampaging emotions back under control. For some inexplicable reason, he felt lightened and peaceful, even safe, within the delicate circle of her arms. Her voice and her touch were soft and warm—like the haven he had been seeking all his life, without success. At the same time, Drake hated himself for his display of weakness. Perversely, he also resented Lucy for having witnessed it.

"You don't understand." He wrenched himself away from her, though his heart cried out to burrow deeper into the sweet nest of her embrace. "It's *my* fault those children were in this cursed mine. If they'd died, I'd never have lived with myself."

"Now you listen to me, Drake Strickland." Lucy forcefully gripped his arm, reestablishing the connection between them. Hard as he tried, he could not bring himself to pull away. "You did not send those children into the mine. I'll wager you didn't even know they were there until half an hour ago."

She seemed to demand some acknowledgement, so Drake nodded. Then, remembering she couldn't see him, he muttered a curt word of agreement.

"I thought so." She sounded vindicated in her trust of his good intentions. "Thanks to you, the Leadbitter boy and all the others have come out alive. I know you'll do everything in your power to prevent this kind of thing from ever happening again."

"Of course I will."

"In that case—" Lucy slackened her grip on his arm and let her hand slide down to grasp his "—you have nothing to reproach yourself for." She tugged at Drake's hand. "If it's all the same to you, I would like to get out of this infernal tunnel before it collapses on *us*."

"You're right. It isn't safe here."

As Drake rose from his seat on the wheelbarrow, a piercing pain in his side made him cry out.

"What's the matter? You're hurt, aren't you?" Lucy draped his arm over her shoulder, preparing to sustain his weight—as if she could. For an instant Drake forgot his injury, marveling at how snugly she fit beneath his arm. His sleep-starved mind conjured absurd images of Eve, created from Adam's rib.

"Ribs." He grunted. "I may have broken one."

"You're certain that's all?" She didn't sound very confident of his veracity. They groped their way toward the mouth of the tunnel. Drake found himself leaning heavily on her.

"Feel dizzy," he admitted. "Got knocked on the head by a rock."

"It's a mercy you have such a good thick skull," Lucy scolded gently. "Why didn't you come down to our aid station and get doctored with the other injured men? Several of those who came to us had less wrong with them than you do, by the sound of it."

"Told you. Had t'get those men out," Drake muttered through his clenched teeth. Each step over the uneven ground jarred his ribs, and made him feel as if he were being repeatedly stabbed with a dull knife.

"Of course. It was your duty." He could hear the exasperation in her voice.

"Yes. Is it so hard for you to understand? What made you come here to tend people you've never met before?"

"Can we stop and rest a minute?" Lucy puffed.

"If you like. We're clear of the worst." Drake eased himself to the ground with Lucy's help, letting out a sharp hiss of pain as his ribs protested.

The muted hubbub of celebration drifted up from the foot of the hill on the still, cold air. Overhead, the sky shimmered with icy starlight. Drake shivered. Immediately, he felt Lucy bundle her heavy shawl around him.

"Don't be ridiculous!" he snapped. "Get this back on your own shoulders. Not the first time I've been cold. I can stand it."

"Well if that's the way you're going to be, you stubborn creature..." Kneeling behind him, Lucy brought the thick folds of wool around to encase them both. Soon Drake could feel the warmth of her body on his back, the soft rounding of her breasts pillowing his neck. He imagined what it might be like if she was kneeling in front of him. Suddenly Drake felt uncomfortably warm, and his breeches felt uncomfortably tight.

He jumped up as though she'd lit a fire under his backside, gasping as the abrupt movement jolted his ribs. "Can you make it the rest of the way?"

Lucy resumed her place by his side. "I can if you can," she announced defiantly.

"You never answered me," Drake pressed. Though speech was an effort, he needed to talk. To take his mind off the pain, and off the pleasure of having Lucy lodged tightly under his wing.

"What was the question?"

"Why did you come to High Head? It wasn't a wise idea...."

"I know," she interrupted. "It is beneath the dignity of a viscountess to consort with common miners."

Drake almost laughed out loud as she aped Phyllipa's pedantic tone. So he'd guessed right. Phyllipa had been filling her head with all this "viscountess" nonsense. By the sound of it, Lucy disdained the whole business as heartily as he did.

"What a load of rubbish!" she continued. "If a viscount can lower himself to wield a shovel and push a barrow, I don't see why his wife can't pitch in, too. A sorry mess you'd have been in if I hadn't come. No food for the rescue party. No one to tend the men who got hurt in that second rock slide—"

"You're right."

"Right? What do you mean? Right about what?" They were nearing the overseer's house. In the glow of torchlight, Drake could make out Lucy's puzzled expression as she stared up at him.

"About everything. We couldn't have done it without you." He nodded toward the crowd, which continued to swell as word of the miners' deliverance circulated though the village.

Lucy just looked at him. Torchlight, starlight and the glimmer of a fresh new dawn glowed in her soft brown eyes. Whatever tight, prim dressing she'd pinned her hair into yesterday morning, it had dissolved into flyaway curls and delicate gold tendrils, gently framing her face. The night air had nipped her cheeks to a healthy pink, and she had a smudge of coal dust on her nose from nuzzling his soot-caked hair.

Drake had never imagined a creature so beautiful.

Braced for a severe reprimand, Lucy hardly knew what to make of Drake's frank admission that he...they...had needed her. He was staring at her in the most disconcerting way. No doubt she looked a fright. She'd have died of mortification if Jeremy had ever seen her in such a state.

"We need to get you home to Silverthorne and have a doctor check you over." As they edged into the boiling crowd, Lucy had to shout directly into Drake's ear. Even then, she wasn't certain he'd heard her.

"There's something I must tell everyone, first," Drake bellowed back.

With mingled admiration and sympathy, Lucy watched his futile efforts to make himself heard above the joyous tumult around them. Each time he took a deep breath, he flinched. Whatever his injuries might be, she did not want him making them worse with such straining. Spying Anthony Brown nearby, she reached out her free hand and tugged on his coattail. He spun around, flashing her a wide grin of recognition.

As he leaned toward her, Lucy shouted, "His lordship has something to say! Can you get everyone's attention?"

Anthony replied with a wink. Drawing his lips taut with two fingers, he issued a whistle as shrill and din-piercing as had ever assaulted Lucy's ears. The noise of the crowd hushed so rapidly and completely, she wondered if they had inhaled their jubilation on bated breath.

"New owner has some'ut to say," Anthony's voice boomed out in the expectant silence. "You mind him, now."

Drake nodded Anthony his thanks. "I'll dispatch the sheriff at once to investigate this *accident*. I expect you to give him your full cooperation. When the investigation is complete we'll make repairs and reopen the mine. I'll to do everything in my power to see that events like these are never repeated at High Head."

Seeing the stricken looks on the faces of several women, Lucy knew just what they were thinking. The mine closed indefinitely. A number of the men injured. Winter almost here. She whispered a suggestion to Drake.

He nodded his agreement. "Everyone connected with the mine will draw full wages until it reopens."

A ragged cheer met Drake's announcement.

"Until I can appoint a new overseer…" A fit of coughing overcame him before he could complete his sentence. The pain each spasm caused was clearly etched on his face. Lucy knew she must waste no time getting him home.

"Until a new overseer comes—" she pitched her voice loud, to project over Drake's raspy bark "—Anthony Brown is in charge."

No one looked more surprised by this announcement than Anthony himself. Tugging off his cloth cap, he held it over his heart, as though swearing a vow. "I'll do my best for you, ma'am. That I will."

Though Drake's coughing had eased, Lucy could feel him leaning more heavily upon her. "I'm sure you'll do splendidly, Anthony. I count myself a very good judge of character and ability. Now, I must get my husband home."

Immediately several men sprang into action, and before Lucy knew it, the tilbury was hitched and ready for the return journey to Silverthorne.

Spying her father nearby, she called out to him, "Will you come back with us?"

Hastening to Lucy's side, Vicar Rushton patted her arm. "Unless you have need of me, my dear, I believe I will stay awhile. I'd like to conduct a short service of thanksgiving."

Several people within earshot nodded or murmured their agreement with the vicar's suggestion.

"What a fine idea." Lucy dropped a warm kiss on her father's ruddy cheek, then glanced up at the driver's seat of the gig. Somehow, Drake had managed to pull himself up there. He sat rigidly erect. In the growing light his face and hands looked almost as black as his hair. What effort did it cost him to sit there, hurt and weary as he must be? To look at him, who would guess the private torment that had fueled his superhuman effort to dig out those trapped miners? With those questions stinging her conscience, Lucy scrambled up beside him.

Drake gave the reins a jog and they were off, leaving High Head less than twenty-four hours after they had arrived. To Lucy it felt more like a month had passed. Part of her wished they could have stayed in the mining village, plain Mr. and Mrs. Strickland, instead of the viscount and his lady hemmed in by protocol at stately Silverthorne.

As the tilbury rattled down the steep road, Lucy heard behind them: "Three cheers for the Stricklands, all!"

Lucy glanced over at Drake, but he gave no sign what he might be thinking or feeling at that moment. When they were finally out of sight of the village, he passed the reins over to her with a weary sigh. For a time the two-wheeled carriage jogged along the winding road from High Head to Nicholthwait. Harness metal and the horse's hooves played a kind of soothing pastoral music, occasionally punctuated by the bleating of Herdwick sheep grazing lazily by the wayside.

A swath of early-morning mist hung over the Mayes Valley. After those few suffocating minutes in the mine shaft, Lucy relished the scent of crisp autumn air. In the wake of those long tense hours surrounded by people, she savored this quiet solitude and Drake's undemanding company. Out of the corner of her eye, she glanced at him. He sat bolt upright with his eyes closed. The firm chiseled lines of his dirt-blackened profile looked more than ever like they'd been hewn from black marble.

Lucy cleared her throat. She had made a promise to herself and she meant to keep it. Something told her it would be easier to begin here and now, rather than wait until they were back at Silverthorne. But where to start?

"I was proud to call myself your wife today. You did well." Her words emerged as a muted murmur. Had Drake even heard her tentative overture? "I've behaved very badly toward you of late. The reasons don't matter now. What matters is that I promise to mend my ways, if you'll forgive me and let us begin again. I would like us to be friends at least...for the child's sake.''

''Very well.'' The reply rumbled from deep in his chest and he did not bother to open his eyes. ''Friends.''

Slowly, as they neared Nicholthwait, Drake began to list toward Lucy, until his head came to rest on her shoulder. There it remained as the gig wended its way back to Silverthorne.

Chapter Nine

Drake strained toward consciousness like a drowning swimmer desperate to breach the surface of the water above him. Everything was dark. Reason dictated that he must be back at Silverthorne, in his own bed. His senses adamantly contradicted that assumption. He heard the soft crackle of a fire, felt its enveloping warmth, smelled the sweet pungency of wood smoke. That was not all he smelled. The savory aroma of lamb and onions. A faint breath of…lavender?

It all conspired to produce an atmosphere of *cosiness*. That was not a word Drake had ever considered to describe his bedchamber. The spacious, airy room occupied one corner of the east wing. It had large windows on two walls that afforded a magnificent view of the lakeland. In the center of the third wall, a wide archway opened into a generously proportioned dressing room.

Sparsely appointed, even by the tastefully restrained standards of the time, his bedchamber contained a small writing desk and chair, a nightstand and a bed. The latter was a curious modern affair without the usual high posts and curtains. Since he spent so little time there, Drake seldom had a fire laid in the hearth.

Until that moment, he'd never thought his bedroom lacking in anything. Lying there, poised on the borderland of dreams, Drake suddenly realized what a cold, bare place it was. Cold and bare as his life. That was a thought he could not bear to dwell on.

Willing his body to respond, Drake tried to sit up. Waves of pain restrained him. He heard someone moan. Was he the one making that sound? The scent of lavender came closer, accompanied by the muted rustle of a woman's skirts. Something cool and smooth came to rest lightly on his forehead.

"Drake, are you awake? How do you feel?"

At the sound of Lucy's whisper, Drake realized he must be back at Silverthorne after all. Wary of the pain provoked by his attempt to sit up, he raised his eyelids to mere slits.

Lucy's face hovered in his field of vision, luminous in the muted glow of firelight, framed by a wispy golden halo. Her fine tawny brows knitted together in an expression of tender concern. The sight brought a pleasant rush of warmth coursing into Drake's loins. He shrank from it as intensely as he had from the pain.

"How do you think I feel?" He twitched his head away from the touch of her hand, gasping as another searing bolt pierced his skull.

"More dead than alive I should think, after what you've been through. I suppose it's a good sign you've recovered sufficiently to complain." She picked up a bowl and spoon from the edge of his night table. "Lie still and have some of this broth. Mrs. Maberley cooked it up especially for you."

When Drake opened his mouth to protest that he could not simply loll in bed for days on end, Lucy shoved a spoonful in. He had no choice but to swallow the most delicious bit of broth he'd ever tasted. Suddenly conscious of the hunger gnawing at his belly, Drake decided he'd better eat something to help regain his strength. For a while he said nothing, obediently opening his mouth each time Lucy offered him a spoonful of soup. Only when the pangs of hunger began to subside did he challenge her.

"What time is it?" He squinted toward the clock on the mantel. He could scarcely make out its face in the dim light. Was it his imagination, or was his vision a bit blurred?

"Teatime," said Lucy. "You've been asleep since we got back from High Head, yesterday morning. I feared you'd never wake."

Jagged recollections of High Head flashed in Drake's mind. "Must get up." He struggled against the pain and dizziness. "There are urgent matters that require my attention."

"Such as…?" Lucy pressed him back gently but firmly with a hand on his chest. His *bare* chest.

Had they not had the decency to put a nightshirt on him? Drake fumed to himself as he felt his face suffuse with color. Lucy's touch was not intended to be the least provocative, he knew. It had a most provocative effect, all the same.

"Don't be obtuse, woman," he snapped. He hated not being in control of his own mutinous body. "The sheriff for a start. Must brief him on the situation at High Head and send him to investigate."

"Done." Lucy tucked the coverlet securely around him.

Drake flashed a glance at the portrait of his mother hanging above the mantel. He had no recollection of her, or anyone else, ever tucking him into bed. In fact, he might have remained entirely ignorant of such intimate domestic rituals, but for Jeremy. When the lad had come to Silverthorne after the death of Drake's stepmother, he had insisted his brother tuck him into bed each night. Reluctantly, awkwardly, Drake had done it. Displays of tenderness had never come easily for him, but until Jeremy went away to school, he had never missed a night.

The gesture held disportionate significance for Drake.

Having never been on the receiving end, he was not sure he liked it. Particularly from Lucy.

"What do you mean, 'done'?"

Lucy rolled her wide-set eyes. "Now who's being obtuse? I sent for the sheriff as soon as we got home. I explained what had happened at your mine and asked him if he would look into it. Did I presume?" she asked with a trace of good-natured irony in her voice.

"Hardly." Drake marveled that she'd shown such presence of mind. "Time was of the essence. You did well. It just never occurred to me that you'd... But, see here, the mine is only the most pressing of my obligations. What of my other concerns? The tannery? The mills? They require my supervision as well."

"At this hour?" Lucy coaxed another spoonful of soup into him. "I think not. Besides, I believe you underestimate your managers just as you underestimate me. I doubt it can be good for them—running to you with every minor problem, looking to you for direction in every decision. What would have become of them if more serious harm had befallen you at High Head?

"Turmoil. Chaos." Lucy answered her own rhetorical question, then posed another for Drake. "Is that what you want?"

He lifted his chin defiantly. "Of course not. What are you suggesting, that I abdicate all responsibility for the enterprises I've built from nothing?"

"Hardly." Lucy's exasperated glare suddenly softened. "I'm only saying your business concerns are like maturing children. You need to let them grow up, make mistakes if need be, but learn to rely on their own judgment and only call on your guidance in truly critical matters. That way, they will be able to continue operating well even if something does happen to you, heaven forbid."

"That makes sense," Drake conceded reluctantly, thinking what a good mother she would be, with such an attitude.

"Can I be hearing right?" Lucy shook her head, a droll expression on her face that made Drake forget everything but the urge to laugh. "The imperious Viscount Silverthorne disclaiming his vaunted infallibility?"

His lips twitched and a chuckle escaped. "Only admitting I recognize good advice when I hear it."

Lucy offered him another spoonful of broth. "Truly, the age of miracles is not past."

As more laughter overtook him, Drake choked on the broth. With each spasm of coughing, his injured ribs throbbed. Lucy hovered anxiously over him, saying over and over how sorry she was to have made him laugh while he was trying to eat.

"I thought you wanted us to be friends," gasped Drake, when his coughing had finally subsided. "Is this your idea of friendship—hectoring a poor invalid in his bed?"

In response to his jest, Lucy's fair complexion took on a furious red cast. "I didn't think you'd remember about that. Besides, I'm only hectoring you for your own good. It'll be far worse for your business concerns if you end up making yourself seriously ill because you've not taken proper care of yourself."

A rumbling bass voice sounded from the doorway. "I agree entirely, your ladyship. Perhaps between the two of us, we can convince this blockhead it is in everyone's best interest for him to take life easy for a while."

Drake's physician, friend and distant cousin, Charles Varoy, swept into the room. Strands of his iron-gray hair had pulled loose from their tie and flew in all directions.

"So our patient is sensible at last?" he asked Lucy.

Drake barely caught her wry mutter. "So he thinks."

"My wife thinks otherwise, Charles." Drake flashed the doctor an exaggerated wink.

"Does she, by Jove?" Dr. Varoy felt at Drake's throat for a pulse. "You're in a jokey humor for a man who's nearly been smashed to a jelly. Are you in much pain?"

Drake shrugged. "Bearable."

"Ever the stoic. Well, let's get a proper look at your injuries. I only took a glance yesterday to assure your wife that neither posed any immediate danger. I knew my doctoring would only interfere with the sleep you truly needed. Can you sit up?"

"I tried, but…my wife would have none of it." Clenching his teeth, Drake pulled himself upright. The pain was not as bad as the first time.

Lucy rose abruptly. Walking over to the hearth, she tossed another stick on the fire, stirring the glowing embers with the poker.

"You've got yourself a wife, Drake." The doctor chuckled again. What did he find so dashed amusing? "You'd better heed her advice."

"I didn't marry her to get advice," Drake snapped before he could stop himself. He glanced at Lucy, who had frozen for an instant in the act of replacing the fire irons. Drake cursed his own thoughtlessness. After High Head, he wanted to make things right with her—start afresh. Somehow, he'd fallen into this abominable habit of opposing her, and it was proving difficult to break. Especially when his pulse sped up every time he looked at her. "Are you going to get on with your examination?" he barked at the doctor.

Gently, Charles probed at a tender spot on Drake's back. Not gently enough. Before Drake could steel himself to contain it, an exclamation of pain broke from his lips.

"I don't wonder it hurts," the doctor said. "The rib is broken, all right, but I expect it's the bruising that pains you." He pulled a roll of bleached cotton from his satchel and wound it tightly around Drake's chest. "There. That'll support the rib while it knits—as much as we can do, I'm afraid."

Drake replied with a stiff nod. The snug binding around his chest was an instrument of torture. He did not try to speak as the doctor cleaned his head wound with ungentle dispatch, directing Lucy to bring him water and hold the basin.

"Well, that's done," the doctor pronounced at last. "Now, let's have a quick look at the rest of you to be sure there's nothing else wrong." He tugged at the quilt, which covered Drake to the waist.

Grasping the edge of the coverlet to prevent the doctor from pulling it off, Drake glanced at Lucy. The basin clutched tightly in her hands, she stared at the quilt, in horrified fascination.

"I'm still hungry," blurted Drake. "Could you fetch me more of Mrs. Maberley's broth?"

Lucy startled at his words. As she fumbled the basin, several drops of water spilled to the floor. "I beg your pardon? Oh, broth. Yes, of course." She quickly returned the basin to his dressing room, all the while chattering in a high breathless voice. "Mrs. Maberley has a huge tureen of it simmering on the fire. Enough to feed the whole house. She'll be glad to hear you have an appetite to eat it." Lucy recovered his soup bowl from the night table. "If you will excuse me, Dr. Varoy?"

"By all means, ma'am." The doctor beamed at her as he continued his tug-of-war with Drake for the quilt. "Rest and proper nourishment—most effective medicine in the world."

As Lucy darted out the door, Drake relaxed his hold. The doctor wrenched the quilt clean off him. "Such modesty in a newly married man." The doctor laughed. "You needn't be embarrassed to let your bride see the effect she has on you…in spite of your injuries. If you like, I can tell her to go easy on you until your rib heals."

Ignoring the pain in his ribs, Drake grabbed the corner of his pillow and swung it, clouting his old friend soundly. The doctor rolled with the blow, laughing more heartily than ever—a sound that was beginning to grate on Drake's nerves.

After a brief look at Drake's sound lower limbs, he twitched the bedclothes back over his patient. "If I catch you out of bed in less than a week, Viscount Silverthorne—" he pronounced Drake's title with genial irony "—I will insist upon thoroughly examining you from top to bottom…with your good lady as my assistant."

For a moment, Drake was too incensed to reply. By the time he worked up a dozen solid reasons why he must be up and about his business, Dr. Varoy had packed his satchel. He departed with a broad grin and a jaunty salute.

Lucy fled Drake's bedchamber, clutching his soup bowl so tightly she almost expected it to shatter in her hands. Her cheeks tingled furiously, and not from her recent proximity to the fire. Fiercely as she'd tried to distract herself, her attention and her gaze had strayed again and again to Drake, sitting naked in his bed for the doctor's examination, with only the quilt covering him below the waist. Stealing surreptitious glances at his hard, lean torso, she'd recalled the feel of his bare chest beneath her fingertips.

The taut smooth flesh and the unexpected silkiness of the thatch of dark hair on his chest—Lucy's mouth went dry at the thought of it. There was no denying that Viscount Silverthorne was a fine specimen of manhood. It was not embarrassment or modesty that had made her run off when the doctor had started to peel back the bedclothes. It was the fear that they might catch her staring with unladylike fascination.

Engrossed in such thoughts, Lucy nearly barreled into Lady Phyllipa.

"Lucinda, my dear, wherever are you bound in such a flying hurry?" Phyllipa recovered her balance. "Is it Drake?" Her pale eyes bulged further than usual. "Has he taken a turn for the worse?"

"Oh no, Cousin Phyllipa," Lucy gasped. Their near collision had startled her and she had the guilty conviction that her carnal musings showed plainly on her face—at least to Lady Phyllipa's gimlet eye. "He's awake now and appears to have his wits intact. Doctor Varoy is checking him over at the moment. I'm on my way to the kitchen to fetch him another bowl of broth. You can imagine how hungry he is."

"Quite." Phyllipa eyed the bowl in Lucy's hands with polite horror, as if it were an overflowing chamber pot. "Is it necessary for you to scurry about the house like a common scullery maid? His lordship employs any number of servants. None overburdened with work so far as I can see. Surely, you don't mean to tend him yourself?"

Lucy opened her mouth to state precisely that intention. Then she realized that opposing Phyllipa would only to serve to keep her dawdling in the corridor, engaged in a futile argument.

"I fear you will have a very uphill battle to make me into anything like a proper viscountess, Cousin." For once Lucy did not try to censor the impatience in her voice. It was going to take all her willpower to forge a more amicable relationship with her husband. She had made no such vow concerning Lady Phyllipa Strickland. "If you will excuse me, I must fetch that broth. I'm sure it won't do Drake's temper any good to wait for food when he's scarcely eaten in two days."

"Drake is in a temper, is he?" A sly smile puckered the corners of Phyllipa's thin lips. "I shouldn't wonder after the way you chased off across the county to dispense half the contents of Silverthorne's larder to a horde of grubby miners."

"As it happens, Cousin Phyllipa, Drake was very…" The look of gleeful expectancy on Phyllipa's face stopped Lucy cold. This toadying, pasty creature was up to something—though Lucy couldn't immediately work out what it might be. One thing was clear to her, however. Mending relations with Drake would be much more difficult with Phyllipa lurking about. Somehow she must dislodge Drake's cousin from Silverthorne, and Lucy could see only one sure way of doing that.

"Well?" prompted Phyllipa, audibly impatient. "Drake was very what?"

"Angry." Lucy came to herself. "You were right. He was very angry with me. One good thing did come of it, however."

Phyllipa's high thin brows arched questioningly.

"Apparently, my husband now sees the urgency of taking me to London." Lucy prayed she would not be struck down for such an outright falsehood. "He insists we must go as soon as he is fit to travel."

"Why didn't you say so sooner?" Phyllipa's fishy eyes bulged to an alarming degree, and her thin lips stretched into the first sincere smile Lucy had witnessed on her. "This is wonderful news!"

"I thought you would be pleased." That was more than she could expect from Drake once he heard the news, decided Lucy. Oh well, in for a penny, in for a pound. One more falsehood couldn't land her in any worse trouble. "Drake asked me to inquire if you might return to London to ready the house for our arrival."

"Mind?" Phyllipa let loose a volley of shrill laughter. "I shall be packed within the hour." She laid one long-fingered hand to her flat bosom. "This is such a relief. The roads are still clear, thank goodness, and we shall be able to celebrate Christmas at home. Could we set out as soon as tomorrow?"

Lucy tried to keep a giddy note of relief from her own voice. "The sooner the better, I should think. The weather is so fickle at this time of year."

"I'll keep the maids packing all night if I have to. Send one or two of them up from the kitchen to help me."

"I'll send someone straightaway, Cousin Phyllipa," Lucy called over her shoulder as she made for the staircase. Under her breath she muttered, "Anything to speed you on your way."

Skipping down the stairs, Lucy found herself humming a merry little tune. Deep inside, however, her joy over Phyllipa's imminent departure was tempered by a qualm of dread. How would Drake react when he found out what she'd done?

Chapter Ten

"London?" Drake stared at Phyllipa, all decked out in a puce-colored pelisse and matching bonnet. He hardly dared to hope he'd heard her aright. "You and Reggie are leaving for London, today?"

Fiercely, he restrained his lips from curving into an eager smile. The chief reason he'd been so anxious to get about his business was the fear that he'd be a sitting target for Phyllipa, if he was confined to bed. For weeks it had been his dearest wish to dislodge her from Silverthorne. Suddenly, without him having raised a hand, it was coming to pass.

"Perhaps it is for the best." He tried to sound regretful but resigned. "I'm in no condition to be agreeable company." He touched his bandaged head in what he hoped was a piteous gesture. "Of course, Lucy will be far too much occupied with tending her poor invalid husband to play the gracious hostess."

Speaking Lucy's name, he cast a furtive glance at her. She stood near the door of his bedchamber in an attitude of timid watchfulness.

"Drake, you are a caution!" Phyllipa dismissed his last remark with a wave of one gloved hand. "You have plenty of servants to tend you. Lady Silverthorne is not some hired girl.'' Her long sallow face brightened. ''I have just had the cleverest thought. Lucinda might accompany Reggie and me back to London, and you can join us once you've recovered.''

''Join you…?''

Darting to Drake's bedside, Lucy pressed a cup of water into his hand. With a skittery glance toward Phyllipa, she gasped, ''You mustn't mind him repeating everything you say. The doctor warned that his wits might be addled for a few days.''

To Drake, she spoke loudly and slowly. ''Remember, my dear? You said we should go to London once you're able to travel. You told me Cousin Phyllipa must go ahead to ready the house.''

''I said no such—''

The pressure of Lucy's slender fingers on his hand arrested Drake's protest. Her face had gone pale and her eyes held an unmistakeable plea. For what, he wasn't sure. Forgiveness? Permission? Drake was of two minds himself. Part of him wanted to put as much distance as possible between himself and this woman who constantly provoked such unfathomable feelings in him. Another part wanted to draw her closer still—as close as she had been in the tunnel at High Head.

''Er…how very agreeable of you to set out so quickly, Phyllipa.'' Drake wasn't certain what he should say about Lucy's going, not until he had a clearer notion of her preference. ''As for my wife, she's at liberty to go with you…if she wishes.''

She clutched his hand tighter still, as if anchoring herself to Silverthorne. ''I *do* think my place is here with you.''

With such a definite sign of her wishes, Drake felt himself well-armed to declare, ''Just so. A houseful of servants is all very well, but a man in my condition needs his wife. Besides, Phyllipa, I know how anxious you are to launch

Lucy in society. Think of the scandal if I pack her off for London so soon after our marriage.''

Phyllipa eyed Lucy with barely concealed vexation. ''I was only thinking of the poor child, and what a dull Christmas it will be for her. You must get well very soon, Drake, so you can bring Lucinda to London in time for the holidays.''

Just then Talbot appeared to announce that all was ready for Lady Phyllipa's departure. After several minutes of effusive farewells and insistent demands that they start for London the moment Drake was fit to travel, Phyllipa left Silverthorne at last.

Dizzy with relief, Lucy threw her arms around Drake's neck. ''Oh, thank you for not giving me away! I'm sorry for all the lies I told, but I simply couldn't think of any other way to get rid of her. I know she's part of your family and you think her the perfect lady, but…''

Gently, Drake withdrew from her impulsive embrace. ''No need to apologize. I only wish I'd realized that a false promise to visit London was all it would take to speed Phyllipa and Reggie on their way. I'd have done it myself, weeks ago.''

''You would?'' Lucy wondered if that bandage around Drake's head might be tied a bit too tight. ''The last time I raised the subject of London, you nearly bit my head off.''

''I know and I'm sorry for it. The truth is, Phyllipa has played us for a pair of fools. I was the greater fool by far, since I knew her and should have guessed her motives.''

''Motives?'' Lucy asked. Whatever Drake was talking about, he sounded sincerely chagrined. ''I don't understand.''

Drake drew a deep breath. ''I'm certain Phyllipa has been stirring up ill feeling between us, ever since our wedding day. For instance, she led me to believe you were desperate to get to London. She also claimed she was only staying on at Silverthorne because you couldn't bear to part with her.''

"What a pack of nonsense!" Lucy jumped from her perch on the edge of Drake's bed and began to pace the room. "I wanted nothing to do with London. I merely gave in to her constant nagging on the subject when I realized it would be the only way to get rid of her." Coming to an abrupt halt, she pointed an accusing finger at Drake. "*You* were the one who insisted on Phyllipa staying...." She could feel herself starting to blush, though she could not fathom why. "To instruct me in proper decorum and make sure I didn't keep 'low company.'"

"Rot!" Drake sat up in his bed, a grimace of pain momentarily flickering across his features. "Utter rot, all of it. The only one who wanted Phyllipa to stay on at Silverthorne was Phyllipa herself. She tried to make each of us believe it was because of the other."

Snatches of Phyllipa's conversation from the past weeks rang in Lucy's thoughts. "Why would she want to make trouble between us? Is it because she disapproves of you marrying beneath your station?"

"Hardly." Drake chuckled. "You could be the Princess Royal and still not suit Phyllipa." He eased himself back down onto his pillows. "With Jeremy gone, and until we have a son, Phyllipa's Reggie stands to inherit Silverthorne. After Neville, of course, but I'd say there's precious little chance of him outliving me or getting any legitimate heirs of his own."

A nauseating pang of shame seized Lucy. She hung her head. "Oh, dear. How stupid of me not to have realized! So you didn't enlist Phyllipa to turn me into a proper viscountess."

"Never." Drake's voice was soft but adamant. "I like you—have always liked you—the way you are."

Swiftly, Lucy glanced up at him, but he refused to meet her eyes. During their brief, intense courtship, Jeremy had paid her many charming compliments, but none had touched her as deeply as this halting admission of Drake's.

"So you don't object if I ride, or read, or visit my old friends in the village?"

He glanced at her waist with an embarrassed grin. "Perhaps the riding can wait a few months. I certainly have no objection to your reading and I would positively encourage you to cultivate all your old friends. Poor Mrs. Sowerby has been quite bereft without you."

"Oh." Lucy gave a choked little gasp. "I will go to see her this very day. What must she think of me for staying away?" An equally distressing notion occurred to her. "What must you have thought? That's why you were so angry with me, wasn't it—the night we quarreled in my room? Because you thought I'd come over all toplofty and deserted my old friends."

"In part." Drake shrugged. "I must apologize for my churlish behavior these past weeks. Compounded with Phyllipa's constant presence, it must have made life at Silverthorne intolerable for you."

Lucy wrinkled her nose. "Not pleasant, I'll admit. That still doesn't excuse what I said to you, and the way I acted."

"You meant what you said about my driving Jeremy to join the army, though, didn't you? I couldn't fathom what made him go. Now I see it was my fault all along."

He looked so stricken, Lucy wished with all her heart she could recall that hurtful accusation.

"Jeremy was a man grown. He made his own choices, for his own reasons. Perhaps I wanted to blame you rather than believe he chose to leave me."

Her words eased Drake. She could tell, because he allowed himself to smile. His dark, sharp-hewn features seemed to radiate a glow from deep within his being. It made Lucy's breath catch in her throat.

A strange sensation of panic assailed her, though she could not think why—a need to escape his presence. As casually as possible, she said, "I believe I'll celebrate my freedom from Phyllipa by paying a visit to the village."

A fresh pang of guilt for deserting him made her add, "Try to get some rest while I'm gone. Is there anything I can fetch you before I go?"

With a slow shake of his head, Drake waved her on her way. "Enjoy your liberty, and give Mrs. Sowerby my fondest regards."

She was halfway out the door when he called. "Lucy..."

She glanced back.

To her questioning look he replied self-consciously, "Come back soon."

Was it her imagination, or did something lost and lonely look back at her from the depths of his stormy eyes? Acting on an impulse she did not understand, Lucy pressed two fingers to her lips, and blew a kiss back toward him.

As she came to the end of the chapter in Livy's *War With Hannibal*, Lucy let her voice die away. The only sounds in the room were the fire's soft crackle and Drake's deep, regular breathing. She glanced at him expectantly. Twice before she had paused in her reading. Each time he'd stirred, opened his eyes and declared himself awake, asking her to continue. This time he lay quiet, his chest rising and falling slowly beneath his nightshirt. Lucy had almost nodded off more than once over this dry Roman history.

She set the heavy volume of Livy on Drake's night table. Quietly resuming her seat, she watched him sleep. Relaxed in slumber, his features had taken on an unexpected vulnerability, completely at odds with their waking demeanor. Seeing him so unguarded, with only the flickering firelight playing over his face, it was almost possible to imagine him as a boy. A starveling, all bony wrists and ankles, with dark, haunted eyes too large and too old for his pinched little face. Like the one Mrs. Sowerby had told her about that very afternoon.

Offering her humblest apologies for not calling sooner, Lucy had nobly resisted the urge to lay the blame on Lady

Phyllipa. No one had held her prisoner at Silverthorne, after all. She should have shown more spirit and stood up for what was important to her. Without a word of reproach, Mrs. Sowerby had made her welcome.

Over a cup of strong tea, Lucy gingerly raised the subject of Drake. "Do you recall that talk we had just before my wedding, Mrs. Sowerby?"

"I do. Stuck my pointy old nose in trying to make you see how fortunate you was to get a fine man like his lordship."

Lucy smiled ruefully. "Some things people can't be made to see, Mrs. Sowerby. Some things people just have to discover for themselves." With that, she launched into a glowing account of Drake's heroism at High Head. Her old friend listened with rapt attention and a proprietary smile.

"You mentioned his lordship had a hard childhood," Lucy said as she concluded her account of the mine rescue. "He never talks about it. Will you tell me what you know?"

After pondering Lucy's request for a moment, the old woman finally nodded. "Aye. I don't reckon it'll do no harm, what with you being his missus and all. Not many folks know the rights of it, you see. They all think he were brought up grand. But our Susan used to do for 'em up to the big house, before she married. The tales she carried home fair rang a mother's heart, they did. His mam died bearing him, you know. A fine lady she was and well liked by the local folk. It was so sad."

Reflecting on Mrs. Sowerby's story, Lucy looked up at the portrait of Elizabeth Strickland hanging above Drake's mantel. No beauty, with the dark, definite features she'd bequeathed her son, the previous Lady Silverthorne had kind eyes and a hint of humor about her mouth. What a shame Drake had never known her.

"The child were a frail, sickly little creature," Mrs. Sowerby had informed Lucy. "The doctors told the old master it wasn't likely to live long without its mam. Leave the child in the country, they said. It'll toughen him up, if it don't kill him. So that's just what his lordship done. Left the boy here at Silverthorne and went off to London to forget his grief at the gaming tables.

"The more brass he frittered away, the worse ruin the estate fell into. Most of the house was shut up—damp from the leaking roof, moldy and crawling with rats, cold as charity in the wintertime. Audrey Maberley and our Susan did what they could for young Master Drake. That governor his lordship engaged for the boy, he was the very devil of a creature.

"Said he meant to toughen Master Drake up with plain food, fresh air, long walks, cold baths and the like. While all the time, he was spending what little brass his lordship sent on drink and bad company. Susan swore the poor child never had a single plaything nor a bit of fun in all his life. Used to make my blood fair boil, it did."

No wonder the viscount was such a stern, cold man, Lucy mused as she watched him sleep. Without a single happy day to recollect from his whole childhood. Not surprising that he spent all his time on dull business matters, either, having never learned how to enjoy himself. Though he would surely deny it, Lucy knew he desperately needed someone to look after him, someone to bring a ray of sunshine into his life. How sad that he had insisted on playing the gallant fool and marrying a woman who could never love him as he deserved.

Lucy rebuked herself for such a thought. After all, the welfare of her baby lay in the gallant folly of his uncle. Laying one hand on her flat belly, now taut as a drumhead, Lucy reached out with the other, passing it gently over Drake's hair.

Strange brooding feelings roiled in her heart. She scarcely knew what to make of them. Was it the child growing within her that made her long to protect and nurture even so assured a man as Viscount Silverthorne?

Lucy smoothed Drake's bedclothes and tucked them securely around him. With a last glance at his tranquil features, she picked up the candle and tiptoed from the room. At some point in the past several hours, she had come to an important decision. Perhaps she could not love Jeremy's crusty, insular brother, but at least she could take care of him and try to bring a little happiness into his life. Did she not owe him that much?

His coverlet piled with sheets of paper like mounting snowdrifts, Drake sat in his bed. A crowd of men surged around it, each trying to make himself heard above the others. This was the first time Lucy had permitted his overseers an audience. All were clamoring for his attention, demanding decisions and solutions for their problems. Lucy had been right. They did need to learn how to take more responsibility. Drake could scarcely hear himself think.

"Milord, about that order from Lichfield…"

"…that new spinning jenny's been naught but trouble to us since we got it.…"

"…though our raw tonnage is up over last month's, we've lost…"

"It's them ships from Nova Scotia, your lordship…"

Drake seized upon that remark. It had been a pet project of his. He'd bypassed the British shipyards, which were engaged in filling naval contracts, to buy cheap little vessels from the North American colonies.

"What about the Nova Scotia ships, Mr. Stokes?" Drake gestured for silence from the others.

"Lloyd's won't rate 'em for better than seven years, milord. Rough built, they claim."

"That's hardly surprising. From what I understand, the builders are small farmers and fishermen. They build a barque or brigantine during the winter months to earn some ready money. I have every confidence their skill will improve with experience. Besides, even at seven years, the

craft are cheap enough to make them a profitable investment."

With a dubious expression on his florid face, Mr. Stokes
stroked his impressive side-whiskers. "That's as may be,
sir. We make a pretty penny on the timber and fish they
bring over to us. After that, they ship home with empty
holds. It ain't profitable, milord and it ain't safe. A ship
light in the hold bobs like a cork in rough seas."

"How do you suggest we allay that problem?"

"A three-way trade, milord, instead of back and for'ard.
Our ships bring lumber and fish to England, send out mer-
cantile goods to the West Indies, then pick up a cargo of
sugar, rum and slaves..."

"Never!" The word reverberated even in the crowded
room. Drake pounded his fist on the mattress, but it failed
to produce a satisfactory crash. "I will see my enterprises
bankrupt before I allow them to turn a ha'penny's profit
from that heinous trade."

In the instant of silence that greeted his declaration, a
brisk clap of hands sounded and Lucy's voice rang out.
"Enough. Have you gentlemen glanced at your watches in
the past hour?"

The crowd around his bed parted like the Red Sea to let
Lucy make her way to his side.

"I'm certain many of you have wives waiting tea for you
at home. It's past time for his lordship's tea as well. I'll not
have you upsetting him while he's recovering from his injuries."

Drake shifted uncomfortably in his bed. In fact, he hadn't
felt so much as a twinge in days—except his conscience.

Fraud! Malingerer! he silently rebuked himself. His business concerns required his urgent personal attention. Yet
here he sat, tucked up snugly in his bed, complaining of
phantom headaches and imagined tenderness around his
ribs. All so he could continue to bask in the gentle, devoted
attendance of Lucy.

She woke him each morning with a cheerful inquiry about how he'd slept and a hearty breakfast of his favorite foods. She scarcely left his side the whole day. They'd compromised over reading matter, putting aside Livy in favor of Dr. Johnson's *Rasselas*. Even that literary masterpiece did not hold the charm of Lucy's conversation. Chuckling over the tale of an odious suitor who had plagued her at Bath, Drake realized he'd laughed more in a single fortnight with her than in his whole prior life.

Every night she insisted on sitting with him until he was fast asleep. More than once he'd woken from the hellish pit of a nightmare to find himself in the fragrant heaven of Lucy's embrace. When he'd calmed and slipped back into more peaceful repose, he would sometimes rouse again as her soft, warm lips brushed his brow.

Suddenly aware that he had lapsed into the befuddled grin of a simpleton, Drake composed his features back into proper severity. "You have heard her ladyship's edict, men." He could not keep a jocular note from creeping into his words. "Even a viscount must submit to wifely tyranny. I will look over the papers you've left and communicate my answers within the next day or two. Don't be shy about making decisions on your own initiative. I'm a family man now. It's high time I stepped back from the daily operations of my business concerns."

His sober, hardheaded overseers stared back at Drake as if they'd all been poleaxed in the midriff. Obviously, they weren't ready to be cut adrift quite yet. He had a responsibility to them that took precedence over his personal inclinations—no matter how strong.

"Off you go." He waved them on their way. "I'll be on my usual rounds in a week at the latest. Call back again if something urgent arises in the meantime."

They filed out of the room, still looking dazed, though somewhat reassured. As Mr. Stokes reached the door, Drake called out to him. "I'm glad you raised the problem of the

Nova Scotia ships. You're right about human cargo making good ballast."

Stokes scratched the smooth, bald crown of his head, his heavy brows drawn together in obvious puzzlement. "But if you're so set against shipping slaves…?"

"I would not oppose transporting paying passengers."

"These is cargo ships, milord," the man objected. "No cabins or other what passengers'll expect."

"Not your high-class of passenger, I'll grant you, but few of that type are anxious to emigrate. It's poor folk who are willing to brave the hardships of a new land for the sake of their childrens' futures. We can knock together deal bunks, have the people provision themselves, and keep our fares low."

"Aye." Stokes's deep-set eyes gleamed with the possibilities. "Even if we only charge a few bob, it beats an empty hold."

"That's the idea." Drake nodded. "Besides, it will mean an increased population in the colonies to provide a growing market for our commercial goods."

The overseer beamed. "I've said it before, your lordship. Never met a gentleman with your head for trade, and that's a fact. Had it ever since you first walked into my office, a tall spindly boy with hardly a whisker to shave. Now I come to think on it, you've scarcely had a day's rest since then. Don't rush your recovery, lad. We'll all muddle along, I daresay, and try not to lose you too much brass doing it."

Bobbing a parting bow to Lucy, he followed the departing managers, closing the door softly behind him. Drake glanced at Lucy to find her gazing at him, clearly deep in thought.

"Why *do* you work yourself so hard?" she asked. "You have more money than you'll be able to spend in ten lifetimes…or so I've heard."

"A man must do something with his time." Drake shrugged. "I'm not much good at anything else."

Lucy's eyes held him. "No need to be flippant with me, Drake Strickland."

He'd tried to explain to others. Neville, Phyllipa, even Jeremy had reacted with amusement and derision. For some reason it bothered Drake inordinately that Lucy might laugh or sneer at his very reason for living.

Some promise of sympathy in her searching gaze pulled the words from him. "You don't know what it was like here…when I was growing up. Time and again I swore to myself that I would live in spite of what the doctors said. I vowed that when I came into my inheritance, I'd make it my business to help my people feed and cloth their families. Provide their children with a decent education and opportunities for the future."

"Your people?" Those whispered words flowed as warm and sweet and comforting as a cup of chocolate on a cold day. "I should have known. That's why you married me, isn't it? Neville and Reggie will never look out for your people as you do, but a child you raise might carry on as you've begun."

"In part. I also felt a responsibility to you and to the child, after the disgraceful way Jeremy used you."

"Used me?" Lucy's delicate features went rigid, and her eyes blazed with golden fury. "You make me sound like a handkerchief…or a chamber pot. Jeremy was an honorable man. He loved me, and I adored him. I did nothing against my will to conceive our child. If I had it to do again, I would not hesitate."

A strangled little cry broke from her lips. Drake ached to take her in his arms and return the comfort she'd offered him time and again. The ferocious anger in her eyes stopped him cold. Somehow of late he had fooled himself into thinking she belonged to him. Witnessing her distress, he understood that she would always be Jeremy's. He opened his mouth to offer an apology, but she cut him off before he could find the words.

"Don't waste your pity on me, Drake Strickland." She darted for the door. "Save it for *your people*."

Chapter Eleven

Lucy paused in her eager ingestion of a generous slice of Mrs. Maberley's hare-and-partridge pie. Glancing at her down the length of the dining table, Drake began to smile in spite of himself. With Phyllipa's departure and the improvement in Lucy's appetite, there had been no further talk of the cook retiring.

"What shall we do about Christmas?" Looking up suddenly, Lucy caught him staring at her.

Forcing his budding smile into a scowl, Drake looked away, pretending a rapt concentration on his own dinner.

"It's less than a fortnight away," she added in a tone that eloquently expressed her doubt he was aware of the fact.

Drake hesitated, uncertain how he should respond. For the past week he had been studiously weighing his every word to Lucy. After all, his ill-considered remark about Jeremy had cost him the continuation of his pleasant convalescence. The very next morning, he'd risen early and returned to work—something he *was* good at.

"What *shall* we do about Christmas?" Though he affected a casual reply, the very mention of that day made him feel like a woodcock during hunting season.

For reasons he could not fathom, everyone else in the world appeared to regard the Yuletide in a spirit of merriment. Drake had always felt like an outsider. Worse yet, he had the bewildering sense that it was wrong for him to succumb to his loneliness and gloom during such a holy season.

"What I mean is..." Patience warred with asperity in Lucy's voice. "Every family keeps Christmas in its own way. Now that I am part of your family, I must follow your traditions."

"Traditions?" Drake gave a bitter chuckle. "Take your pick. The long-cherished ritual of hiding out on the attic landing to avoid my tutor and his pack of drunken revelers? Or perhaps the merry custom of staying behind at a boarding school after all the other boys have left for a holiday with their families?"

Seeing the stricken look on Lucy's face, he checked his outpouring of bile. No use expecting her to understand that he did not begrudge others their merriment. As an employer, he was acclaimed for the generosity of his "Christmas box," the customary annual gratuity. If a man had friends and family with whom to celebrate the holiday, Drake had no wish to see it marred by the want of mere money.

All he desired at this time of year was that he be left alone to keep the day in his own quiet manner. Reading the lesson at Christmas matins. Worrying down a portion of the enormous goose and plum pudding Mrs. Maberley always prepared. Then going for a solitary ride, so as not to inflict his ill humor on others. On his lonely rounds in the early twilight of winter, if he happened to pause and stare longingly at some homely cottage, straining to catch an echo of tinny music or mildly inebriate laughter, contemplating the elusive mystery of human happiness—whose business was it but his own?

With a jolt, Drake came to himself to find Lucy kneeling beside his chair, her delicate hands clutching the wrist cuff of his coat. "Forgive me, Drake. I should have realized..."

Blast and confound the woman! He scowled. Why must she persist in doing the complete opposite of what he ex-

"Precious little fear of that." Drake permitted himself a faint mordant grin, fleeting as a heartbeat.

Lucy's heart beat queerly as she sat alone in the Silverthorne pew on Christmas morning. It fluttered rapidly, high in her chest, leaving her light-headed and breathless. Ridiculous to feel this way, she castigated herself. Jeremy had been dead for months. To be strictly honest, in all that time she had not thought much about him. Why, on this of all mornings, had the full weight of his loss descended upon her?

Perhaps because he had spent so little time at Silverthorne in recent years, she reasoned. Until now it had been possible to fancy that he was simply off in London, or in Spain with his troops, apt to show up on leave at any time. But Christmas morning at Saint Mawes, without Jeremy? Unthinkable!

For more years than she cared to remember, Lucy had huddled in a drafty balcony pew, gazing in adoration at his pure, exquisite profile. That fleeting hour of worship had been all the gift she'd ever asked of Christmas. Now the balcony pew was empty, but for the ghost of her timid yearning, and she occupied the spot where Jeremy Strickland would never sit again.

In a daze of renewed grief, she stumbled through the familiar responses in the Book of Common Prayer—sitting, standing, kneeling, bowing her head, moving her lips all by rote. Then Drake strode up to the lectern and began to read the lesson. As head of the family that endowed the vicar's living, reading the lessons was Drake's privilege and duty. In all the years of their acquaintance, distant though it had been, Lucy had never known Drake to shirk his duty. And in all those years, she had scarcely noticed him carrying it out. Certainly never at Christmastime, when she'd had eyes only for Jeremy.

Perhaps it was Jeremy's absence that made her aware of his brother this morning—suddenly and forcefully. Or perhaps it was the consciousness of new life growing within her that made Lucy hear the Nativity lessons charged with deep personal significance. Whatever the reason, she found herself attending to Drake's reading with rapt concentration.

Lord Silverthorne looked very distinguished in his crisp white surplice, Lucy realized with a bewildering jolt. It set off his fierce dark aspect in a most compelling manner. She had always acknowledged Drake Strickland as a powerful man. Unlike expensive finery or the ermine robes of a peer, the stark simplicity of the surplice drove home the realization that his was a power not of wealth or rank, but of character and honor.

"'In the sixth month the angel Gabriel was sent from God,'" read Drake in a firm, resonant voice, "'unto a city of Galilee, named Nazareth.'"

As he continued to read the familiar words of Saint Luke, Lucy pictured the scene vividly in her imagination. Gabriel, an angel, an eloquent golden creature of manly perfection, announcing to a reverently adoring virgin her privilege and burden to bear the Christ Child. Instinctively, Lucy pressed one gloved hand below the waist of her pelisse. She could not detect the first subtle swelling of her belly under the thick warm velvet.

"Reading from the Gospel of Saint Matthew," announced Drake, breaking in on Lucy's reverie. Glancing up from the pages of the massive Bible, he shot her a swift, piercing look.

"'Now the birth of Jesus Christ was on this wise: when his mother Mary was espoused to Joseph, before they came together, she was found with child of the Holy Ghost. Then Joseph her husband, being a just man and not willing to make her a public example, was minded to put her away privily.'"

Joseph. What a contrast to Gabriel! That rough, practical workman, with his dark looks and yeoman manners. Yet there must have been more to this Nazarene carpenter than

first met the eye. For one thing, he had been a kind man—
"just" as Saint Matthew had called him, reluctant to see
poor Mary publicly disgraced. He had done her a matchless
service, providing her vulnerable child with an earthly father
to protect and nurture him. A special man indeed, entrusted
by God with such a task. A task not without its penalties.

"'Then Joseph, being raised from sleep,'" concluded
Drake, "'did as the angel of the Lord had bidden him, and
took unto him his wife: and he knew her not till she had
brought forth her first born son, and he called his name
Jesus. Here endeth the reading of the second lesson.'"

As she watched Drake withdraw from the lectern, a faint
sigh escaped her lips. Had Mary come to appreciate all her
husband's fine qualities? Lucy wondered, hoping so. Had
she come to love him at last? Or had she clung to the shimmering memory of her brush with an angel?

An angel.
She looked for all the world like an angel, Drake thought
as he held out his arms to lift Lucy down from the sleigh.
How fitting that those celestial beings should appear in blue
and white and gold—a compound of sky, clouds and sunshine. Lucy had wrapped a soft white shawl over the shoulders of her blue pelisse. At the brow and nape of her matching blue bonnet, fine curly tendrils clustered, like filaments
of shimmering gold.

His hands closed around her waist, nearly able to span it
even through the thick fabric. She felt so light in his arms
as he eased her to the ground—almost incorporeal. Alarm-
ingly so.

The concern must have shown on his face, for Lucy
flashed him an encouraging smile. "It won't be as bad as
you think, Drake. You'll see."

Scarcely had the words left her lips when she suddenly
went limp in his arms.

"Lucy! What is it? Are you all right?" He gathered her

up, holding her close to his chest, as he had on the night he'd found her weeping in the churchyard.

With a weak apologetic laugh she pressed one gloved hand to her brow. "Just a passing dizzy spell. I'll be fine." So he alone could hear, she added, "Expectant mothers are prone to them, you know."

The tone of her whispered confidence was warm, but for some reason her words chilled Drake. Why had she suddenly seen fit to remind him she was carrying another man's child?

"Oh well, if that's all..." Abruptly he set her back on her feet.

She clung stubbornly to his arm, nodding toward the path. The light snow had been trodden repeatedly underfoot and the resulting slush frozen by the icy upland wind. "It looks slippery." Again she lowered her voice confidentially. "I'm sure you would not want to risk my taking a fall and jeopardizing your future heir."

She cast him a mischievous look, together with a bewitching smile that twined around Drake's heart. "Besides, it's chillier than I expected. I need you to shield me from the wind." With a movement as quick and graceful as a dance step, she insinuated herself just under his shoulder.

Instinctively, he placed his arm across her back, crooking around to hold her securely under his wing. Unbidden images flashed in his thoughts. Of that dark hour before dawn when she'd supported his broken frame down from the High Head mine. Now it was his turn to support her.

"There now, I'm warm and safe." Lucy snuggled tightly against him.

For an instant it occurred to Drake what a slippery emotional incline he was treading in his feelings for this woman. Resolutely, he banished the thought, committed to honoring his promise that he would help her celebrate Christmas.

"Talbot. Mrs. Maberley," he called to the cook and butler, struggling out of their fleece lap robes. "The overseer's countinghouse is over there. We'll leave it to you and the others to prepare for this evening's festivities, while we pay our calls round the village.''

"It was so kind of you to offer your help," piped up Lucy. "I'm certain this will be the most splendid Christmas celebration High Head has ever seen.''

Mrs. Maberley beamed. "My pleasure, your ladyship, I'm sure. I do fancy cooking for a crowd at Christmastime. Puts me in mind of the old days. The puny little geese I've roasted the past few years were hardly worth the trouble.'' She shot Drake a look of mild reproof. "Come along, Mr. Talbot," she fussed at the butler. "I must get a kettle boiling if I'm to steam those puddings proper.''

"We must be on our way, too, Drake," said Lucy. "If we are to pay all our calls and invite everyone for our little revel this evening.''

She peered around at the junior servants, unloading provisions from their small fleet of sleighs. "Now where do you suppose Father is? I thought he meant to come with us.''

"You know what he's like." Drake hoped he sounded convincingly innocent. "Got talking to some old dame about her rheumatics and forgot all about us. I vote to be on our way. He'll catch us up sooner or later.''

To himself, Drake wondered whether his absentminded father-in-law would follow through on their carefully laid plan. If he did, would Lucy approve? She hadn't shown any sign of disappointment when no presents had been forthcoming at breakfast or at luncheon. He might not have given any thought to a gift, if Mrs. Maberley had not posed an innocent question about it. Drake had spent any number of days pondering what he could possibly buy for his wife.

It had finally occurred to him that, unlike the few other women of his close acquaintance, Lucy always appeared more happy to give than to receive. In that realization had been born his plan for today. For a solid week afterward he'd been quite useless at business matters, preoccupied with secret visits to shops in Kendal and clandestine conferences with Vicar Rushton. Drake had never approached the Christmas season with such a sense of anticipation. Now that the moment was at hand, he felt a certain misgiving about how Lucy might react.

A shiver went through her, communicating itself to Drake, "Let's be on our way. The wind here makes it feel so much colder than at Silverthorne."

Word must have gone forth of their arrival in the village, for they were met at the door of their first stop with a cordial, noisy greeting and speedily drawn inside to sit by the fire and take a cup of mulled cider.

Drake gratefully curled his fingers around a mug, toasty from the introduction of the host's hot poker into the cider. He watched with quiet gravity as Lucy launched into an animated dialogue with the family. She inquired after the soundness of their host's ankle, which he had injured in his brave effort to dig out the trapped miners. The lady of the house she commended on her tireless help at the aid station that night. The children she praised for their size, beauty and cleverness. Basking in the warmth of this exchange, Drake wondered that they needed the cheerfully crackling hearth fire to fend off the winter chill.

While he was savoring the last drop of mellow, spicy cider, the baby of the family staggered over and clung to his knee. A sturdy boy, not yet in trousers, he lavished Drake with a wide, wet smile—all but toothless. Some mysterious impulse prompted Drake to lift the child onto the toe of his boot and bounce him up and down several times. The boy responded with an infectious gurgling chuckle in which Drake joined.

It suddenly occurred to him that in a year's time he might be sporting with a young one of his own. A son to clasp his fingers in a chubby fist, grin adoringly and call him *Papa*. The thought warmed and intoxicated Drake more thoroughly than his cup of cider. He was scarcely aware of the silence that had fallen in the room.

"Will ye look at that now." The child's mother spoke in a tone of hushed wonder. "Our Colly's right strange of folks as a rule. When me own Ma comes, he screws up his eyes and sets to howling the minute she's through the door."

Drake worked hard to keep a sober face. Clearly this wee lad's grandmother was cut from the same cloth as his own.

Ignoring the astonished interest caused by his behavior, the little fellow wriggled up onto Drake's lap. There he settled contentedly, popping a plump thumb into his mouth. Gradually, Drake became aware of Lucy's gaze fixed on him. Her eyes shone with a radiance she must once have turned on Jeremy, to beguiling effect. What could it mean? Had the sight of a small child in his arms smitten her with the reality of the one growing within her? Whatever had made her look so, Drake only knew it made him long to kiss her.

Just then a hearty rap sounded on the door, and a deep masculine voice boomed from outside the cottage. "Are there any good little boys and girls in this house?"

"Father Christmas!" The children scrambled for the door, fighting good-naturedly for the honor of opening it.

A short portly figure made his way inside. The children clung excitedly to his fur-trimmed robe, assuring him repeatedly of their impeccable behavior.

"I see I've come to the right place." He patted small heads and shook small hands.

Drake hoped his eager admirers would not tear the beard of brushed fleece from their guest's chin. He caught Lucy scrutinizing Father Christmas with a gleeful grin of recognition. When she cast him a questioning glance, Drake could only avert his eyes sheepishly.

The family exclaimed in loud, appreciative tones over their gifts. Toy soldiers for the oldest son. A daintily painted fan for a girl on the verge of womanhood. Poppets and books for the younger ones. Mother received a pretty work basket and father, a fine leather pouch of tobacco. Master Colly surveyed the scene with suspicious solemnity, from his sanctuary on Drake's lap. At last he did condescend to accept a brightly colored spinning top. When his sisters turned it for him, he crowed with delight.

As each gaily wrapped parcel emerged from the bulging pack of Father Christmas, Lucy's smile widened and her eyes grew more starry. A sense of fulfilment swelled in Drake's chest.

It was the same at every house they visited that afternoon—a cordial welcome, modest hospitality, eager greetings for Father Christmas and ardent appreciation of his bounty. After all their calls, the villagers crowded into the countinghouse for a short service of lessons and carols. If any of the older children saw a likeness between the ruddy little vicar who read the lessons and the jolly figure of Father Christmas, they tactfully refrained from sharing this intriguing information with the little ones.

There followed a merry supper of Mrs. Maberley's best board, crowned by the very choicest of plum puddings. Groaning with repletion, the diners helped to clear the floors for dancing, while mothers spirited their young ones home to bed, under the watchful eye of a grandparent or a trusted older child.

Only when they had paused for breath after a succession of spritely line dances was Lucy able to corner Drake for a private word.

"Papa told me you financed his little turn as Father Christmas today," she remarked softly as they stood in the doorway. "I was hoping we could do something like that, but I hadn't the face to ask you, what with all you've done for me already."

Drake kept his eyes studiously fixed on the dancers. "I was at a loss for a Christmas present to give you." He shrugged, unable to frame the proper words to explain his intentions. No doubt Jeremy would have found the perfect bauble to delight her, and delivered it with the proper gracious flourish. Suddenly his own Christmas surprise seemed to Drake the height of ridiculous sentimentality.

"You needn't have gone to so much trouble," Lucy persisted. "Father told me you got a list of all the villagers from Anthony Brown, with his guess of their ages. He said you haunted the shops for miles around, hunting up just the right gifts for everyone."

"I enjoyed it." Drake pretended to spare their conversation only a crumb of his attention. "This is the first year I ever looked forward to Christmas." Try as he might, he could not sound indifferent.

Beside him, Lucy chuckled. "As my Christmas present to you, I promise to refrain from saying, 'I told you so.'"

"A rare gift from any wife," Drake quipped wryly, venturing the dangerous luxury of a sidelong glance at her.

The final notes of the music were fading away. He knew it would be his duty as a good host to take the floor again, when the musicians struck up their next tune. Yet he could scarcely bear to break the spell of quiet intimacy between them.

"I could not be better pleased." Her eyes glittered like tawny gemstones, and Drake sensed a tremulous thickness in her voice. "Not if you'd showered me with diamonds. Hearing those children laughing, watching their faces glow...this has been my happiest Christmas ever."

Before Drake could trust himself to reply, she pointed to the door frame above them. Someone had secured a wilted sprig of mistletoe there. The leaves almost brushed the top of his head. How had he failed to notice it until now?

Lucy reached up and curled one hand around the nape of his neck, drawing his face down to hers with gentle insistence. As she kissed him, Drake held himself severely still. It was a soft kiss, utterly chaste. And for a wondrous instant,

Drake felt himself gifted with a treasure of inexpressible sweetness.

Then, as her lips lingered on his, they innocently ignited a flame beneath his long-simmering desire.

Chapter Twelve

Her happiest Christmas ever.

Had she truly uttered those words? Lucy asked herself as she tossed restlessly in her bed a few nights later. Of course she'd been anxious to assure Drake how much she appreciated everything he'd done on her behalf. Still, to have called a Christmas without Jeremy her happiest was the romantic equivalent of sacrilege.

Yet even after the most rigorous inquisition of her feelings, Lucy could not bring herself to recant the heresy. It had been a rare sweet day, one whose tender magic would shimmer in her memory for years to come. However, that innocent magic had spawned another enchantment—one dark and potent. Ever since the moment her lips had met his, Lucy had found herself consumed by carnal yearnings for Drake.

As he ate dinner, she followed every motion of his large, deft hands. She found herself imagining how masterfully they might dispatch a woman's clothing in a moment of passion. When he happened to glance up and catch her gaping, she ducked her head, hoping to conceal the hot blush that mantled her cheeks.

More than once, when he was standing close enough to catch her, she had pretended to fall into a swoon. The contradictory sensations of his strong arms enfolding her, and the gentle flutter of his breath on her hair made Lucy's whole body tingle with desire. The mere sound of his firm, swift footsteps set her heart racing. What had come over her?

Not love.

Of that she was certain. This strange fascination she had suddenly conceived for Drake bore no resemblance to the delicate, dreamy devotion she'd nursed in her heart for Jeremy. Every book she had ever read, every poem, every romantic ballad affirmed that such feelings were true and everlasting—experienced but once in a lifetime.

What she felt for Drake was only a physical, sensual interest, like an unquenchable thirst or an itch in that hard-to-reach spot between one's shoulder blades. Persistent. Impossible to ignore. Yet how good it might feel to slake that thirst. To scratch that bedeviling itch.

"Stop scratching yourself, Neville!" snapped his grandmother. "If you will frequent those low taverns and gaming hells, I'll thank you not to carry their vermin into my house."

She eyed Neville and Phyllipa suspiciously. "You're here for money, I presume. I know better than to expect a call from either of you when you're flush."

"Well, since you mention it..." began Neville.

"Quite the contrary, Grandmama." Phyllipa fetched him a vicious gouge in the ribs with her pointy elbow. "Neville and I are here to wish you greetings of the season."

"Indeed." The marchioness rang for tea, with a grudging air. "By my calculations, it's nearly Twelfth Night. A trifle late in the Christmas season for the pair of you to be overcome with family feeling."

Neville prompted Phyllipa with an expectant look. This kind of toadeating was her forte.

"Late? Yes. Well, as a matter of fact..." She groped for

a polite excuse. If his own interests had not been at stake, Neville would have enjoyed watching her squirm.

"Drake and his wife!" she declared at last, her pale cheeks flushed with triumph.

"What about them?" The marchioness sounded dubious.

"We were expecting them for Christmas," replied Phyllipa. "Any day. Naturally, Neville and I wanted to wait until we could all celebrate together as a family."

Just then a maidservant appeared with the tea tray. While his grandmother occupied herself with its disposition, Neville treated Phyllipa to a covert grin of approbation. She'd managed to placate the old girl, while simultaneously introducing the true reason for their call. Though she might irritate him beyond bearing by times, Clarence's widow clearly had her uses.

"Drake coming to London voluntarily..." said the marchioness. "Are you certain?"

Phyllipa sipped her tea, which was loaded with enough sugar to make Neville's mouth pucker. "He assured me so himself, just before I returned home. I can't think what has detained them, though I fear Lucy may be behind it."

"This bride of Drake's not anxious to get to town?" The marchioness sounded surprised.

Phyllipa sighed. "Tried to pretend she was, but I knew better. I fear Lucy has little taste for the kind of company she ought to cultivate. An altogether unsuitable wife for a viscount."

"I see." Her ladyship helped them both to more cake. "Perhaps you'd better tell me how things stand."

As Phyllipa gleefully recounted Lucy's indecorous behavior in the matter of High Head, Neville watched his grandmother grimly absorb the news. He could scarcely refrain from beaming. The marchioness had been against Drake's marriage from the start. She might make a formidable ally in their quest to bring it down. Still, they must tread carefully, for the old lady had no desire to see him inherit Silverthorne.

"So you see," concluded Phyllipa, breathlessly, "it's imperative we get the pair of them down to London, so you and I can take Lucy firmly in hand."

"How do you propose we do that?" asked the marchioness. "Drake is unlikely to heed any summons of mine."

"Not a summons, perhaps." Neville bolted a mincemeat pastry. "I doubt he'd ignore a letter claiming you were ill and asking to see him."

His grandmother looked long at Phyllipa, then at Neville, in an enigmatic way that made him fairly break out in a sweat. She might be older than Methuselah's mother, but the old love had her wits about her. Was it possible she divined their scheme?

"Very well," she said at last. "I'll dispatch a letter within the week. Though I have my doubts Drake will come, for all that."

Breathing easy for the first time since they'd arrived, Neville summoned enough cheek to ask his grandmother for a drink of something stronger than tea. To his vast surprise, she obliged, and they had an unwontedly convivial visit for a further hour.

As they departed, finally, Phyllipa whispered to Neville. "I'll send my own letter to elaborate on Grandmama's. No matter what the stakes, I don't fancy she'll lay it on quite thick enough."

Neville nodded his approval. "We don't want to take any chances."

From the window of her sitting room, the marchioness watched them go. What were they talking about? she wondered.

It didn't take an oracle to divine they were up to something. What could it be?

Drawing his eyebrows into a stern frown of concentration, Drake pored over the company ledgers in Harold Stokes's

Ullswater countinghouse. For the first time he could recall, the meticulous columns of figures meant nothing to him. Ordinarily, he could glance over a page and spot a missing farthing, or project revenues for the next quarter. Today he did not trust himself to sum one and one.

"Some'ut wrong lad?" Stokes leaned back against the low windowsill, eyeing him with paternal concern.

In the early years of their association, when he'd been no more than a lanky boy with a nose for trade and a burning need to prove himself, Drake had appreciated his shipping manager's respectful deference. As he'd moved from one commercial triumph to another, the balance of their relationship had undergone a subtle shift.

"Wrong?" Drake stiffened. "No, of course not. Just anxious to get back in the traces after all that Christmas nonsense." He peered at the entry for dry dock expenses, hoping by sheer dint of concentration to wrest some meaning from the bald number.

Out of the corner of his eye, he saw Mr. Stokes take a long ruminative draw on his pipe, then blow the smoke out the side of his mouth in one long sustained stream.

"What you did at High Head this Christmas weren't nonsense, lad," he muttered gravely. "Show a man you give a damn about him and his family, that he's not just another name in the wage ledger. He'll pay you back with the kind of loyalty brass can't buy. You mark me—when that mine at High Head gets back into production, it'll be more profitable than you can imagine. Those men will break their backs digging that coal out for you, and all because you brought smiles to their children's faces."

"That's what Lucy said." It surprised Drake to find himself musing aloud.

"A right good head on her shoulders has your wee missus." Harold Stokes chuckled. "A strong backbone to boot, no mistake. I could see that the day she tossed us all out of

Silverthorne on our arses, because she reckoned we were tiring you out.''

All Drake could manage in reply was a sickly grin. He did not dispute Mr. Stokes's admiring assessment of his wife. She certainly did have a good head and a strong backbone. Those were not the physical attributes that had come to preoccupy him until he could no longer concentrate on his work or get a sound night's sleep.

With the earlier rigors of her pregnancy past, Lucy had recently blossomed like a sweet, wild rose. Fortunately, the high-waisted gowns would hide the most obvious sign of her condition for a few months yet.

Ever since Christmas, when he had first tasted her kiss, Drake had often found his gaze lingering upon Lucy, tantalized by the enticing feminine sway of her walk. He did not dare to indulge in such behavior when she was facing him. If he'd chanced to let his eyes dwell on the honeyed sunshine of her hair, the ripe sweetness of her lips, or the creamy bounty of her bosom, his face might have betrayed the wistful hunger that threatened to devour him. His tongue might have lolled out like a poor starving hound's.

Even in the sterile atmosphere of the countinghouse, such thoughts made his body ache for her.

''Besides, lad,'' Mr. Stokes interrupted Drake's provocative fancies. ''You've been in the bliddy 'traces' a sight too long. Broke to the yoke young, you might say. You've had no chance to sow your wild oats and enjoy a bit of fun.''

Drake raised his eyebrows dubiously. ''Fun? In my experience, that is an innocent-sounding title for all manner of dissipation and vice. I assure you I've never felt I was missing out on anything worthwhile by applying myself to my duty.''

''Duty's a fine ideal, lad,'' Mr. Stokes conceded. ''World would be a better place if more folks attended to theirs. But there's all kinds of pleasure in the world, too, and not all of it's a sin. I reckon the secret of a good life is striking the right balance between duty and pleasure. Bit like baking a cake. Too rich with butter, eggs and spices and it's hard on the digestion. Leave them out, and it's scarcely worth the eating.''

This bit of sage advice was leavened with such obvious respect—even affection, that Drake could not bring himself to resent the unwarranted intrusion upon his privacy.

"I had no idea you were such a philosopher, old friend. How would you suggest I go about seasoning this stale cake of mine?"

Looking much relieved that Drake had not taken umbrage at his unsolicited counsel, Mr. Stokes took several short puffs on his pipe. His grin stretched the considerable width of his broad face. "Well, since you've asked…"

Both men laughed.

"I'd say you should spend every spare minute with that fetching lass you've wed. Soon enough she'll have a nursery full of young Stricklands to keep her occupied, I shouldn't wonder. Enjoy this time while there's only the two of you."

Drake felt his features freeze into a tight smile that no longer reflected his mood. There was no such unit as Lucy and him, only the two of them. From the very beginning there had been a third in their marriage—the child, vicariously representing Jeremy.

Even that was not quite accurate, Drake reflected bitterly. He was the third party in the triangle. The interloper. The intruder. An unsatisfactory substitute for the man Lucy wanted by her side and in her bed. The very thought of claiming his place in Lucy's bed roused Drake's body anew, and he found himself resenting it bitterly. He was a begrudged guest at a feast. Not only forbidden to taste the delicacies arrayed before him, he must not touch, smell or even look.

"Take her off to Brighton or Bath for the winter," continued Mr. Stokes, oblivious to the change in Drake's humor. "Enjoy a bit of society. Your overseers have had a taste of running the operations without you. They can manage for a month or two. Trade always slows in the winter anyroad."

"I suppose…" Drake ventured. Perhaps it would do the two of them good to get away from Silverthorne, crammed to the rafters with reminders of Jeremy. "I've a notion to put in an appearance at the House of Lords, to remind our noble peers what their accursed American blockade is costing this country. Particularly those of us who work for a living."

"Capital, lad. Mark me, though. If you mean to go, do it soon. We've had a mild winter so far, but it'll only take one bad storm and who knows but you might be stranded here 'til spring." Mr. Stokes leaned forward to pat him on the arm. "Now quit pretending you see anything worthwhile in that ledger and come join me for a quick pint before you head back to Nicholthwait."

As Drake rode home from Ullswater in the gathering winter twilight, doubts began to nag at him.

London.

For years he had avoided the city, concluding his business on each infrequent trip as swiftly as possible. He'd taken little part in the social doings of his fellow aristocrats, no matter how numerous and insistent the invitations. What man in his right mind would put himself out to be stalked by ambitious mamas, eager to foist their reluctant daughters upon him? Furthermore, Drake had no inclination to expose his painfully inadequate social skills to the derision of people who placed such a high value on eloquence and charm.

Exchanging a desultory greeting with Talbot upon his return to Silverthorne, Drake wandered off to his rooms to bathe and change for dinner. As he went through the motions of his toilette, he continued to ponder the problem. Even if he could reconcile himself to wintering in London, Drake concluded, how would he convince Lucy? It was only when he paused to peruse his mail that the answer became obvious.

"Mr. Talbot?" Lucy intercepted the butler on the way to her rooms to dress for dinner. "Please inform me when his lordship returns." She clutched a crumpled letter tightly in one hand. "There is a matter of some urgency I would—"

"The master's home, Madam." Talbot managed to blurt out this announcement when Lucy paused to gasp a breath. "Has been for nearly a half hour, now. I expect he'll be having his bath at the moment."

"I see." Lucy could feel herself blushing an agonizing shade of scarlet. "In that case, I suppose it must wait until dinner."

As Talbot drifted almost silently toward the stairs, Lucy took a few tentative steps in the direction of her rooms. Once the butler was out of sight, she darted back down the corridor toward the east wing. Not a single second's reflection crossed her mind as she hurried down the dimly lit gallery. Some unknown force animated her body, propelling her against her will—certainly against her better judgment.

On the threshold of her husband's bedchamber she hesitated at last. Her rational self began to protest her mindless, instinctive actions. What did she hope to accomplish by interrupting Drake in the middle of his bath? She was about to turn away when she noticed his door was slightly ajar. All sensible inhibitions drowned in a ravenous wave of curiosity.

Holding her breath, Lucy peeped through the slender crevice between door and jamb. The bedchamber lay in darkness. Only a soft flicker of firelight illuminated the dressing room beyond. It was more than sufficient to show Lucy what she longed to see. Perhaps due to the colder weather, the bathing tub had been set near the hearth, directly in her narrow line of vision.

Wisps of steam rose from the bathwater as Drake bent

forward, splashing a palmful of it on his face. He shook the wetness from his hair and side-whiskers, like a lithe, lean hound. Abruptly, he rose to his feet—naked as Adam. Lucy drew in a sharp gasp of air. All her senses reeled at the sight.

Water sluiced over the long, taut muscles of his flanks. The last drops slid more slowly, in a sinuous caress that Lucy's fingertips ached to trace. As he turned slightly toward her, she could see the beads of moisture glistening on his chest. They clung to the dark, curly thatch matted between two bronze buds. With reluctant anticipation she let her gaze slip lower. Following the crease of fine black hairs that started below his navel, it trailed down to the dense nest at the apex of his hard, lean thighs.

Before she could properly contemplate the rest, Drake grabbed a towel from the back of a nearby chair. He began to rub himself dry with quick, vigorous strokes. With a start, Lucy came to her senses. She shrank from the brooding rapacity that had surged within her as she'd watched Drake. She wanted him—at least her traitorous body did. Wanted him with a deep, savage need she had never felt for any other man. Not even Jeremy.

No!

She'd sworn fidelity to Jeremy's memory. Even if she hadn't, Drake Strickland was the last man for whom she dared entertain such desires. Lucy wrenched her gaze from the alluring, disturbing sight of his bare body. Turning away, she fled back down the gallery as though the hounds of hell were baying at her heels.

She sensed the new intensity which charged his feelings for her—Drake could tell. Judging by her manner, it was obvious she did not approve the change. During the first three courses of dinner, Lucy had scarcely ventured a word. Accustomed as he'd grown to letting her lead their table talk, Drake had no idea how to broach the subject of Lon-

lon. The silence between them spread almost imperceptibly, like the thin, brittle ice of early winter that crept out from the shores of Mayeswater.

Whenever he happened to glance up at her, she appeared determined to avoid his eyes. Drake wished for all the world that Dr. Varoy and Lucy's father had been able to accept their invitations to dinner that evening. Unfortunately, there'd been an outbreak of diphtheria in a poorer section of the village. Both the physician and the vicar had been summoned. Drake could not help feeling like a general charging into battle with his battalion deserting in droves behind him.

He fortified himself with an ungentlemanly swig of his wine. "See here, my dear —"

"Drake, I have a great favour to ask—"

Their abruptly blurted words clashed in the echoing stillness of the dining room.

They both began to laugh. Drake liked the harmony of their voices mingled in mirth. High, clear and sweet, Lucy's laughter trilled a pleasant counterpoint to his own deep chuckle, somewhat rusty from disuse. Holding up his hand to claim the right of first speech, he felt inordinately pleased when Lucy met his eye without glancing skittishly away.

"Name your favor."

"Well..." She did look away then, biting her lip in a manner Drake took to betray nervousness. "I have had a letter from Lady Phyllipa today, coaxing us to come down to London while the weather holds. She says your grandmother is ill."

"That part is true enough," said Drake. "I have a message from Grandmother, herself. She makes light of her ailment, but I can read between the lines. Would you mind terribly if we did go to London? Grandmother and I didn't part on the best of terms, and she is getting on in years."

"Of course we must go." Relief infused Lucy's words,

but also an anxious catch, both of which Drake was at a loss to explain.

"Very well, then. Set to packing. We are for London."

"I suppose we will have to stay with Lady Phyllipa." Lucy's nose wrinkled expressively.

"I can't say I care for the prospect, myself. It would look rather odd for us to rent premises, when I already own the house on Grafton Square. Once we get there, I expect Phyllipa will waste no time trying to pit us against one another again. When I think of all her mischief making this fall, I would dearly love to repay her in kind."

Leaning back in his chair, Drake sipped his wine, mulling over the possibilities. As one particularly amusing notion developed, a slow smile ripened on his lips.

"You've thought of something?" Lucy prompted him.

"Perhaps, but I'd need your cooperation to affect it."

Amber merriment danced in Lucy's eyes. "If you can guarantee it will vex Lady Phyllipa, I am your creature."

"Don't foreswear yourself until you hear what I have in mind," Drake cautioned her. "My cousin appears intent on sowing strife between us. Therefore, I doubt anything would gall her more than to see us billing and cooing like a besotted pair of turtle doves. I propose we play the adoring newlyweds, fawning over each other in a manner quite sickening to behold. Now what do you say to my idea? Are your acting skills equal to the enterprise?"

Young Devonshire press us to stay that extra day. They'll
be looking for us at Alscot and Prees and Blenheim—all
down the line. I don't care much for the looks of that sky
either."

Thick slate-gray clouds brooded menacingly over the
Derbyshire peaks and a few flakes danced on the mists
of lying inland.

grim manner. Lucy could not fathom why. He'd begun their
visit to Chatsworth in good humor, but his manner had deteriorated

things

Surely it was not...

Chapter Thirteen

Were her acting skills equal to playing Drake's lovestruck
bride? That question resonated in Lucy's thoughts as she
stared out the window of the barouche, at the rolling Derbyshire countryside. She stole a quick glimpse at Drake
seated opposite her. Perhaps a more apt question was
whether she could continue to feign indifference for a man
whose physical presence captivated her more with each
passing day.

At least in London there would be welcome distractions.
That had been the chief reason she'd urged him to make the
journey—she needed every distraction available. Her shock-
ing behavior, spying on Drake as he rose from his bath, had
convinced her she could not trust herself alone with him at
Silverthorne.

Besides, London society might not be so terrifying after
all. Not if the rest of the ton treated her as graciously as
their hosts of the past several nights. To break their long
journey south, they had stopped along the way to visit with
relatives of Drake's. They were now an hour out from
Chatsworth where the young Duke of Devonshire had made
them most warmly welcome.

As if her silent musings had somehow communicated
themselves to Drake, he spoke up. "I should never have let

young Devonshire press us to stay that extra day. They'll be looking for us at Anstice and Prees and Blenheim—all down the line. I don't care much for the looks of that sky, either.''

Thick slate-gray clouds brooded menacingly over the Derbyshire peaks and a few tiny flakes danced on the gusts of biting upland wind. Drake's expression looked equally grim, though Lucy could not fathom why. He'd begun their visit at Chatsworth amiably enough, but his humor had deteriorated hourly. By the time they took their leave, his brusque, almost surly, farewell mortified Lucy.

"Surely, you can't hold His Grace to blame for the weather?'' She wondered why the duke had bothered to extend his hospitality to such an ungracious guest.

"Of course, I don't hold him to account for the weather.'' Drake sounded every bit as impatient with her as she was with him. "Only for detaining us.''

"I should never mind being detained in such charming company and such splendid surroundings,'' Lucy retorted.

Drake made no reply for fully a quarter of an hour. The time felt much longer to Lucy. Silence swelled between them, punctured only by the muted tread of the horses and the rattle of the carriage.

Finally, he reached over and rubbed a patch of frost from the carriage window. "You appeared quite as taken with the master as with his house.'' Drake peered out the circle of glass he had cleared.

Even from her seat opposite him, Lucy could see the snow falling at an alarming rate. "As well I might be. Chatsworth is among the finest houses in England. The Duke is a charming gentleman and an attentive host. What a pity he's had to come into the responsibilities of his title at such a young age.''

"Harrumph!'' Drake's expressive dark brows knit together in a look of mingled vexation and concern. "The boy is a good five years older than I was when I came into my inheritance. The Devonshire estate is also considerably more solvent than my father left Silverthorne. Not that I have much confidence of it remaining that way."

"Nonsense," said Lucy before she could stop herself. The young Duke had put her much in mind of Jeremy, with his graceful compliments and subtle gallantries. His company had temporarily eased her foolish infatuation with Drake. She would not stand by and listen to anyone disparage him.

Drake looked away from the window, staring her intently in the eye for the first time in several days. "Give me credit for understanding finances, my dear. All that talk of renovations to the estate—a new wing for the house, improving the grounds, fountains. No fortune is bottomless. Mark my words—he'll end up selling some of those fine pictures to pay for his extravagance."

"Drake Strickland, I do believe you're jealous." She was lying, of course—she believed no such thing. Somehow, though, she sensed it would put him on the defensive.

"Jealous? Me? Of that pup, Devonshire?" Drake looked for all the world as though he wanted to storm away indignantly. If they had been dining at Silverthorne instead of driving along some country lane in Derbyshire, perhaps he would have. "Now who's talking nonsense?"

"Jealous," Lucy persisted, compelled for reasons she could not fathom to goad him into a display of passion—if only a passionate denial. "You can't stand anyone making an unfavorable comparison between Chatsworth and your beloved Silverthorne. Such a ridiculous attitude. Silverthorne needs take second place to no other house in the kingdom."

As the words left her lips, Lucy knew they were true. When they had taken their leave of Nicholthwait, she'd been so absorbed with apprehension about their journey, that she'd scarcely spared a thought to how much she would miss Silverthorne. An unexpected pang of homesickness struck her.

"I have no interest in squandering my fortune on a show-place," said Drake. "Traipsed through by every Tom, Dick and Harry in the county with sixpence to tip the house-keeper."

No sooner had he spoken than the barouche ground to a dead halt. Above them, Lucy heard a volley of anxious shouting between the coachman and the footmen.

Reaching up, Drake gave a peremptory rap on the ceiling of the coach. "Hallo! What's going on out there?"

Lucy heard the driver scramble down from his perch. A few seconds later there came a polite tap on the carriage door. When Drake swung it open, Lucy gasped at the sight outside. The sky, the hills, the road were all an indistinguishable blur of whiteness. Lucy could scarcely see the coachman's blue livery beneath an overcoat of snow. On the top of his hat, flakes had accumulated to a height of several inches.

"What's all the commotion out there?" demanded Drake.

"Begging your pardon, milord." The man bobbed his head, sending a flurry of snowflakes cascading from the top of his hat. "We've overshot our turnoff for Anstice. Missed it in the snow. This bit of road we're on is getting worse by the minute."

"Where are we exactly?" Drake squinted against the glare from the snow as he peered out the carriage door.

"Not sure, milord. This here might be the Nottingham road."

"I'll wager there's not an inn or a house of any consequence between here and Nottingham. Stranded in Sherwood bloody Forest."

"Wouldn't care to push them horses more than another mile in weather like this, milord," said the coachman. "We did pass an inn half a mile back, though. With luck we might make it there before the carriage lands in a ditch or the horses give out.''

"Very well.'' Drake sounded reluctantly resigned. "No sense lolling about on the open road when we can weather the storm under cover.''

"Very good, milord.'' The coachman looked to be drawing his first easy breath in hours.

"You were right,'' said Lucy as Drake pulled the carriage door closed. "We shouldn't have lingered at Chatsworth in January without expecting to pay the price. We should have pressed on for London while the weather held.''

Drake shrugged. "What's done is done.''

"It may not be so bad.'' She tried to reassure him, to ease the anxious tension she read in his eyes. "A country inn can scarcely compare with Chatsworth for accommodations, but I expect we can bear anything for a night or two.''

Drake looked ready to agree with her. Before he could say so, the barouche lurched backward, sending Lucy sprawling into his arms. An instant of heart-pounding shock gave way to equally heart-pounding arousal. His side-whiskers caressed her cheek. Her nostrils flared to inhale his scent. Time slowed for her, drawing out each frantic heart-beat and each erratic breath over many minutes. Tentatively, she began to move her lips across the sharp-hewn plane of his cheek, questing toward his mouth.

"Lucy! Dear God, are you all right?'' Clutching her upper arms, Drake pushed her away, depositing her on the seat beside him. The coach was listing badly back and to the left. "We must have dropped a wheel into the ditch trying to get turned around. Are you hurt? You've gone white as the snow.''

"Just startled, that's all.'' She struggled to regain the tiniest measure of her composure.

"If you're sure,'' said Drake. "The men can probably

use my help with the horses.'' The shrill sound of frightened whinnying confirmed his guess.

"I'm fine." Lucy waved him away. "Go."

Alone in the carriage, she could hear the men calling sharply to one another while the horses continued to protest. The barouche rocked forward and backward several times. Lucy braced herself against this buffeting. It scarcely compared to the emotional tempest that raged within her. She'd been wrong to claim she could stand anything for a day or two.

She could scarcely stand a second or two in Drake's arms without surrendering her self-control.

"I'm afraid this is the best our innkeeper could do." Drake pushed open the door to a tiny gable room so Lucy could enter. "The maidservant usually sleeps here," he continued apologetically. "When she heard me pleading with her master for lodgings, she offered to let us rent it."

Since there was nowhere else in the room to sit, Lucy sank down on the narrow corner bed while Drake shrugged himself out of his sodden greatcoat and hung it on a peg beside the door.

Cramped, drafty, and of dubious cleanliness, even the servants quarters of an indifferent inn provided a welcome haven from the blizzard outside. As he'd struggled to coax the horses on in the teeth of a howling wind, Drake had almost despaired of reaching shelter. He had driven them on, driven himself by a desperate, consuming urge to protect Lucy and her child.

When they finally stumbled into the courtyard of the remote country inn, numb with cold and fatigue, Drake thought he had never seen a more welcome sight. Of sturdy lathe-and-beam construction, the modest old manor house easily dated from Tudor times, if not earlier. His relief had soon given way to dismay, upon finding The Black Cygnet stuffed to the rafters with other guests, also seeking refuge from the storm. When begging and blustering did not move the landlord, Drake had commenced to bribe. An outrageous sum in gold sovereigns changed hands before their party received a belated welcome.

Lucy sniffed the air. "I wonder what's for tea? I'm famished."

"So am I. A more apt question is, what might be *left* from tea? I'll wager this inn is housing more guests just at this minute than in the whole month past."

A most unladylike growling issued from Lucy's stomach. She groaned. "I'll eat anything—bread and drippings. What I wouldn't give for a taste of last night's dinner leavings at Chatsworth."

"Chatsworth! Of course!" Drake's spirits buoyed. "Devonshire's cook packed us a hamper for the road. I'd forgotten it entirely. I'll go fetch that hamper before someone else gets hold of it."

"While you're gone, I'll try to hunt us up a candle." Lucy's stomach gurgled again, even more insistently than before, which set them both laughing.

"Be as quick as you can," she begged.

Drake managed to lay hands on the hamper, blessedly unmolested. Finding it well provisioned, he parceled out some of its bounty to his grateful coachman and footmen. They had found sleeping quarters in the inn's taproom. By the time Drake arrived back at their room, Lucy had secured a candle. It flickered precariously as a chill draft whistled in the chinks around the window casement. The sound made Drake shiver.

"For so small a cupboard, it's not exactly snug, is it?" He set the hamper down beside the bed and bent to inspect the casement. "I doubt this window's been properly caulked since the Restoration."

"We can worry about that later." Lucy burrowed into the hamper, pausing now and then to exclaim over its bounty. "His Grace's cook must have meant to provision us all the

way to London. Here's some of that Derbyshire cheese…
and dried apples…half a pudding. We'll have to eat that
straight away. See here, Drake. I managed to wheedle a little
kettle of hot water. This looks like…why, yes it is…a box
of tea."

Sitting on the bed tucking ravenously into Chatsworth
dainties, they laughed over the day's misadventures. Somehow the food tasted better than it had on the previous evening, piping hot and served on bone china in the Duke's
formal dining room. Tonight Drake had Lucy all to himself—a luxury he basked in.

After they had eaten their fill, Lucy repacked the hamper
with enough to last them several days more. Meanwhile
Drake stuffed the cracks around the casement with strips of
linen torn from one of the napkins. The muted sound of
lusty singing rose from the taproom below.

Drake and Lucy exchanged smiles. "It doesn't sound as
though the men will get much sleep tonight."

Amusement twinkled in Lucy's eyes. "When it does
come, I expect it will be a very sound sleep indeed."

"I hope their racket won't keep you awake. I know it's
early yet, compared to the hours we kept at Chatsworth. If
candles are as scarce as everything else around here, we
should conserve this one by turning in for the night."

"I suppose you're right." A strange, wistful look momentarily crossed Lucy's face. "Try not to match your servants drink for drink, if you please."

"I beg your pardon?"

"You *are* planning to sleep downstairs with the men
aren't you? I thought you said this was the very last room
available."

"So it is." Drake pulled his greatcoat from the peg where
it had been hanging. Though still a trifle damp, it would
serve. He threw it around his shoulders. "However, there's
nothing like a lock on this door. Not that it would do much

good on such a flimsy bit of board. I have no intention of leaving you alone here all night."

Seeing her cheeks suffuse with color, he added brusquely, "Don't worry. I'll roll up in my coat and sleep on the floor." Licking his thumb and forefinger, he quickly snuffed the candle.

Out of the darkness Lucy spoke. She sounded different, now that he could not see her—the pitch of her voice high and thin. "If you think I'll let you sleep on that cold, hard floor, think again, Drake Strickland. Your broken ribs may not have knit completely. You must have put a strain on them today, pushing our carriage out of the ditch and leading the horses."

"I've recovered." Drake eased himself to the floor. In truth, he could feel his muscles beginning to stiffen. The site of his old injury gave a twinge.

Tentative, shuffling footsteps came nearer until...

"Dash it, woman! Do you mean to break my ribs again, kicking me in the back?"

"If you hadn't snuffed the candle in such a hurry..." Lucy grasped his arm forcefully. "Up with you. I don't intend to take no for an answer. If you must sleep in this room, we will share the bed. It might keep us both from freezing."

"If you're cold, I can hunt you up a spare blanket," Drake offered. "That pallet hardly looked big enough for one, much less two."

"I can assure you, there is not a spare blanket to be had in this establishment tonight at any price. I asked while I was after the candle and the water. The landlord laughed in my face. As for size, I do not take up much room. For all your length, you aren't very broad. Provided you don't thrash about in your sleep, we should manage well enough. You needn't fear for your virtue on my account. I give you my word I won't transgress upon your person."

She was laughing at him—the little minx! Drake could

hear it in her voice. If only she knew. It was not the possibility of her transgression that worried him—but his own. Could he abide the temptation of spending a whole night in her bed without succumbing to his desires?

Suddenly the exertions of the day overtook him. He yawned deeply. Easing himself down, he began to pry the Hessians off his cold, stiff feet.

"I'm glad you've decided to be sensible at last." Lucy sounded amazed that he'd given in with so little struggle. "What say we spread your greatcoat and my manteau over this thin counterpane?"

They spent a few awkward minutes trying to find a workable sleeping position. They ended up lying on their sides, like two spoons in a silver chest. Drake faced out, his knees tucked up due to the shortness of the bed, while Lucy snuggled at his back. Much to his surprise, he did not lie awake throbbing with passion for her. That came in the next morning when he woke to find her arm draped over his hip, her limp hand poised tantalizingly over the front of his breeches.

If Lucy had needed further proof of Drake's indifference, his behavior the next morning would have convinced her beyond doubt. While she lay there, wrapped in a stuporous doze that followed a restless night, he leapt up as though he'd been doused with ice water.

"Morning already?" He danced clumsily around the room on one foot, trying to force the other into his boot. "It must be true what they say—if a man is tired enough, he can sleep anywhere."

Lucy slid over to the patch of thin lumpy mattress still warm from Drake's body. "I congratulate you," she grumbled sarcastically, pulling the pile of blankets and coats around her. "I wish I could say the same. Now, *if* you will oblige me, I would like to keep my eyes closed awhile longer."

"Please yourself." Drake retrieved the kettle from the

floor. "With such a crowd here, there'll likely be considerable competition for breakfast, hot water and everything else. I mean to be the early bird."

"Enjoy your feast of worms." Lucy rolled over, pointedly turning her back on him.

After he left on his errands, she heaved a deep sigh of relief. Never in her life had she spent so unsettled a night! Huddled against Drake's back, feeling the gentle rhythm of his breathing, she'd greedily soaked up his warmth. Even through the many layers of clothing they both wore, she could feel the firm lean strength of his body.

Over and over she relived the most intimate moments of their otherwise chaste marriage. Gazing hungrily at his naked body, steaming from the bath. Touching his bare chest while tending his injuries. Clasping him to her bosom in a pitch-dark mine shaft. With each remembrance her physical yearning for him had grown. A queer tingling ache, it had pulsed in her wrists, at her throat, and in the sensitive tips of her breasts. It throbbed most insistently at the apex of her thighs, straining in vain for some relief.

Only twice had she lain with a man, and the two encounters could not have been a greater contrast. Burrowed under musty bedclothes in this chilly little room, Lucy found it almost impossible to imagine the sun-dappled glade where Jeremy had made love to her. It had been like a rosy, lyrical dream—one from which she'd awakened with brutal abruptness.

She'd traded that luminous illusion for a far harsher reality—clinging desperately to a man who promised safety, even warmth. One who turned his back on her at every opportunity, leaving her cold and alone. Why? Lucy asked herself yet again. Why had Jeremy's tender, eloquent seduction failed to rouse the tempestuous desire that Drake went out of his way to discourage?

Last night, it had taken all her restraint to keep from slipping her hand beneath his shirt and making the intimate acquaintance of his bare torso with her fingertips. Lucy shuddered to imagine Drake's reaction if he'd woken to find her fondling him. No doubt he would have hauled her out of bed by the hair and subjected her to a summary lecture on the sin of wanton lust.

Though he protested otherwise, she knew he considered her a scarlet woman for having conceived a child out of wedlock. If not, why did he shy away so skittishly or lash out in righteous wrath whenever she tried to draw close to him? She could not afford to alienate the man any further—her child's future depended upon it.

How was she supposed to stand another night in this tiny room with him, without falling prey to her reckless urges? She must concentrate on Jeremy, Lucy decided at last. Think about him. Talk about him. Encourage Drake to talk about him. Perhaps his gallant spirit would help to subdue the licentious demons that threatened to overpower her.

Booted footsteps sounded in the corridor, coming to a halt before the door. With a light tap, Drake called through, "Are you decent, my dear?"

That, she reflected with a wry smile, was a highly debatable question. "I'm still in bed, if that's what you're wondering. I'm decently covered, however. You may enter."

Enter he did, flashing a triumphant grin and bearing a squat iron brazier. "This may ward off the worst of the cold. If I can scavenge enough coal to fuel it."

He set it in the corner farthest from the bed, then began to ferry other items in from the corridor.

"This shouldn't take up much room." He slid in a small trunk, part of their luggage from the barouche. "It can double as a seat or a table. You might find a change of clothes in it."

Though she knew very well it contained only her undergarments and nightclothes, Lucy did not say so.

After the trunk came the kettle, steam rising from its

spout. A dented, but serviceable enamel basin followed, along with the lap robes from the carriage.

"I let the men have these last night." He piled the lap robes at the foot of the bed. "I hope you don't mind. I fear my charity was misplaced. They assured me this morning that the taproom was quite snug. A few mugs of mulled ale can keep a man as warm as any blanket."

Lucy had never heard Drake rattle on like this. She was not sure what to think of the forced heartiness in his voice, either. It made her uneasy. Emerging from her carapace of coats and blankets, she surveyed his modest bounty. "A profitable expedition I see."

Setting the basin atop the trunk, she poured a frugal measure of hot water from the kettle. "Has the cold lessened since last night, or have I just grown used to it?"

Drake peered out the tiny latticed window. "The wind has veered to the southwest and turned our falling snow to rain. If it keeps up all day, who knows but we might be able to escape this place in another day or two." He could not disguise the eagerness in his voice—if he was even trying.

"The sooner the better," Lucy muttered under her breath. With a day's growth of dark whiskers not yet shaven, Drake looked dangerously attractive. Better they should be on their way, lodging in stately houses that afforded the civilized amenity of separate quarters for a husband and wife.

Desperate to distract herself from the thought of spending another night in bed with Drake, Lucy splashed a palmful of rapidly cooling water on her face. "Tell me about Jeremy. What was he like as a boy?"

Drake wheeled sharply from the window. "I didn't get to see much of him when he was a small child. I was away at school." His voice took on a well-honed edge. "Why do you ask?"

"No reason." Lucy shrugged, trying to keep her tone convincingly casual. "I worshipped him from afar for so long, but I was close to him for so short a time. Is it not natural that I should want to know about the father of my child? You're the only person who can supply me with that information. Anyone else might grow suspicious of my questions.''

Anxious to divert attention from her true motives, she demanded, ''Did your school have no holidays, that you hadn't an opportunity to spend time with your only brother?''

''Oh, we had holidays. I never got invited to pass them in London.'' Almost to himself he added, ''My stepmother had little use for me.''

All that long dull day, as rain melted snow on the Derbyshire hills, Lucy persisted in questioning Drake about his brother. Whenever she ran out of questions, she fell back on recounting the story of her brief courtship with Jeremy. As a distraction from her unchaste desires for Drake, it proved a mixed success at best.

Chapter Fourteen

Perhaps because she'd exhausted herself during the previous wakeful night, Lucy fell asleep before the press of Drake's body overwhelmed all her scruples. Now it was his turn to writhe on the rack of his own desire—and writhe he did.

Heightening his torture was their state of undress. The weather had turned mild and the glowing coals in the brazier further warmed the room. There had been no excuse for them to sleep fully clothed. Extracting a nightgown from her little trunk, Lucy'd told Drake to keep his back turned while she changed for bed. Once he doused the light, Drake reluctantly shed his stock, breeches and boots, to sleep in his long shirt.

Now the blasted garment kept riding up, exposing his bare backside to the occasional brush of Lucy's hand, a sensation that roused him unbearably. Even through the fine linen of his shirt, he could feel the warmth of her breath every time she exhaled. His own breath came faster. But the most exquisite torment was the soft, steady pressure of her deliciously ripe bosom at the base of his rib cage.

How he longed to turn and bury his face in the creamy cleft between her breasts, filling his nostrils with the lush feminine scent of her. His hands ached to explore every delectable inch of her body. His palate craved the intoxicating nectar of her lips. By daybreak, when he could stand it no longer, he was quite delirious with need.

To what end? He could suffer, bleed, even perish for want of her. Lucy had made it abundantly clear that she preferred his brother, dead, to any man alive. Especially him.

She had never talked of Jeremy so constantly as during the past day. Perhaps he had been constantly in her thoughts all these weeks, but she'd refrained from discussing him excessively within earshot of the Silverthorne servants. With that impediment removed, she had shown Drake where her heart lay—where it would always lay.

In the most secret bastion of his own heart, had he cherished a foolish hope that she might forget Jeremy, eventually, and turn to him? If so, he had been a most pathetic idiot. Drake berated himself as he hastily dressed in the feeble light of a grey winter dawn. Had twenty-five years taught him nothing? There was not a soul in the world who had not preferred his handsome, engaging half brother to him. Beginning with their father…and ending with their son, no doubt. Somehow Drake knew, with bitter foresight, that no matter how diligently he toiled to nurture Lucy's child, the boy would inevitably come to venerate the memory of his supposed uncle.

Stealing out of the inn, Drake walked aimlessly for several hours in a cold mist, until his fevered body felt blessedly numb. Returning to The Black Cygnet past noon, he joined the company in the taproom, determined to quench the last embers of his passion for Lucy with the landlord's potent brandy.

But as any wise man knows, alcohol only fuels a blaze.

The candle sputtered to a fitful demise in a puddle of molten wax. The room plunged into darkness, save for the last few embers glowing in the brazier. With a sigh Lucy acknowledged the obvious. Drake had chosen to abandon her for the night in favor of more congenial company.

She'd been sick with worry when, after waking to find him gone, there had been no sign of him by midday. Gazing out the window, she happened to spot him returning to the inn. She worked herself up to give him the scolding he deserved for frightening her so, but he did not put in an appearance. Several hours later, she recognized his distinctive resonant baritone joining in the chorus of a song, in the taproom below. Still, she'd assumed he would return for the night.

Tossing from side to side in the narrow bed, Lucy told herself it felt good to have room to move. How much better she would sleep by herself, as she usually did. She wouldn't need to battle her wayward desires. An altogether more satisfactory arrangement. Save for one minor detail.

She wanted him more than ever.

The cramped little bed felt cavernous and empty without Drake. Grudgingly, Lucy admitted to herself how much she had craved this one last opportunity to be close to him.

An unpalatable question wheedled its way into her thoughts. Where was Drake sleeping tonight, if not with her? If he was downstairs in the taproom, snoring away in some corner chair, she could accept that. But what if he had found his way into some other woman's bed? He was rich, titled and fiercely attractive, in his way. Many women would welcome even a fleeting liaison with such a man.

Perhaps Mrs. Esmond, the stylish young widow stranded here on her way to visit friends in Melton Mowbray? Or Cherry, the innkeeper's buxom daughter? Despite Drake's claim that he cared little for women and his persistent lack of interest in her, Lucy knew men had physical needs they could not long deny. Had their bodily contact over the past two nights stirred a slumbering hunger within him, as it had whetted her own desires?

Gradually, Lucy fell into a fitful doze that was not quite

sleep. Thoughts and images ran through her mind in an exhausting, bewildering spiral. Several times she woke from the grip of a tantalizing dream in which Drake had come to bed and begun making love to her.

When she heard unsteady footsteps approaching in the corridor, some rational portion of her mind insisted she was dreaming again. This time more vividly than ever. Only when the door swung open to reveal Drake's rangy figure silhouetted against the feeble light from the corridor, did Lucy believe he was truly there.

He stumbled into the room, emanating fumes of brandy that Lucy could smell even from the bed. Fearing he might kick over the brazier with his fumbling, she scrambled out from under the covers.

"Be careful, now," she scolded in a whisper, pushing the door closed. "What a state you're in!"

"Ah, Lucy." His slurred words were barely intelligible. He leaned upon her so heavily, she almost gave way beneath his weight. "Did you miss me in your bed, little wife?"

Had she heard him right, or was she hearing what she wanted to hear in his inebriate ramblings? There could be no mistaking the sensations that engulfed her as she felt his hands through the light cloth of her nightgown. During the past two days and nights, desire had saturated her being like oil soaking into dry tinder. It had left her vulnerable to the slightest spark.

"You need to sleep this off." She strove with all her might to ignore her body's pleadings. Her breath came fast and shallow. Her limbs trembled to contain their wanton inclinations. "Let's just get your coat and boots off and untie your stock, so it doesn't strangle you."

Somehow she managed to pry his coat off. He staggered, and she caught him in her arms, driven to extremity by the delicious prickle of his unshaven whiskers against her brow. She remembered the taste of his kiss on Christmas night.

That was not the kind of kiss she wanted from him now.

Her fingers fumbled with his neck linen as he steadied himself by grasping her hips. Compelled by some elemental force that defied all logic and all propriety, her quivering hand brushed his bare neck. It trailed down to his breastbone.

"Dear God, Lucy, don't tempt me!" The plea broke from his lips. Or was it a warning?

Suddenly, she did not care. She was past mercy and miles beyond caution, caught in the potent undercurrents of forbidden desire. Her hand snaked back up his neck, twining her fingers in his hair. She felt him clutch convulsively at the rounded, sensitive flesh of her backside.

Gripping his hair with savage strength, she thrust his face toward hers, assaulting his lips. He fought back, vanquishing her with a deep, probing kiss that tasted of the brandy—hot, sweet and potent.

"Please," he moaned, even as his lips ravished her face. "Understand…a man has needs…a husband's rights."

Though she heard his barely coherent ramblings, Lucy was deaf to everything but the rapid hiss of his breath and the pounding gallop of her own pulse. He might have pulled her down, or she might have pushed him. Perhaps they both collapsed under their reckless assault on one another. As Drake fell, he clutched at the throat of her nightgown. The cloth rent from collar to hem with a high, ecstatic screech.

Lucy gasped as the cool air licked her fiery skin. She gasped again when she landed on top of Drake, and her bare thigh brushed the straining iron of his arousal. They grappled with each other, rolling sideways, until he hovered above her. His chin scratched an incendiary trail over the aching fullness of her breast. His lips parted and his tongue licked out, swiping thirstily over the responsive peak. In a rush of anguished urgency and wild pleasure, Lucy cried out.

In that pulsating instant, she could imagine no greater fulfilment than yielding to his strength. Obliterated beneath the onslaught of his power. Consumed in the white-hot flame of their shared passion. Her body resonating to the thrilling sensations unleashed by his ravenous attentions, she thrust herself against him. Returning kiss for bruising kiss.

As though from a far distance, Drake heard Lucy's frantic cry. For a moment it only spurred him on in his urgent quest for release. Then, vaguely, he sensed her desperate struggle beneath him. Even as it inflamed some ancient urge to mastery, a faint voice deep within his heart whispered for restraint. What if he hurt Lucy—or damaged the fragile life growing within her?

The very thought made him recoil from the precipice. Profoundly as he wanted this woman, he could not risk doing harm to her or the child. Summoning his last shred of self-control, he pushed free of her. As he lurched from the room, her terrified sobs dogged his footsteps.

Drake's ears had not deceived him.

As he lumbered away from her, Lucy lay on the bed, exposed and vulnerable, weeping the bitterest tears of her life. In part, they were tears of fear. Fear that she might have harmed her unborn child while in the grip of her feral passion. In part, they were tears of disgust. Disgust with herself for betraying Jeremy's memory. More than Lucy cared to admit, they were tears of frustration.

She had been racing toward the brink of some unimaginable delight, poised to soar. Now she was empty and alone, thwarted in her desire. Curling herself into a tight, protective ball, she whimpered Drake's name.

Tonight, for the first time, he had succumbed to the exigency of his own manhood, enough to admit that she "tempted" him. No doubt that was how he had always viewed her—as a temptress. One who had enticed his brother into an unwise alliance, then parlayed the result of that liaison into an advantageous match with him. What a wonder that the rigorously moral viscount should consider besmirching himself to bed such a woman. Even if she was his wife.

Yet he had been willing. Downright eager, in fact. Until she had betrayed her true colors by responding to his advances with wanton aggression. Then he'd pushed her away in revulsion. Now she would never experience the bliss she had dimly glimpsed in his arms.

God in Heaven, how could she ever face him again?

His own shivering jarred Drake to consciousness the next morning. Peering through eyelids he could not open more than a slit, he wondered exactly where he was and how he had managed to get there. The pungent aroma of horse muck was his first clue.

Trying to still his chattering teeth, he pulled something tighter around his upper body. Evidently, it had kept him from freezing in the night. Drake recognized the coarse weave of a horse blanket—his second clue. It reeked of stale brandy and vomit. The smell made his gorge rise ominously. Drake dimly recalled that the vomit was probably his own.

So he had spent the night on the rough floor of the stable, with only a stinking horse blanket for cover. Where was his coat? How had he come to the stable in the first place? The last he remembered was ordering a cup of brandy in the taproom. Drake tried to rise, but the abrupt explosion of pain in his head made him drop to his knees again. Mother of mercy, had he been waylaid and bludgeoned on his way to bed?

Bed.

The thought sent a chill through Drake more intense than any caused by the January frost. It sickened his stomach to a far worse pitch of nausea than that inflicted by his drinking binge. His head alternately whirled and throbbed with memories he would rather have kept at bay. They refused to retreat tamely.

He recalled staggering up the narrow back staircase of the

inn, the fire in his loins conquering all reason. The room had been dark and Lucy asleep. She'd wakened, though, and come to him. His next recollections were a chaotic tangle of sound, touch…and taste. As the memory of nuzzling Lucy's bare breast returned to him with breathtaking clarity, Drake felt himself harden.

For a moment he concentrated avidly on retrieving every sensation from their brief, frenzied tryst. No matter how he tried to savor each sensual detail, there could be no denying the sordid facts. Blind drunk, he had forced himself on her, torn her nightgown and thrown her across the bed. In spite of her passionate resistance, he had very nearly taken Lucy against her will. Even Jeremy, who had casually seduced and abandoned her, had not been so gross a cad. Waves of nauseating shame constricted Drake's innards. There, on the stable floor of a third-rate country inn, Viscount Silverthorne retched the last drops of bile from his heaving stomach.

"Waste of expensive brandy, that, if you don't mind my saying so, milord," boomed a cheerful voice.

"I do mind your saying so." Drake spat, but the acrid taste of guilt clung to his tongue. "I mind anyone saying anything at that volume and with such vexing good humor. Why do you look none the worse for last night?"

The towering young footman doffed his coat and wrapped it around Drake's shivering form. "Not that I weren't obliged by your hospitality, milord. 'Specially after the brass you put out for those two bottles. Landlord'll be able to retire on what he charged you. I stuck with the local ale. What yer doin' out here in the cold anyroad, milord? Couldn't find a basin to puke in?"

"If it's any of your damned business, I took a wrong turn on my way to bed. I spent the night out here."

"Shall I run and tell her ladyship I've found you?" the boy offered eagerly. "She'll be right worried that you never made it up to bed."

"Don't trouble yourself," Drake headed out into the

courtyard at a cautious pace. No doubt, Lucy's only worry was that he might return in the night to hurl himself upon her again, like some heat-maddened beast.

"It's time we got the hell out of here," he said. "Tell the others we'll be leaving as soon as I can make myself presentable."

The entry hall of The Black Cygnet seethed with activity as Drake ventured in. Clearly, the other guests were in no mood to linger when an opportunity of escape had presented itself. Haphazard piles of luggage leaned drunkenly against the wainscotting, while their owners barked directions to servants and pestered the innkeeper to prepare their bills.

Spotting the innkeeper's wife waddling down the stairs, he advanced to meet her. With every jarring step, his temples throbbed. As much as any of the guests jostling for the landlord's attention, he wanted to be clear of The Black Cygnet, and its shameful memories. Yet he could not possibly appear at Prees in his present state.

"Begging your pardon, ma'am." He bowed slightly to the harried-looking woman. "Might I trouble you for the temporary use of a vacant room?"

She swiped a lock of dingy graying hair from her broad forehead. "Take your pick, milord, I'm sure. At this rate the whole inn will be empty by noon." With that she descended into the fray in the entry hall.

Drake turned to his footman. "Go fetch my brown leather case from the carriage. Then see if you can chase me up some hot water. I need a wash, a shave and fresh clothes before we get back on the road."

That was precisely what he needed. Soap and scalding hot water to purge the stench of drunken lechery from his body. A lethal-edged razor to shear his face smooth and make him look less like a ravaging black beast. Fresh, pristine clothes, that did not exude a faint tantalizing scent of Lucy. Perhaps if he did all that, he could begin to forget what he had done last night. And perhaps he could convince

Lucy that he had no memory of his actions. It might be his only hope for holding on to her.

Drake quailed at the thought of facing her again, and of the enforced intimacy of their carriage ride to Prees.

He handed the footman back his coat. "Once you've done all that, go tell my wife to prepare for our departure two hours hence."

If he wondered why Viscount Silverthorne did not choose to deliver that message himself, the lad was wise enough to hold his tongue.

Chapter Fifteen

As their barouche rolled along the king's highway into London, Lucy felt the lump of apprehension in her throat swell with every mile. She stole a glance at Drake, who leaned back in the seat opposite her with his eyes shut. He was only feigning sleep, she suspected. Possibly for the same reason he had pretended intense curiosity in the news from *The Spectator*. Both were useful dodges to avoid speaking.

They had scarcely exchanged a dozen words since their abrupt departure from The Black Cygnet. On that first day, as they rode to Prees, she had cringed in terror at his every glance. She knew he would soon castigate her for her licentious behavior. Perhaps he would go even further. Might he decide that a wanton woman had no business raising his heir?

From the moment she realized her condition, Lucy had conjured up a vivid image of her future child. Fair, like his father. All plump and dimpled, with soft golden curls and a gurgling laugh. For a time she clung to that vision, as the one solace for her aching heart. As the hurt eased, she came to love her dream baby for his own sake.

She fancied herself beaming with pride as she passed him to his grandfather at the baptismal font of Saint Mawes. She pictured herself holding his tata-laces as he took his first staggering steps in the Silverthorne nursery. She imagined herself keeping a slow pace on her horse, as he jogged along beside her on a sturdy pony. His birth was still months away, and already she cared for him with fierce maternal affinity.

Of late, Drake had begun to figure in her sweet musings on the future, but now he loomed as a possible threat. Her insides constricted at the realization of how much power he held over her and her child. Three words returned to haunt Lucy. Words she had scarcely heeded in the grip of passion, intent only on stilling Drake's lips with her own.

A husband's rights.

In the heat of her desire, they might have sounded like a most seductive invitation. In the cold light of day, Lucy recognized them for a dire threat. A husband had rights— to a woman's property, to her body, to her children. A wife had none. Even the grievous right to dissolve a marriage belonged to the husband alone. No matter how he abused, neglected or betrayed her, she was his for as long as he wanted her. If he no longer wanted her, he could divorce her on false charges of adultery.

Sneaking a furtive glance at Drake's closed, dark countenance, Lucy wished she could read his thoughts. Anything, to gain an idea of where she stood with him.

Gradually, the scene outside the carriage window caught her attention. Buildings now clustered more densely along the roadside and the traffic had grown heavier, particularly in the opposite direction. As the winter daylight faded and twilight fell, the market vendors and street hawkers had begun wending their way homeward to small farms on the fringe of the city.

Opening his eyes at last, Drake adjusted his cravat and cleared his throat.

Casting her own eyes modestly downward, Lucy tried to swallow the astringent taste of fear in her mouth. Would it come now—the blast of wrath she'd been dreading for the past three days? In the stately houses where they'd stopped, their hosts had carried the conversation, with only occasional answers from her and Drake. For fear of rousing in him any slumbering memories of their last night at The Black Cygnet, Lucy had held her tongue. What kept Drake silent, she could only guess.

He cast her a searching glance. "I trust you have not forgotten your promise?"

Lucy felt herself blanch. Her promise—never to love him. She had given Drake ample cause to believe she'd broken that vow. How could she explain that love was not the reason she had flung herself at him that night at the inn? It would only confirm his worst opinion of her character and morals.

As she desperately searched for words, their carriage drew to a halt before an elegant town house on Grafton Square.

"Well?" Drake sounded impatient, to say the very least. "Are you still willing to help me repay Phyllipa for her meddling by playing the lovebirds?"

A wave of relief broke over Lucy, almost as intense as the previous wave of panic. "Oh, that promise! Yes...of course."

He held her hand as she lit from the barouche box, tucking it securely into the crook of his elbow as they mounted the steps to the entry.

"You'll have to bear more than your part in all this," he muttered, sidelong. "I'm no good at love talk and such. No practice."

"It won't be so bad," Lucy found her voice at last. "If you run into trouble, just pretend you're Jeremy, and say what you think he would say."

"What will you do when you run into trouble?" Drake asked.

Lucy felt her vital organs knotting. Her greatest trouble

would be keeping her feelings for this man in the realm of playacting. Straining to keep her tone casual, she replied, "Why I shall pretend you are Jeremy, too."

"Still no sign of the newlyweds, what?" Neville Strickland surveyed the drawing room of Drake's town house through his monocle, as though he might conjure them by sheer dint of concentration. "You're certain they're on their way?" He gave Phyllipa a faintly suspicious look.

"I have Drake's letter." She clutched the paper like a talisman. "It's dated over a fortnight ago and he writes that they planned to set out at once."

"You don't suppose any ill has befallen them?" Despite his effort to feign familial concern, Neville could not fully censor a note of gleeful calculation from his voice.

"The way matters stood between them when I left Silverthorne, it would not surprise me if they tore each other to pieces before they ever reached London."

From her simpering smile, Neville got the feeling Phyllipa wanted him to pat her on the head for a job well-done. He forced a wan grin in reply. His own head still throbbed in retribution for a very gay rout at Randall's the night before, aggravated by the worrisome attentions of his creditors. At the reports of his cousin's sudden marriage, most of them made no secret they regarded his expectations as transient, at best. He'd show them. He'd show them all.

"I still say it was deucedly irresponsible of you to return to London without them." Though he reminded himself they were allies, Neville could not resist pricking Phyllipa's bloated air of self-satisfaction.

She wrinkled her long nose. "That's all very well for you to say, Neville. You weren't exiled to that godforsaken wilderness, without a scrap of proper society, and the most idle, insolent pack of servants. Poor Reggie was quite fading away from the dreadful food."

Neville rolled his eyes. Could her maternal partiality truly see that bun-shop-on-legs as the frail, sensitive creature she made him out to be?

"Besides—" Phyllipa turned to the mantel, fussing with several curios, arranging and rearranging them. "—by the time I took my leave of Silverthorne, Drake and Lucy could scarcely abide the sight of each other. With him facing a protracted convalescence from his injuries—you can just imagine the state of his temper. Like a badger with a sore head."

"Indeed." Neville felt himself lapsing into a smile, just picturing the scene. His own headache began to subside. Perhaps all was not lost.

"I have done my part." Abandoning her preoccupation with the objects on the mantel, Phyllipa rounded on him. "Now don't you think it high time to tell me about yours? What brilliant plan have you hatched to send our young viscountess bolting for the Continent?"

Could he trust her with such information? Neville asked himself as he eyed his cousin's widow dubiously. The bulging eyes were as bland a blue as ever, but he detected a slight tilt of resolution in the pointy little chin.

"On one condition. Fetch me a spot of brandy. I'm parched."

With a reproachful sigh, Phyllipa swept over to a low table by the window and unstopped a decanter. Tipping a parsimonious drop into a glass no bigger than a thimble, she bestowed it upon him like Lady Bountiful dispensing largesse to the poor.

Neville inhaled the brandy's bouquet and made a face. A potion of such indifferent quality scarcely merited his telling her the time of day.

"Oh, very well," he snapped in response to her expectant goggling. "If they are as much at odds as you say, it shouldn't be difficult to part them for good and all. First I shall drop a few well-placed hints to make certain her ladyship receives a very chilly reception in London society."

"Is that all?" Phyllipa sniffed. "A country parson's daughter snares one of the wealthiest gentlemen of title in England and you think it'll take *your* urging to have her shunned?"

Neville bolted his mean little allowance of brandy in a single gulp. "I didn't say it was going to be difficult, though we must tread carefully. You know how Drake loves to champion the underdog. If he takes a notion that his wife's being unfairly persecuted, he'll stick by her in spite of the ton. No. We must subtly goad her into committing several breaches of etiquette. Perhaps then our dear cousin will see how imprudent it was for him to rush into a match with such disparity of birth and fortune."

"Can we make life unpleasant enough for Lucy that she will abandon the security of a wealthy marriage?"

"That is where the second phase of my plan comes in. Having rendered life with Drake quite intolerable, we must present her with a superior alternative."

"What sort of alternative?"

"A young, handsome, charming alternative, my dear Phyllipa. While everyone else is treating her with icy contempt, we'll find a gallant blade to give Lucy a very warm reception indeed."

For a moment Phyllipa looked blank, as though his words were having difficulty penetrating her torpid mind. Then a look of transparent admiration came over her. "Oh, Neville. You are clever! Have you anyone in mind?"

Neville could not resist preening a little. Admiration, even from the likes of Phyllipa Strickland, was heady stuff. Drake's young bride would soon find that out—to her detriment. Puffing up his cravat he replied, "As a matter of fact, I…"

The sound of voices and footsteps in the entryway arrested his words. After a hasty knock, the butler appeared briefly to announce the arrival of Viscount and Lady Silverthorne.

"Take their wraps and show them in, Moss. Then let Cook know we'll have company for supper." Phyllipa glanced at Neville. One pale thin brow raised and a gloating smile tugged at the corner of her bloodless lips. "Will you join us?"

"To welcome our dear cousins to London?" Though his stomach rebelled at the mere notion of food, Neville could not resist. "I would not miss the opportunity on any account. I believe this calls for a celebration. Moss, why don't you scour the cellar for a decent bottle of claret?"

When the butler looked to Lady Phyllipa, she nodded, though not before treating Neville to a petulant frown. "Pray, show the viscount and his wife in, Moss, *before* you go poking about in the wine cellar."

"Very good, madam."

The travelers soon entered, looking none the worse for their long journey, so far as Neville could see. He and Drake exchanged a manly handshake, while the ladies gingerly touched cheeks.

"What a time you have taken getting here," Phyllipa fussed at Drake. "We were beginning to worry."

For a man reported to be at odds with his wife, Drake hovered around her a good deal more closely than Neville would have liked. "I must apologize, Cousin Phyllipa. Did my letter create the impression we'd be pressing straight through? We broke our journey with relatives along the way." He laid a hand on Lucy's shoulder. "Made a delayed honeymoon of it."

"Oh," said Phyllipa.

When Drake started to withdraw his hand from her shoulder, his wife reached up and caught it in her own. "A snowstorm stranded us in the Midlands for a few days, but no harm befell us." She glanced back at her husband, and the pair exchanged a look that Neville could not read.

He did mark the blush that rose in Lucy's cheeks, however. He marked something else as well. Drake's bride was a deucedly fine-looking filly. He had not thought so at the time of their wedding—too scrawny and pallid. Though she still fell short of his plump, saucy ideal of her sex, she had acquired an indefinable luster. The kind that might melt even as implacable a pillar of granite as Viscount Silverthorne.

A surge of panic rose in Neville's gorge.

"Is there time for us to wash and change before supper?" asked Drake.

"What?" The question roused Phyllipa from her stupor. "Oh, of course." A lifetime of toadeating asserted itself. "You are our honored guests. We dine at your pleasure."

"You forget yourself, my dear," snapped Neville. All his banked irritation with Phyllipa burst into open flame. "Drake is the master of this house. It is you and Reggie who live here by his sufferance."

She shot him a poisonous look, her thin lips drawn into so tight a line as to be almost invisible. "Do you never forget *your* reliance on Drake's charity, Neville?"

"Come now, cousins." Drake chuckled with a warm note of genuine amusement, such as Neville had never heard from him. "I may hold the deed to this place. However, since I scarcely darken the doorstep once a year, even I think of it as Phyllipa's home. For the duration of our stay, she is our hostess and we are her guests."

"Her honored guests." Lucy's eyes twinkled with a kind of merriment Neville neither liked nor understood. It was as though the pair of them were privy to some joke, which no one else shared.

"If you wish to change for supper, your rooms are ready. As they have been for almost a fortnight." Clearly, Phyllipa could not resist needling them further on that score. "I have repapered your room since last you were here, Drake. Lucy, I have put you in the west corner bedchamber. It has a fine view of the square."

"Oh." Drake sounded disappointed. "I suppose separate

quarters are a good idea. Lucy complains so of my taking the lion's share of the bedclothes.''

"Drake Strickland!'' His wife slapped his arm in playful horror. "Such things to talk of in company!''

Seizing her from behind, Drake wrapped his arms around Lucy, resting his chin on the crown of her head. "Neville and Phyllipa are family, my sweet. Besides, everyone excuses newlyweds for their foolish fondness.''

Neville could scarcely believe his eyes. He knew superstitious country folk talked of the fairies stealing infants and leaving changelings behind. He wondered what horde of elfinkind it had taken to abduct his cousin. The man in this room must be an imposter. No other explanation could account for his present behavior.

Nuzzling Lucy's ear, Drake murmured, just loud enough for Neville to catch, "Never fear, my angel. I'm not so unfamiliar with this house that I cannot find my way around in the dark.''

Pressing her fingers to his lips, Lucy protested, "I must get you out of here, before you embarrass me beyond recovery. The west room sounds fine, Cousin Phyllipa. Thank you for coming ahead to London and preparing so warm a welcome for us.''

The pair of them ambled off, arm in arm. Looking deep into each others' eyes. Whispering and laughing together.

When he judged they were well out of earshot, Neville turned on Phyllipa. "I wonder they didn't tear each other to pieces on the journey from Nicholthwait—in a bloody fit of passion! If that's your idea of a couple at odds, I'd hate to see a devoted pair.''

Phyllipa wilted onto the settee, fanning her face with her hand. "They weren't like this when I left. Of that I can assure you. They were scarcely speaking. I can't think what has come over them. I have never seen Drake…''

"Smile?'' hissed Neville. "Laugh? Jest? Behave like a

love-struck schoolboy? Perhaps the dunt on the head he took at that mine has addled his wits.''

''Whatever shall we do now?'' Phyllipa wailed into her handkerchief. ''All is lost!''

''I'll be damned if it is.'' Neville paced the Persian hearth rug furiously.

''Be sensible.'' Phyllipa wiped her ruddy nose. She was a revolting sight with those pale eyes swollen and her sallow complexion all blotchy. ''We've lost. If we ever had a chance of winning in the first place. We're right back where we started before Jeremy died.''

''Not quite. Until that filly foals, I am my cousin's heir. This is no time to lose our nerve. We must redouble our efforts—hold fast to our plan and see it through.''

''Plan?'' The word burst from Phyllipa like a hiccough. ''Get the ton to snub her and set some rogue to woo her?''

''Not just any rogue.'' Neville toyed with his quizzing glass, turning it over and over with his fingers as he rummaged his memory for faces and names. ''We need the very prince of rogues. He won't come cheap, though, if he's to be had at all. Can you lay hands on some money?''

''You're quite mad, Neville, if you think I'll sink a ha'penny into this ridiculous plot of yours.'' Phyllipa blew her nose quite forcefully, as if to signal the end of their discussion.

Neville sank onto the settee beside her. ''You'll find the money,'' he predicted in a smooth mocking tone. ''Because you can't abide the notion of Reggie bowing and scraping to that woman's children and living on their charity.''

Her bland features hardened then. The flesh of her face drew taut. Squeezing her innocent handkerchief in a death grip, she kept her eyes averted from Neville, staring straight ahead. She sat silent for some little time, while he waited patiently for the answer he knew would come.

''How much will you need?''

* * *

Drake and Lucy were barely halfway up the stairs, when she put a hand to her lips in a vain effort to stifle an ungovernable burst of laughter.

"Ssh!" Drake nodded at the stiff back of the housemaid striding several brisk steps ahead of them.

"I can't help it," whispered Lucy. "Did you see their faces? I feared your Cousin Neville was going to take a fit of apoplexy."

Suddenly, Drake found it difficult to restrain his own laughter. His heart lightened for the first time in weeks. It felt good.

"Phyllipa's eyes—did you ever see a toad stepped on?"

Lucy almost bent double with silent mirth, perhaps unaware that he still held her hand in his. For a fleeting moment, the ever present fear had left her eyes. Drake felt like his heart had escaped from somewhere dark and suffocating. He almost warmed to Phyllipa and Neville for making this ruse necessary.

"You put on a most convincing act." As he bent to whisper the compliment, a stray tendril of Lucy's hair brushed against his cheek. Drake had never been struck by lightning, but just then, he could imagine how it might feel.

She turned her gaze full upon him, her eyes twinkling with mischievous merriment and a hint of warmth that pierced him to the core. "You, on the other hand, laid it on far too thick. I may blush all over again remembering it—usurping the bedclothes!"

"I seem to recall you grumbling something to that effect after our first night at The Black Cygnet." The instant the words left his mouth, Drake longed to recall them.

Lucy stiffened and averted her eyes.

Fortunately, at that moment they reached her bedchamber. After a brief flirtatious exchange, staged for the benefit of Phyllipa's housemaid, they took leave of each other to dress for supper. As Drake washed and then changed his clothes, he sensed his pulse quickening in anticipation of the meal.

Lucy might be prepared to ignore or excuse his outrageous conduct at The Black Cygnet, but she had obviously not forgotten it. In the coming weeks, he must do everything within his power to convince her he posed no threat.

Drake ran a finger along his cheek, where the merest brush of her hair had seared him. Was he equal to the challenge?

Chapter Sixteen

From her corner seat in a quiet receiving room at Almack's, Lucy raised her fan and gave it a dispirited flutter. The purpose of her action was twofold. The first, to cool a bright flush that blazed in her cheeks. The second, to make her as inconspicuous as possible. This evening was their first true "night out" since arriving in London. If it was a sample of what she could expect for the duration of their stay, it boded for a very long winter indeed.

Drake had put on his attentive show beforehand, for Phyllipa's benefit. Upon their arrival he had dutifully made her introduction to the Lady Patronesses who welcomed her with gushing cordiality that scarcely masked their predatory eyes. After a single stiff dance, he had wandered off to engage some political acquaintance, abandoning her to Lady Phyllipa's chaperonage.

In the hour that had followed, Lucy had discovered the penalty for daring to interlope in a class to which she'd not been born. Everyone had been unfailingly courteous. Behind their mannerly facade, however, they'd made her run a gauntlet of innocent-sounding questions calculated to trip her up, and jests that she did not comprehend. All the while, they'd watched and judged, declaring their opinion of her subtly with a raised eyebrow or the flare of an aristocratic nostril.

More than anything, she longed to flee their civilized baiting and never venture out into London society again. All that held her back was the thought of her child—and her husband. These people represented her child's future, and she meant to win them over. Tonight was not the time to start. Let them have their fill of staring and laughing and gossiping behind her back. If she deported herself modestly, some of them might relent later.

"My dear Lady Beechum, good evening." A smooth, masculine voice hailed the ancient relation of Drake's to whom Lucy had attached herself. "What a pleasant surprise to discover you in town! I trust Godfrey and Horace are well."

"Eh? What do you say?" Her ladyship inclined a less-than-sound ear to the gentleman who had taken the seat beside her.

"Your nephews." He pronounced the words slowly and at great volume. "Godfrey and Horace—they are well, I trust?"

Fixing the questioner with a rheumy glare, Lady Beechum snapped, "Flourishing, like all scoundrels."

He greeted her testy remark with a gust of free, amiable laughter. "Dear madam—as bracing a wit as ever!"

Lowering her fan by a degree or two, Lucy scrutinized the man who had so agreeably engaged a neglected old lady. First she spied a well-groomed head of ash-blond hair, and expressive eyebrows in a darker shade. Then, an appealing pair of eyes, a clear candid blue in color. As Lucy watched, they glanced her way, transfixing her in a gaze of obvious admiration.

Blushing, she abruptly raised the fan and ducked her head.

"I vow, Lady Beechum, the unexpected pleasure of our meeting has quite driven off my manners. I fear I have escaped the happiness of an introduction to your fair companion.''

"Oh, this chit. She's Silverthorne's bride.''

He replied so quietly, Lucy knew he did not intend the words for Lady Beechum. "Has the new viscountess a name of her own?''

Letting her fan fall again, she marked his straight slender nose and wide, frank smile.

"Lucy," she murmured.

"Lucy," he repeated, lingering over each syllable as though savoring their taste on his tongue. "'Gayer than the blush on roses are the glories on her face.' I consider it a grave misfortune for the company that our most beautiful adornment should conceal herself in a dim, quiet corner. Would you do me the honor of a dance? I feel it my aesthetic duty to put your charms on greater display.''

Lucy hesitated. "I am a married woman, sir. Should you not be dancing with the debutantes?''

"On the contrary, dear lady.'' A shadow of wistful sorrow darkened his clear blue eyes. "You see, I have recently suffered a grave disappointment in love.''

Lucy's heart warmed in sympathy at the regretful catch in his voice.

"This is my first social engagement since it happened,'' he continued. "I could not bear to risk my vulnerable affections so soon again.''

He smiled bravely. "I do enjoy a dance, though. A married lady like you would make the ideal partner.''

"I suppose…'' Lucy glanced at Lady Beechum, ready to ask if she would object to their deserting her.

She discovered that her companion had lapsed into a peaceful doze. Common sense informed Lucy that it would be the better part of valor not to disturb her ladyship.

"I earnestly entreat you, dear lady. Take pity on a heartbroken man. Do him the favor of providing a few moments' precious distraction from his sorrow.''

Extending her hand, Lucy smiled. "I count your invitation as great a favor as you deem my acceptance, sir."

"Then you are gracious as well as beautiful, Lady Silverthorne. Your husband is a fortunate man indeed."

Lucy bit her lip. "You may be the only person present who holds that opinion, sir." Marking the censorious stares that followed their progress to the dance floor, she explained, "Perhaps you have not heard of my origins. My father is a simple country vicar in the Lake District. I am quite devoid of fortune or aristocratic connections. I have nothing to recommend me as a wife to His Lordship."

They paused a moment before joining the other dancers marshaling for a set of Sir Roger de Coverley.

"Nonsense! I recognize no fortune but abundant wit and no peerage but that of superior understanding."

Buttressed by her partner's charming reassurances, Lucy took the floor on his arm with her head held high. The new lightness in her heart soon communicated itself to her feet. Almost before she realized it, she had executed three separate dances with ever increasing confidence and gaiety. As the music concluded for the third, however, she protested a need to stand out and take some refreshment before continuing.

"How thoughtless of me, dear Lady Silverthorne! Pray let me get you a cup of punch. I can't think when I last committed such a lapse in manners. I can only plead my enjoyment of your company, and my pride in squiring you this little while."

Lucy hastened to assure him that she had also enjoyed their dances. She did not take the least notice of Lady Phyllipa until Drake's cousin suddenly appeared directly in front of her.

"Enjoying your first evening in society I see, Lucy. To think how you resisted coming to London. I had no notion you were such an accomplished dancer."

"There are assembly rooms even in the wilds of Cumberland, Cousin Phyllipa,'' Lucy answered in a bantering tone born of her newfound assurance.

''Of a kind, I suppose, but do you find many partners as agreeable as your present one? I don't believe we have met. Will you do me the kindness of an introduction?''

''Of course. Lady Phyllipa Strickland, may I introduce…'' Plundering her memory for a name, Lucy realized in horror that she had not the slightest clue of her partner's identity. ''I…that is…''

That instant of utter mortification stretched on interminably. How could she have committed such folly? To dance—not once but thrice—with a man to whom she had not received a proper introduction.

As Lucy stammered and reddened, trying desperately to fight back a burst of tears that would complete her humiliation, her partner spoke. His words were the sweetest she had heard in a very long time.

''I fear the excitement of the evening has affected Lady Silverthorne's memory. I am of far less consequence than most of the persons she has met so far this evening. My old friend, Lady Beechum, was good enough to introduce us. I am Eugene Dalrymple. Perhaps you have heard of my aunt, the Duchess of Swansea.''

Mr. Dalrymple glanced up at Lucy as he bowed over Phyllipa's hand. Merriment twinkled in his blue eyes. A look of shared confidence passed between them, of such intimacy that Lucy dared not sustain it.

''Mr. Dalrymple, of course,'' Phyllipa gushed. ''Who has not heard of your lady aunt? She is abroad, I believe?''

''Indeed, Lady Phyllipa. How kind of you to inquire. She has taken up residence in Naples where the climate is better suited to her delicate health. I am in London temporarily to oversee her affairs, but I expect to rejoin her soon.''

''Her Grace is fortunate to have such a devoted nephew.''

Mr. Dalrymple nodded toward Lucy. ''Your family is fortunate to have gained such a delightful addition.''

Lady Phyllipa gave a fleeting and insincere smile, even by her usual standards. "Where has Drake got himself off to, Lucy? He has been somewhat lax tonight in his duties as an attentive bridegroom."

Again the gallant Mr. Dalrymple rode to Lucy's rescue. "Viscount Silverthorne? Why, I saw him some little while ago, deep in talk with Lord Lonsdale. Urgent Parliamentary business by the sounds of it. His Lordship asked me to deputize for him on the dance floor, until he could extricate himself from the conversation."

Lucy felt certain that Drake had done nothing of the sort. However, the explanation appeared to mollify Phyllipa, as well as several blatant eavesdroppers nearby. As she sipped her punch and chuckled appreciatively at Mr. Dalrymple's amusing stories, she was struck by his similarity to Jeremy in both looks and manner. Why was it then that her heart picked up tempo only when Drake appeared behind the younger man, looking for all the world like a raven looming over a goldfinch?

"It's high time we left," he announced. For Lucy's ears alone, he muttered, "You have made yourself enough of a spectacle for one evening."

Ignoring the arm he held out stiffly toward her, Lucy turned to Eugene Dalrymple. "Thank you for taking such pains to make me feel welcome, sir. I hope we may meet again while we are both in London."

He held her hand to his lips for a heartbeat longer than decorum dictated. "I look forward to it with the greatest pleasure, dear lady."

As Lucy and Drake settled into the carriage for their return trip to Grafton Square, a contentious silence fell between them.

Then Drake spoke. "You'll have nothing more to do with that man."

"I beg your pardon? Even you could not be so unfeeling

as to warn me away from the one person in London who has extended me a sincere welcome.''

"Sincere?" Drake exhaled a derisive breath. "I wouldn't trust him to spell the word."

"What a cynic you are!" Lucy bristled. "If you must know, I danced with Mr. Dalrymple out of pity. The poor man has recently suffered a romantic disappointment and he couldn't bear to dance with any of the eligible ladies so soon."

"Poppycock!" Drake glared pointedly at Lucy's abdomen. Its gentle swelling was more noticeable when she sat. "You would do well in the future not to swallow every story some suave fellow slips you."

His malicious dig ignited weeks of seething, combustible emotions within her. "And you would do well not to act like a jealous husband. The pose does not become you."

"Jealous?" Drake flared. "Of all the absurdities!"

"Precisely so." Lucy fought to douse a flicker of disappointment that he had denied her charge so vehemently. "We made a vow, if you will recall. A prior contract—never to mar our association with common jealousy. Under those terms I believe I'm quite within my rights to enjoy an innocent dance with such an agreeable gentleman whenever our paths cross. It is not as though I am bestowing any favors you crave from me."

Whatever Drake meant to reply, he did not get the opportunity to smite her with it. At that moment, their carriage halted before Number 17 Grafton Square. For the benefit of any servants who might be watching, Lucy took his arm as they alighted. When at last they reached to door of her bedchamber, Lucy hesitated.

"Will you…? Do you…?"

Since their arrival in London, it had been Drake's custom to "visit" awhile with her before retiring to his own bed. The look on Phyllipa's face was worth any price in lost sleep, he'd declared. In spite of the persistent temptation to throw herself at him, Lucy had come to enjoy these quiet talks in the darkened room. This might be the perfect opportunity to resolve their silly dispute over Mr. Dalrymple.

His dark features an impenetrable mask, Drake shook his head decisively. "I've had enough of playacting to last me the rest of my life."

With that, he turned on his heel and strode away.

Drake scarcely gained the sanctuary of his own chamber when his limbs gave way to violent trembling. It was so bad he could neither untie his stock nor pry off his boots. Incapable of undressing, he paced the floor. Vividly, he recalled how Lucy had slapped his face on their wedding night. That momentary sting was nothing to the blow she had just dealt him.

It is not as though I am bestowing any favors you crave from me. Her words gouged his heart like the knotted tips of a lash. Had she no notion what he craved after their tumultuous night at The Black Cygnet? He craved her—body, heart and soul. As a starveling craved bread or a drowning man his next breath of air. That craving gnawed at him more fiercely with each passing day…and night. Tonight, having watched that suave dandy Dalrymple feast at a table from which he'd scarcely sampled a crumb, Drake feared it would devour him whole.

Lucy peered out from the alcove of the sitting room, squinting at the mantel clock. It would soon be time to dress for the theater party this evening. A fine kettle of fish she'd got herself into, as Mrs. Maberley would say.

Occupied with penning a letter to her father, she'd scarcely heard Phyllipa and her friends enter the main part of the room. Fearing they might invite her to join them if she showed herself, Lucy had kept on with her writing. Precious little worry that the soft scratch of her pen would be heard above their shrill chatter.

However, as the afternoon waned, more guests had arrived. Long since finished her letter, Lucy was now too embarrassed to come out and admit she'd been there all the time, eavesdropping on some rather scandalous gossip. By and by Phyllipa had called for a claret cup to be served round. The level of the conversation had sunk lower still.

"I hear Lady Hargreaves is with child at last," said one of the women. "At White's they are laying five to one odds the offspring is not his lordship's."

"I shall soon have to retire from society…again," sighed another member of the party.

Her comment met with some laughter and much sympathetic clucking.

"Does Spenser give you no peace?" someone asked, her words slurring audibly. "You simply must find him a mistress."

"Pooh, they're such a bother!"

More laughter.

"Wait until this one is born, at least. If you're anything like me, you might enjoy his attentions now."

There were one or two gasps of mock horror at the indelicacy of the comment—one, Lucy was certain, from Phyllipa.

"I should say," chuckled the expectant mother. "I'm quite shameless. If my husband is absent more than a day or two, I start casting covetous glances at the footmen!"

It was not long before they all began telling tales of the wantonness brought on by their pregnancies. Even Phyllipa, much to Lucy's amazement. They were still airing the topic when the clock in a nearby church steeple chimed the hour of six.

"Oh, hear that?" Phyllipa squealed. "Six already and we are for Covent Garden this evening."

Before Lucy knew it, she was all alone in the sitting room once again. After waiting a moment to be sure no one would return, she hurried off to her bedchamber where she began to dress for the theatre.

Removing her day gown, she let her hand rest a moment against the gentle rounding of her belly. A sly smile rippled across her lips.

In a whisper, she addressed her unborn child. "So you are responsible for the naughty feelings I've developed toward your Pa—" She caught herself. Drake was not the father of her child. What a foolish thing to say—to even begin to say! This baby was all she had left of Jeremy. He would live on in his son. How could she deny him in the secrecy of her most private thoughts, the one place she was at liberty to acknowledge her baby's true paternity?

Still, it was a relief to understand, at last, the source of her dangerous preoccupation with Drake. If what she'd overheard was true, her wanton longings were simply another troublesome symptom of her pregnancy. Like the biliousness of those first months, or the cravings for strange foods that still plagued her at times. Hurriedly slipping into a new gown, she laughed at her own foolishness. How could she have imagined it was anything more serious than that?

She almost laughed again when she found Drake in the entryway, impatiently awaiting her.

"I arrived home not twenty minutes ago from Westminster," he bristled, drumming his fingers on the balustrade. "Yet I have managed to wash, shave and change into evening clothes. Meanwhile, you ladies, who have had all day to don your frippery, are in real danger of leaving us late."

Not a single word about her new gown, or how the yellow hair ribbons brought out the color of her eyes. Lucy stifled a smile as Drake stiffly held her wrap. How could she have imagined herself harboring tender feelings for this brusque, taciturn creature? Yet, when the back of his hand brushed the sensitive flesh of her upper arm, a strange, white-hot energy surged between them.

Much to Lucy's dismay, she could scarcely keep her eyes upon the Covent Garden stage that evening for a lively production of *The School for Scandal*. Again and again she found her gaze straying sidelong to Drake's crisp profile, or lingering on his strong, shapely hands. Safe in the knowledge that her interest held no deeper significance, she seized this rare opportunity to indulge it fully.

She remembered the sensuous dichotomy of Drake's unshaven chin scraping across the responsive flesh of her breast, followed by the intoxicating tickle of his sidewhiskers. Her errant thoughts dwelt on the first moment she'd felt herself lifted in Drake's arms. Though she'd scarcely noticed it at the time, Lucy now realized that she'd never felt so completely vulnerable, yet so completely safe.

When the audience broke into applause at the end of Act Three, Lucy came to herself with a start. Busily, she plied her fan, to cool the wanton flush that smarted in her cheeks. She did not notice the usher entering their box, until he held a folded note card before her.

Before she could touch the paper, Drake snapped it up. After a mere glance, he tossed it onto her lap without a word or a look.

"It's from the gentleman across the way, with his compliments," the usher nodded toward a box on the opposite side of the stage.

Looking up, Lucy saw Mr. Dalrymple eagerly trying to catch her eye. When he realized he had succeeded, he smiled broadly and bowed. She nodded briefly in response, then glanced down at his note.

"Your vibrant beauty eclipses even the best Covent Garden has to offer," it ran in a copperplate script.

Somehow, Lucy could not summon the thrill such a gallant compliment should have evoked. In truth, she had become a trifle impatient with Mr. Dalrymple's constant attentions. She was a married woman after all, with a reputation to consider. Not that he had overstepped the bounds of propriety...yet. This note came perilously close.

If only Drake hadn't played the tyrant and warned her away from Dalrymple, she would never have encouraged him in the first place. Lucy stifled a sigh of exasperation. As far as she could tell, Drake no longer cared with whom she consorted. Gone all day on business or to the House of Lords, he had dropped all pretense of affection—even for the fun of goading Phyllipa. During their evenings at the various routs and balls that presaged The Season, he left her to her own devices. If Eugene Dalrymple had not come to her rescue so continually, she would have suffered a very dismal time indeed. Lucy chided herself for failing to appreciate his friendliness. Looking over at the young man again, she flashed him her warmest smile.

As the play recommenced, she noticed that Drake's gaze never veered from the stage. Gradually, she noticed something else. One actress kept looking up at their box.

"Cousin Phyllipa," Lucy whispered. "Who is playing the part of Lady Teazel?"

"Goodness, Cousin Lucy, do you know nothing? That is Mrs. Beaumont—she's only the most celebrated actress in the country next to Mrs. Siddons."

"She's very beautiful."

"My, yes. They say she has her pick of gentlemen. They swarm around her like moths to a candle."

Again, Lucy caught Mrs. Beaumont glancing up at them—at Drake. She forced herself to smile and flutter her fan. Really it was too ridiculous a notion even to entertain. Even so, a chill of apprehension lodged in her heart.

Chapter Seventeen

A week after the theater party, Drake hesitated on the threshold of his grandmother's bedchamber, letting his eyes become accustomed to the gloom.

"Are you awake, Grandmother? You can dispense with your pose of illness. I'm alone today."

He drew several quick breaths of the close, stale air, faintly perfumed with the scent of desiccated rose petals. Having received no reply to his whispered question, he backed toward the door.

"Francis?" The deeper shadows at the head of the bed stirred slightly. "Is that you my dear?"

Perhaps she hadn't been putting on an act, after all, Drake reflected. Never had he heard his grandmother's voice so soft, so affectionate. And in all his life, no one had dared to call him by his given name.

With reluctant steps, he propelled himself deeper into the room. He would have given half his fortune for the liberty to throw open the draperies and raise the window sash. "Yes, Grandmother. It's Drake. I've come to visit with you—alone."

Since their arrival in London, he and Lucy had been coming to call at least once a week, often with Phyllipa or Neville in tow. Drake had realized from the start that the marchioness was not ill in the least. That's why he'd come alone today, resolved to discover what was behind her charade.

"Drake? You sounded so like your grandfather. For just a moment..." Her words trailed off wistfully, but she soon rallied. "Well, I'm glad to have you to myself at last. We need to talk, you and I."

This sounded more like the woman he knew. Pulling a chair closer to the bed, Drake took a seat. Before he was able to phrase any of the questions he'd come to ask, his grandmother confounded him with one of her own.

"How are you finding this honest business arrangement you call a marriage?"

Her words hit Drake like a solid blow to the stomach. During their previous visits, his grandmother had maintained a cool, but painfully correct facade. Though she scarcely acknowledged Lucy's presence, at least she'd refrained from overt hostility. He should have known it couldn't last.

"It's not what I'd expected." No lie, that. Why then, did he find it so hard to meet his grandmother's discerning gaze? "But not unpleasant," he hastened to add.

"Not unpleasant." The marchioness chuckled, a dry rustling sound, like an autumn breeze stirring the fallen leaves. "You are like your grandfather and growing more so every day. I never found another like him, though not for lack of trying. She's very beautiful, this wife of yours."

It was not a question, but Drake felt compelled to reply all the same. "That is an understatement."

"Is it, indeed? How would you describe her then?"

"You're asking the wrong brother," Drake replied with a rueful sigh. "Jeremy could have found the right words to do her justice. I have not that happy facility."

The marchioness reached out one tiny, wrinkled, indomitable hand and brought it to rest upon Drake's. "No you don't, child. And no bad thing, either. The world is full of wags and poets these days, when it needs more men of heart and deeds.''

This truly left Drake bereft of words. Never had his grandmother spoken to him with such approval, almost fondness. He savored the softness of her touch.

''So, my wishful old eyes haven't deceived me. You've come to love this girl. That's what you didn't expect of marriage.''

All Drake's defenses bristled. He sprang from his seat and began pacing the room. ''Why do you care?'' The atmosphere stifled him worse with each breath he drew. ''After the way you set your face against my marriage, the last thing I expected from you was a full interrogation on the subject. Why did you feign this illness to lure us to London?''

''Sit down and behave yourself, Francis Drake Strickland! Of course I disapproved of your rushing off from the supper table and appearing at breakfast, betrothed. What was I to think, but that you'd fallen prey to a fortune huntress? When I came to hear of your bride's character, naturally I wanted to see the truth for myself. And to heal the breach between us. You may not believe this, child, but I did want to see you make a love match.''

''I'm sorry to disappoint you on that score, Grandmother.'' Drake strode for the door.

He had been a disappointment to everyone in his life from the moment he'd been born. Disappointment to his father, who had wanted a live wife and a healthy heir. Disappointment to Jeremy, who had chafed under his stiff paternalism. Disappointment to Lucy, who wanted a handsome charmer for a husband.

''You've had too little love in your life.'' The words stopped Drake in his tracks. ''For which I take my share of the blame. You do not disappoint me, though I think from your tone that you disappoint yourself. I sensed there was something not right between you and Lucy, for all the show you put on to vex Phyllipa. Come tell me all about it. No need for frills and furbelows—I prefer my information straight and plain.''

Reluctantly, Drake turned back.

Any other woman so slight and small might have looked lost in that cavernous bed. Yet his grandmother, in her wrap and nightcap, looked as self-possessed as any empress on her throne. She held out her hand to him—a gesture at once imperious and entreating.

''Are you certain she cannot love you? If that's so, then she is a fool. Would you even recognize love if she offered it?''

Something in that frank question pierced Drake's armor, lodging in his heart as surely as Cupid's arrow.

''Perhaps I wouldn't, Grandmother.'' He took his seat again and reclaimed her hand. ''You've had plenty of experience with marriage, though. I shall tell you about Lucy and me, and see what you think.''

A grudging ghost of a smile fluttered on his grandmother's thin, resolute lips. ''Now you're talking sense.''

''And when I'm finished—'' Drake's voice warmed ''—I'll tell you a piece of news that should make you very happy.''

''You're home at last,'' Lucy said to Drake, as the butler took his hat and gloves. ''Had you forgotten that Cousin Neville is taking tea with us today?''

Turning on her with eyes that seemed truly to see her for the first time in weeks, Drake took her arm. ''I must admit, it had slipped my mind, but I am home, at last. I doubt Neville will take offense if I don't change for tea. We have an engagement this evening besides, do we not?''

Something about his casual, relaxed tone disturbed Lucy, even as it warmed her. Was it her imagination, or did his coat smell vaguely of a woman's scent—dried roses?

''Engagement? Why, yes. Don't say you've forgotten that as well? We're invited to a ball at Holland House.''

"A coveted invitation from Lady Holland—how could I forget such a social coup?" Drake ushered her through the door to the sitting room, where Phyllipa was already pouring tea. "To what do we owe the honor, do you suppose?"

Lucy could not help smiling, despite the ridiculous suspicions that buzzed softly but insistently in her thoughts. This sardonic good humor sounded so like the old Drake of Silverthorne days. Would they ever return to her beloved Lake Country?

"I can't imagine why Lord and Lady Holland have invited us." Taking a seat on the sofa, she took the cup and saucer Phyllipa held out to her. "We are hardly the toast of the ton…at least I am not."

"Perhaps that is our entrée." Drake plucked up a dainty square of bread thickly spread with butter, and ate it in two quick bites. "As I recall, our dear Lady Holland was something of an outcast herself, when she and his lordship returned from Florence as newlyweds. In the past fifteen years most people have conveniently forgotten that she was a divorcée."

Neville's monocle fell from his staring eye. "Surely, you don't count your charming bride on the social level of a divorcée, Drake? Cousin Lucy has won any number of admirers. That young nephew of the Duchess of Swansea, for instance."

Phyllipa bobbed her head in vehement agreement. "If dear Lucy was not a married woman, I should say Mr. Dalrymple was smitten with her."

Seeing a darkness shadow her husband's expression, Lucy blurted the first remark that entered her head. "How was your day, Drake? A lively debate in the Lords?"

Before Drake could reply, Neville spoke. "I was down to Westminster this afternoon, Cousin. Didn't see any sign of you. Not playing truant, I hope?"

Nibbling on her cheese sandwich, Lucy listened intently

for Drake's answer. If not at the House, where *had* he been until such a late hour?

"I gave my final speech just before noon and left them to chew on it," said Drake. "They'll find it a bitter mouthful, no doubt. I demanded the immediate suspension of this cursed American blockade. Before it cripples British industry and makes paupers of half the country with the price of bread spiraling." He shot his cousin a dubious look. "What on earth were you doing in the Commons, Neville? Taken a sudden interest in politics?"

"Dear me, no!" Neville flicked his wrist dismissively. "A few of the fellows do like to take over the gallery now and then to heckle the Prime Minister. Perseval is such a sober pedant, he makes fine sport!"

"You'll get no quarrel from me," said Drake. "I've done with them all, frankly. I've tried my best and I believe I've managed to win a measure of support over the past few weeks. It's going to take more than reason for this government to shift from its blinkered course. A hungry mob storming Westminster like the Parisians stormed the Bastille, most likely. I'd prefer to be as far from London as possible when the storm breaks. All I can do now is return to Silverthorne and tend to my own enterprises."

"Return to Silverthorne?" Phyllipa wailed. "But the Season has scarcely begun. There'll be ever so many more amusing things to do now that spring is here."

"Think of the roads," chimed in Neville. "You'll be up to the axles in mud all the way to Nicholthwait."

Whatever had Drake's cousins so flustered, Lucy could only sip her tea demurely and make every effort to suppress her amusement. Her heart swelled with pleasure at the thought of an early return to her dear home, and gratitude to Drake for making it possible.

"If we wait a week, I fear you might be correct, Neville." Drake popped a morsel of gooseberry tart into his mouth and bolted the last of his tea. "The cold weather has lingered far past its usual limit, and I mean to take advantage of it. We'll be on our way tomorrow.''

''Why so soon?'' Phyllipa's receding chin began to quiver. ''You've been here such a short time. Can't you at least stay long enough for me to arrange a proper send-off?''

Drake shrugged. ''This do at Holland House will have to serve as our farewell. It could be dangerous for us to tarry.''

''Dangerous?'' Neville and Phyllipa spoke together, looking from Drake to each other.

Lucy wondered what he meant as well. She was as astonished as the cousins when he reached over and caught her hand.

''If we wait for the roads to thaw and the spring mud to dry, I fear my dear wife will be too close to her time for making such a long, jarring journey.''

''Her time?'' Neville croaked.

Phyllipa dug him soundly in the ribs with a sharp elbow. ''Cousin Drake means that Lucy is expecting a baby. What…exciting news. Con…gratulations to both of you.''

Lucy sat mute while Drake beamed as proudly as any new father-to-be, and the cousins stammered their unenthusiastic good wishes. She'd known they would have to announce the news eventually—before her swelling belly outstripped even the concealing fashions of the day. If only Drake had given her a little warning.

''So.'' Phyllipa turned to her. ''How long have you… known?''

Now it was Lucy's turn to stammer. ''A…while. I should have guessed much earlier…but having no experience of such matters…''

''This calls for a toast,'' declared Neville, with forced heartiness. ''Got anything potable left in your wine cellar, Drake? This promises to be a night of celebration indeed.''

During the weeks that followed, Lucy was to recall those words again and again, with great clarity.

* * *

In the entry hall of the London house where he'd never felt master, Drake waited for Lucy and Phyllipa to join him. Three times he retied his stock. Twice he brushed invisible specks of dust from his gray trousers. A few weeks earlier, at Phyllipa's insistence, he'd visited a fashionable Bond Street tailor for a whole new wardrobe. His familiar old suits were threadbare and ten years out of style, she'd fussed until he agreed to go. Despite the bother of fittings, Drake had to admit the new styles suited him. Streamlined, manly and businesslike, the long trousers and cutaway coats were infinitely preferable to the fussy, effeminate styles of his boyhood.

For reasons Drake could not fathom, ever since the talk with his grandmother, he'd felt an easy confidence beginning to sprout within him. Perhaps it was the unexpected discovery of the fondness and respect she bore for him. Or perhaps it was her salty common sense that, in a long life, had looked on many tempests and been little shaken.

"So your bride believes her heart is buried with her first love?" The marchioness had chuckled privately, recalling a time when she had been so full of naive idealism. "Heaven spare any woman the grief of marrying her first love! The qualities that make a girl's silly heart flutter are not the kind that stand even the mildest test of time."

"You don't understand, grandmother," Drake protested, anxious not to betray too much of the truth. "This man was everything I am not. While it's true his charms might have paled if he'd lived, he's now beyond criticism. Beyond competition."

"Pshaw! You hold the trumps in this hand, my lad. For you are alive, flesh and blood. Your Lucy sounds too sensible a girl to cling to a ghost when she can have a man like you. Let her know your feelings have changed, and that you'll no longer settle for the crumbs of her affection. I wager you'll find her more than willing to make a go of this marriage, if you are."

He'd promised he would try. The first step must be getting them both out of London and back to Silverthorne, where they could be alone. Without the constant presence of Phyllipa and that benighted bounder, Dalrymple. Once they were back at Silverthorne he would begin to show Lucy how his feelings had altered and...

A rustle of muslin.

Drake looked up in time to see Lucy descending the staircase—a vision in the most breathtaking confection of a gown he had ever contemplated. A soft rose color with the fashionable high waist that hid any sign of her condition, it had a filmy pink overslip embroidered with rosebuds. If there was a goddess of springtime, Drake could only imagine she must look just so.

Catching sight of him, Lucy bit her lip, smiling uncertainly. Drake realized his mouth had fallen open.

"Will I do for Holland House?" she murmured, casting her eyes downward, then looking up at him through her luxuriant lashes.

Drake felt his tongue turn to stone and his innards to quivering jelly. There could be no question of waiting for their return to Silverthorne. He must win this woman, and he must set about winning her tonight. Nothing in his life had ever felt so imperative.

"Well?" Lucy prompted him expectantly. "Am I presentable for our last night in London?"

"Yes." He felt like an ass. The way she looked, the way she made him feel—he should be spouting poetry worthy of Shakespeare. Not a word of more than a syllable would enter his head. "Quite," he managed to add, mentally berating himself. "Your gown is very...it's new, yes?"

"Do you think it cost too much? I felt faint when the seamstress told me the price, but Phyllipa says all the ladies in London spend..."

Bewildered at her onrush of words, Drake regretted that his stupid fumblings had caused her to reach such a conclusion. Now, even the simplest utterances deserted him. For lack of any other recourse, he hushed her with the most delicate pressure of his forefinger against her lips.

Only when the tender flesh trembled slightly beneath his fingertip did Drake realize his error. Lucy feared him, and he had given her cause. Now, if he hoped to make any progress with her, he would have to move slowly and deliberately. He could not afford to unleash his straining passion again and risk frightening her off for good and all.

Wrenching his hand back as though her lips had scorched his skin, he stammered, "Spend…what you like. Lord knows…we've money enough. The gown is…lovely."

He winced at the sound of his own words. *Lovely*—what a tepid, commonplace, two-a-penny word to describe how she looked. For the first time that night, Drake yearned with all his heart for even a scrap of his late brother's ingenuous charm.

But not for the last.

In spite of his resolve to win Lucy, or perhaps because of it, his efforts went awry at every turn. Dance partners flocked to her until Drake found himself shunted aside. He fumed in silence as he watched her gliding through the steps, a smile of genuine pleasure lighting both her lips and her eyes. As the music concluded and a bevy of swains rushed up to claim the honor of the next dance, Drake shouldered his way through the press.

He fixed the importunate gentlemen with the legendary Silverthorne glare. "Is it thought bad manners nowadays for a man to dance with his *own* wife?"

Lucy's admirers dispersed like a covey of quail set upon by a bloodhound.

"Did you wish to dance?" Suppressed amusement shone in her eyes. "I thought I was sparing you the obligation."

"We will dance." The words came out like a curt command, not at all as he'd intended.

He moved woodenly through the steps. If he allowed himself to look too long at Lucy or savor the touch of her hand, he might lose concentration and trip over his own feet. By the time he had stomped through two sets, treading at least once on Lucy's toes, he was ready to explode with vexation at himself.

"I could do with a dipper of punch." She sounded eager for any excuse to remove herself from the peril of his clumsy dancing.

"Punch. Of course." Eager to redeem himself by doing her bidding, he rushed to return before she was once again mobbed by prospective dance partners. In his haste, Drake jostled the rotund Earl of Weymouth. Struggling to regain his balance, he lurched toward Lucy. The entire contents of the punch glass splashed down the front of her beautiful new gown.

She gasped, staring at her sodden skirt. A furious blush rose in her cheeks. Her eyes held Drake in a gaze of wounded puzzlement that made him feel a thousandfold more culpable.

"So sorry…my…dear." He fumbled with his pocket handkerchief, daubing at her gown. "Damnably clumsy of me. Shall I call for our carriage?"

As Lucy swept past him, she spoke just loud enough for his ears alone. "If you wished to go home, sir, you might have asked, rather than subjecting me to this humiliation."

Chin tilted proudly, she walked to the staircase and mounted the steps with deliberate dignity.

A harsh profanity rose to Drake's lips. He swallowed it again as his gaze met the triumphant smirk and insolently cocked eyebrow of Eugene Dalrymple. With languid grace, the young dandy pivoted on the toe of his silver-buckled shoe and strolled to the foot of the staircase. There he lounged, sipping his punch and patiently eyeing the stairs for Lucy's return.

Drake cursed aloud.

When the Countess of Weymouth bleated in protest, he

skewered her with a piercing glare and strode to take up a post opposite Dalrymple. It was a futile gesture, he knew, but one which Silverthorne honor demanded.

Relieved to find the tiring-room blessedly deserted, Lucy took a linen towel from the wash stand and pressed it to her damp skirt. Alternately, she mopped the moisture then shook out the fabric to let it air dry.

Giving herself a critical look in the pier glass, Lucy chuckled. If Drake had to douse her with liquid, thank fortune he had chosen a champagne punch. And thank fortune her new gown was made of muslin, not silk.

What had got into Drake tonight? Seldom had she seen him so stiff and self-consciously solicitous. Almost as if he were trying to expiate his conscience. The now familiar frost of suspicion chilled in Lucy's heart. At the same time, her womanly pride reared.

If he had done something of which he was ashamed, let him salve his conscience without spoiling her last evening in London. Given the choice between his usual aloof neglect and tonight's awkward attentiveness, Lucy wondered if she did not prefer the former.

Shaking her head, she heaved an exasperated sigh and slipped behind the screen to relieve herself. She had just finished when she heard the door open and two loudly chatting women enter. Having no inclination to be caught again as she had during Phyllipa's impromptu tea party, Lucy began to clear her throat to signal her presence. A remark from one of the women stopped her.

"Did you see it? The whole glass of punch down the front of his wife's gown! The years haven't cured Silverthorne of his boorishness. Aren't you glad you didn't marry him after all?"

Lucy froze. If these ladies should discover her, it would be ten times more embarrassing than on the other occasion.

"Oh, I don't know." The second woman mulled over the

idea. "Who'd have guessed he'd grow so very rich. Handsome, too, for all his lack of refinement."

"Are you saying you're sorry you eloped with Lucius?"

"Of course not. Lucius was so gay and amusing. Always the perfect gentleman. It's true what they say about Drake Strickland—he's nothing but a tradesman with a title."

Both ladies erupted in high-pitched squeals of laughter over this malicious quip. After lampooning several other of their acquaintances, and checking that their petticoats were not showing, the giddy pair left Lucy in peace. After a decent interval, she followed, her thoughts churning.

Small wonder Drake had been so reluctant to marry, after having his pride, and possibly his heart, mauled by that razor-clawed cat. Small wonder he acted so ill at ease in aristocratic society.

Tradesman with a title. True, Drake had little in common with the general run of noblemen, who showed no interest in anything beyond their own pleasure. He'd been much more convivial with his foremen, and the miners' families at High-Head than among the aristocratic parasites of high society.

At the top of the stairs, Lucy paused to draw a deep breath. In the ballroom below, she could see Drake and Mr. Dalrymple positioned like a pair of sentries on either side of the balustrade. For a moment her heart lifted at the sight of Eugene Dalrymple. No doubt he would have some ready quip to deflect gossip and diffuse her embarrassment.

Marking the black look Drake fired at the young man, Lucy thought back to the conversation she'd just overheard. Suddenly, she glimpsed the reason for his animosity to Mr. Dalrymple. It had probably been just such a mannerly, amusing lightweight who'd robbed young Drake of his fiancée and made him the laughingstock of the ton to this day. Surely, he could not believe she'd ever humiliate him in such a way? With a flutter of chagrin, Lucy reluctantly admitted that she might have given him reason to doubt her.

Well, no more.

Working up the pretense of a carefree smile, she glided down the stairs, steeling herself to run the gauntlet of raised eyebrows and covert smirks. As she stood on the last step, Mr. Dalrymple turned to her. Taking her hand, he swept her an exaggerated bow.

"I kneel in awe of your poise, Queen Lucy. Beautifully recovered, indeed. Shall we take the floor and show the company that it takes more than a little wetting to quench your grace and vivacity?"

Though he sounded entirely sincere, Lucy could not help thinking that a subtle shift of inflection might turn his impeccable compliment into the most caustic sarcasm.

A marked coolness infused her reply. "Tempting as I might find your invitation, sir, I fear I must decline."

Withdrawing her hand from his grasp, she turned to Drake. "My husband still owes me a drink of punch and I mean to collect on my debt."

Ignoring Drake's dumbstruck look, she took his arm and spoke teasingly. "Shall I help *you* to a glass, dear husband? I promise to refrain from wetting you down, provided I don't catch you casting admiring looks at the other ladies."

She could feel the tightly wound tension in Drake's body begin to subside.

"A simple enough feat when I have you to look on."

It was not a very eloquent compliment compared with the verbal confections of Mr. Dalrymple, or Jeremy. Yet the very economy of Drake's words and the tone of tender earnest in which he had uttered them made his tribute precious to Lucy. A strange sweet warmth swept through her.

Fluttering her lashes to dispel an inexplicable stinging in her eyes, she tried to speak past the unaccountable constriction in her throat.

"Flatterer! I shan't let you off that easily. This is our last night in London and you owe me a good time. I've been very patient all these weeks while you've skulked away to talk politics, leaving me to the company of any gentleman who might invite me to dance out of pity. So I give you fair warning—you are mine for the night.''

With exaggerated care, he offered her another glass of punch. Then he tipped his own glass toward her. ''I am entirely at your service, my lady.''

The heat in Drake's dark gaze rekindled a wild yearning which had flamed in Lucy on that night at The Black Cygnet. Would he tender such an offer, she wondered, if he had any idea how far she might press it?

Chapter Eighteen

Drake might have suspected he was dreaming that night at Holland House, but for one thing. Never in his life had he dreamed anything half so wonderful. It was quite beyond the bounds of his practical, limited imagination. He'd steeled himself for Lucy to spurn him when she returned to the company. He fully expected her to lap up Dalrymple's fluent compliments and then to take the floor on his arm.

Never would he have dared to hope she might turn on him with a gentle rally and the unlooked-for gift of a second chance. Whatever angel had intervened on his behalf, Drake could only thank providence from the bottom of his heart.

As the night wore on, it became increasingly clear that his wife had resolved to think well of anything he should say or do. She praised his barely adequate dancing, coaxing him to take the floor with her again and again. She hung upon his most banal utterances, laughing merrily at his feeblest jests. Most pleasant of all, she held his arm at every opportunity, as though she never meant to let him go. What it all meant, he felt too puzzled and befuddled with happiness to cypher out. Was there no boon so rare that fortune would deny it to him this night? And did he dare to test the ultimate limits of whatever benevolent enchantment had overtaken him?

So reluctant was Drake to risk breaking the spell, that they were among the last guests to leave Holland House.

After they had gone off arm in arm, Lady Holland turned to her husband, her eyes shining fondly. "I don't know when I've seen such a devoted pair. We must be sure to invite them again whenever they come to London."

Drake was even quieter than usual on their carriage ride home, but Lucy sensed a different quality in his silence. It had none of the cold, mute antagonism of previous nights when they had returned from social engagements. Social engagements where she had kept company with Mr. Dalrymple. Tonight he appeared content to listen as she prattled on, a tad nervously, about the superior company and entertainment of the Holland set.

She was conscious of him watching her, with approval and admiration at once more subtle and more sincere than the overt regard of Mr. Dalrymple. Though she scarcely knew what to make of it, Lucy could not help savoring his appreciative scrutiny, after so many weeks of unspoken censure. Liberated by the knowledge that her fancy for him was no more than a curious quirk of her pregnancy, she allowed herself to imagine making love with her husband.

Vivid, compelling images flashed in her thoughts like bolts of lightning. She felt herself growing more and more aroused. Gradually the effort to keep her tone of voice casually animated became too great, and she lapsed into silence. Even then she had difficulty in keeping her rapid breathing from betraying the pitch of her suppressed desire.

The young footman who admitted them to the house on Grafton Square looked ready to fall asleep on his feet. An early spring dawn was not many hours away.

"Get yourself to bed, boy," advised Drake, when the lad had taken their wraps.

"Won't you be wanting your port in the library, milord?" The boy tried to stifle a yawn.

Drake shook his head. "I've too much wine punch in me already. I fear the port wouldn't sit well on top of it. Hate to end a pleasant evening by shooting the cat, what?"

The footman hiccoughed with laughter at Drake's use of the fashionable slang for retching.

Lucy smiled, too, though she did not believe Drake for a moment. Ever since that drunken night at The Black Cygnet, he'd been strictly temperate in his consumption of spirits—tonight had been no exception. In recent weeks he'd taken to lingering downstairs with a glass of port while she retired to bed. Perhaps he'd wanted to avoid an awkward parting at her bedroom door. Tonight, however, he followed her up the stairs.

With every step, Lucy was achingly conscious of his presence so close behind her. Could he not feel the emanation of raw need that pulsed through her? It licked at her limbs, and made her mouth alternately water and dry out. On the fourth stair from the top, her slipper caught on the hem of her gown and she faltered. Shadowing her so closely, Drake was on top of her before he could stop himself.

"I'm sorry. Did I hurt you?"

Righting herself, she clung to him. "It was my fault. I'm fine—truly."

Somehow they managed to ascend the final three steps, their bodies entwined.

If she did not get some relief for herself soon, Lucy feared she might burst into flame. From a throat suddenly dry as parchment, she tried to dredge the words that would keep Drake with her. Before she could master her wayward vocal organs, he spoke. His voice was scarcely more than a whisper, hoarse with his own wanting.

"Let me stay, Lucy. I beg you."

Before she could reply with her own entreaty, he rushed on, as if to counter an expected protest. "I don't mean to go back on our original agreement. I know Jeremy's memory will always have first place in your heart. As for my-self…''

She pressed her fingertips to his lips, as he had done to her scant hours before. Just then she could not bear to hear Jeremy's name spoken, could scarcely bear to think of him at all.

''A man has needs.'' She finished his sentence, loathing herself for the worst kind of hypocrite. It was her own need, not Drake's, that compelled her.

With fumbling, trembling hands she turned the knob of her bedroom door and drew her husband inside. A dying fire in the hearth bathed the room with a soft, welcoming glow. The quilt had been turned down and her nightgown laid out. Silently leading Drake toward the bed, Lucy grappled with a sense of shame that threatened to smother her.

This was no betrayal of Jeremy, she sternly insisted to herself, almost believing it. She was simply seeking relief from the carnality brought on by her pregnancy, as well as submitting to the lawful demands of her husband. She was at his mercy, for by the law of Church and State, he had every right to her body. Conveniently forgetting how close she had come to begging him, Lucy absolved herself, determined not to repulse him this time with any unseemly eagerness.

Nothing had prepared her for Drake's deliberate, re-strained lovemaking.

With measured movements, he shed his coat. Loosening his stock, he unwound the white neck linen from around his bronzed throat. One by one, he unfastened the buttons of his waistcoat and then his shirt. Lucy watched the nimble manipulations with jealous attention. He slipped off the fitted kneeboots of fine, supple leather. Shrugging off his upper garments, he stood clad in only his narrow-legged trousers. The sight of him almost unmastered her. Lean, lithe and dark, he looked for all the world like some dangerous but compelling predator.

Now he turned his attentions to her, and she could scarcely keep her knees from buckling. Deftly, he liberated each tiny pearl button that secured the back of her gown. Then, standing behind her, he laid a hand on each of her shoulders with no more pressure than a moth lighting on a rose petal. His lips found the exquisitely sensitive flesh of her neck. Skimming upward in a deliciously ticklish caress to the base of her ear, they began again on the other side.

Languorously, he eased the insubstantial sleeves off her shoulders and down her arms. The low-cut bodice of her gown parted company with her breasts. Silently, she willed Drake to touch them. She yearned for him to cup each ivory mound in his warm dark hands and flick his thumbs over the ruddy brown nipples, erect and pleading for his attention. He made no move to do so.

When the sleeves slid over her hands, Drake allowed nature to finish the task he had begun. The gown continued to fall with leisurely grace, until it lay in soft folds about her ankles along with her single light undergarment. Swallowing an immense lump in her throat, Lucy closed her eyes. Other than her stockings and slippers, she stood quite naked, more completely exposed than she had ever been in her life. Her pulse raced in her ears, and her whole body tingled, anticipating Drake's touch.

She sensed his movements behind her as he slowly drew off his trousers, then he bent his concentration upon her once again. At the base of her neck, he bestowed a lingering kiss that made her heart clench in her chest. Slowly, maddeningly so, his lips traced a sinuous path down her back. She could feel the moist heat of his breath. Its ragged pace betrayed a fierce eagerness, in sharp contrast to his leisurely seduction. Now and then his tongue would flick out, setting her senses aquiver.

He dropped to his knees, his voyaging lips exploring farther south. Lucy steeled herself for the feel of his lips or his hands on the rounded, oh-so-receptive flesh of her backside. He stopped short of that.

Instead, he turned his face, pressing his cheek and silken side-whiskers into the small of her back. Lucy clenched her lips to stifle a groan of pleasure and almost intolerable yearning, but she made no move. She had sworn to rein in her wanton urges—and rein them in she must. If she drove Drake away now, when he had coaxed her to such a pitch of arousal, how would she bear the torture of such frustration?

She gasped as he touched her ankles, his hands traveling upward until they reached the rolled tops of her stockings. With a delicacy scarcely imaginable from hands so large and powerful, he inched the sheer silk down her legs, drawing off her slippers and her stockings. Completely disrobed at last, Lucy waited impatiently for what would come next.

Suddenly deprived of his touch, she strained to hear what Drake was doing. Unable to stand the suspense, she opened her eyes. There he stood, silhouetted against the dim glow from the embers in her hearth. A magnificent creature, all taut, lean strength and dark, brooding potency. Though she longed to explore his body with her hands and lips, she could not trust herself.

With a smoldering intensity in his gaze, he nodded toward the bed. Lucy sank down gratefully, not certain how much longer her quivering limbs could have sustained her. She held out her arms to Drake, wordlessly pleading with him to quench the rapacious desire he had so deliberately kindled. He stretched out beside her, cupping her head with one hand, while the other played over her body at will. She prepared herself for a deep, demanding kiss like the ones they had forged together on their wild night at the inn. It never came.

Instead his mouth hovered, almost out of reach. He enticed her with fleeting, shallow kisses that made her strain toward him. His fingertips—those sweet, capricious tormenters! They whispered over her skin, turning the hollow of her shoulder or the base of her lowest rib into the apex of sensual delight. All but ignoring those parts of her body that pleaded most desperately for his attention. Higher and higher he coaxed her until her very bones throbbed with excruciating need.

Forgetting the promise she had made to herself, forgetting everything in the world, she parted her legs, beseeching him to take her. Take her he did, in one deft, fluid motion, sliding home in a single smooth deep thrust. At the same instant his mouth clamped down on hers, muffling a cry that would have otherwise raised the whole house. For as Drake eased into her, Lucy lost herself in a rapturous, shattering release.

By degrees she returned to full consciousness, and the blissful but disconcerting sensation of being borne on a warm breeze like a wisp of thistledown. She found herself lying on her side, nestled in Drake's arms. Her cheek pressed to his chest where she could hear his heart racing. Why had he stopped? she wondered drowsily. Unless she had been misled by her meager experience with men, he had received no satisfaction from their coupling. Yet he made not the slightest move—as if *her* pleasure had been his goal all along.

She wanted to say something, to give Drake a sign that would acknowledge the unique and precious gift he had bestowed on her. However, she could not puzzle out the contradictory emotions that vied for control of her heart. Neither could she comprehend why Drake had begged permission to make love to her, only to leave his own desires unappeased. What an enigmatic creature! Almost as unfathomable as the feelings he provoked in her.

She was still mulling it over when a deep, mellow drowsiness overtook her.

Only when he was certain she'd fallen asleep did Drake stir himself to twitch the bedclothes over them both. Still buried within her, he clasped Lucy to him. In the darkness he smiled to himself. Unless all he'd heard and what little he'd experienced of physical love was completely in error, he had just taken Lucy to a place few women voyaged. Certainly, it was *terra incognita* to him.

The strangest part was that he hadn't meant to do it. Though not altogether bereft of experience, he had never considered himself an accomplished lover. His temperate, almost chaste seduction of Lucy had risen from a desire not to frighten her. No torn clothes. No savage grappling. Nothing to stir distasteful memories of their first aborted encounter.

He had also refrained from speaking, for fear that anything he might say would only spoil it for them both. Afterward, when Lucy lay silent and spent, he had clasped her to him, satisfied that his body had spoken most eloquently on his behalf.

In spite of his delight at having roused and sated the woman he adored, his own long-denied hunger now threatened to engulf him. In the faint light of that spring dawn, he could make out the sumptuous contours of Lucy's body. The tempting fullness of her breast rose and fell gently in sleep. The subtle, fragrant musk of her desire filled his nostrils. The tight, moist grip of her intimate embrace carried him to the brink of madness…and beyond, in a soundless, motionless climax of devastating intensity.

Chapter Nineteen

Lucy woke around noon, or so she judged it, roused by the singing of a lark outside her window. The little bird sounded as though he were bursting to warble his delight at returning home to England after a winter exile in warmer climes. For a moment Lucy wondered why her own heart resonated with the same boundless joy and exultant sense of homecoming.

As she lay there, basking in an aura of sublime contentment, she felt the baby move within her for the first time. Her fragile peace of mind shattered like a bauble of spun glass dashed on a marble floor. Guilty tears stung in her eyes, and uncertainty roiled in her heart once more.

Slumbering memories stirred of her child's conception. Memories she had suppressed until this very moment. Jeremy had tried to use her gently, knowing she was a maid. In the end he was overcome by his own need. Raining kisses on her face, he whispered hoarsely that he loved her, and that it would soon be over. He lied. By the time he gave one final grunting thrust and rolled off her, she was whimpering like a wounded animal.

For months she had thrown a rose-colored curtain over those memories. Now they surged back to life, raw and shameful. Over and over, she'd insisted to Drake and to herself that she would never regret what she had done, what she'd allowed Jeremy to do. Now she was no longer sure. Of that, or of other old certainties.

Was it possible she had grown to love her gruff, pensive husband, the complete opposite of his boyishly engaging half brother? And what were Drake's feelings for her? Had they also changed since the day the two of them had made their foolish compact never to burden one another with unwanted affection?

As Lucy wrestled with these vexing questions, a rapid, insistent tapping sounded on the door of her bedchamber. For an instant her heart leapt, thinking it might be Drake. Then she realized the sharp, staccato knock could not possibly come from him. Lucy almost called out to bid the person enter. The words caught in her throat as she realized she was naked beneath the bedclothes.

Scooping her nightgown from the floor, she pulled it over her head. "A moment, please. I just woke up."

Quickly donning a warm wrap and slippers, Lucy opened the door to Phyllipa. Drake's cousin eyed her disheveled hair with ill-disguised interest. Lucy felt herself blushing. Like most ladies of the time, she made a ritual of brushing and braiding her hair for bed, no matter how late the hour. Following Phyllipa's gaze to the pile of discarded evening clothes beside the bed, she blushed deeper still. Mixed up with her ball gown and underclothes, were Drake's stock and waistcoat.

Her eyes fixed on the garments, Phyllipa's mouth opened and closed several times. Finally, she managed to gasp, "What time did the two of you get in this morning? When you didn't come down, I thought I should check to see if you were ill."

"Aside from being a little tired, I am quite well thank you."

Lucy sternly reminded herself that Drake's clothes on her floor should not be any cause to blush. They'd been married for months now and during that time they'd gone out of their way to convince his cousins they were physically intimate. But that had been playacting. This was not. In spite of the wedding band on her finger, it felt furtive and illicit.

"I only thought…" Phyllipa continued to stare at the telltale pile of clothes. "That is, Drake said you'd be leaving today. And you haven't anything packed."

Lucy shrugged. "Perhaps we'll wait until tomorrow."

Seeing Phyllipa's tight little smile of triumph, she couldn't keep from adding, "Or perhaps I'll throw some traveling clothes into a trunk and you can send the rest of our baggage on later."

"I suppose it will depend on how long Drake takes with his interview." A note of sly triumph sounded in Phyllipa's reply.

"Interview?" Lucy knew she should not rise to the bait, but she couldn't help herself.

"I thought perhaps you were aware of it."

"I wasn't." Turning from Drake's cousin, Lucy began to pick up the fallen clothes and fold them. "No doubt it's some Parliamentary business or other he has to finish before we leave."

Phyllipa chuckled, a sound that made Lucy's skin crawl. "I know of no women who sit in the House."

When Lucy persisted in ignoring her, she snapped, "Are you not going to ask me who he's seeing?"

Lucy pretended to busy herself with choosing clothes—traveling clothes. "Why ask when I know you'll tell me in any case?"

"I do feel it's my duty, as I am so very fond of you. It's that actress," said Phyllipa. "Remember? The one you asked about that night at Covent Garden."

A cold dagger of dread slashed at Lucy's entrails. "I remember."

"She arrived out of the blue half an hour ago, *demanding* to see Lord Silverthorne. They've been together in the library ever since—with the door shut."

"Then by all means go and press your ear to the keyhole, Phyllipa. I'm content to wait until my husband informs me what Mrs. Beaumont wanted."

"But, Lucy...I only thought—"

"You only thought it a pity to waste this chance of making trouble between Drake and me before we return to Silverthorne. Save your breath, Phyllipa. My husband is the most honorable man I know and I trust him completely. No doubt there is a perfectly innocent reason for Mrs. Beaumont's call. Now if you'll excuse me, I must dress and get packed."

She all but pushed a sputtering Phyllipa out the door. Then Lucy sank onto the bed, fighting to make herself believe her own vehement protestations. If she did not care for Drake, why on earth should she mind what was going on in the library?

"You're quite certain of this?" Torn between disbelief and outrage, Drake stared at the woman sitting across from him.

"As certain as any woman can be, Lord Silverthorne." Rosalind Beaumont allowed herself the ghost of a smile. She'd dressed rather too fashionably for a morning call, in a pale-green gown and darker green jacket that set off her fair complexion perfectly. A tiny scrap of a bonnet hid little of her plentiful dark hair. "The child I am carrying belongs to your late brother."

"Half brother." Never before had Drake made that distancing distinction.

"I'm sorry, ma'am, but you must understand my scepticism."

She inclined her head slightly to acknowledge his point. "I did not come here to make wild claims I cannot support, your lordship. I can provide you with proof of everything I've said."

"I fail to see how that's possible, under the circumstances."

Rummaging in her reticule, she drew out several badly creased letters and passed them over to him. "I trust you recognize the hand?"

Drake gave a convulsive nod, not trusting himself to speak. It was an unsettling sensation to see unfamiliar words penned in a familiar hand, now dead. Somehow they brought the writer momentarily to life. No question the writing was Jeremy's. The spiky, boyish hand, the effortless fluency. The young fool had been quite smitten with Rosalind Beaumont. Addressing her in disturbingly intimate terms, making her any number of imprudent promises—including marriage. Had Jeremy actually entertained the notion that his brother would sanction such a match, to an actress several years the boy's senior?

His exasperation with Jeremy sharpened Drake's tone. "I'm willing to concede my brother was in love with you, Mrs. Beaumont. As for the rest..."

With obvious reluctance, she surrendered one final letter. Despatched from Spain, it bore a date only days before Jeremy's death. It mentioned their "special night together" and once again hinted at marriage, without actually asking for her hand. Drake felt his stock growing increasingly tight around his neck. Between Lucy and Mrs. Beaumont, his brother's final leave had been most...productive.

Somehow his hardheaded practicality asserted itself. "Very well. He was in love with you and you took him into your bed."

"What further proof can you need?"

"At the very least I need to be certain that what you say about your condition is true."

Eyes blazing, she rose from her seat. Drake assumed she meant to flounce out of the room in high dudgeon. By the time it dawned on him that she was lifting the hem of her gown, he was too astonished to even avert his eyes. For a moment she stood there with her gown kilted up to her bosom and her rounded belly exposed. Along with much else besides.

Hearing a gasp, Drake assumed it was his own.

"Convinced?" She twitched her clothing back in place and resumed her seat.

"A-and you're certain no other man could have fathered your child?"

For the first time during their interview, her self-control looked in danger of faltering. "By rights I should slap your face for that question, Lord Silverthorne. Unfortunately, I cannot afford to. I fear you have only my word that I'd no other lovers but Jeremy. Despite what you may have heard about actresses, we are no less moral than other women."

"I count myself a fair judge of character, Mrs. Beaumont. I withdraw the question with my apologies."

Drake thought he detected a momentary tremor of her chin.

"What do you need from me?" he asked.

She reached back into her reticule, this time producing a handkerchief. "I am not accustomed to asking for charity, sir. Never would I stoop to it on my own account. But for the sake of Jeremy's child, I am prepared to swallow my pride."

"I can understand that." Drake caught himself in a sigh. He had to admire Jeremy's taste in women and envy the devotion he inspired. Almost as much as he abhorred the way his brother had treated them.

Rosalind Beaumont's green eyes searched his and appeared to approve what they found. "I want to raise this child, Lord Silverthorne. I'd given up hope of ever having one. When I realized my condition, it was as though your brother had left me a parting gift."

Drake bit back a sardonic quip. Who was he to strip this woman of her romantic illusions?

"I refuse to farm my baby out and scarcely ever see it.

However, to raise an illegitimate child openly would spell the end of my stage career. I have a little money put by, but nowhere near enough to retire on.''

''Set your mind at rest, Mrs. Beaumont.'' Now that he was convinced of her story, he could at least spare her the final humiliation of asking for his help. ''I will not see my brother's child in want. I commend your decision to raise it yourself.''

He turned to the writing desk behind him and jotted down a number on a scrap of paper. ''Will this capital sum in trust provide a sufficient income?''

When he handed it to her, the woman stared at the paper with widening eyes. ''I had no intention of asking for so much, your lordship. It is not my wish to use my child for financial gain.''

''Of course not. But prices continue to rise. I want Jeremy's child to enjoy a comfortable upbringing and the finest possible education. I also feel you should be compensated for giving up your stage career. Have you given any thought to where you'll go?''

''I mean to stay in London until the child is born and I can arrange to let my house. Then I'll find a quiet country village in Devon, perhaps, or the Cotswolds, where no one will know me. I'll claim I'm an officer's widow.''

''Close enough to the truth.'' Drake nodded. ''I would be honored if you and your child decide to bear the Strickland name.''

She broke down then, so abruptly and completely that Drake could not resist reaching out to her. Kneeling on the floor before her, he held the weeping woman to his shoulder until her tears subsided. Before Lucy, he never would have dared make such a personal gesture. His wife had nurtured a side of him that Drake had never suspected, let alone taken pains to cultivate. Yet he knew he was a better, happier man for it.

When at last she mastered her turbulent emotions, Mrs.

Beaumont seemed eager to conclude the interview. Drake promised to postpone his departure from London until he had consulted his solicitors and arranged a mutually agreeable settlement. Peering out around the library door, he satisfied himself that the hall was empty. He tried not to betray his haste to get Mrs. Beaumont out of the house.

At the front door, she turned and grasped his hand. "Bless you, sir." She spoke in a choked whisper. "Your generosity is legendary, but those reports scarcely do you justice. Your permission to use the Strickland name is more precious to me than all the money in the world. Your wife is a fortunate woman indeed."

His wife. Lucy. Here was his chance to wrest her from Jeremy once and for all. Introduce her to Rosalind Beaumont. Show her the evidence of how Jeremy had used her—going straight from her arms to the bed of another woman, passing false promises of marriage as his romantic currency.

Mrs. Beaumont gave Drake a strange look. "I'm sorry, your lordship. Was it something I said?"

Drake shook his head to dispel the rash impulse. He knew of other captains of industry who had clawed their way to the top by ruthlessly destroying all competition. That had never been his way. Whether in business or matters of the heart, Drake wanted to succeed on his own merits, not by eliminating his rivals.

Besides, how could he face himself if he gained Lucy's love at the cost of her fragile romantic ideals? How might she feel about herself, knowing the man she'd worshipped had exploited her with such casual indifference?

"I attach only one condition to our arrangement, Mrs. Beaumont."

"Yes?" She looked wary, as if unsettled by the sudden intensity in his voice.

"My wife must know nothing about this."

"You have my word."

* * *

As she collapsed onto the second step above the staircase landing, Lucy's thoughts resonated with Drake's parting words to Mrs. Beaumont.

My wife must know nothing about this.

Talk of shutting the barn door after the horse had bolted!

It was her own fault, she supposed, for eavesdropping. Listeners seldom overheard anything good. Not that she'd meant to spy on Drake. On her way to fetch a small trunk for packing, she'd happened to overhear a couple of the maids gossiping.

"Just had a quick peek in the keyhole and I thought I'd faint dead away. There she was hauling her dress off—in our library in broad daylight!"

"Never!"

"Swear it on my life."

When the girls had moved out of earshot, Lucy couldn't keep herself from perching on the stair landing. From there she had a clear view of the library door, while remaining all but invisible herself. Though it could not have been above ten minutes before Drake and that woman emerged from the room, it felt like hours to Lucy. Hours during which she made up her mind and changed it a hundred times.

So absorbed was Lucy in this debate with herself, that the sound of the library door opening made her start guiltily. She eased farther back into the concealing shadows of the upper stairway. Though she could not distinguish the words her husband exchanged with the actress, the urgency of their tone was unmistakable. Drake's final words had floated up to her, distinct and emphatic—the last damning indictment to sway her verdict.

Yet set against all the other evidence wavered one faint but stubborn hope. If Drake did care for the actress and she, Lucy, meant nothing to him, how could he have made such exquisite love to her only hours before?

Suddenly Lucy felt she could endure anything but this

guessing and wondering. After what had passed between them last night, she could not bear to confront Drake. To look into his regret-filled eyes and hear the harsh words of confirmation from his lips. No. Whatever distasteful truth she must face, she would brave it better from a stranger.

As Lucy tied on her bonnet, she puzzled how to order a carriage and escort without alerting Drake. Just then, she heard a mannerly tap on the front door. Thinking Mrs. Beaumont might have returned, she didn't know whether to feel dismayed or relieved.

Lucy tugged the door open.

There stood Eugene Dalrymple, dapper in a high beaver hat, buff-colored trousers and a well-tailored coat.

"Lady Silverthorne!" He looked both surprised and amused to find a viscountess answering her own door. It did not take him long to regain his poise, however. Sweeping a courtly bow, he offered her a bouquet of poseys.

"Dear Lady Silverthorne. Please accept this humble token of my most abject apologies and assurance of my continued regard."

"Apologies?" Glancing nervously behind her, Lucy took the flowers and stepped outside, quietly closing the front door behind her. "What on earth have you done that might require an apology?"

"Then you aren't angry with me?" The anxious set of his eyebrows relaxed visibly. "Perhaps I've only been foolishly sensitive. But after you rebuffed my dance invitation last night and then went out of your way to avoid me...I concluded..."

Lucy clasped his hand. After what she had seen this morning, she couldn't abide the thought of causing anyone else emotional distress. "Of course I'm not angry with you. Why, you have been kindness itself to me ever since I arrived in London."

"An honor and a pleasure, dear lady. Nothing could give

me more joy than being of even the slightest service to you." He lifted her gloved hand to his lips.

Spying his carriage on the curb gave Lucy an idea.

"You could do me a most signal service this very moment, Mr. Dalrymple. I have an appointment at Covent Garden and no carriage at my disposal. Might I importune you for a drive?"

His handsome features blossomed into an expression of utter felicity. It put Lucy in mind of how Jeremy had looked the day she'd agreed to a tryst in the woodlands of Silverthorne. For some reason that made her uneasy.

Her budding doubts dissipated when Mr. Dalrymple replied, "I am entirely at your disposal, dear lady."

A brief word to his driver, and they were off.

"What a fortunate coincidence," said Mr. Dalrymple. "It leads me to wonder if Lady Fate may have taken me in hand."

"I beg your pardon?" Lucy buried her face in the poseys to avoid the intensity of his gaze.

"I had hoped for a private word with you, and what could be more private than this?"

Lucy glanced around the tastefully appointed interior of the carriage. She was suddenly mindful of the breach in propriety she was committing by driving alone with a man other than her husband. Steeling herself against such thoughts, she decided it was no greater indiscretion than Drake "entertaining" an actress in the library.

"You'll have to speak quickly," she said. "We won't have many minutes to the theater." As the carriage made a sudden right turn onto King Street, Lucy cast Mr. Dalrymple a questioning look. "This isn't the way to Covent Garden. Please, sir, it is urgent I get to the theater."

Airily, he waved her objections away. "All in good time, my dear Lady Silverthorne. I took the liberty of instructing my driver to take us on a short detour through Hyde Park.

I trust you would not deny me ten minutes of your time, when we may not meet again for who knows how long.''

Lucy tried to summon the indignation she knew should readily rise, but it flickered and died in the face of that charmingly wistful smile and entreating eyes.

''Oh, very well.'' She gave an indulgent sigh. ''What have you to say for yourself?''

''Something I have longed to say from the moment we met. First, though, I must tell you some important news. I have just this hour received word from Florence that my aunt, the Duchess of Swansea, has died. I expect to sail for the Mediterranean tomorrow at the latest.''

Though he looked far from heartbroken by the news, Lucy expressed her sympathy for his loss.

''Indeed, I shall miss the old girl, but it was hardly un-expected...most fortuitous, in fact. As my aunt's sole heir, I'm now master of a fortune at least the equal of your husband's.''

''How lovely for you. I trust your new wealth will ease your grief.'' She could not fully censor a note of scorn from her voice.

''Don't you see, Lucy?'' Kneeling on the floor of the carriage, he took her hand. ''Now that I've come into my inheritance, I am free to tell you how ardently and passion-ately I have come to love you. Say you'll sail with me tomorrow, and we shall live like royalty in the courts of Europe.''

After an instant of complete shock, Lucy found her voice at last. ''Do get off the floor, Mr. Dalrymple.'' She wrenched her hand away. ''And kindly refrain from address-ing me in such a manner. I will thank you to remember that I'm a married woman.''

He made no move to rise. ''Bah! A loveless marriage to that awkward excuse for a viscount. I know how miserable you are with him. He doesn't begin to deserve you.''

''You have no idea what my husband deserves, young

man. Now stop spouting this foolishness and take me home at once.''

Instead Mr. Dalrymple took her face in his hands and kissed her. A thorough, practiced, expert kiss, that might have turned another woman's knees to water. It only made Lucy's gorge rise as high as her temper.

"Let go of me, Mr. Dalrymple and stop this carriage so I can find my own way home. Driver! Stop now!''

Dalrymple backed off slightly, though he did not resume his seat. Remorse and affront plainly warred for control of his handsome features. "I must apologize, dear lady. It never occurred to me that you might not return my feelings. Now I fear you are overset. Here, take my handkerchief.''

The white cloth fluttered before Lucy's face. Then came an explosion of pain and darkness.

Chapter Twenty

"Gone?" Drake sputtered. "What do you mean, gone?"

"It's a common enough word," replied Phyllipa, her tone uncommonly sharp. "I mean Lucy is nowhere to be found and no one has the slightest idea where she might be."

Drake felt as if someone had just pulled a very comfortable chair out from under him. Still, he tried to sound casual. "Perhaps she thought of some last minute purchases she needed to make before we leave for Silverthorne. Did you check if she took one of the carriages?"

"That was my first thought." Phyllipa shook her head, negating that possible explanation.

"When was the last time anyone saw her?"

Phyllipa thought for a moment before answering. "Martin saw the two of you when you got back from Holland House, but none of the servants saw her this morning. I'd say that makes you the last to see her. You don't suppose she went out before the servants were stirring this morning?"

"She was still here at six." He refused to elaborate, though her blatantly curious stare all but demanded it. At six he had slipped out of Lucy's bed and stolen away. He hadn't known what he should say when she woke, fearing whatever he said would be wrong.

"Are you telling me no one in this house has seen Lucy between then and now?" he demanded gruffly.

"I've asked everyone."

"You didn't ask me." Young Reggie spoke from the staircase. Traces of jam stained his ample mouth.

His mother threw up her hands in horror. "Reggie, darling, get back to the nursery this instant!"

"Oh, Mama! I'm too old for the nursery. I want to go away to school like other chaps my age."

"Reggie, dear, you know your constitution is too delicate for the rigors of school. Besides, the good ones are so expensive."

Drake might have laughed at their exchange, if he hadn't been so anxious about Lucy. "The boy has a point, Phyllipa. High time he went to school. I'll draw you up a bank draft to cover his expenses."

Reggie's petulant frown spread into the most sincere smile Drake had ever seen on his round face.

"Now, Reggie, I'm asking—did you see Cousin Lucy today?"

The boy bobbed his head vigorously. "Round noon. A posh-looking cove with yellow hair called. Lucy went away with him in his carriage. He gave her flowers," the boy added helpfully.

"Did you see which way they went?" Drake managed to ask from a painfully constricted throat.

"That way." The boy cocked his thumb in the direction of central London.

"Anything else you remember?"

"The horses were brown."

"You've been a great help, Reggie. Thank you."

The boy was scarcely out of earshot when Phyllipa erupted. "Dalrymple! She's bolted with Mr. Dalrymple, and my poor impressionable Reggie had to see it all!"

"We don't know it *was* Dalrymple," Drake snapped. "And we certainly don't know Lucy has bolted."

Phyllipa contemplated him with a look of pity usually reserved for harmless imbeciles. "Who else in London does she know well enough to accept a drive? The man certainly answers to Mr. Dalrymple's description."

"They may only have meant to exchange a few words of farewell." Silently conceding the identity of Lucy's escort, Drake wondered if this suggestion rang as hollow to Phyllipa's ears as it did to his own.

Apparently so, for she nodded toward the clock in the east corner of the library. It showed the hour as half past three. "If that's the case, they're taking their own good time about it."

He could not stand to continue this conversation with Phyllipa. As he desperately tried to pretend everything was all right, his heart screamed that something was terribly, terribly wrong.

"Go check her room. See if she took anything away with her. Ask Reggie if she was carrying any luggage when he saw her."

After Phyllipa had hurried away, clucking and fussing, Drake locked the library doors and sank into a chair. Was it possible that Lucy had bolted with that suave dandy, Dalrymple? Had they planned it in advance? Was that why she'd let him into her bed last night, to allay his suspicions? Or had she fled on impulse, because he'd insisted on claiming his marital rights? If he had driven her into the arms of a rogue like Eugene Dalrymple, Drake knew he would never forgive himself.

Lucy woke in the pale light of a spring dawn to the sound of a lark piping outside her window. For an instant she burrowed beneath the blankets, chuckling over the vivid but ridiculous dream she'd been having. Then she felt the insistent throbbing in her head and smelled a dank, musty odor Lady Phyllipa would never permit in 17 Grafton Square.

Cautiously, Lucy opened her eyes. Wherever she was, it

bore no resemblance to her airy corner room in Drake's elegant town house. The dimensions of the two chambers were roughly comparable, but all similarity ended there. Instead of flower-sprigged wallpaper, this room had been paneled with dark wood—in Tudor times, by the scarred look of it. In place of her bright chintz-covered chaise sat a sturdy wooden armchair of ancient pedigree. The lone window looked only half the size of her one at Grafton Square. Rather than soft damask draperies, it boasted a set of stout iron bars—the newest item in the room.

Holding her head and swaying from dizziness, Lucy staggered from the narrow tester bed to the door. It was locked securely from the outside. At the base of the door a slot had recently been cut and fitted with a hatch. Lucy knelt to inspect the dimensions of the hole. A small child or a dog might have been able to wriggle through, she decided. A grown woman, particularly a pregnant one, would not have a hope in the world. Weaving her way to the window, past the crumbling hearth and an archaic washstand, Lucy glanced outside. Her heart sank.

Even without bars, the three-story drop to the ground would have made the window an unappealing avenue of escape. The building that housed her prison room stood well back from a country lane—within sight, but out of earshot. There were no other dwellings nearby. No one she could call for help.

Slowly Lucy wilted to the floor, tears of impotent rage and self-reproach stinging in her eyes. How could she have been so imprudent as to trust a scoundrel like Dalrymple, in spite of Drake's express warning? She'd been misled completely by his good looks and facile gallantry.

This was not the first time she'd allowed herself to be deceived by appearances. How could she have imagined herself in love with a man she hardly knew? She'd been drawn by Jeremy's golden beauty, by his easy charm. In every way that counted, though, he'd been a stranger to her.

If he'd been half the peerless gentleman she'd imagined, he never would have pressured her to make love before she was ready.

Make love? A hiccough of tearful, ironic laughter broke from Lucy's lips. Jeremy Strickland hadn't made love to her in that secluded glade on the Silverthorne estate. He had made use of her body to satisfy his own needs, with no thought at all about her feelings.

Drake had made love to her, with no regard for himself. In the months of their marriage she had come to glimpse his true worth. Knowing Drake, there was probably much more to discover—all of it good. She'd been a fool not to heed his warning about Dalrymple. She'd been wrong to suspect anything amiss between him and Mrs. Beaumont. If only she could find her way back to him....

The sound of approaching footsteps intruded on Lucy's thoughts. Hastily brushing her tears away, she scanned the room for anything she might use as a weapon. Her options were depressingly limited. Careful to make as little noise as possible, she pried a good-size stone from the crumbling mortar of the hearth. Twisting it into a corner of her shawl, she wished for a clear shot at Eugene Dalrymple's golden pate. By heaven, she'd repay him for the tender goose egg that throbbed behind her left ear.

The steps came to a halt on the far side of the door. The hinged hatch raised to admit a small basket of food. Lucy held herself still as a statue, until the steps began to retreat again.

Though she longed to berate her captor in the foulest possible language, she called out in as soft and appealing a voice as she could feign. "Mr. Dalrymple, is that you? Won't you come in so we can talk?"

The footsteps approached, but Lucy heard no rattle of keys or lifting of the latch.

"Dear lady, awake at last," came the sickeningly familiar voice. "I trust you slept well."

If she could have reached his throat, she would happily have throttled him. Still, he represented her easiest means of escape.

With good cheer, which she hoped did not sound too forced, she replied. "Very soundly, thank you. If you brought me here to consider your proposal at greater leisure, I am sorry to have put you to the trouble. I had every intention of accepting you, eventually. I only protested at first for fear I might lose your respect by agreeing too readily. I'm flattered you were prepared to take such extreme measures to win me."

"Nicely tried, dear lady." Dalrymple mocked her with exaggerated courtesy. "You pretend to fly with me, only to give me the slip at Dover."

Lucy cursed silently. How could she have hoped to dupe the master of duplicity?

"I would like to believe you, if only to salve my wounded vanity," Dalrymple continued. "Though, to be perfectly candid, your answer yesterday would not have influenced your present circumstances. This was our destination all along. Your initial reluctance simply forced me to employ less subtle tactics to secure your cooperation."

His oily mock civility goaded Lucy worse than outright impudence. Like an overwound spring, her composure snapped.

"Villain! How dare you abduct me and hold me against my will? How long do you mean to keep me here? Are you aware that I am…in a delicate condition?"

"Indeed? If you think that will influence my actions, I regret to disappoint you. In fact, your…condition is an advantage to me, if anything. I doubt you would wish to endanger your unborn child in some foolish effort to escape my custody. I can assure you, dear lady, we are miles from anywhere. Even if you were to find a way out of this house, you could not waddle far before I hunted you down. As for the length of your stay, that depends on how long it takes Lord Silverthorne to secure a Bill of Divorcement.''

"Drake?" Lucy almost gagged on his name. "Do you mean to say he is behind all this?"

After a short pause, Dalrymple replied, "Very clever, dear lady. You have managed to trick more information from me than I meant to divulge. However, since you have, I might as well tell you that I have been in your husband's employ from the moment we met. He is most anxious to sever your ill-advised union."

"Liar! Drake warned me away from you. He said he would not trust you to spell the word *sincere*."

Dalrymple sniggered. "As well he should know, having secured my services. Your husband is a surprisingly effective actor when properly motivated. Of course, it was I who suggested he forbid you to consort with me. I thought it would create a favorably repressive atmosphere from which you might seek to escape."

Lucy choked on her own furious retort. How could she stake her life on her faith in any man's integrity? Hadn't she proven herself gullible time and time again?

"Enjoy your breakfast, dear lady, and do make yourself as comfortable as possible under the circumstances. I regret the amenities here are so…limited. I look forward to more of your delightful discourse when I return with your dinner."

Slowly, Lucy sank to the floor, sucked into a well of despair too deep for tears. Would her father believe she had abandoned her husband to run off with another man? How would he bear the disappointment and disgrace? And what would become of her child? Would Drake claim the baby and take him away from her as soon as she'd given birth? He would never see the child come to harm—that Lucy still believed. What of Mrs. Beaumont, though? Might Drake's new wife see the child as a threat to her own? Infants were so vulnerable…

How long she crouched on the bare wood floor, alternately battered by hopelessness and self-reproach, Lucy could not tell. She only came to herself when the baby gave several insistent kicks from within her.

Laying a hand on her belly, she rubbed it in sweeping circles. "You're hungry aren't you, little one?"

Poking through the basket Dalrymple had left, she discovered four slices of coarse bread, a dried apple, cheese, a cold hard-boiled egg and a small pitcher of fresh milk. At least her captor did not intend to starve her. Lucy ate the egg, the apple and half the bread, washing her breakfast down with the milk. Two pieces of bread she set aside with the cheese. She'd need an emergency supply of food, so as not to be altogether dependent on Dalrymple's dubious mercy for nourishment.

Listlessly, she walked over to the window and stared out. Part of her mind registered the first swelling buds on the massive old oak tree. Its wide-flung branches almost brushed the house. Out on the road, a loaded haywaine trundled past. No doubt it was headed for the fodder market of some nearby town. Tugging up the moisture-swollen window sash, Lucy longed to call for help. Then she considered the consequences.

Even if the distant wagoner did hear her, the not-so-distant Mr. Dalrymple surely would. Dependent on him for food and water, she did not dare antagonize him. Besides, if a passerby heard her and came to investigate, the unctuous Dalrymple was quite capable of fabricating a plausible and innocent-sounding explanation. Frustrated beyond bearing, Lucy slammed her fist against the window casement. The wet, rotten wood splintered beneath the savage force of her blow.

A faint ray of hope flickered to life in her heart.

With no one but herself to consider, she might have lain on the bed and given up. She might have wallowed in the heartbreak of Drake's betrayal and the brutal shattering of all her romantic ideals. But she was not alone.

Some instinct warned her that she dared not risk giving birth to her child in this house. No longer certain who she could trust, she knew she could not trust her captor. While she was in his power, her child would never be safe. No matter how difficult or dangerous, escape was imperative.

She could not afford to approach it in her usual impetuous manner, though. She needed to cultivate practicality, vigilance, and above all, patience. She would get only one chance, so her plan must be foolproof. With each passing day of her placid, uneventful captivity, Dalrymple would relax his guard, until she was ready to make her move.

"Are you certain of all this?" Drake glanced up from the report he'd been reading. Even on this mild April day, the ice of January gripped his heart.

"Certain as I can be, milord," answered the author of the report. He was a small man, with an agile, inquisitive air that had probably served him well on the force of the Bow Street Runners. "The trail was clear enough for a blind man to follow."

"I see you questioned the carriage driver. How did you manage to track him down?"

"Notice in the papers, milord, promising a small reward for information. Draws 'em out of the woodwork every time, it does. One chap correctly supplied me with details purposely omitted from the newspaper notice."

"I see. And he drove them around Hyde Park before continuing to the river. Did that not strike you as odd?"

The man shrugged. "When you've been in this business as long as I have, milord, you find out people do odd things. Often for reasons none of the rest of us can understand. I believe that driver is telling the truth about his passengers boarding a barque flying the Portuguese flag."

Once again Drake looked down at the report, written in

a crabbed, barely decipherable hand. "The *Santa Inez,* bound for Florence, which cast off shortly after they boarded."

Neville, who'd been listening to the exchange with uncharacteristic restraint, could not keep his opinion to himself a moment longer. "What more evidence do you need, Cousin Drake? She ran off with Dalrymple on a ship bound for Florence...."

"...where he has wealthy relations," chimed in Phyllipa. "I'm certain that will be ample evidence for Parliament."

"What business of Parliament's is my private life, exactly?" Drake strove to keep a rein on his temper. If his cousins kept it up much longer, he'd be sorely tempted to smack their heads together. He'd suffered three days of their ill-disguised gloating, and he didn't think he could stand one minute more.

Neville stared at him as though he'd grown a second head. "It's the House that will decide whether or not you get your Bill of Divorcement, of course. It'll be an open-and-shut case. Most of the Honorable Members got a chance to see your bride disporting herself all over London with that Dalrymple cove."

"I don't recollect asking for your opinion on any of this, Neville." Seeing Phyllipa preen self-righteously, Drake widened his glare to include her. "Nor yours, madam. What will it take to dun it into your thick skulls that I have no intention of airing my private life before Parliament?"

Phyllipa's meager lower lip trembled, and her watery eyes brimmed. "We are only thinking of you, Drake, and the family name."

Placing his arm gingerly around her shoulder, Neville offered his handkerchief. He cast his cousin a reproachful look, using Phyllipa's tears as an excuse to get in one last dig. "She's right, old fellow. You're going to have to divorce Lucy one of these days. Why not now while public sympathy is running high for you and the press is keeping strangely quiet about the whole affair? If you let it go and then bring a bill forward later, it'll simply dredge everything up again. Quickest mended, soonest forgotten, what? You need to put this behind you and get on with your life."

"Don't!" Drake only realized at what volume he'd bellowed when Phyllipa jumped back, emitting a strangled squeak. With every remaining shred of self-control, he resumed in a quieter, but no less menacing tone. "Don't have the effrontery to lecture *me* on how I should live my life, Neville. There will be no divorce. The subject is closed. Now I would like a private word with Mr. Langstroth."

The pair of them vacated the library, shamelessly milking Phyllipa's distress for the benefit of the investigator. When the door finally closed, Drake exchanged a glance with Langstroth. The two men shook their heads.

"I like the work you've done on the case thus far, Langstroth. You've shown yourself to be thorough, discreet and trustworthy—difficult virtues to come by singly, let alone in consort."

"Just trying to give good value for the pay, milord."

"A policy I fully endorse. I have another mission I'd like you to undertake on my behalf, if you're willing. How do you fancy spring in Italy?"

"I've always had a fancy to travel, milord. What sort of mission did you have in mind?"

Drake handed over a heavy envelope, well-sealed with wax. "I want you to find my wife and give her this. The English colony in Florence is not that large. You shouldn't have much trouble tracking her down through Dalrymple's aunt."

"Very good, milord. I'll leave as soon as I can book passage." Langstroth turned the envelope over several times in his hands. If he wondered about its contents, he did not ask.

"Don't come back right away after you've delivered it," Drake added. "Let Lady Silverthorne know you'll be staying awhile and where she can reach you. If she requests your help, you are to give her your complete cooperation. I will compensate you handsomely for your trouble.''

''So, if she asks, I'm to bring her home to you, milord.'' Langstroth looked a little doubtful, as though he could not fathom a man willing to take back his errant wife.

Drake shook his head. ''If she asks, you are to take her wherever *she* wishes to go.''

When his agent had gone, Drake dropped heavily into the nearest chair, raking a hand distractedly through his hair. The letter now en route to Lucy, accompanied by a large sum in gold, had been the most difficult he'd ever written. He'd labored over it day and night, consigning draft after draft to the fire. Somehow, from the depths of his heart, he had dredged up the words to tell her something of what she meant to him.

Begging forgiveness for what he had done to her, he swore it would never happen again. And he meant every word. Wondrous as it had been to commune with her physically, that was but a small part of his love for her. Though it might exact a gruelling cost from him to keep her at arm's length, that is what he would do if only she would come back. Her presence in his life was all he asked.

Drake prayed that by the time his agent reached Florence, Lucy would have discovered Dalrymple's true character. Perhaps when he realized she was carrying another man's child, his passion would cool and she would see he was no fit father for her baby. Then, perhaps, she would return to Silverthorne.

Nursing that spark of optimism against all common sense, Drake returned to Nicholthwait a week later. There he immersed himself in business, working doggedly to keep himself from thinking. After each long day he would ride out for an hour or two, galloping over the steep roads as if to outrun the doubts that bayed at his heels.

As each week gave birth to the next, and spring blossomed into summer in the Lake Country, Drake waited for news from his agent. With each passing day, and no word, his hope suffered a painful and protracted death.

Chapter Twenty-One

"Hurry up, Dalrymple, you vile bounder," Lucy muttered to herself as she lay on the bed listening for the sound of his approaching footsteps.

Having spent three interminable months as a prisoner in this run-down garret, she doubted she could tolerate another hour without going mad. Besides, her opportunities for escape were dwindling rapidly. By her own inexpert calculations, the baby would soon insist on making his appearance. Fortunately her body had not yet become too unwieldy, but she could not count on that continuing. Nor could she risk the exertions of her escape bringing on labor.

It had taken almost two months of slow, painstaking preparation to ready everything for her flight. She'd pressed every available drop of moisture into service to keep the rotting wood of the window casement constantly damp. Then, a splinter at a time, she had gouged out the weak frame around those sturdy iron bars. Now, a single push should send them hurtling to the ground below.

She'd torn her bed linen into strips. Braiding them together for strength and tying the lengths into a serviceable rope, she hoped to climb down it to safety. Ever since that first day of her imprisonment, she'd eaten only the perishable food from her meals. Any foodstuffs she could safely save for a day or two, she had saved, eating what she'd kept from the previous days. That way, she always had emergency rations on hand.

Observation had been the final key to her plan. She knew Dalrymple had been right in boasting she could never reach safety on foot. With a bit of charcoal from the hearth, she'd drawn a crude calender on a corner of the floor. For days she had kept watch by the window to see if any traffic passed regularly. Her diligence had been rewarded. As it happened, the haywaine she'd watched going past on her first morning of captivity was a regular weekly fixture. All she had to do was arrange to get out of the house on a Tuesday morning in time to catch a ride to town hidden in the pile of hay.

That had proven no mean feat.

Two weeks earlier, she'd been all set to put her plan into action. Dalrymple had proven most uncooperative, however, showing up so late with her breakfast that the haywaine had long since passed. He'd been bright and early the following week, but a vicious rainstorm had dissuaded Lucy from trying.

The weather this morning was perfect for her purpose. A light fog would mask her activities from any curious passersby. Not that it would matter if that blackguard Dalrymple didn't come soon…

Lucy could not stifle a squeal of frustration.

"Something the matter, dear lady?"

Dalrymple's words took her so much by surprise, she almost forgot what she meant to do next. Almost….

"Ooo!" she groaned biliously.

The footsteps drew nearer. "What's wrong?" he demanded. "What's going on in there?"

"What do you think, fool? My baby's coming, of course! Ooo! The pains have been getting worse for hours now. I didn't think you'd ever come." That part was true, at least. "Please go fetch me a midwife. You promised you would.

Please. Ooo!'' She dredged up a most impressive groan from the depths of her bowels.

Lucy heard the sound of something hitting the floor—her breakfast no doubt. For a moment she feared Dalrymple might venture inside to attend her himself. She redoubled her thrashing and moaning.

''Yes. Yes. Stay right there.''

During the past weeks, it had been Lucy's dubious pleasure to become well acquainted with her captor. What she had discovered frightened her deeply. In some ways he reminded her of a badly spoiled child. Behind his mask of exaggerated civility lurked a vicious temper, which flared when his will was thwarted. Their weeks of isolation had made it worse. Yet for all his cold-bloodedness, he'd betrayed a disquieting squeamishness about childbearing that puzzled Lucy. At the moment, she thanked heaven for his exploitable weakness.

''Hold it in!'' he cried. ''I'll be back with the midwife before you know it.''

He sounded in such a panic Lucy could scarcely keep her pretended sobs of pain from turning into hysterical laughter.

She kept up her charade of childbirth all the while she crept to the window and watched Dalrymple ride off. As soon as he was out of sight, Lucy sprang into action. Tying a bundle of food in a sling over her shoulder, she secured the end of the plaited rope to one sturdy bedpost. Using the washstand as a light battering ram, she pushed the iron bars free of the eroded window casement. They fell to the ground with a muted but satisfying thud.

When Lucy eased herself out the gaping hole where the window had once been, her nerve momentarily deserted her. It was such a long way to the ground and she had no head for heights.

Too late for such thoughts now.

Inhaling as if it might be her last drawn breath, she grasped the thick braid of linen tightly with her hands and her knees. Slowly she began hitching herself down. Teeth clenched together and every muscle of her body knotted with tension, she kept her eyes fixed on the stone wall before her as she descended.

After one heart-stopping moment when she feared her rope would tear, Lucy reached the ground safely.

By the time she ran across the open field to the hedgerow, she was panting—partly from the exertions of her escape, partly from heightened nerves, and partly from a sense of imminent triumph. Soon the haywaine would rattle by, and she would scramble aboard without its driver being any the wiser. Some minutes passed before an uneasy chill crept into her heart.

Where was the wagon? Could she have miscalculated the days? As a host of doubts assailed her, Lucy heard the distant pounding of hoofbeats. For an instant her roiling stomach settled. Then she realized the approaching horse was far too light and fleet to be the farmer's lumbering dray.

Her worst fears took shape when Dalrymple rode by on a chestnut cob, with the midwife riding pillion. A sob of vexation broke from Lucy's clenched lips. There could be no question of staying where she was. Soon Dalrymple would be after her.

But where to go? Lucy looked down the road. A town lay that way, one large enough to host a weekly haymarket. Had she any hope of reaching it before Dalrymple caught her? Not likely. Turning her face in the other direction, she set out. Somewhere this way she would find the farm that was home to her familiar haywaine. But would Dalrymple find her first?

Drake looked up from a ledger to see the compact figure of his agent, Langstroth, entering the countinghouse. For a moment his pulse sped up and the room wobbled dizzily in his vision. Then he marked the grim expression on the little man's freshly tanned face. Ruthlessly, Drake clamped down on that heady rush of hopeful elation.

"What news?" he asked, dispensing with the usual pleasantries. "My wife—did you see her? Speak to her? Is she well? The baby?"

Avoiding Drake's demanding stare, Langstroth shook his head. "Wherever your wife is, Lord Silverthorne, I can assure you she's nowhere near Florence."

"Nowhere near...? That's absurd! That hired driver saw them boarding the ship." Could there have been a wreck? Barbary pirates? His blood fairly congealed with dread at the terrifying prospects.

"Oh, the *Santa Inez* made port in Florence right enough, milord. Your wife wasn't on it, though. Nor Mr. Dalrymple, if that's his true name."

"What are you saying, man?"

"Well, milord, I poked around Florence awhile trying to track them down, and not a sign. Finally, I made contact with a man who works for the Duchess of Swansea. Turns out Her Grace *did* have a nephew named Eugene Dalrymple—but the young fellow died two years ago in Barbados."

"Then who was the man...?"

"Begging your pardon, milord, but I'd say that's what we have to find out next. That, and where the pair of them left the *Santa Inez*. My guess is they disembarked as soon as that hired driver was out of sight. Someone went to a good deal of trouble to make it look like your wife eloped to Florence, milord. I don't mind telling you, I smell something foul afoot."

Drake sat down hard on the high counting room stool. His head spun with questions, possibilities and gutwrenching fear.

"What do we do now?" Langstroth's news had unsettled him to such a pitch that he could scarcely think.

"I reckon all we can do, milord, is start fresh with the facts we know for certain. I'll hunt up that driver and question him again. Find out if anyone on the docks saw anything unusual that day. The trail will be cold after this many weeks, but it's all we have to go by. I take it you've had no communication from your wife, milord. No ransom demands?''

The very word, *ransom,* struck Drake like a hard, unexpected fist in the stomach. Mechanically, he shook his head.

''Would you be able to get away, milord? Come back to London and help me out with my inquiries?''

''Why, yes…of course. I have a day's work to settle and then I'll come. In the meantime, I want you back in London pursuing the case. I'll give you carte blanche, Langstroth. Whatever it takes. More manpower. Rewards for information. Bribes.''

How could he have neglected the prospect that Lucy might not have gone willingly? Drake berated himself. It had just seemed so reasonable that she should forsake him for a man so much like Jeremy.

''I won't rest until I get to the bottom of this.''

''Very good, milord. I'll meet you back in London.'' Langstroth took several short strides toward the door before he stopped suddenly and scurried back. From the pocket of his coat he withdrew the sealed envelope he'd carried to the Mediterranean and home again. Drake's love letter to Lucy.

''Under the circumstances, I think you'd better hang on to this, milord.''

After the agent had gone, Drake sat on the countinghouse stool, slowly turning the envelope over and over in his hands. Try as he might, he could not keep them from trembling. Though it had tormented him to think of Lucy sharing a Florentine villa with a wealthy young scoundrel, it was worse having no clue where she might be, or with whom.

Lucy brushed away a stalk of hay that tickled her nose, praying the chaff wouldn't set her sneezing. She had managed to reach the farm—a far nearer neighbor than she'd ever suspected. There in the lane, listing on a broken wheel, stood the loaded haywaine. With not another living soul in sight, Lucy dove into the pile of hay, covering herself completely. Cradled in the prickly, sweet-smelling cocoon, under a star-strewn summer sky, she had enjoyed her first peaceful sleep in months.

Bright and early that morning, the farmer and his son arrived and began to repair the old wagon. Willing herself to complete stillness, Lucy prayed they would soon finish and be on their way to town.

"Pardon me, good man." At the sound of Dalrymple's voice, a garotte of fear tightened around Lucy's throat. "Have you by any chance seen a young lady wandering this way? She is my sister, poor creature. Hasn't been right in the head since her husband was killed fighting in Spain."

"Haven't seen no one." The farmer did not bother to pause in his task.

Hardly daring to breathe for fear of discovery, Lucy still allowed herself the luxury of a faint smile. Clearly some people were immune to Dalrymple's vaunted charm.

He did not let the brusque reception deter him. "If you do see her, I'd be obliged if you could return her to me at Vinelands. The poor dear is with child and due to deliver any day. I can't imagine what made her run off. I shudder to think what harm might befall her if I don't recover her in time."

Lucy shuddered to think what might become of her if Dalrymple *did* find her. Only when he had ridden off and the haywaine had begun its ponderous progress, did Lucy allow one silent tear after another to slide down her cheeks.

Some while later, seeing the open countryside give way to the fringes of a town, she heaved a deep sigh of relief. Surely, she could find one kind soul to hide her and help her reach the safety of her aunt's house in Bath. Could she be so fortunate that this might be the outskirts of Bath itself? Certainly some of the buildings did look familiar.

But…wait.

With a start of amazement, Lucy realized they were not riding into Bath, but London. This must be Oxford Street. If the hay that concealed her was destined for Covent Garden or Smithfield, the old wagon would pass within yards of Grafton Square. Finding herself suddenly and unexpectedly back at the site of happier times overwhelmed Lucy. She experienced a surge of elation. Sanity had been restored again and the past three months felt like nothing but an unpleasant nightmare from which she'd finally awakened.

Before she quite knew what she was doing, Lucy scrambled out of her hiding place and slid off the slow-moving haywaine. Brushing the chaff from her clothes and picking long straws from her hair, she hurried towards Number 17.

Only when she was practically on the doorstep did she realize that she might be walking straight into the lion's den. After the measures he'd already taken to rid himself of her, what might Drake do if she suddenly appeared at his house? Would she find Mrs. Beaumont ensconced at Grafton Square, or had Drake taken his beautiful mistress back to Silverthorne?

As Lucy paused to consider a wiser course of action, a hired carriage pulled up before Number 17 and a man hastily alighted. Lucy instantly recognized Eugene Dalrymple. For a split second she froze, like a wild creature caught in the sights of the hunter's firearm. Then she dove for cover, into the narrow alley that led to the mews behind Drake's town house.

Pressing herself back against the bricks, she prayed Dalrymple had not noticed her. Gradually, over the deafening pounding of her own heart, she heard voices—agitated, angry voices. Lucy glanced up. Just a few feet above her head, the sitting room window had been opened to let in the balmy air. Resisting every instinct that screamed for her to flee at once, she listened carefully to the conversation. Her ears strained to catch the sound of Drake's voice.

*   *   *

For some time Neville Strickland had harbored the feeling that he was caught in the cogs of an enormous machine. He had set the mighty engine in motion. Now it was smoking and churning out of his control, and he could neither stop it, nor free himself from its pull. Just this minute his gathering apprehension had risen to a head at the sight of an unkempt and agitated Dalrymple in Phyllipa's sitting room.

Dalrymple's presence appeared to unnerve Phyllipa every bit as much. "How dare you show yourself here? That Bow Street Runner of Drake's passed through town just a few days ago, on his way north. He came around asking more questions. What if one of the servants recognizes you?"

"Gag her with something will you, Strickland?" Dalrymple honed in on the brandy decanter like a trained falcon swooping down on a hare. Disdaining the thimble-size glasses, he tipped the whole decanter back and all but drained it.

Flinching under Phyllipa's glare of outrage, Neville addressed their *guest*. "I say, old fellow. You're about the last person we expected to see. Thought you were off trysting under the Mediterranean sun."

He was lying. For some time Neville had suspected that the man he'd hired was not who he claimed to be. The look of utter contempt Dalrymple cast him in reply made Neville wonder if he had suddenly sprouted the head of an ass.

"Did you honestly suppose I could get to Florence, let alone live in any kind of style on the pittance you furnished me? I have been hibernating in a little hidey-hole of mine out past Ealing. Has that cousin of yours got his divorce yet? I've seen nothing about it in the papers, when I've been able to come by them. What's he dragging his feet over?"

Neville's sense of alarm escalated tenfold. "Drake claims he doesn't want a divorce—reluctant to air a scandal. What does that matter to you?"

"And what are you doing here?" added Phyllipa, her mouth puckered like a prune.

"The lovely Lady Silverthorne has escaped my custody," announced Dalrymple, his mannerly words laced with a bitter dose of sarcasm.

"Escaped?" squeaked Neville. "You mean she didn't go away with you of her own accord?"

"She might have if I'd been patient, but when she pretended reluctance I simply knocked her on the head and dragged her off. All the while making it look like we were bound for Italy. Clever, no?"

As one, Neville and Phyllipa collapsed onto the settee. Fetching him a furious blow, she burst into hysterical tears. "We're ruined! Doomed! This is all your fault, Neville. I never should have listened to you. She'll run straight to Drake, and then... Ooo! I daren't think what he'll do to us!" She ended in a doleful wail.

Dalrymple swooped down and gripped her by the arm. "Button up you wet goose, or I'll give you something to bawl about. The last place she's likely to run is back to Silverthorne. I told her he was the one who hired me to dispose of her. Fortunately, she's almost as gullible as the pair of you. Now we've got to get her back before she draws any unpleasant attention to us."

Her face pale as a sheet, Phyllipa wrenched her arm from Dalrymple's grasp. "To you, you mean. We didn't pay you to kidnap the woman, just persuade her to run off with you."

Dalrymple brought his handsome face within inches of hers. His reply was almost too quiet to hear, yet it carried a lethal edge. "Depend upon it, Lady Phyllipa. If I go before a judge, you and your dear cousin here will be standing either side of me. Swinging there, too, if it comes to that."

He straightened up, assuming his accustomed air of cynical composure. "We must get her back at all costs. And you are going to help me, or I swear I will skip the country, leaving Lord Silverthorne a very convincing message incriminating the pair of you."

Neville felt his head bobbing furiously up and down in agreement. "What must we do?"

"Place a notice in all the papers. Say we're looking for a poor mad woman who has run away from her loving family. Say she must be found before she comes to harm. Offer a reward for information."

"Very well." At that moment Neville would have given up all his expectations simply to turn the calendar back before any of this started. From his lackluster schooling he dredged up the old story of Pandora and her box.

In a daze, Lucy stumbled away from Grafton Square, scarcely conscious of where her legs were carrying her. The conversation between Neville, Phyllipa and Dalrymple hummed in her thoughts. Her heart raced and her empty stomach curdled, knowing they were on her trail like a pack of bloodhounds. All the same, a curious lightness buoyed her step, for Drake had not been the one behind her abduction after all.

She did not deserve him. Through her impulsive folly, he had once again been exposed to public ridicule as a man no woman would suffer. In spite of everything she knew about her husband's honorable character, she had swallowed Dalrymple's lies—believed him capable of the treachery committed against her. He was better off without such a wife.

If not to Drake, where could she turn?

Suddenly Lucy became aware of her surroundings again. Lost in her musings, she had wandered into Covent Garden. If only she'd been sensible enough to walk here on that fateful day in March, instead of rashly appealing to Dalrymple for a drive…

With that thought came the recollection of Mrs. Beaumont. Obviously she had no part in Dalrymple's plot after all. However, she did know something Drake wanted kept from his wife. Perhaps that was all the influence Lucy would need to prevail upon her for help.

Asking at the theatre for Mrs. Beaumont's address, Lucy received directions to a side street quite nearby.

"She don't see callers as a rule these days," the charlady informed Lucy. "Retired from the stage she has, and planning to leave the city, I hear. Pity that. Her so pretty and popular with the crowds."

Without a coin to tip, Lucy offered the woman her warmest smile of thanks. By the time she reached Mrs. Beaumont's house, she was footsore and weary to the bone. So the actress was planning a retirement to the country—the Lake Country, perhaps? Just because Drake was innocent of engineering the kidnapping did not mean he hadn't taken advantage of her absence. Still, if she promised to stay away, Mrs. Beaumont might at least advance her the coach fare to Bath.

As she knocked on the door of Mrs. Beaumont's modest house, Lucy tried to come up with a plausible excuse to gain admission. Before she could open her mouth to speak however, a stern-looking housekeeper eyed her up and down and motioned her inside.

"This way. Come along."

Swallowing her astonishment, Lucy followed. Down a long dark hall. Up a narrow staircase. Stopping before a closed door, the housekeeper knocked softly, then held the door for Lucy to enter. As she stepped over the threshold, the door closed almost soundlessly behind her.

Dainty, cream-colored draperies filtered the warm June sunlight, giving the room a luminous aura. The same tranquil glow exuded from the woman who hovered over a tiny cradle. In a dressing gown the color of Lake Country daffodils, she looked like the Madonna, as Gainsborough or Lawrence might paint her.

Lucy stood transfixed, caught in a maelstrom of conflicting emotions.

Mrs. Beaumont looked up at her and smiled. "You must

be here about the wet nurse position." She spoke in a low voice so as not to disturb the sleeping infant. "I believe you'll do admirably once we get you cleaned up a bit. How soon is your baby due?"

Chapter Twenty-Two

"I...I'm due...s-soon," Lucy stammered. "May I sit down? I've walked a long way today, and I'm feeling rather faint."

"Why, of course, my dear." Mrs. Beaumont ushered her to a comfortably upholstered chair near the baby's cradle. "How thoughtless of me. You don't look as if you've eaten properly in a while, either. Shall I ring for Janet to bring you a biscuit and some tea?"

"Later perhaps." Lucy could not keep herself from returning the other woman's smile. It spoke volumes for Mrs. Beaumont's character, this concern for the well-being of a virtual stranger. Here was a woman worthy of Drake.

"I hope you won't object to answering a few questions about your background," said Mrs. Beaumont.

Lucy shook her head. Her conscience pricked her for misleading such a kind lady. However, it might be the only way to discover if this child was the secret Drake had wished to keep from her.

"It won't pose a problem for you, removing to the country?" The actress looked visibly ill at ease with this necessary avenue of inquiry. "You have no strong ties to hold you in London? Friends? Family? A husband?"

"I'm a widow," Lucy replied, wondering if a trained

actress would recognize a blatant falsehood when she heard it. "I have no friends or family of any kind, which is why this post would be a godsend."

"You poor dear." Mrs. Beaumont clasped Lucy's fingers. "What a desperate situation for any woman, particularly with a child on the way. I am recently widowed as well. Fortunately my child has been provided for."

This salved Lucy's conscience somewhat. At least she was not the only liar of the two. Did this mean Drake had abandoned his mistress and child, leaving only hard cash to represent him? She scarcely knew whether to feel pleased or disillusioned. She detected a moist gleam in Rosalind Beaumont's eyes.

"I'm very sorry about your husband," Lucy murmured.

As she was about to inquire what had become of the lady's fictitious husband, the baby gave a thin squall, like the mewing of a cat. Mrs. Beaumont reached out and gently began to rock the cradle. Lucy's gaze fixed on the child—his head of fine dark hair and the thick, black eyebrows that looked oddly out of place on an infant.

Before she had time to think, the words were out of her mouth. "He does look like his father."

"I beg your pardon?"

Lucy caught herself. "I mean, does he look like his father at all?"

"No," Mrs. Beaumont whispered. She gazed intently at the baby, now peacefully asleep once more. A faint sound escaped from her lips—a chuckle with the slight catch of an arrested sob. "He takes after me entirely in his looks. Though they say a baby's first hair is often dark, then the second comes in lighter. If that happens, he still may be a handsome golden-head to remind me of…"

A single tear escaped her eye and slid slowly down her cheek.

Lucy's breath caught in her throat, and her own eyes suddenly brimmed with unshed tears. One last question, and she would know the truth she suspected. "Will you call him Jeremy?"

Perhaps Rosalind Beaumont was too deeply immersed in a melancholy mingling of love for her child and renewed grief for his father. Whatever the reason, she gave no sign that she recognized the significance of Lucy's question.

In a dreamy, faraway voice she replied quietly, "No. I would not presume. Lord Silverthorne has been generous enough, allowing us to use—" Her reverie shattered into shards of bewilderment and alarm. "Why did you ask that? How do you know? Who are you?"

Covering her face with her hands, Lucy wept in soft shuddering sobs. She knew she should be shedding tears of anguish for this final betrayal of Jeremy's—this proof that she had meant nothing to him beyond a passing conquest. In truth, those feelings might have accounted for a drop or two. But they were lost in the ocean of joyous brine, a wave of buoyant relief that Drake was the gentleman of honor she had long believed him to be.

Perhaps their wondrous night of love, the one she had tried in vain to forget, had meant as much to him as it had to her.

Gradually, she regained her composure. "Forgive my deception, Mrs. Beaumont, but I had to find out about the paternity of your son. I promise no harm will come to either of you by my knowing the truth. My name is Lucy Strickland. Lord Silverthorne is my husband."

Mrs. Beaumont's pretty mouth fell open. She stared at Lucy as if speculating whether she had welcomed a madwoman into her home.

"Lady Silverthorne? But, how? I thought…I mean, it was being said…that you'd…gone away with a man…." She passed Lucy a handkerchief.

Mopping up the last of her tears, Lucy gave a bitter chuckle. "I was abducted."

"Against your will?"

"If I'd cooperated, it would hardly be an abduction, would it?" Lucy ran a hand through her hair and came up with several short switches of straw. "I managed to escape yesterday and rode to town in a haywaine. I came to you because I hoped you might help me. I have no money, nowhere to hide, and the man who kidnapped me is on my trail."

As Lucy related the events of her abduction, imprisonment and eventual escape, Mrs. Beaumont's eyes widened and her breath quickened. When the story concluded, she fairly burst out, "Of course you must stay here. I will do anything I can to help you. Come now, let us get you a proper meal. Then a bath and fresh clothes..."

Suddenly Lucy felt famished and disheveled and exhausted. "Thank you," she breathed. "You are very kind."

"It is the least I can do to repay your husband's generosity to me. I must say, I never did understand his insistence on keeping this all a secret from you." The implied question struck Lucy dumb for a moment. Clearly, Mrs. Beaumont suspected nothing of her relationship with Jeremy. That was precisely the way Lucy intended to keep it.

"You probably realize my husband is a very scrupulous man. My father is the local vicar. Perhaps his lordship thought I might take some moral offence. I assure you, I am the last person qualified to sit in judgment."

Drake checked his saddlebags one last time. The Spaniard tossed his black mane and whinnied, as if anxious to be on the road, tearing up the miles between Nicholthwait and London. The horse was not one whit more anxious than his master. Drake had rushed through all the arrangements required for his absence, uncertain how long it might be.

Logically, he knew a day or two's delay would make no difference at this stage. In rational moments he conceded there was nothing he could do to find Lucy that his agent Langstroth could not accomplish with greater ease and skill.

Common sense decreed that Lucy might not be within a hundred miles of London in any case.

None of that mattered. London was the last place he had seen her. He blamed himself for believing the worst of her. He had allowed precious time to elapse before beginning a serious investigation into her disappearance. Her time was near, and he could not live with the thought that she might give birth far away from him—frightened and perhaps in terrible jeopardy.

Hearing a hubbub outside the stables, he led the Spaniard over to see what was causing all the fuss. A boy broke from his animated exchange with the butler when he saw Drake coming. The boy thrust a paper into his hand.

"From the magistrate in Carlyle, milord. They've taken that fellow Crook who blew up your mine."

Drake scanned the letter impatiently. The authorities had apprehended Janus Crook, the swindling overseer from High Head, as he had tried to escape the country. The magistrate needed Drake to come north at once to swear out a warrant against the miscreant.

"Why now?" he muttered to himself, crushing the paper in his fist. "The damned rascal's been at large for near half a year, and *now* they take him."

Remembering the messenger, he fumbled in his pocket and tossed the boy a small handful of silver. Bobbing his head and grinning from ear to ear, the lad departed.

"How will this affect your traveling plans, milord?" asked Talbot.

Drake sighed. "I have little choice in the matter. I'm for Carlyle. The minute I've dispatched my business with Mr. Janus Crook, I shall head south again. I don't fancy an extra two days added to my journey, but…" He shrugged. Sometimes he wondered if the fates were conspiring against him.

"Safe journey, sir." Talbot held Drake's hat while he mounted the Spaniard. "Any idea when we may see you back at Silverthorne, sir?"

Drake stared down at the man, suddenly aware of the deep concern imprinted on those normally impassive features. "I may stop in here again on my way south. After that, I'll return when I can bring my wife home, Talbot. Though I have no idea when that may be."

"Soon, I hope, milord."

"Yes." Drake gave the Spaniard a subtle nudge to go. "The sooner the better."

"There it is." Lucy scanned the paid notices in *The Times*. "'Lady sought.' It's all there. A description of me. That I am with child and near my time. Not to mention all that balderdash Dalrymple concocted about my being in 'a state of extreme nervous distress.' I'd like to lock him up for three months and see how well his nerves stand it!"

Rosalind Beaumont glanced up from nursing her young baby. She had not much cared for the looks of the other women who'd inquired after the position as wet nurse. At Lucy's urging, she had decided to take the unfashionable step of nourishing the child herself.

"What else does the notice say?"

Lucy read on. "It directs inquiries to a Mr. Clarke at the Piazzo Coffeehouse. Oh, dear! That's just round the corner. And…they're offering a reward of fifty pounds for information leading to my *recovery*."

"Fifty pounds?" Mrs. Beaumont blanched. For many in London, fifty pounds represented a vast, scarcely conceivable fortune. "Do you think anyone might have seen you come here?"

"I don't doubt it. The Market was teeming, as usual, and I asked directions of that charwoman at the theater. I must leave at once. You have been so very kind to me. I would not place you and the baby in jeopardy on any account. Dalrymple is a dangerous man."

"Don't worry." The actress held her son to her shoulder,

rubbing his tiny back. "We can hide you here at least until Lord Silverthorne comes."

Lucy's head snapped up. The newspaper wafted out of her slack fingers. "Drake is coming? But…how…?"

"The very day you arrived, I sent Janet to find a fast post rider who would carry a message north."

Lucy heaved herself from the chair. In the past week, her girth had increased dramatically. "This is terrible news! I can't face him. Not now. I don't begin to deserve a man like him—exposing him to scandal and ridicule because of my heedless behavior. Even if he would take me back out of some misplaced sense of duty, he's better off without me."

"I don't believe that for a moment." Mrs. Beaumont tucked the sleeping infant back into his cradle. "And I doubt your husband does, either. You must stay."

"I must go." Lucy took the other woman's hand. "But you have done me a service. I'd intended going to my aunt in Bath. If Drake is on his way to London, then I am free to return home to my father in Nicholthwait."

Mrs. Beaumont squeezed Lucy's hand. "I will gladly provide you with coach fare, of course. But how to spirit you out of town practically under the nose of that blackguard, Dalrymple?"

Lucy nodded ruefully. "With fifty pounds at stake, people will be quizzing any expectant mother who ventures abroad."

"True." A slow, cunning smile lit Mrs. Beaumont's face. "Though I suspect no one will look twice at a fat old crone in mourning."

Early the next morning, the Royal Mail coach set off from London for Manchester and points north. It carried a plump woman in deep mourning weeds, her bonnet swathed in a heavy black veil.

Lucy watched the outskirts of London melt away, her

relief growing with every mile the fast mail coach put between itself and the city. She counted herself fortunate that the only other inside passenger was an uncommunicative older man, thoroughly absorbed in his book. This would not be a leisurely progress, like she and Drake had enjoyed on their trip to London. The Mail kept a strict timetable and prided itself on speed. They'd be fortunate to get two thirty-minute stops for refreshment on a continuous journey of nearly a day and a half.

As that June day wore on, Lucy felt increasingly stifled in the greatcoat that concealed her condition and the heavily veiled bonnet that further disguised her identity. Mrs. Beaumont had even thought to pad her black gloves with cotton, so her slender fingers did not betray the masquerade. When evening fell and the Royal Mail raced along the deserted roads of the Midlands, Lucy shifted in her seat continuously. It was almost impossible to find a position sufficiently comfortable that she could snatch an hour's rest.

Her thoughts offered her no comfort, either. Hour after hour without the slightest diversion, she mulled over the events of the past months. What a fool she had been. Fate had put her in the way of a fine man like Drake Strickland, and she had disdained him. Instead, she'd clung to the memory of a thoughtless, selfish boy not worth a tenth of his brother's measure. At every turn she'd valued fair appearances instead of true merit, putting style before substance. Too late she'd learned the bitter lesson—*all that glitters is not gold.*

It had eased her brooding heart to discover Drake was not the father of Rosalind Beaumont's infant son. That she could have entertained such a suspicion proved yet again how unworthy she was of him. His insistence on hiding the child's existence from her also boded ill. If she meant anything to him, if he wanted her for himself, shouldn't he have been eager to expose Jeremy's betrayal?

How glad she would be to see her father again, to convince him she was well, and innocent of any wrongdoing. As soon as she could possibly travel with her child, however, she would have to quit Nicholthwait for good. No sense trying to fool herself that she and Drake had a future together.

As the morning sun rose on the second day and the mail coach rolled north from Manchester, Lucy set her teeth and tried to ignore her first twinges of labor.

Chapter Twenty-Three

"What's all the row? Who's there?" Silverthorne's butler demanded sharply, holding a tall wax candle to light the dark corners of the larder.

"I'm your culprit, Talbot." Grinning ruefully, Drake held his hands above his head until the butler recognized him. He wouldn't have put it past Talbot to be carrying a loaded blunderbuss.

"Milord!" Expelling a gasp of relief, the butler shuffled forward in his dressing gown. "Why did you not ring the bell?"

"Who is it, Mr. Talbot? Have you caught a prowler?" Mrs. Maberley called from beyond the kitchen door.

"Sorry to wake the house," said Drake. "Considering the hour, I thought I could forage up a bite on my own."

Near midnight he'd ridden into the forecourt at Silverthorne, weary, hungry and desperately anxious to be on his way to London. He had pressed on from Carlyle several hours after he was ready to fall from his saddle. What was the sense of supping and trying to rest at some indifferent inn? A few miles more and he could enjoy the food from his own good kitchen and sleep in his own clean bed.

"Light the fire for us, Mr. Talbot, like a good fellow." The cook bustled about, sweeping up the remains of a crockery bowl, now smashed into a thousand pieces by Drake fumbling about in the dark. "How'd it go in Carlyle, Master Drake?"

"As well as can be expected, I suppose." Too hungry to wait for a proper meal, Drake filched a biscuit and devoured it in two wolfish bites. "Crook has been caught. He'll be in the custody of the Carlyle authorities until he stands trial. My solicitor is taking steps to regain what we can from the funds Crook embezzled. I mean to use part of it to compensate the people of High Head. Build a school, perhaps."

It was on the tip of his tongue to say how much Lucy would like the idea. He checked the impulse. Instead he asked, "Any word from London?"

"From London?" said Talbot "Why no, milord. Were you expecting a message?"

Drake shook his head. Not expecting. Hoping, though. Hoping Langstroth had somehow tracked Lucy down, in spite of the stone-cold trail he had to follow.

"If you ask me, Master Drake—" Mrs. Maberley placed before him a plate of bread, cold meat and cold pie "—you ought to get a decent night's rest and a few good meals before you head off to London. Galloping from one end of the country to the other at a moment's notice. You'll wear yourself out and make yourself ill."

Drake shook his head wearily over the suggestion. "No, Mrs. Maberley. I appreciate your concern, but I must be off again at first light. If I stay, I'll only fret myself into a worse state."

How could he stay here at Silverthorne when he could be on the road to London? Ever since his interview with Langstroth, Lucy had preoccupied his thoughts more than ever. What had become of her? Would he ever see her again?

It was well past noon when Drake finally stirred. Picking up the mantel clock, he held it to his ear, to check if it was running. Hearing the muted *tick-tick-tick* and realizing it must be showing the correct time after all, he dashed the timepiece onto the bricks of the hearth, growling a long string of profanities. Striding into his dressing room, he threw open wardrobe doors and hauled drawers out, thrusting various parts of his body into more or less appropriate articles of clothing. The litany of curses continued unabated.

"What is the meaning of this?" he barked at the butler as he flew down the stairs two at a time. "I left instructions to be woken at dawn."

From his post in the entry Talbot glanced up, imperturbable as ever. "I beg your pardon, milord. I do recall you saying you meant to ride out early, but I didn't realize you intended anyone should wake you. I assumed you'd decided to catch up on your sleep before undertaking that long journey south."

Being caught with no one to blame did not sweeten Drake's temper. "I've lost the better part of a day already. I'll have to make up lost time tonight. Tell the grooms to saddle the Spaniard."

"Surely, sir, you'll have a hot meal before you go."

"Dash it all man, can't you understand? I've lost more time than I can afford as it is."

"Before you go, sir." Talbot drew a slender envelope from his breast pocket. "This just arrived. From London."

Drake snatched the paper, broke the unfamiliar seal and tore the letter open. Expecting a communication from Langstroth, he stared in bewilderment at scarcely a dozen words, penned in a woman's delicate hand. "Your wife has escaped and is in hiding with me. Come at once. R. Beaumont."

Over and over he read the words until two of them at least began to make sense to him—*wife* and *escaped*.

"Is everything all right, sir?"

"Talbot! Thank God!" Throwing his arms around the butler's stout trunk, Drake lifted him clear of the floor, spinning several times around.

Setting Talbot down at last, he thrust the letter at his reeling servant and sprinted for the door. "I'll saddle the Spaniard myself."

The Royal Mail coach pulled into Nicholthwait's Three Tuns Inn, at four o'clock precisely, for a change of horses and driver scheduled to take no more than five minutes. Teeth clenched against the mounting pain of her labor contractions, Lucy alighted. Swaying slightly at the feel of solid ground beneath her feet, she could scarcely contain her joy at coming home.

Saint Mawes and the vicarage were not far from the inn, no more than half a mile. However, as the force of her next contraction bent Lucy almost double, she wondered how she would make it even that short distance. When the pain finally passed, she stripped off her gloves, bonnet and greatcoat. The clement June breeze and the sweet scents of a Lake Country spring embraced her, welcoming her home at long last.

Home. As much as she yearned for her father and the vicarage where she'd grown up, part of her felt the pull of Silverthorne. Ridiculous, her logical self protested. She'd lived there only a few months. It was not as though she had conceived her child there or Viscount Silverthorne had fathered him. On the long coach ride from London, Lucy had often caught herself daydreaming along those lines. She'd imagined how it might have been, if she'd never succumbed to Jeremy Strickland's suave blandishments. Her wedding night with Drake might have matched their blissful tryst following Lady Holland's ball.

The gathering power of another birth pang roused Lucy from her reverie. She shook her head to clear it of such wishful foolishness. Lord Silverthorne would never have spared her a second glance, let alone wed her, if he had not desperately needed an heir and she had not been carrying his dead brother's child in her womb.

"Oh." She gave a plaintive little gasp as the mounting pain clutched her abdomen like a giant invisible hand and squeezed. She simply could not go another step. The next wave of pain would surely push her fainting into the wayside to bear her young like some poor stray animal.

When the pain receded at last and Lucy opened her tightly clenched eyes, she saw a carriage halted before her, its door held open invitingly. It looked like the phaeton belonging to Squire Lewes. Perhaps he had recognized her, even after the months of her absence. More likely, he had assumed her to be a stranger in distress. Lucy thanked heaven for Lake Country hospitality. His carriage would bear her to the vicarage in a trice.

Eagerly she tottered toward the waiting phaeton, determined to get inside and explain who she was and where she was bound, before the next labor spasm overtook her.

"How kind of you, Squire." She climbed aboard with the assistance of a gloved hand held out to her. "I can't thank you enough. I'm not going far, just—"

The carriage door swung shut behind her with a sharp, irrevocable *clack.* In the darkened interior of the coach, Lucy squinted to make out the face of her benefactor. The carriage lurched off at a greater speed than necessary to cover the brief distance to the vicarage.

"You have led me a merry chase, Lady Silverthorne." Eugene Dalrymple's face came into focus for Lucy. In contrast to his mannered words, his tone was coldly menacing. "I believe the last time you saw me we were driving in a carriage. What do the French call that—déjà vu?" He chuckled, as though making polite small talk at Almack's. But his narrowed eyes glinted with frightening intensity.

Another wave of pain engulfed Lucy. She pressed herself back into the seat, a soft moan escaping her lips. As the contraction gripped her, she heard Dalrymple cluck his tongue.

"You have used up that dodge, dear lady, remember? At

least do me the courtesy of coming up with something more novel. Frankly though, I'd suggest a wiser course of unconditional cooperation.'' A ray of afternoon sunlight pierced the grimy carriage window, gleaming on a lethal-looking knife he held. ''Since your husband appears unwilling to be rid of you, I'll make him pay dearly to get you back.''

The pain eased, leaving Lucy limp and bone weary. What was the use in struggling? She had schemed and fled, eluded him, hidden, disguised herself and fled farther away. In the end she had fallen right back into his oily, loathsome clutches. Now she was too tired to run and too weak to fight.

For herself.

Some spark of rebellion flickered to life in Lucy's heart. Never would she let her child come into the power of this smarmy blackguard. As that conviction surged within her, she spotted a familiar black horse galloping toward them, carrying a familiar dark rider. In a single desperate burst, Lucy threw her greatcoat over Dalrymple's head. Diving for the carriage door, she screamed Drake's name at the top of her lungs.

Neville Strickland also recognized the dark horseman bearing down on them. Though sweating like the proverbial pig, he hunched deeper into the bulky greatcoat of his coachman's disguise. Pulling the dust scarf up just below his eyes, he felt in imminent danger of retching from fear and overwrought nerves.

Silently, he cursed Phyllipa. It had been her suggestion that Lucy might return to her father in Nicholthwait, despite her mistaken belief that Drake had ordered her abduction. The fact that Phyllipa had guessed correctly did nothing to soften Neville's spite. He'd been in this whole mess up to his neck, anyhow, with Lucy at large and Dalrymple maniacally resolved to recapture her. Now Neville was in over his head, with a riptide sucking him down to hell.

He had the sinking suspicion Dalrymple meant to betray him, by letting Drake ransom his wife. Yet, he dared not cross the fellow, considering the incriminating secret Dalrymple was holding over his head. What in heaven's name had possessed him to recruit such a ruthless cardsharp in the first place? One who made his living bilking weak, greedy, stupid noblemen out of their inheritances. Neville cursed himself for a weak, greedy, stupid...

"Drake!" Lucy's scream pierced even the thunderous tattoo of the horses' pounding hooves. It startled the overset Neville almost out of his greatcoat. Common sense insisted he should whip the team on to greater speed. Instead, some long-buried instinct made him pull the reins tight, checking their headlong rush.

Drake must have heard the cry, too, for his black stallion wheeled and made straight for the carriage horses, stopping them cold. The hired hacks tossed their manes and broke into a chorus of high, nervous whinnies. Neville could guess how they must feel. The sight of his towering dark cousin vaulting from the saddle filled him with the same elemental terror. Scrambling down from his perch, Neville could think of nothing beyond putting the maximum distance between himself and the whole benighted enterprise.

He got as far as the concealment of the hedgerow before curiosity lured him to glance back. He saw his cousin wrench open the door of the phaeton and reach inside. Instantly Drake flew backward, propelled by a black-booted foot on his chest. Obviously winded, he struggled to rise from the dust. Before he could gain his feet however, Dalrymple came sailing out, too, expelled by some unseen force. He landed squarely on top of Drake, knocking him back to the ground.

Neville could see Lucy watching helplessly from the door of the carriage. Eyes wide with fear in a face pale and twisted with pain, she held one hand protectively over her bulging belly. The men grappled on the ground for a moment. The light, agile Dalrymple regained his feet first. The afternoon sun glinted off a slender blade which suddenly appeared in his hand.

Damn! What if Dalrymple should kill Drake outright, here and now? Neville didn't want to be Lord Silverthorne, with all those tiresome tenants and workers to consider. All he'd ever wanted was his expectations. Gingerly picking up a fist-size rock from the ground at his feet, he moved tentatively toward the combatants.

With the speed of a striking viper, Dalrymple slashed at his opponent. Drake raised an arm to protect his neck. Drops of bright blood spattered the dust. In a blind rage, Drake lashed out. Dalrymple danced beyond his reach, then skipped in again to inflict another quick slice. An anguished wail from Lucy made all three men pause for a heartbeat and turn toward her.

Dalrymple recovered first. With Drake's attention momentarily diverted, he took his chance and lunged in for a deadly strike. Gritting his teeth and squinting his eyes in distaste, Neville raised his rock. With all the force he could muster, he brought it down on the back of Dalrymple's blond head. Dalrymple staggered and his aim went wide.

With a guttural bellow of rage, Drake dashed the blade aside and sent Dalrymple flailing to the ground. Leaping upon his foe, he straddled the smaller man's chest and began to punish his pretty face with blow after blow. Each one made Neville wince just to watch.

"Drake, the baby!"

Lucy's tormented cry woke Drake from his blood lust. Not bothering to check if his enemy was dead or alive, he leapt from the ground and raced to her side, oblivious to the blood still seeping from his wounds.

"You!" Drake barked. He pointed toward the coachman's perch on the phaeton. "Get back up there and drive, man! Follow this road until you see a big house on a hill. Make for that."

Catching Lucy in his arms, he drew her back into the carriage. The phaeton surged forward up the narrow road, past the old stone church toward Silverthorne.

"Lucy, what are you doing here? I thought you were in London." Drake held her in his arms, the way he'd cradled her on that long-ago night when he'd proposed. He wanted desperately to kiss her, but he did not dare. Some half-mad instinct told him this might be an illusion. If so, he did not want to risk shattering it.

"What are *you* doing here?" Lucy gasped. "Didn't you get Mrs. Beaumont's...message? I never would have... come if I'd known you were still—"

Another birth pang robbed her of speech.

Her words wounded Drake far more deeply than Dalrymple's toy of a knife. She would never have come to Nicholthwait if she'd known he was still here. When would he learn to stop hoping?

If she'd been with Rosalind Beaumont, Lucy must have learned the truth about Jeremy. For as long as Drake had known her, she'd been an idealist and a romantic. Had the knowledge of Jeremy's betrayal irrevocably poisoned her capacity for trust and love?

Chapter Twenty-Four

An hour later, Drake descended the main staircase at Silverthorne, his usual brisk stride subdued to a hesitant, rather unsteady walk. They had settled Lucy into her own bed, the household scrambling to prepare for the birth. After what she had said to him in the carriage, he'd expected she would not want him near her. To his surprise, she'd clung to his hand until the doctor arrived and then made him leave. Suddenly conscious of the two knife wounds Dalrymple had inflicted, he let Talbot clean and bind them. Then he changed out of his blood-soaked clothes.

Urgently trying to distract himself from what was happening in the room upstairs, Drake latched on to the village constable when the man appeared.

"Have you got Dalrymple under custody? I want to press charges for kidnapping, assault and attempted murder."

The constable scratched his chin. "We have him all right, your lordship, but he'll not be standing trial."

"Not standing trial?" Drake flared. "That's impossible! The blackguard abducted my wife, not once but *twice*... came after me with a—"

"You mistake me, Lord Silverthorne." The constable raised his hand to halt Drake's voluble indignation. "Dalrymple may not face a judge in this world, but he'll have to answer to a higher court.''

"I killed him?" Drake blanched. "It was purely in self-defense, I assure you constable. If you'd care to question Dalrymple's driver, I had him detained. I don't believe he took part in Dalrymple's criminal activities. I owe the man my life. He came to my assistance when Dalrymple attacked me with a knife.''

"Rest assured, your lordship, I will want to question the fellow, whoever he is. As for killing Dalrymple, don't trouble your conscience. He was battered but alive when you drove away. I've a witness who saw it all—said that scoundrel made the mistake of trying to escape on that bad-tempered black stallion of yours.''

Drake scarcely needed to hear the constable's next words. In all the commotion, he hadn't spared a thought for the Spaniard.

"The beast threw him," said the constable, confirming what Drake already suspected. "Snapped his neck like a twig.''

That came as no surprise, either. He nodded mutely in reply. The world was well clear of a dangerous malefactor. His overwhelming feeling was a sense of relief. He had no blood on his hands and no murder charge hanging over his head.

"If you'll allow me to speak to the driver, constable," he said at last. "Then I'll turn him over to you for questioning.''

"Very good your lordship. No hurry about it. I understand you've got your hands full just now.''

As if on cue, one of the housemaids came rushing down the stairs. "Milord, the doctor says come at once! The mistress is calling for you. She won't settle and the doctor says it's making the birth go all the harder.''

Drake shot up the steps, three at a time, his own pain and recent blood loss forgotten. He also forgot the constable until he was halfway up the stairs. Halting abruptly, he called down, "Dalrymple's driver is in the library. I don't know how long I may be. If you want to question him now, go ahead. I can offer him my thanks later."

"Thank you for your cooperation, Lord Silverthorne. I do hope all goes well with your lady."

Drake bounded up the last of the stairs and down the hall.

When he pulled open the door to Lucy's room, he heard her voice, sharp with pain and raw with fear.

"Where's Lord Silverthorne? I must speak to him. Please. It's urgent."

A jumbled chorus of voices responded in various tones of entreaty, reassurance and appeasement. She must lie still. They had sent for Lord Silverthorne. He was on his way. She must not upset herself.

When he stepped into the room, they all turned their faces to him, like flowers to the sun. He swept them with his most commanding stare and uttered a single word.

"Go."

Only Varoy, the doctor, offered even a show of reluctance to comply. "Don't stay too long, Drake. Just calm her down, then call me back. I'll be right outside if you need me."

When Drake gave no response but a continued steady look, Charles Varoy backed toward the door. "Five minutes, Drake. I won't give you any longer. A birthing room is no place for a husband—especially a gentleman."

Not waiting to see the doctor go, Drake rushed to the bed and knelt by Lucy. She paid him no mind at first, lost in the strain of bearing her child. A whimper broke from her lips. Catching her nearest hand in his, Drake twined their fingers together, wishing he could leech part of her pain with his touch. Perhaps he did—or perhaps the pang eased in the natural ebb and flow of nativity.

Lucy looked into his face then, with a bright wonder of recognition, as though her spirit had just then returned to her body from afar.

"Thank you for coming," she breathed.

As if he would voluntarily stay away.

"I haven't much time. I can't talk when the pain takes me. I want you to know how sorry I am for the trouble I've brought on you. Such a little fool from start to finish. Never deserved the kindness you've shown me."

Drake opened his mouth, but no words would come. Couldn't she see it had nothing to do with kindness and nothing to do with deserving? He loved her with every nerve and sinew in his body. He would move heaven and earth for her, without ever once considering whether she deserved his service. Love was not bestowed on the basis of merit. It took hold of the heart powerfully, sometimes painfully. As the elemental force of birth took hold of a woman's ripe body.

All this Drake knew as he knew how to walk and how to breathe. But he could not put it into words. His heart was full to bursting, but his mind had suddenly emptied of all but the baldest, most prosaic phrases.

"You mustn't say that. You're home now and safe. That's what matters."

She shook her head, determined to be all the more severe with herself in spite of his clemency. "I've been a wet goose. For all my book learning, I knew nothing about life. Judging by appearances, never recognizing true value. You deserve better."

More talk of deserving and value. Drake's heart sank. She could not begin to reciprocate his feelings, or she would never use such words.

She gripped his hand harder. "I must make you understand. I never meant to go with Dalrymple."

Drake sensed another spasm gathering power within her. "Of course you didn't. I know what happened. I don't blame you."

"I *am* to blame. Overheard you and Mrs. Beaumont talking. Heard you tell her I mustn't know her secret. I thought you and she…''

''Mrs. Beaumont? You thought I…?'' The very notion bewildered him completely. Even if he'd known she overheard them, he never would have dreamed she'd jump to such a conclusion. An obvious one perhaps in the case of any other man. To think Rosalind Beaumont would want him, though. To consider he would take a mistress when he longed day and night for his wife. No. Even hearing the suggestion from Lucy's own lips, Drake could scarcely credit it.

He had no time for rebuttal. Gasping for air like a swimmer breasting the waves, Lucy gripped his hand. The force of it almost made him cry out. He watched the pain wring her, feeling more completely helpless than at any other time in his life. Only when her hold relaxed did he draw breath again.

For a moment she seemed to search for the thread of her previous words. ''Don't be angry. Forgive me. Should have known you'd never stoop to…anything…dishonorable. I was so confused by my feelings then. Beginning to realize I loved you.''

The very thought of it robbed him of all thought. He could only stare at her like a dumb animal.

She must have misunderstood his silence. ''I know this isn't the time. It goes against the…promises we made. I don't ask you to return my feelings, just to hear me.''

He yearned to reassure her that there could be no *bad time* to receive such news. The very fact of receiving it, even on the brink of doom, transformed it to a wondrous time. The words would not come.

Tears welled in her eyes, and Drake wished he could drown himself in them.

''I love you, Drake. Some wise part of me…always has. The foolish part…tricked me into believing…I cared for Jeremy.'' She shook her head. ''I never *knew* your brother.

Just wrapped him in an ideal…from my books and day-dreams. I know you, Drake. You're no…romantic paragon, but you're…ten times the man your brother was. Wish I'd realized that sooner—for both our sakes.''

He longed to tell her that she had just transformed his world. That in a single stroke she'd made him more nearly whole than at any time in his life. He found himself scarcely capable of framing the thought, let alone the words.

Her grip on his hand tightened again. ''One last thing…must ask you.''

The intensity of her gaze wrenched the promise from him. ''Anything.''

''Something's wrong. With me. With the birth. I see it when Dr. Varoy…looks at me. Promise me, Drake…you won't let them harm my baby.''

''Harm the baby? Of course not. Everything will be well—you'll see.''

''Swear it?''

''Of course, I swear. I'd never let anyone harm our child.''

Her fierce concentration bled away quietly. ''Thank you. I'm content to die, myself. Just wish it didn't…hurt so much.''

''You're not going to die, Lucy. You can't.''

She chuckled softly, her eyes glowing with all the love she'd confessed for him, and more. ''Not something you can forbid…my lord. Better this way—I know it. Such disgrace on your good name…never live it down. Couldn't be content in our marriage…feeling as I do.''

He tried to interrupt her then. He wanted to ask why in the world she could not be content when she loved him and he adored her. She persisted, perhaps sensing she did not have much time before the next wave of labor hit.

''Know you'll cherish this child…give him the love you missed.''

"Yes, I will, but...please don't talk like this, Lucy, as if you won't be here to help me."

"Don't spoil him...like Jeremy. Want my son to grow up a fine man...like you. Worthy successor...to... his...father."

He started to protest again, when another contraction racked her. Feeling a firm hand on his shoulder, he spun around to see Charles Varoy. Lucy was right. His old friend's face betrayed more than the usual concern.

With a sideways nod of his unkempt head, the doctor motioned toward the door. "Get away with you now, like a good fellow. Your lady's in capable hands."

"Dash it, Charles, is there nothing I can do?"

The doctor's voice dropped to a low whisper. "If I were you, I'd head down to the chapel. Put in an earnest word with *The Great Physician.*"

Drake's eyes widened. "As bad as that?"

Glancing at Lucy, who was stirring in the ebb-troth of her labor, Varoy gave only a curt nod in reply.

As Drake stalked from the room, he heard Lucy call after him. "Don't forget your promise, Drake. I'll hold you to it."

He did not turn around to answer her. He was suddenly possessed by a wild, superstitious certainty that if he did, it might be the last time he would see her alive.

Scarcely conscious of what he was doing or where he was going, he wandered down to the family chapel. It was all that survived of the original Silverthorne Manor, which had burned to the ground during the Restoration. There was not much to it beyond an altar and a couple of pews. The family no longer used it, even for weddings or funerals. Inside, Drake found Vicar Rushton kneeling in prayer.

"My boy." The old clergyman beamed when Drake laid a hand on his shoulder. "I came as soon as I got word. I was visiting with Mrs. Sowerby when your man finally tracked me down. She insisted on coming with me. I hope you don't mind. She's very fond of Lucy and she was a midwife before her sight failed. One of the maids took her up. Since Lucy's mother can't be here..."

His voice trailed off, but then he appeared to recall his original train of thought. "I just paused here to offer a prayer of thanksgiving for my daughter's safe return to us. May I see her now? Or should I wait until...after?"

Drake clenched his features tight. His feelings, too, for fear they might overwhelm him. In terse, almost brutal terms, he told his father-in-law how matters stood.

"Charles said I should pray," he concluded with an exhalation of bitter, ironic laughter. "You can tell a doctor hasn't much faith in his own powers when he acknowledges a higher one."

Though his face looked stricken, the vicar's voice remained warm and steady. "I expect our good doctor meant the prayers to help *you,* through this—not Lucy. Come. Kneel with me, then and we'll administer the doctor's prescription."

Drake did drop to his knees, as much out of emotional exhaustion as anything. "I don't know where to begin, Vicar. I'm up at the lectern every Sunday, reading the Scripture, but it's just a part of my duty. I'm not a godly man at all."

The vicar's face blossomed in a smile of tender, paternal benevolence. "My boy. Oh, my dear boy. For as long as I've known you, you have been living your life for others. The well-fed faces of the children in these parts, the decent homes families are able to keep—these are all testament to the workings of our Lord in you. 'By their fruits, ye shall know them.'"

Though the affirmation warmed him, Drake shook his head. "What can I say? How dare I ask for special consideration from the Almighty? Other men lose wives and children in childbed—men in far greater need and far worthier than I."

"It is not a question of worth, you see. Ask only for God's will to prevail and for the strength you need to bear it."

A deep, wrenching sigh shook Drake's frame. "I don't often surrender control, Vicar, but I'll try."

For several minutes, the two men prayed together in the receptive silence of the old chapel, communing with their deepest fears and dearest hopes. For no logical reason that he could fathom, Drake felt a strange sense of peace steal over him. At first he did not hear the muted footsteps approaching behind him. Then someone cleared his throat.

Drake turned. "Constable. What can I do for you?"

"Forgive the intrusion, milord. I've questioned Dalrymple's driver and I think you ought to come see what you can make of him."

"I'm rather...preoccupied at the moment, Constable. Can't it wait?"

"Begging your pardon, sir. I don't think it can."

"Neville! What's the meaning of this? Where's Dalrymple's driver?"

Neville's knees knocked together so violently it was a wonder he could keep on his feet. He held up the greatcoat and scarf. "At your service, Cuz."

Never had he seen his self-controlled cousin so greatly at a loss. Features slack and expressionless, Drake looked like someone had just clouted him in the face with a sack of horseshoes.

"But how? What connection have you with Dalrymple?"

"Quite simple, really." A vain attempt at his old sang-froid rang thin and hollow. "I hired him to seduce your wife and wreck your marriage." Neville wasn't certain what inconvenient flash of honor kept him from betraying Phyllipa's part in the whole sordid scheme.

Now Drake looked as though he'd taken that sack of

horseshoes square on the kneecaps. The pain in his eyes unmanned Neville entirely.

"Why? What have I ever done to you?"

"Other than setting an insufferably sterling example and putting me continually in your debt—nothing."

"I don't understand."

"No. I don't expect you would understand greed and self-ishness and plain blinkered stupidity on that scale." Neville hung his head. "You have every right to doubt me, but please believe I never meant any harm to come to you or to Lucy."

"No harm? My God, Neville. You let him tear us apart." Drake held up his bandaged arms. "These are nothing compared to what I've been through in the past months. As for Lucy…"

"I expect you'll want to have me tried as an accomplice." Neville squared his shoulders, determined to take his downfall like a man. Inwardly, though, he trembled. Theft of goods above five shillings was punishable by hanging. The abduction of a peer's wife—did they still burn criminals at the stake?

Slowly, as if still dazed by these revelations, Drake shook his head. "I don't believe you meant us any real harm, but you foolishly managed to get involved with a much more dangerous character. When it came to a choice at last, you intervened and saved my life. I'm sure that took more courage for you than for most men. You'll have to pay for the havoc you've wreaked in our lives, Neville. But I don't see how it serves any good purpose for you to pay in blood."

Neville sank to his knees. "Thank you Drake. You won't regret this, I swear. I'll do anything to make it up to you."

He might have completed his abasement then and there by bursting into grateful tears, but one of the maids intervened.

"Come quick, milord! The doctor and Mrs. Sowerby are fit to kill each other and the poor mistress is beside herself!"

Looking into his cousin's face, Neville saw written there all the harm his machinations had wrought. Suddenly the gallows seemed no excessive punishment for him.

Drake headed for the door. "Don't leave Silverthorne until I've had a chance to speak with the constable and decide what to do with you."

Neville nodded. "Is there anything I can do now?"

Drake spun around. The question appeared to surprise him—but pleasantly. "The only thing any of us can do now, Neville. Pray for my wife and child."

With those words, he dashed out behind the nearly hysterical servant girl.

In the deafening silence of the library, Neville considered his cousin's request. True, he was already on his knees. But he hadn't said prayers since school, and then only by rote. What would it avail anyhow, the prayer of a repentant villain?

Chapter Twenty-Five

Pounding up the stairs, Drake heard the signs of strife before he saw them.

The doctor's voice rose, perturbed to a pitch of vexation such as Drake had never heard. "Damned if I'll let you back in there, you meddlesome old witch. You've got that poor girl worked up to a fit of hysterics on top of everything else."

"Now see here, you ham-handed sawbones!" Could that be placid old Widow Sowerby? "You're the one who got her in that state with your mutterings about killing her baby. You should learn to keep your voice down. A woman doesn't go deaf the minute she starts to give birth, you know."

"You're only making it worse, encouraging her to think there's any chance we can save them both."

Dr. Varoy's last words landed like a solid punch to Drake's stomach. As he strode up to the combatants, they quieted for a moment, both gathering breath for a verbal assault on him, most likely. In that instant of silence, Drake could make out Lucy's faint, hoarse cries emerging from behind the solid bedroom door.

"Don't let them hurt my baby. Please!"

His own impotent rage boiled up. Forgetting that Mrs.

Sowerby could not see him, Drake glared murder at the pair of them. "What are you doing out here, going at it hammer and tongs, when my wife needs you—" he stabbed a forefinger at the door. "—*in there,* cooperating to help bring her and the child safely through this."

They both began to talk at once, but the doctor's deep imperative tone drowned out Mrs. Sowerby. "That's the point, Drake, and it's cruel to let you fantasize otherwise. We have a choice to make, and we must make it soon. It's either Lucy or the baby. The child is big, particularly for an eight-month baby."

For a split second, the offhand remark puzzled Drake. Then he realized the doctor was calculating from his wedding to Lucy.

"At least he has a big head," continued Dr. Varoy. "And your wife's a slender little thing, especially around the…hips." He stumbled over the indelicacy of the word, but professional necessity won out.

"If we want to save the child, I'll have to perform the necessary surgery. There's not a moment to lose."

"C-cut her?" Drake swayed on his feet.

Avoiding his eyes, the doctor nodded. "It's the only safe way to deliver the baby. I won't lie to you—not many women survive the procedure."

Drake did not need to be told that twice. His mother had died as a result of his own Caesarian delivery.

"I can't lose her, Charles. Not now."

"Then we need to…compress the baby's skull to get it out before she dies from the strain and blood loss."

"Kill the child?"

The doctor raked a hand through his disheveled hair. "Isn't that what I just said? I don't care for the options any more than you do, Drake, but it's not as though we have a choice. We must make a decision and act soon, or we'll lose them both."

"She made me swear not to let you harm the baby."

Drake clamped a fist to his mouth, suddenly realizing what that rash promise might cost him.

Dr. Varoy waved that objection away. "You can't hold a woman responsible for the daft things she says in the extremity of childbirth, Drake. As her husband and the child's father, this is a decision only you can make."

All his life Drake had trained to make hard choices. Hitherto he had prided himself on his ability to weigh all the factors and make a rational determination that would best serve his long-term interests. Never once had he shrunk from the necessity of decision making.

Until now.

Now he stood paralyzed, unable to face the consequences of either option Charles Varoy had presented to him. How could he sentence Lucy to death, even at her insistence? Never to see or hear her again. Never to bask in the sunlight of her smile. Never to relish the fresh breeze of her bracing humor

As for the other so-called choice, it was not one whit more appealing. If she survived her grief, would Lucy ever forgive him for breaking his oath and allowing the destruction of her child? Would having her alive, but hating him, be any better than letting her die with words of love on her lips? Two unbearable choices, yet if he did not sanction one or the other the result would be doubly tragic.

Dear God, let me choose well.

The sound of Mrs. Sowerby's voice called Drake back. "Don't listen to him, your lordship. How many babies has he delivered, I'd like to know?"

The doctor sputtered. "Enough to know what needs to be done here."

"Nonsense," snapped Mrs. Sowerby. "You only attend a birth if the folks are rich. Even then you think it beneath you."

She turned to Drake. "If you'll trust me, milord, there is another way. 'Tisn't easy, but I believe we must try. I know

Miss Lucy will pine away for that baby. And the little one? You managed to cling to life without your mam, but most babies don't.''

It was true, Drake realized. This was not a business judgment about cutting losses or salvaging partial assets out of a bad investment. Choosing death, for either Lucy or their child, he could not live with. He must cast his lot with life—with hope.

Drake took Mrs. Sowerby's hands in his own. Wizened little claws they were, but soft as kid leather. For all their smallness and softness, they possessed a strange primal strength, as though accumulated from woman to woman through the centuries, since the first human infant had been hauled squirming and squalling into the world.

On the back of each gnarled hand he bestowed a kiss. ''Do what you can, Mrs. Sowerby.'' He cast a silencing glance at Charles Varoy. ''I understand the risks and I take full responsibility. Whatever the outcome, I thank you for being here when Lucy needs you.''

She offered no false reassurances, but turned and felt her way back into the bedchamber. From the triumphant expression she turned on the doctor, Drake wondered if she could see more than she cared to admit.

''For the love of God, Drake!'' Charles Varoy blustered. ''The strain of all this has unhinged you, man. Do you realize you've just entrusted your wife's life to a blind old woman? You'll lose them both—see if you don't.''

Drake shook his head. ''Breeding is a woman's province, Charles. A man sows his seed and after that the woman grows a child and brings it into the world with no further help from him. We have no right to interfere now.''

The doctor stalked toward Lucy's bedchamber. ''You, my friend, are addle-witted.''

''That may be,'' replied Drake calmly. ''But if you try to interfere with Mrs. Sowerby, I'll break your arms.''

His ruddy face mottled with fury, Varoy shouldered his

way past Drake. "Never fear. I won't do a thing 'til she begs me to salvage what she's botched. Then I'll do what I can."

For all his confident pronouncements, Drake felt far less certain than he'd tried to sound. What if he had doomed both the child and Lucy?

Gasping as though she had run a mile, Lucy pressed her head back into the pillows, determined to savor this brief respite from her labor. She'd been vaguely aware of the raised voices out in the gallery. Certain that the fate of her baby hung in the balance, she'd managed to wail out her wishes in the matter. Not that they were likely to pay her any mind.

Surely Drake would honor his promise to her. That was one reason why she had confessed her love for him—so he would see how intolerable a future stretched ahead of them if she lived. The other reason had been purely selfish. Though he might not love her, though he might actually shrink from the unbidden love she bore him, she could not slip into the dark uncertainty of death without him knowing.

The strident voices outside her door had fallen to a grave murmur. The battle must be over. She only hoped they had not resolved to save her life in spite of her wishes. If she had to, she would fight them with every last ounce of her strength to protect her baby. But she could feel that strength ebbing away.

The door opened and Mrs. Sowerby felt her way inside. The servant girl who was bathing Lucy's forehead dropped her cloth and ran to guide the old woman over to the bed.

Lucy could feel another pain beginning to build—a very bad one, unless she missed her guess. She had to talk quickly, before the doctor returned.

"What did they say? Won't hurt the baby will they?"

Mrs. Sowerby fumbled for her hand. Finding it, she gave a reassuring squeeze. "Nobody's going to touch that baby, my dear. Not until he's born at any rate, and then only to take the very best care of his wee lordship.''

In spite of the pain, Lucy's whole body relaxed. Tears of relief stung in her eyes. She clung to Mrs. Sowerby's tiny hand until the contraction spent itself.

"How…how soon will the doctor operate?" It was what she wanted, but her nerve still quailed at the thought of the knife.

"He won't." Mrs. Sowerby patted Lucy's arm. "I'm going to see to you and do what I can to help you bring this strapping young Strickland into the world."

"Help *me?*" Lucy writhed in the tangled bed linens. She wished she could crawl away from her own body and the frightening forces that now possessed it. "I can't do this. I'm so tired, I want to sleep forever, somewhere dark and quiet where there isn't any pain."

"You're not a flighty girl anymore, my dear. You're a woman. This baby is going to need you warm and alive. Not cold in your grave. Think of Lord Silverthorne. He needs you, too."

Lucy pushed a damp curl back from her forehead. "I'm the last…person he needs. Brought him nothing but turmoil. He's better off…without me."

"Nonsense." Mrs. Sowerby leaned close and whispered. "He's been without you these past weeks, and there isn't a soul in Nicholthwait who'll tell you he was better off. Don't desert him again, now that he's got you back."

Before Lucy could reply, another contraction gripped her. The pain was less with this one, but the pressure unbearable. She felt like an orange being squeezed for every last drop of juice by an enormous hand. It forced a deep, rasping moan from her.

"You need to push, don't you?" asked Mrs. Sowerby.

Limp and spent in the wake of it, Lucy could only nod.

"Then your rest may be coming soon, my dear. For the next little while, though, you're going to have to work hard and do as I tell you. For the child's sake, and his lordship's. Can I count on you?''

Again Lucy nodded. Knife or no knife, there was no way she could survive many more spasms like the last one. If Mrs. Sowerby needed her help to bring her baby safely into the world, she would try. After all she had put him through, she owed it to Drake to bear him a healthy heir.

She felt the forces gathering again. As she began to strain, the older woman coaxed her. ''Let it build my dear. Don't fight. Give yourself over to it. When it reaches its crest, bear down with all your might. Push from deep in your bowels. Someone clear these bedclothes out of the way and help me get her knees up.''

Lucy started at a gentle probing touch inside her birth passage.

''Don't fret, my dear,'' the midwife soothed her. ''I have to feel what your body's doing. Just as I thought—you're all ready. It shouldn't take much longer to bring this wee one into the world.''

Easy enough for Mrs. Sowerby to say. The next hour felt like an eternity to Lucy, as the midwife crooned encouragement for her to push through one strong contraction after another.

''Almost there. I can feel the head coming!'' Mrs. Sowerby cried triumphantly.

Several more contractions racked Lucy. Then, as if from a long distance, she heard Mrs. Sowerby. ''There's the head crowned. Go easy now. There's a good lass. Just let the rest of this wee one ease out.''

A sharp, intense pain, different from the others, made Lucy scream in agony.

''The baby's shoulder must be fetching up on her pubic bone.'' Lucy heard the doctor say as the contraction passed and the pain receded—slightly. ''I knew something like this would happen. How you talked Drake into—''

''Keep your mouth shut, or I'll call for someone to toss

you out," barked Mrs. Sowerby. "Someone rummage in my bag and find that crock of tallow I brought."

To Lucy's surprise, the doctor did not say another word.

"Brace yourself, my dear," urged Mrs. Sowerby. "What I've got to do now is going to hurt like the very devil, but it's the only way to save your baby."

Lucy sucked in a great breath of air. "Do it," she gasped, clenching her teeth against more pain to come.

It was even worse than she'd feared—a wrenching, rending torment of unplumbed depths. Then a peaceful, painless darkness opened before her, and she fled into it. Later there was light, and ministering angels fed her with the nectar of heaven.

The vicar looked hopefully into Drake's eyes. "You've been gone quite a time, my boy. Have you glad tidings for a proud grandfather?"

Not trusting himself to speak at first, Drake shook his head slowly and dropped onto the kneeling bench beside his father-in-law. How he envied the older man's childlike faith. A lifetime of carefully cultivated pessimism weighed down his own heart. "I put Mrs. Sowerby in charge. She thinks there's a chance to save both Lucy and the baby. Varoy doesn't agree."

The vicar laid a comforting hand on Drake's. "At least this way, whatever happens, they'll be together."

Drake sighed. He could not take much consolation in that thought.

Squeezing his eyes shut and clenching his hands in supplication, he let his lips move in the familiar words of prayers he'd uttered all his life. His thoughts ranged beyond the confines of the chapel and beyond the present hour. Opening the treasure chest of his memory, he drew out image after image of Lucy from their brief marriage.

Lucy, as she had looked on their wedding night, brushing out her golden curls before the looking glass. How the sight and scent of her had inflamed him! Lucy, smudged and tousled amid the jubilant celebration of the miners' rescue. Lucy, quivering at his touch, then lying spent and contented within the circle of his arms. Now those memories glowed with a special new aura—the priceless knowledge that she had grown to love him.

"...deliver us from evil..." Drake stumbled in his prayer by rote. The crushing weight on his heart was more than he could bear. He almost wished Lucy had not confessed her love for him. It would make her loss infinitely more painful, glimpsing what they might have shared together.

Hearing the deliberate tread of footsteps behind him, he glanced around. Charles Varoy wandered into the chapel, looking utterly dazed. He dropped heavily into the pew beside Drake.

"Charles!" Drake grabbed the doctor by the arms. "Is it over? What's happened?"

Neither Drake's rough grasp, nor his abrupt interrogation penetrated the doctor's strange bemusement.

"Damnedest thing I ever saw," he murmured to himself. "She just greased her hands up with tallow and..."

"And what, Charles? Who greased whose hands? For pity's sake, man, come down to earth and tell me, are my wife and child alive?"

"I could never have done it." The doctor shrugged, holding up his hands. "Far too big. It's not the kind of thing a gentleman would do, even with lives at stake...."

Drake was just about to strike some sense into the man when the chapel door eased open and one of the maidservants led Mrs. Sowerby in. Her face looked drawn and exhausted. Her clouded eyes glistened. Pushing past the befuddled doctor, Drake approached and took her hands.

He was about to ask the question he dreaded putting into words, when he heard a sound approaching from outside the chapel. Closer and closer it came—the high, almost feline howl of a newborn infant. Even with his scant experience of such things, Drake thought it sounded like a lusty, healthy cry.

Mrs. Sowerby turned and held out her arms as a maid-servant entered, bearing a well-swaddled baby. Taking the child, she offered it to Drake.

"My wife?" he asked in a harsh whisper.

A triumphant smile spread across the old woman's face and Drake recalled a Bible verse he'd read during many a matins and evensong. "Beautiful are they...that bring good tidings."

"She's a brave, hardy lass. We've given her a sleeping draught, but she should be right as rain in a week or so."

Gingerly gathering the tiny but vocal creature into his arms, Drake bowed his head. His heart was suddenly too full, and his throat too constricted to speak. Clutching the squalling infant to his breast, he baptised it with a father's tears.

Chapter Twenty-Six

She couldn't be dead after all, Lucy decided as she groped feebly toward consciousness. For one thing, she hurt too much. Not the excruciating rigors of childbirth, of course, which her memory had already begun to mute. Her body did throb with a dull ache, though. A dying echo of the pain that had propelled her into merciful oblivion.

If she had managed to survive the ordeal, what of her baby? The thought sent Lucy scrambling up the slippery slope toward full awareness. Her eyelids fluttered, letting in the soft, warm sunlight of an almost-summer morning. Her other senses reached out, searching for signs of her baby. She heard no cries or cooing. She felt no squirming bundle tucked into bed beside her. During her stay with Rosalind Beaumont, she had become familiar with the irresistible milky scent of an infant. She could detect no such smell now.

Fighting down her mounting panic, Lucy wrested her eyes fully open. Her skittery glance swept the room. One of the maids stood at the window looking outside, the only other person in her bedchamber. Lucy saw no evidence of a baby's presence, nor that one had ever been there.

"P-please," she croaked from a parched mouth.

The girl at the window started. Quickly regaining her

composure, she approached the bed. Though she smiled brightly, Lucy could see she bore a look of strain and fatigue around her eyes.

"So you're awake at last, ma'am. Is there something I can get for you?"

The answer seemed so obvious, Lucy wanted to scream. She held out her empty arms.

"My baby," she rasped. "What's become of my baby? Is he alive? Is he healthy?"

The girl smiled more broadly than ever. "Indeed, ma'am—alive and well."

Lucy let her feeble arms drop to the coverlet. As tears gushed from her eyes, she was powerless to stop them.

"Strong and healthy, according to the doctor, and such a cunning wee one. The first lass born into the Strickland line in five hundred years—or so Mr. Talbot says. I'll go fetch her for you, ma'am, now that you're awake."

Before Lucy could voice any of the insistent questions that clamored in her thoughts, the maid slipped away. Tears of relief turned rapidly to tears of another kind. Dumbfounded by the sudden revelation, she could scarcely grasp it. A girl? Her child was a girl. The propensity for Stricklands to breed sons was legendary in the Lake Country. The Silverthorne title and estates had passed down father to son, without fail, since the Middle Ages.

Through her tears, Lucy laughed bitterly at the irony. Wed for the sole purpose of furnishing a male heir, she had borne the first Strickland daughter in centuries. Lord Silverthorne would find it no laughing matter. Now he was saddled with a wife he did not want. And a girl child, who could do nothing to stop his unscrupulous relatives from inheriting the estate he'd labored most of his life to restore.

"Here she is, ma'am." The maid breezed back in bearing Lucy's child. "Such a bonny baby. The way she's chewing on her wee fist, I'd say she's hungry."

She tucked the baby in beside her mother.

Lucy reached over with her free hand and ran her little finger over the downy pink cheek. Grabbing on with her own tiny red claws, the baby popped the fingertip into her mouth and began sucking energetically.

"They're right," Lucy breathed. "You are a precious little creature."

Extricating her finger, she tugged down the low-cut bodice of her nightgown and rolled gingerly onto her side. Pinching her nipple erect, she brushed it across the baby's cheek toward her mouth, as she had watched Mrs. Beaumont do with her infant. The child shaped her tiny rosebud mouth into a ravenous O, and began to suckle.

"What a clever girl you are," Lucy crooned, nuzzling her chin against the baby's modest thatch of dark hair. Overcome by potent maternal passions, she could not bring herself to regret that the tiny miracle enfolded in her arms was not a boy.

"His lordship looked so peaceful, with his wee princess nestled in his arms, I hadn't the heart to wake him," said the maid.

The words were so contrary to anything Lucy had expected, that for a moment they refused to have meaning for her.

"Lord Silverthorne...was holding the baby?" she ventured at last.

"I should say!" The girl gave an indulgent chuckle. "From the minute Mrs. Sowerby gave her to him, he wouldn't let anyone else have her. 'Cept the vicar, of course, and then not for very long. I never would've taken the master for a man to dote on a baby so."

Lucy pondered the idea. A year ago, she would have agreed entirely. Now, she knew better. Drake had a wealth of tenderness in him, together with protective instincts of primal ferocity. Perhaps all that kept them in check was a fear of rejection. If any man had cause to fear such a thing, surely it was one who had never known a family's love.

Until now, Drake had been obliged to lavish all his care upon his people. Whatever affection he might feel for her, a daughter could not continue his work.

"So…" She hesitated, scarcely able to frame the words. "Lord Silverthorne wasn't disappointed…in a girl?"

"Disappointed? Ma'am, have you not heard a word I've said? If that was disappointed, I'd hate to see him jubilant. Why, the way he took on, you'd think he was the first man ever to become a father. I'll go get you a bite to eat, ma'am, now that you're awake. You'll need to feed well if you mean to nurse young Missy, yourself."

As the maid bustled away, Lucy pressed the baby even closer. Though her body lay torpid, her thoughts ranged far and wide, at an anxious gallop. This crumb of hope frightened her, after the peaceful resignation of despair.

Drake loved the baby. Even though he hadn't sired her. Even though she was not the heir he so desperately needed. Was it possible he could love a wife even though she had brought disgrace on his proud name?

"Lucy! Miranda-a-a!!"

Drake lurched bolt upright in his bed, still fully dressed from the night before. Sweat beaded his hairline and his heart pounded like the Spaniard's hooves at a dead gallop. He had dreamed of two smiling, golden-haired men. Men who took his wife and daughter away while he lay bound and helpless to stop them.

The baby! Drake hauled the bedclothes this way and that, searching for some sign of his missing child. They hadn't been able to pry her from his arms the previous night, after Mrs. Sowerby had laid her there. He had borne her throughout the house, showing her off to all the servants. He'd ordered the finest vintages in his wine cellar breached, so the household could toast his daughter's safe arrival. If it had been within his power, he'd have ordered the whole county roused from their beds with a twenty-one gun salute.

A tidal wave of paternal pride and love had demolished the once invulnerable dam of his reserve. When she'd dozed, he'd declared her a well-behaved little angel. When she'd squalled, he'd laughed delightedly at her spirit. He'd held her, kissed her and crooned to her. From out of nowhere he'd named her Miranda, for Prospero's beautiful, beloved daughter in *The Tempest*. When Mrs. Maberley and the maids had begged leave to hold her for just a minute, he'd jealously resisted their entreaties.

Miranda's less faithful admirers had taken to their beds at last, in the early hours of the morning. Her besotted Papa had remained awake and watchful, whispering of the grand future he planned for her. Ponies, seaside holidays, beautiful gowns, books, the finest education money could procure. At last, with his precious daughter cradled protectively in his arms, he'd stretched out on his bed and closed his eyes. He only meant to rest them for a minute.

He'd wakened just now to find the baby gone—spirited away as if by black magic.

Barreling out of his bedchamber, he almost bowled over Talbot, bearing a well-laden breakfast tray. In spite of his agitation, the aroma of food made Drake's stomach rumble piteously. He could not remember having eaten since that midnight snack in Mrs. Maberley's kitchen. Hungry as he was, food would have to wait on more urgent matters.

"Talbot, raise an alarm. Someone has taken the baby!"

The butler tried to look solemn, but an indulgent smile tugged at the corners of his mouth.

"Yes, sir. Nell fetched the child. The mistress was anxious to see her."

Drake's alarm waned in a long, slow hiss of exhaled breath. After all Lucy had done to protect the child, even putting her own life at risk, Drake knew he could rest easy if Miranda was with her. Lifting a cover from one of the dishes on Talbot's tray, he bolted a scrap of fried ham. Never had he tasted anything so delicious. Drake relieved his butler of the tray and headed back through his open bedroom door. Now that he knew Miranda was safe, he was in no rush. Let Lucy enjoy some private time becoming acquainted with their daughter, as he had.

"One more thing, milord," said Talbot.

Drake raised his eyebrows expectantly.

"About Master Neville," continued the butler. "As far as I can tell, he slept the night in the library. Will he be staying? Should I make up his usual room?"

Drake shook his head. "Get him a bite to eat, though. Something to stay his stomach for a journey."

Half an hour later, Drake entered the library, feeling like a new man. He found his cousin doggedly consuming an enormous breakfast with the air of a convict devouring his last meal.

"I'm glad to hear it all went well last night," said Neville between bites. "With your wife, I mean." He sounded subdued, but sincere. "Have you decided yet what you plan to do with me?"

Drake seated himself opposite his cousin, who looked to have aged several years in a single night. Was there hope this perpetual adolescent might yet mature into a man?

"I don't mean for you to get off from this with merely a scare. It would be an exercise in folly sending you back to London—too great a temptation to lapse back into bad habits and worse company. What you need, Neville, is a clean break from your old life and a chance to prove yourself."

Neville's pasty complexion took on an even paler cast. But he squared his shoulders with an air of desperate resolution. "Where will you send me?"

"The Nova Scotia colony. I recently bought a shipyard in a garrison town called Halifax. I need a manager who's willing to apply himself and learn the business."

"Halifax? Never heard of it." Neville brightened. "Sounds a bit of all-rightish just the same. Who knows but I couldn't master the operation?"

"One other proviso, Neville."

"Yes?"

"Phyllipa and Reggie are to accompany you. I want you to take the boy in hand. He's not a bad little chap, just needs someone to keep his mother from molly-coddling him."

"Phyllipa, eh?" Neville looked less enthusiastic about this part of the scheme for his rehabilitation. "I don't suppose that point's negotiable?"

Drake smiled ruefully. "I'm particularly resolved upon it. With the birth of my daughter, it is altogether likely that you and Reginald will inherit Silverthorne one day. I want you both prepared to continue the work I've begun."

"You had a daughter *this* time, against all odds," said Neville. "Plenty of chances to breed a whole nursery full of potential heirs, though. Why bother putting Reggie and me through our paces?"

Drake rose abruptly. Neville had alluded to the one dark cloud on his presently bright horizon. "It was a difficult birth. My wife may not wish to go through something like that again."

Though Mrs. Sowerby assured him Lucy would be quite capable of bearing more children, Drake had his own misgivings. He'd been with her for little enough of her labor. From what he had seen, though, he doubted she would want to go through another ordeal like the one she'd barely survived. If she decided against having more children, he would honor her wishes…difficult as it would be to refrain from making love to her.

Neville grimaced. "Rum luck, old man."

Suddenly, Drake remembered that his cousin's machinations might have cost Lucy her life. He savored his parting words to Neville.

"By the way, for propriety's sake, you and Phyllipa will have to get married."

He tossed the remark over his shoulder, never looking

back. Not even when he heard something of substantial bulk hit the floor.

Hearing the door of her bedchamber slowly ease open, Lucy glanced up, then quickly averted her eyes again. Drake had come at last.

Fiercely, she pretended to concentrate on the baby nursing lazily at her breast. From what Lucy could tell, her daughter was not drawing much actual milk, but she seemed content to suckle anyway. Keeping her eyes trained on the dark silky down of the baby's hair, she waited and waited for Drake to speak. He stood near the door for the longest time, quiet and motionless. When at last she worked up the nerve to slant a covert glance in his direction, she thought his dark eyes glistened suspiciously.

As well they might. He had gone to great lengths, even wedding a wife he didn't want, to secure a suitable heir to his title. Now all his plans lay in ruins and he was saddled with a spouse who had inconveniently fallen in love with him, contrary to her express promise.

"I'm sorry." Though she tried to keep her voice steady, it broke, and unbidden tears brimmed in her eyes. Inwardly Lucy raged at her uncontrollable emotions. She did not want to coerce Drake into maintaining their marriage out of guilt or a sense of duty. She had failed to fulfil the conditions of their union. Why should he remain bound to keep up his side of the bargain?

He took a cautious step nearer the bed. "Sorry?" he murmured in a voice thick with emotion. "Why should you be sorry?"

"Must you make me say it?" She could not bring herself to meet his gaze, for fear of what she would see there. "Sorry I brought disgrace on the Silverthorne name. Sorry I…"

Lucy hesitated. Never in a million years would she regret the birth of her daughter. In spite of what the maid had told her, she could scarcely expect Drake to share those feelings. The child was not his, after all. She could not save his life's work from falling into unworthy hands.

"Sorry I did not bear you the heir you need. Sorry…"

Again the word stuck in her throat. She would never regret loving Drake. She was proud to have achieved the perception and maturity to care for a man so vastly worthy of it. For his sake, though, for the burden of unwanted obligation it placed upon him, she was sorry.

"Sorry I broke my most important promise to you. I swear I will make amends for all of it. Only a trusted few know that I am not in Florence with Mr. Dalrymple. If I went away, took an assumed name, you could still petition Parliament for a divorce. I would only ask for my baby's sake that you provide for us as you have provided for Mrs. Beaumont and her son."

Drake staggered his last few steps to her bedside, where he fell to his knees.

"No, Lucy. No. You must never leave me again. Never. If you do, I will die. Dear God in Heaven, don't you see? I love you better than my next breath." Brokenly, he poured out his heart to her. "I would give my last breath to keep you from harm—both of you. And I would not exchange our priceless daughter for a brace of boys."

"But…the scandal. Everyone thinks I left you and ran away with—" Lucy's voice caught. "I could never expect a proud man like you…"

"Pride be damned, Lucy." Drake's dark eyes glowed with the earnestness of his declaration. "Pride's cold and hollow. Any man with a crumb of sense would trade it for…love."

With all her heart, she longed to believe him. But did she have the courage?

"I'm not worthy of you. I've proven that a hundred times."

"Worthiness has nothing to do with it, either." The intensity of Drake's tone and his gaze convinced Lucy. "For years I struggled to be worthy of love—from anyone, without success. Then you came into my life, bringing love, like an unexpected gift. You never said the words until last night, but I felt it just the same. Haven't you felt my love, all these months?"

In the garden of the English language, his words were not the most beautiful flowers, nor the most fragrant. Yet they spoke of a love with deep, tenacious roots—one that would bear fruit of inexpressible sweetness.

Not trusting herself to reply any other way, Lucy nodded. With her eyes, she begged Drake to kiss her.

He brushed her cheek, and the baby's, with delicate kisses. Then, finding her lips, he kissed her again, softly but deeply.

One last obstacle remained.

Silverthorne.

Drake's deep sense of duty to his people was what had made him wed her in the first place.

"The baby. She can't inherit your title, can't look after your people."

A hint of regret now shadowed Drake's loving gaze.

Lucy ached for him.

"I'll do everything I can to ensure that Silverthorne doesn't fall into unsuitable hands. But you and our daughter are all the world to me. I wouldn't give you up, even for Silverthorne."

He kissed her again. In his fervent but gentle salute, Lucy had no choice but to acknowledge the truth of his love for her. Perhaps the past did not matter. Perhaps only the future mattered. In the years to come, she would strive with all her heart to be worthy of Drake and to love him as he so richly deserved.

As he continued to kiss her, Drake's hand stole up, cupping Lucy's free breast. Suddenly, she felt the soreness in her body melt into the delicious ache of desire.

Drawing back from her, Drake looked deep into her eyes as a wry smile played across his expressive mouth. "Besides, Mrs. Sowerby tells me there's no reason in the world why we cannot try for a boy in a few months. After what you've been through this time, I wouldn't blame you if you decide against it...." His voice trailed off wistfully.

Her eyes shining with tears of happiness, Lucy drew Drake's head down to rest upon her breast beside the baby, now sated and sleeping. Nuzzling her cheek against his dark hair, she replied in a husky whisper.

"I can hardly wait."

* * * * *

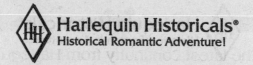

Harlequin Historicals®
Historical Romantic Adventure!

Receive 75¢ off your next Harlequin Historicals® book purchase.

75¢ OFF!
Your next Harlequin Historicals® book purchase.

RETAILER: Harlequin Enterprises Ltd. will pay the face value of this coupon plus 8¢ if submitted by customer for this product only. Any other use constitutes fraud. Coupon is nonassignable. Void if taxed, prohibited or restricted by law. Void if copied. Consumer must pay any government taxes. For reimbursement submit coupons and proof of sales to: Harlequin Enterprises Ltd., P.O. Box 880478, El Paso, TX 88588-0478, U.S.A. Cash value 1/100¢. Valid in the U.S. only.

Coupon expires March 31, 2003.
Redeemable at participating retail outlets in the U.S. only.
Limit one coupon per purchase.

109894

```
5  65373 00075  5   (8100) 0 10989
```

HARLEQUIN®
Makes any time special ®

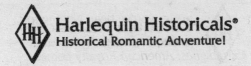

Harlequin Historicals®
Historical Romantic Adventure!

Receive 75¢ off your next Harlequin Historicals® book purchase.

Receive
MOULIN ROUGE™
on VHS video

with two proofs of purchase
from any four specially marked
Harlequin® collector's editions.

Special Limited Time Offer

MOULIN ROUGE

VIDEO!

1 Proof of Purchase

YES! Please send me my *MOULIN ROUGE*™ VHS
video without cost or obligation, except for shipping
and handling. Enclosed are two proofs of purchase from
specially marked Harlequin® collector's editions and a
check or money order for $3.50* shipping and handling
fee made payable to Harlequin Books.

*New York State residents please add applicable sales tax.
*Canadian residents please add 7% GST.

Name (PLEASE PRINT)

Address   Apt. #

City   State/Prov.   Zip/Postal Code

097 KJL DNC9